"Don't touch i[t] fingerprints."

"I doubt it," Katerina said. "I think I felt gloves, not bare skin."

He lifted the folded paper with two fingers at a corner and laid it on a bare spot atop the dresser, then used a pencil to carefully unfold it. He stepped back and watched her reaction as she scanned the note.

"'Turn over the stash and we'll leave you alone'?" she read aloud. "What's that supposed to mean? I don't know anything about any stash. Do they mean drugs?"

"Your guess is better than mine," Max countered. "What do you think?"

She threw up her hands and began to pace. "How should I know? I don't have a clue."

"I wish I could believe you."

"Yeah," Katerina said, scowling at the piece of paper, "I wish you could, too."

USA TODAY Bestselling Author

Valerie Hansen
and
Lynette Eason

Pursuing Justice

Previously published as *Special Agent* and *Bounty Hunter*

⊕ HARLEQUIN® LOVE INSPIRED®CLASSICS

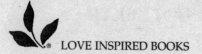

ISBN-13: 978-1-335-14303-7

Pursuing Justice

Copyright © 2019 by Harlequin Books S.A.

First published as Special Agent by Harlequin Books in 2017 and Bounty Hunter by Harlequin Books in 2017.

The publisher acknowledges the copyright holder of the individual works as follows:

Special Agent
Copyright © 2017 by Harlequin Books S.A.

Bounty Hunter
Copyright © 2017 by Harlequin Books S.A.

Special thanks and acknowledgment are given to Valerie Hansen and Lynette Eason for their contributions to the Classified K-9 Unit miniseries.

CONTENTS

Valerie Hansen was thirty when she awoke to the presence of the Lord in her life and turned to Jesus. She now lives in a renovated farmhouse on the breathtakingly beautiful Ozark Plateau of Arkansas and is privileged to share her personal faith by telling the stories of her heart for Love Inspired. Life doesn't get much better than that!

Visit the Author Profile page
at Harlequin.com for more titles.

SPECIAL AGENT

Valerie Hansen

For You have delivered my soul from death,
my eyes from tears, and my feet from falling.
—*Psalms* 116:8

Many thanks to fellow series authors Terri Reed,
Laura Scott, Lynette Eason, Shirlee McCoy
and Lenora Worth—plus editor Emily Rodmell,
who keeps us all on track.

And to my Joe, who is with me in spirit.
He always will be.

ONE

FBI agent Max West squared his shoulders and forced himself to walk away from the latest scene of destruction.

His job there was done. Unfortunately, the Dupree family crime syndicate, at least what was left of it, seemed determined to keep him and his team scrambling by randomly setting off bombs. Opal, his K-9 explosives detection partner, worked very well but it was frustrating to be called in after the fact.

He paused in the shade of an enormous oak and phoned Dylan O'Leary, the team's computer guru, on his cell. "I'm done with this one. Just the usual leftover components and a lot of jumpy people." Max sighed. "At least there was no loss of life *this* time. That family caught in the blast zone on the last one nearly made me turn in my badge."

"So, what now?" Dylan asked. "You thinking of leaving Northern California and heading home to Billings?"

"Maybe soon. I thought I'd look into the backgrounds of some of the Dupree underlings we've scooped up while I'm in the neighborhood. See if we missed anything on the first sweep."

"Little fish in a big pond," Dylan reminded him.

"We got Reginald Dupree, the real brains behind the drug operation."

Max nodded. "While his uncle Angus kidnapped one of our best men and escaped. Has there been any word on Agent Morrow's whereabouts?"

"Sorry. No."

"Okay." Max opened the rear door to his black SUV to air it out before letting his brown-and-white Boxer, Opal, get in. "I checked our files last night and was on my way to the Garwood Horse Ranch when I got diverted to this call. Vern Kowalski, one of the Dupree drug runners, had ties there. When we arrested him he insisted he was working alone but it won't hurt to check. I can use a break and so can Opal."

"You're the boss, *Boss*."

Max barely chuckled. Being SAC, special agent in charge, of the Classified K-9 Unit was no picnic. A lot of responsibility rested on his shoulders, responsibility that weighed heavily. Yes, he considered this job his calling, but that didn't mean he never felt the pain of loss, never wished he'd been more successful and had prevented every explosion, every injury. Every death.

Closing his eyes for a moment he reminded himself that he was just a man, giving his all in terrible situations. Then he loaded his dog, climbed behind the wheel and continued his interrupted trip to the nearby ranch.

Katerina Garwood was halfway between one of the stables and the house, heading for her old suite, when she saw an imposing black vehicle pass beneath the ornate wrought iron arch at the foot of the drive. Unexpected company was all she needed. If her father came outside to see who it was and caught her trespassing on his precious property he'd be furious. Well, so be it. There was no way she could run and hide in time to avoid encountering the new arrival—and perhaps her irate dad, as well.

Chin high, she paused in the wide, hard-packed drive and shaded her eyes. The SUV reminded her of one that had assisted the county sheriff on the worst day of her life. The day when all her dreams of a happy future had gone up in flames.

Darkly tinted windows kept her from getting a good look at the driver until he stopped, opened his door and stepped partway out. Prepared to tell him to head up to the house if he needed to speak to someone in charge, she took one look and was momentarily speechless. The blond, blue-eyed man was so imposing and had such a powerful presence he sent her usually normal reactions whirling. When he spoke, his deep voice magnified those unsettling feelings.

"Katerina Garwood?"

"Do I know you?"

"No, but I know you. I'm Special Agent West. I'd like to talk to you about Vern Kowalski."

"I have nothing to say." She started to turn away.

"This is not a social call, Ms. Garwood." He flashed a badge and blocked her path. "I suggest you reconsider."

"FBI? You have to be kidding. I am so unexceptional that until recently people hardly noticed me."

"They do now, I take it."

She blushed and rolled her eyes. "Oh, yeah."

"Then you'll understand why I need to speak with you."

A quick glance toward the house told her she and the hunky agent had not yet been noticed. That was too good to last. As soon as one of the hands or the fore-

man, Heath McCabe, spotted her, word would get to her
father and he'd be on the rampage again.

"Not here. Not now. We can meet in South Fork later.
I work at the Miner's Grub diner, on Main, near where
the American River forks."

He quirked a brow. "What's wrong, Ms. Garwood?
You seem nervous."

"It's personal."

"Everything is when you get right down to it." He
reached for her arm as a familiar white pickup truck
pulling a matching horse trailer rounded the nearest of
three identical, rectangular stables and came to a stop.

She jerked free. Backed away. Her sky-blue eyes had
widened and she was trembling. "I have to go. Now."

"Care to tell me why?" Max's gaze was unwavering. "Perhaps you'd better come with me and wait in
the car while I have my K-9 partner check this place."

"What? No. I'm not going anywhere with you. I
haven't broken any laws. All I did was believe Vern's
lies and fall in love with him. It's not my fault I was
duped. And I don't know anything about his secret life
as a crook, okay? Despite all the nasty rumors, I'm a
good person."

"Then why are you so jumpy?" Max continued to
crowd her until she was ready to literally shove him
away.

Unable to help herself, Katerina darted glances back
and forth between the immense house and the complex
of stables where the foreman had stopped with the horse
trailer. Was he on the phone to her dad already? There
was no way to tell. And no way to avoid another terrible scene once Bertrand was notified.

There was only one sensible course of action. She
had to plead her case in person, and to do that she had

to reach Heath McCabe despite the determined agent. Staring into the distance on his opposite side, she used that momentary distraction to slip away.

Max was on her in a flash, grasping her arms and holding fast. Katerina began to thrash around. If her father saw her now he'd be even more positive she was worthless. Tears of frustration filled her eyes.

I will not cry, she insisted to herself. *I'm through letting any man make me cry.* Nevertheless, a few drops escaped and trickled down her flushed cheeks.

Suddenly, she was pulled free. The middle-aged foreman had come to her rescue. His arm was drawn back, ready to deliver a punch, and the agent's hand was reaching for his sidearm.

Katerina intervened. "Stop!" She gestured at McCabe. "This is just a misunderstanding. I wanted to keep you from telling Dad I'm here and Agent… West? Agent West must have thought I was running away."

The adrenaline in her system had bolstered Katerina's courage and she faced him as boldly as she could while her insides quaked.

Max met her gaze head-on. "Your father? Why didn't you just say so?"

"I did. You weren't listening."

"No, you were acting guilty, behaving like a scared kid trying to make a run for it."

"I'm not a child. I'm twenty-two."

"I know. I read your file."

She was thunderstruck. "There's a *file* on me? An FBI file?"

"Yes, of course."

"Why am I not surprised?" She felt the starch go out of her like a sigh lost on the wind. Her concentration moved to the foreman. "Please don't tell Dad I'm here and make him mad all over again. It was bad enough when he threw me out the first time because of my horrible love life. I just want to pick up a few of the personal things I left behind."

McCabe doffed his cowboy hat. "I'd never do you that way, Miss Katerina. You know I wouldn't." He gestured back at the truck and trailer. "If I didn't have to get these horses to the vet for checkups I'd stay here and help."

"Do you have Moonlight with you? I looked for her in the stables when I got here and she wasn't in her usual stall. That whole section was empty."

"Your horse is safe and sound with me." The wiry foreman eyed Max. "All right if I leave or are you plannin' to shoot me?"

"I just came to talk to Ms. Garwood. If she had explained the reasons for her reluctance in the beginning we'd probably be done already."

"You gonna be okay if I go, ma'am?"

Katerina smiled. "The horses come first with me. You know that. I'll be fine." She noticed both men staring at the house across the driveway. "If Dad catches me here and starts yelling again I'll just do what I did before. I'll leave."

"Okay, then. You and this cop goin' into the house now?"

She looked to Max for confirmation.

"I do need to speak to Bertrand Garwood. If that's a problem for Ms. Garwood I see no reason to confront her father while she's present. She and I can talk out here."

"Now there's a good idea," Katerina said. "You can go, Heath. Take good care of Moonlight and the others."

"Yes, ma'am."

Watching him drive off, Katerina turned to Max. "All right. If you want to ask me questions let's get it over with. There's nothing I can tell you that I haven't already told the local police and the agents who arrested Vern, but I suppose it won't kill me to go over it again." She made a face. "I learned a hard lesson."

"Oh? Did you?"

Her grimace grew and her eyebrows arched. "Yes, Mr. Agent, I found out that my loving father will disown me and throw me out if I make a mistake. I also learned to never trust a glib-talking man, and that includes you."

She would have been happier if he hadn't seemed to find that final statement amusing.

"Let's sit in my car," Max said, gesturing with his arm. "After you."

"Can't I go get my clothes and stuff first? It took a lot of courage for me to drive back out here and as long as Dad hasn't noticed me yet, I'd like to finish what I came for."

"I take it you expect me to just hang around while you do as you please."

"Why not? I'm no criminal."

The unwavering look she was giving him as she spoke demonstrated determination. And she was right. Law enforcement had nothing on her, personally. He'd merely hoped that some small fact she didn't even think was important would point the way to more of the Dupree associates, perhaps even to herself, although at this juncture he viewed the young woman as more of a pawn in a crooked chess game than a true player.

Blowing out a breath, he conceded. "Okay. Do you want any help?"

"No. The less noise I make, the less likely I'll be noticed. It's a big house and when my father works on his accounts he always shuts the den door."

"All right. I'll wait in the car."

As soon as she started toward the garden leading to the nearest door of the ranch-style home, Max turned back to his SUV. There was something appealing about Katerina Garwood; something he couldn't quite put his finger on. She was far too young for him, of course. It was too bad she hadn't been born ten years earlier.

Max's thirty-three wasn't exactly ancient but there were times when he felt like Methuselah, particularly when he and his team failed to prevent mayhem.

Movement at the edge of his peripheral vision snapped him around. *Now* what was she up to?

"Hey, where do you think you're going?" he called.

Turning to walk backward, Katerina waved. "I left some empty boxes in my truck. I'll be right back."

"Sure, you will," Max muttered. He wasn't taking any chances that she'd try to flee so he fired up his SUV, made a U-turn and headed for the main gate to block it. If worse came to worst and she got away from him he could always call for backup, but it would sure be embarrassing.

Katerina paused to watch his maneuvers. The man was paranoid. What did he think she was going to do, try to outrun his powerful vehicle in her little ol' pickup truck? Talk about David and Goliath.

"Yes, but David won," she mused, happy to have been reminded of a Bible story where the seemingly weaker combatant triumphed in spite of everything.

Before she had time to pivot and continue on her previous path toward the stable, an intense light flashed.

She instinctively ducked and covered her head with her arms.

Her eardrums felt as if she had plunged to the depths of the sea. Debris hit her as the blast concussion sent her—and pieces of one of the barns—flying.

Landing on the hard-packed dirt with the realization that a building had exploded, her last conscious thought was for the well-being of her favorite mare, and others. "Thank You, God. Moonlight is safe with Heath."

Max's heart was in his throat. Nothing in the files had suggested that Katerina was involved in the recent rash of bombings, nor had there been any threats against the ranch. Not that he knew of, anyway.

He was running toward her as he called 9-1-1, identified himself and reported the explosion. "At the Garwood Ranch. That's right. Between South Fork and Groveland. Send an ambulance and the fire department. I see a lot of smoke."

Dropping the phone on the littered ground beside Katerina he fell to his knees and began to check her over. "Lie still. Don't move. An ambulance is on the way."

She moaned and shifted position.

Max held her shoulders gently but firmly. "I said don't move. You could have broken bones or spinal damage." He could tell by the way her eyelids fluttered that she was only half-conscious. That was the worst time for exacerbating injuries. Out cold she wouldn't move. Conscious, she'd probably try to do as she was told.

People were running to evacuate frantic horses from the remaining, undamaged barns. Dogs circled and barked, adding to the mayhem. A heavyset man stomped across the dirt drive. He was wearing boots, a Western shirt and hat, and jeans belted with the biggest gold buckle Max had ever seen.

"Who are you?" the man bellowed.

"Max West, FBI. You must be Bertrand Garwood."

"Smart man. What're you doing on my ranch?" He pointed at the prone figure of his daughter. "And what is *she* doing here?"

The coldness of the older man almost gave Max the shivers. No wonder Katerina didn't want to face him. Well, *he* wasn't backing down. Although he couldn't safely release her until paramedics arrived he looked up and glared. "Your daughter is unconscious, Mr. Garwood. I'm not certain how bad her injuries may be. I don't see any bleeding other than a split lip so she may have escaped the worst of the blast. It's too soon to tell for sure."

"Just get that trash out of here as soon as you can." He started to turn away. "I've got valuable livestock to see to."

If Max had not been busy tending to Katerina he might have resorted to language he hadn't been tempted to use in ages. What a pompous excuse for a parent Garwood was.

Max gazed down at the injured young woman and gently stroked strands of honey-blond hair off her forehead. There was a first aid kit in his car but he didn't dare leave her unattended to fetch it. Close by in the SUV, his trained K-9, Opal, was using her deep boxer bark to alert the world to danger, even though the worst of it was probably over.

As soon as the ambulance and fire department arrived, Max planned to assert authority and insist that he and his K-9 partner perform a bomb sweep for additional devices. It was his job—and Opal's—to ensure no one else got hurt without actually revealing the overarching mission. It was going to be tricky to investigate Kowalski's crimes without exhibiting too much interest in the man's former connection to the Duprees.

He looked at Katerina again and realized he didn't want to turn her over to the care of the EMTs. He would, of course, because it was the right thing to do, but he wasn't going to like relinquishing control before he was certain she was okay.

TWO

Katerina could hardly breathe. Disoriented, she opened her eyes. The back of her head throbbed and her ribs refused to allow her to fully inhale. Gasping, she fought to regain her senses, to sort out confusing memories.

A weight was on both her shoulders, holding her down.

"Don't try to get up," someone ordered gruffly. "An ambulance is on its way."

Nevertheless, she tried to move.

"I said, hold still."

There was a gentleness underlying the otherwise firm tone and it gave her a sense that she was being well cared for. "Who? What?" Flashes of reality returned. "The stable! The horses!"

"They'd been taken out. Remember?"

"Only—only from the one barn."

"That's the one that blew."

"Oh." Blinking up at the face of her companion she saw mostly shadow. Sunlight behind him gave his short blondish hair a haloed look. The brightness kept her from reading his shadowed expression. She sank back down with a moan. "My head hurts."

"I'm not surprised. You hit the ground hard."

Her heart sped as she realized she could have been even closer to the barn when it disintegrated. What could have caused an accident like that? There was nothing more volatile than horse liniment kept near the animals. Even the tack room was safe.

The man restraining her shouted, "Medic! Over here. Everybody else stand clear."

"I'm all right. Really. I need to get out of here."

"The only place you're going, Ms. Garwood, is to the hospital."

"No. I don't have insurance. I can't afford to be hurt." She pushed against his hold momentarily, then sagged back.

Bright flashes of colored light sparkled behind her eyelids. Shooting pain banished any thought of trying to stand. Escape was unthinkable.

Katerina felt as if she were falling into a bottomless abyss. Fog surrounded her, bearing her ever deeper into unconsciousness. Longing for release, she ceased to fight it. Rational thought fled.

The world, and her troubles, faded away.

Max stayed on at the Garwood Ranch to assist local authorities in searching for additional devices in the unaffected outbuildings and house after Katerina had been stabilized and transported in the ambulance. From what he could deduce from the damage, the explosion in the stable had packed a lighter punch than the others he'd recently investigated. Unfortunately, an ensuing fire had wiped out much of the evidence and what the flames didn't consume, the firefighters' high pressure hoses had dispersed.

By now the place was swarming with law enforcement, fire personnel and crime scene investigators. He was relieved that he and his K-9 had not discovered more bombs because a crowd like that was hard to safeguard.

When he reported to the incident commander, a fire department battalion chief, he brought Opal with him. "My dog and I have completed our search. All clear."

"You sure?"

Max laid a hand gently on the boxer's head and stroked between her ears. "Opal is positive. That's good enough for me."

"Okay. Thanks. I can't believe you were already on scene when this happened. Is that some new FBI deduction technique that we haven't heard of?"

Max chuckled. "Not hardly. I was here to follow up with the Garwoods regarding another case my team is working. What can you tell me about Vern Kowalski?"

"Not much." The chief paused to radio instructions to an engine crew. "Pull down that west wall. I don't want to see a rekindle and lose another barn."

As soon as the man turned back to him Max asked, "Had you met Kowalski?"

"Briefly. The guy wanted to join our volunteers but he didn't make the cut. Katerina seemed to like him, though."

"I gathered, since she was going to marry him."

"Yeah. I hope she's gonna be okay. Nice girl. Her daddy's a real piece of work, though. He was hard to get along with before he got elected mayor of South Fork. Now he's impossible."

"Any word on her condition?" Max asked, remembering her attempt to avoid treatment and her father's unfeeling reaction to her condition. How could any parent see his child injured and just walk away?

"Not yet. We shipped her to the hospital in Mariposa.

Paramedics said she could have a concussion. Hard to say without X-rays."

"What became of Garwood? I know he was here for a while." Max made a sour face. "He's hard to ignore."

"Yeah. Sheriff Tate took him off the property in a patrol car. They're old buddies."

"I see. Then I'll talk to the Garwood I can find and head for Mariposa." Max scanned the scene. "Just make sure your people bag and tag as many clues as possible. I'll notify Quantico and have an agent pick up the evidence for processing."

The chief didn't look particularly pleased to share jurisdiction but didn't argue. Instead, he nodded and returned to the smoldering wreckage.

Max was pouring fresh water into Opal's bowl in the backseat as he checked in with Dylan at headquarters. "The ranch owner is AWOL at the moment so I'm going to follow up with the injured daughter, providing she's conscious."

"The one who was engaged to one of the men arrested in the Dupree sweep?"

"Yup. That's the one."

"Just watch your back," Dylan cautioned. "I don't care how idyllic it looks up there, you're in more danger than a gold prospector defending himself against claim-jumpers back in '49."

Max had to smile. "I have Opal and a cell phone and radio, and I'm armed. I'm covered."

"The dog will always work but don't count on electronics if you get down in some of those deep valleys. Besides, the Duprees play rough."

"I know. Thanks," he said, ending the call and drawing his fingers down the ridge of the old scar remaining on his left cheek as he recalled the events originally surrounding that injury five years before. Max knew that nobody lived forever, but he simply could not accept the premature death of a child on his watch. Worse, he had unknowingly contributed to that disaster by trusting the boy's father when the man vowed he'd cut all ties with the drug culture.

Clenching his jaw, he shoved aside the painful memory. If that senseless tragedy had taught him anything, it was to be far less gullible. No one had fooled him since, nor would they do so in the future. Criminal minds were devious in myriad ways. All he had to do was keep himself from accepting anything—or anybody—at face value without concrete proof of innocence.

Take the Garwoods, for example. The young woman he was on his way to see may have looked harmless but she was so unnaturally nervous he was having second thoughts about her. It was hard to attribute all that angst to a strained relationship with her father. Yes, the man was vindictive, but lots of people experienced difficult family situations without quaking in their boots. A more likely scenario was that Katerina knew about the bomb and had miscalculated the timing.

The worst kinds of criminals were the ones who were able to fake innocence so well. Katerina might have fooled the firefighter he'd spoken with but Max would not be as naive. He had not risen to a command position on his team by letting himself be tricked by pretty faces or sweet smiles.

He didn't care if the whole world thought he was inflexible and opinionated. He did his job. And he never lost focus. Not anymore.

Katerina was exhausted. She'd been poked, prodded, x-rayed and scanned. All she wanted to do at the moment was sleep despite the nurses who kept coming into her room and waking her to check her vitals.

The door to the hospital room made a swooshing sound as it opened. She squeezed her eyes shut against the bright overhead lighting. "I'm awake. Please let me rest."

The ceiling-mounted curtain was pulled to isolate her bed. Someone's latex-covered hand clamped hard over her mouth and she tasted fresh blood from the cut on her lip. Tightening her muscles sent pulses of pain shooting through Katerina's battered back. She tore at the glove and tried to see who was attacking her but a ski mask covered his features. A harshly whispered warning came next, "Stop fighting." She tried. Panic argued against it. All she could manage was to hold a little more still after he planted a heavy arm across her chest.

"Don't scream."

Although she managed a weak nod she was not agreeing. This was a busy hospital. If she could manage to shout, even once, help was bound to arrive. Hopefully, it would be enough for a rescue.

The gloved hand eased its pressure. The arm lifted. Trembling, Katerina froze and stared at the figure hovering over her bed. He seemed tall, although it was hard to tell for sure when she was lying down. What she could see of his bare arms beyond the short sleeves of the faded green scrub outfit he wore told her he was tanned but not unusually so. If she'd been able to see his hands they would have given her a better idea of whether he worked inside or on a ranch or farm.

Should she speak at all? she wondered. If he was planning to kill her, surely he wouldn't have awakened her first. But why bother her at all? Why was any of this happening? She gritted her teeth in frustration.

"Vern sent me," the man gritted out.

Anger mingled with her fear. So that was it. "Why?"

He didn't answer. She could see the rapid blinking of his eyes through the holes in the mask as he swiveled his head nervously. Finally, he reached for the IV needle taped to her arm and started to pull it out. "It's too dangerous for me here. You and I are leaving."

Katerina pushed his hand away, took a deep breath and screamed, "No. Help!" at the top of her lungs.

Her attacker jumped away as if he'd been shot with a Taser. At that moment she wished she had one to make it real.

He lunged to cover her mouth once more, but she evaded him by rolling to the side. "Help me!"

The physical pressure lifted. Katerina continued to shriek with primal fear, no longer articulate.

A hand touched her shoulder. Voices mingled.

When she turned her head there were two nurses at her bedside, one blond, one graying and motherly looking.

Katerina peered past them. "Where did he go?"

"Who, dear?"

"The man. He had a mask on and he—"

"You've been through a severe trauma," the blond nurse interjected. "We can't give you a stronger sedative just yet, because of your head injury, but the doctor said we could take the edge off your pain. You may be having a delayed reaction to what happened to you or to the IV meds. I'll report it to him."

"I am not hallucinating," Katerina insisted hoarsely. "There was a strange man right here in this room. He threatened me." She lost hope when she saw the nurses exchange knowing glances.

"All right. Just lie back and rest," the motherly one

said, patting Katerina's hand. "I'm sure you'll be released soon. In the meantime, one of us will be close by. Use your call button if you need anything."

"You're not even going to look for the guy, are you?"

"As I said, we'll report your symptoms to your physician, dear."

Meaning, they still thought she'd been hallucinating or dreaming. Was it possible? *No*, she concluded. A trick of her brain would not have made her cracked lip bleed again. There had been a man's hand pressed over her mouth. And he'd intended to take her away with him.

Vern was in jail. So who had accosted her?

Max knocked before entering Katerina's room accompanied by a nurse. He'd expected to see her in bed but had not anticipated the reaction he got. She took one look at him, fisted her sheet and gathered it up under her chin like a shield. Her skin was pale, her mouth slightly swollen and her eyes reddened and puffy as if she'd been crying.

He hesitated, raw emotion churning through him. despite outward calm "The staff says you've been having a rough time, Ms. Garwood. Do you remember who I am?"

"FBI. You were there when the barn exploded."

"Right. I looked after you until the ambulance arrived. How are you feeling?" he asked gently. "Are you up to finishing our conversation?"

As he watched, Katerina tried to raise herself into a sitting position and blanched. She looked ill beyond her injuries. Max beat the nurse to her bedside and steadied her. "Easy."

With the weight of her shoulders resting on his arm,

Katerina sighed. "Sorry. I forgot myself for a second. It's been a rough day."

Max stepped back as the nurse raised the head of her bed slightly, and then he asked, "Better now? Or do you need a few more minutes?"

"I'll be fine as long as I don't try to move too quickly." She eyed the young nurse in the background. "Would it be possible for us to talk alone?"

Max nodded. "I see no problem with that. Leave the door ajar on your way out, please," he told the nurse. As soon as she had left he took out a small digital recorder, clicked it on and renewed his interest in the patient. "What can you tell me about the incident at the ranch this morning?"

"Me? You were there, too. I don't know any more about it than you do. One minute I was yelling back at you and the next thing I knew I was knocked off my feet." Her voice softened a notch. "Thanks for looking after me."

"You're welcome. Now think. Did you see or hear anything unusual earlier?"

Her brow furrowed. "No. I wasn't actually there for very long. I'd just stopped by to pick up the last of my clothes and things. I told you that."

"I understand you no longer live there."

"No. I don't. My father was so angry when Vern was arrested for smuggling and distributing drugs he blamed me for ruining the family reputation and threw me out."

Max struck a pseudo-relaxed pose. "And you're surprised by that? It was pretty risky to keep company with a lowlife like Kowalski in the first place. You must have suspected he'd eventually be caught."

"I had no idea he was a crook."

That he didn't believe for a second. "You were supposed to be marrying the man. How could you possibly not have known?"

"Because he was slick and because I was naive, I guess." Her cheeks warmed visibly and his chest constricted when he saw moisture glistening behind her lashes. But he reminded himself he had a job to do. "Look," Katerina went on, "I'm not stupid. I actually have a pretty decent IQ. But Vern wasn't like the other men I'd met. He said all the right things at the right times and I fell for him. How was I to know he was using my father's horse business as a cover to distribute drugs?"

"Intuition? Didn't Kowalski ever say or do anything that made you suspicious before he was arrested?"

"No." She broke eye contact. "Later."

Aha! Now they were finally making progress. "When?"

"Promise you won't look at me like I'm a horse short of a full team?"

"Yes. Go on, Ms. Garwood."

"When I had a scare earlier this afternoon, the nurses said I imagined everything and blamed it on my injury and pain medicine."

Leaning closer, Max listened carefully. "Is that what you think?"

"No. Well, maybe. I know I was terrified. I was drifting in and out of consciousness when somebody clamped a hand over my mouth and told me not to struggle."

"Here?" Every instinct in him was on alert. "They told me you'd been having nightmares but what you claim is highly unlikely."

"I know," Katerina agreed. "The nurses who came after I shouted for help insisted I'd been dreaming. I've started thinking they may be right. It's just that my lip bled and hurt more afterward and I can't see any other reason for that much physical change, not even my screaming when I got so scared."

"Describe your assailant."

She huffed. "Pick up any mystery novel and you'll know. Ski mask, hospital clothes and gloves. No prints, no ID, no nothing. He wasn't as tall as you are and not as muscular, but…"

"Okay. What makes you think he had anything to do with Kowalski?"

"Because he told me Vern sent him," Katerina said haltingly. "I—I thought he was going to kidnap me. That's when I started yelling."

Max gave her the kind of stern, menacing look he usually reserved for perps he was grilling. "You didn't want to go with a friend of your fiancé?"

He saw her fists clench. "No."

"Because he scared you?"

Despite the obvious discomfort of pushing herself up with her elbows, she met his severe gaze with one of her own. "No," she almost shouted before lowering her voice, her throat raw. "Because I am an honest person and I want nothing to do with criminals, their friends or their disgusting business. When is everybody going to get that straight?"

The glistening of her unshed tears was more convincing than her insistence. Either she was a great actress or she was truly upset.

Max stood and backed away to make a call. He arranged to have the police check recent activity on the security cameras monitoring the halls and place a guard outside Katerina's room for the night. Then he returned to her. "When you're released from here I'll come back and drive you home. Then, if you're up to it, I'd like to take you back to the ranch and walk you through exactly what you did before I arrived." He handed her a business card after jotting his private cell number on it. "Call me when you're ready to go."

"What if I refuse to take orders from you and arrange my own ride?"

"I don't advise it."

Katerina nodded. "I'll call, but not because you're scowling at me. And not because I'm guilty of anything and hope to fool you. I'll call because you believe there really was a stranger in my room when everybody else insists I'm crazy."

THREE

In retrospect, Katerina was not keen on asking the taciturn federal agent for a ride home the following day. The problem was, she had few other options. Her poor pickup truck was probably toast after the barn blew up and except for a few friends who worked in town and maybe the ranch foreman, there was nobody she felt she could call. Heath McCabe would be in deep trouble with her dad if she asked him, so she did the sensible thing and dialed Max West's private number.

"West."

"Um, hi. It's Katerina Garwood. They've discharged me and I need a ride if your offer is still open."

"Of course. Did you have a quiet night?"

"As quiet as it gets in a hospital," she said with a wry smile.

"Understood. I can be there in twenty. Does that work?"

"Yes, I think I'll last that long. I'd walk down to the cafeteria for a latte if I wasn't still a little dizzy."

"Are you sure you're okay to leave?"

It was refreshing to hear genuine concern reflected in his question. "The doctor says I am so I'm going. This is not a fun place. I want out."

"Hang tight. I'm on my way."

She wanted to tell him how truly thankful she was that he'd made himself available but did not. Her instinct to trust had been so ravaged by Vern's betrayal and her father's rejection she couldn't rely on her instincts. Not yet. Besides, considering all she'd learned about law enforcement in the past few months, Max was probably only being nice to her in order to catch whoever had menaced her or set the bomb at the ranch. Or because he still had doubts about her innocence. Given his job and her background, she figured the agent would become even more suspicious if she acted overly friendly.

Katerina let her thoughts wander as she perched on the edge of the bed in the too-big green scrub outfit the nurses had provided. Her own clothes were ruined. The back of the shirt she'd been wearing looked as if it had been blasted with a shotgun, as her tender shoulder blades kept reminding her. Jeans were tougher but hers were so dirty she'd refused to put them on. Her leather cowboy boots were about the only thing she could still wear, although they slipped without thick socks.

"I should fix my hair," she muttered, wondering why it mattered when she wasn't meeting anyone but Agent West. Nevertheless, she slid off the bed, took a second to steady herself, then made her way to the bathroom mirror. Nurses had helped her shower and the hospital had provided a comb but her long, wavy hair resisted efforts to tame it. Pulling on tangles made her scalp hurt unless she carefully held each portion, so the job took a while and was less than perfect. Well, too bad. If her volunteer taxi driver didn't approve, so what?

That hostile attitude not only struck her as wrong, it made her blush. Whatever his motives, Max was no chauffeur. He was going out of his way to be nice to her. The least she could do was try to look presentable.

A knock on the door startled her. She steadied her balance on the sink and called, "Come in."

One look at him today, when she was fully lucid and aware, took her breath away. Not only was he tall and ruggedly handsome, his dark blue uniform shirt fit the way it should, displaying a powerful form with broad shoulders and a narrow waist, unlike many men his age. How old was he? she wondered. It was impossible to tell, although her best guess put him somewhere in his early thirties. Definitely not over-the-hill. Far from it.

Max acknowledged her with a brief nod. "Ready?"

"Absolutely." She began to move toward him, hiking up her sagging scrubs as the pants started to slip.

He eyed her. "Nice outfit."

"The boots are mine. The rest is borrowed."

He cleared his throat but Katerina still heard the chuckle he was trying to mask when he said, "Glad they had your size."

"I could fit two of me and a couple of the ranch dogs in here at the same time," she quipped, stopping and spreading her arms to better display the two-piece scrub ensemble. That was an error. The room started to tilt and she made a grab for the doorjamb. "Whoa."

Beside her in a fraction of a second, Max caught her around the waist. "Easy. You sure you're ready to leave?"

"I'm signed out and everything. Just had my chickens scattered, as Mom used to say."

"Your parents are divorced?" He was guiding her toward the open door.

"No. My mother passed away when I was fourteen.

That's when I started putting all my efforts into training horses."

"So, last year?"

Katerina knew he was teasing to try to lift her spirits and played along. "I'm twenty-two, going on forty, which my file should tell you." Leaning on his big, strong arm as they walked, she asked, "How about you?"

Max gave her a wry smile. "Older than dirt."

"That old, huh?"

Pausing at the doorway he looked back. "Do you have anything to take with you? Meds or bandages or anything?"

"Just that plastic sack of ruined clothing at the foot of the bed. Since I'm on a tight budget I need to try to salvage the jeans."

Making sure she was well balanced, he fetched the bag and picked up where they'd left off. They were almost to the exit when a nurse spotted them and tsk-tsked. "You're supposed to leave in a wheelchair, ma'am. We don't want you falling."

"As you can see I'm in good hands," Katerina said, smiling and leaning her head toward her stalwart companion, genuinely glad he was by her side.

It wasn't until they left the hospital and she saw his formidable black SUV that she sobered. Lighthearted moments aside, there was big trouble in the little towns in and around historic gold country. First there had been the drug busts and now somebody was setting off bombs. Other incidents had been reported on the local news so she knew her family ranch was not the only target. The question was, did somebody destroy the barn as retribution for her former ties to Vern? It was certainly possible, and terribly disconcerting.

She remained silent as Max helped her into the SUV. Above all, she wanted him to find the perpetrator and put him in jail.

And not blame an innocent bystander. Like her.

"So, where do you live?" Max asked casually.

She arched an eyebrow. "You mean you don't already know? That's not very comforting."

"Okay, I know," he said with a smile, flicking a brief glance across the seat at her. "I figured you might have a shortcut or better way to get there. These winding roads are hard on Opal."

"Who?"

"My K-9 partner. She usually rides closer to me but I put her in her portable kennel box in the back when I have a passenger. You'd have met her if you hadn't been knocked unconscious."

"Oh, I love dogs! Is she a German shepherd?"

"No. And don't you dare laugh. She's a boxer."

"A *what*?"

"You heard me. I get teased almost everywhere we go. She's really great at detecting bombs but people are more used to seeing breeds with longer noses."

"No kidding. Why in the world would they train a boxer for that? I mean, they can't have as keen a sense of smell with such a short muzzle."

"You'd be surprised."

"I'd like to meet her. Dogs and horses were my best friends while I was growing up. There's a darling black lab at the ranch that I'd adopt in a heartbeat if Dad would let me." She hesitated, seeming sad. "So, tell me more about your dog. How old is she and how long have you had her?"

"She's about four. My team has begun rescuing at least one pup for every mission we go on and we don't rule out any capable canine, purebred or mutt. Opal's a good example of hidden talent. She showed aptitude for detecting explosives and hearing or smelling electronics such as detonators, et cetera, so she was trained and assigned to work with me." He cleared his throat before continuing. "We're not master and dog, we're partners. We both have badges. I just happen to be the only one with a driver's license and a gun."

Katerina chuckled quietly. "That's comforting." Pointing to an upcoming turn, she said, "May as well take 49 and double back a little. My place is between here and the ranch."

"I'm surprised you didn't ask more about the horses in that burning barn." He was surreptitiously watching her expression and most likely wondering if he would find out more than she intended to reveal.

"Heath had Moonlight and her stablemates in the trailer, remember?"

"Yeah. Handy."

"What was?"

"That that barn was totally empty when the bomb went off."

"You don't think Heath was responsible, do you? I mean, he's been with the family since he was a teenager. I trust him like an uncle."

He hardened his jaw. "What about your father? Could he have needed insurance settlement money?"

"Of course not. Don't be ridiculous."

"Then you realize who that leaves." His gaze was telling, as it was meant to be.

"Me? No way. I'd never endanger people or animals. How many times do I have to say it? I am one of the good guys."

"Until I believe it." Another sidelong glance caught her evident consternation.

"I don't care if you believe me or not, Mr. Big Important Government Agent, except that you're wasting time. Instead of harassing me you should be out looking for whoever is really behind the bombing, not to mention the lowlife who tried to grab me from the hospital."

"I'm keeping my eyes open," he vowed soberly.

"It's not your eyes I'm worried about," Katerina countered, "it's your closed mind." She turned her face to the window and added, "'There is none so blind as he who will not see.'"

Max knew she was quoting scripture, although he couldn't recall exactly where in the Bible that phrase was found. He didn't mind her doing that. What bothered him was the slim possibility she might be right.

Katerina's apartment was a tiny space above a boarded-up, vacant storefront on a side street in South Fork. It had been all she could find when she'd been ousted by her father and, although she was now employed, anything else was still beyond her budget. If she hadn't worked at a diner, eating might have been, too. Not that she wanted anyone to know. The way she looked at it, as long as she had a roof over her head and enough to eat, she was blessed.

If the K-9 cop/agent was surprised by the appearance of her current dwelling in contrast to the posh Garwood Ranch he hid it well. That pleased her. She'd already had so-called friends from her ranch days turn up their noses at her efforts to make a home out of a veritable hovel. This handsome man with his perfectly pressed uniform and gleaming car never batted an eye.

"I'll get Opal." He eyed her scrubs and smiled. "That shade of green sure isn't your color."

Katerina returned his grin. "Oh, I don't know. It matches my skin whenever I move too fast and get dizzy."

He was chuckling to himself as he opened the hatchback and released his dog. Katerina waited to see what a boxer in uniform looked like. Since the idea was ludicrous she assumed the image would be, too. Opal, however, jumped down on command and stood at the ready, a picture of the perfect canine standing at attention as if she were a seasoned soldier ready to do battle.

"Can I pet her?" Katerina asked. "I don't want to mess up her training."

"Glad you asked. When our dogs are wearing their vests or special harnesses like this it's best to keep your distance. I'll let you play with her later. Okay?"

"Okay. She really is beautiful and impressive. I'm sorry I made fun of her breed." Katerina continued to smile, only this time she was focused on the dog. "Please convey my sincere apologies?"

"Opal never holds a grudge," Max said with a slight smirk. "I think you'll enjoy watching her work. She's intense when she's on the trail of dangerous substances."

"Wonderful. Well…" She eyed the building. "I'll go on up and change before we go back to look at the ranch. That was what you wanted to do, right?"

"Right. After Opal and I have scoped out your apartment."

It was hard for Katerina to stifle an unladylike snort. "I don't think there's much danger of anybody even finding this place, let alone wanting to blow it up. It will probably fall down on its own soon enough."

"Still, we should go with you. Opal can always use

the practice and there's no lead on whoever was in your hospital room yesterday."

Reminded of this, Katerina was willing to let him accompany her. After her recent close calls she was unsteady in more ways than one. Her nerves were firing like kernels of popcorn in a pan of hot oil and she didn't like the feeling one bit.

"Okay. I have an outside stairway in the rear. That way I don't have to bother opening the old hardware store to get in."

"It looks unique." Max squinted to peer through the dusty windows. "I almost expect a prospector to step out carrying a pickax and a gold pan."

"You aren't far wrong. The date over the doorway says the building goes back to the mid-1800s. I suspect it was expanded as needed during the gold rush." She paused when she reached the base of the wooden stairway in the rear. "Single file from here. Be my guest."

Max hesitated and raked her with a solemn stare. "If I didn't have Opal to alert me, I might wonder if you wanted me to go first because you already knew it was dangerous."

"Oh, for…" Katerina pushed past him and stomped up the stairs in her loose boots. The door wasn't locked. Almost nobody in South Fork locked their homes. She straight-armed the door and barged in. One gasp and she skidded to a halt.

Max caught up. "What's wrong?"

"Look! It's awful!"

He took one peek and agreed. "Wow. I take it you're usually a neater housekeeper than this."

"Well, duh." Katerina rolled her eyes cynically. "I never tear the stuffing out of my only chair just for fun.

And I don't have a pet tiger, so those slashes must have been made with a knife."

He drew Opal closer with the leash and placed his other palm on the grip of his sidearm. "Wait here."

He didn't have to tell Katerina twice. Her boots felt nailed to the floor. Trembling, she watched the dog put its nose to the carpet and lead the handsome agent toward her bedroom. Was it simply searching for a scent or had it picked up the odor of an explosive? What if there was another bomb? What if it went off? She shivered involuntarily. The old hardware store was rickety at best and there was no telling what kind of combustibles might be stored below. She had never wondered before. Now she wished she'd been more paranoid.

Taut nerves insisted she not linger despite the agent's orders to the contrary. Checking to see if he was visible and not seeing him or his dog, she began to sidle out the open door. One step. Two...

Max's shout of "Hey!" startled her and she thought he was yelling at her until he added, "Federal agent. Freeze."

Katerina tensed. A darkly clad figure came barreling toward her. There was no time to move before the onrushing man lowered a shoulder and smashed into her like a quarterback trying to make a touchdown. She spun. Fell. Heard more shouting and sensed someone jumping over her prone figure.

Wood cracked. Splintered. The outside railing gave way. A dog yipped. *Opal!*

Katerina flipped over and scrambled for footing. Her head was pounding. Her vision blurry. Unsure, she blinked rapidly, astounded.

Max was hanging from the remains of the broken railing by one hand while his canine partner clung to the partially collapsed stairway edge, legs splayed and claws digging in.

The moment Katerina peered over at him he shouted, "Get the dog!"

It never occurred to her to argue or hesitate. Only after she had hold of Opal's harness and was hauling her to safety did she wonder why she hadn't been bitten. As soon as the K-9 was out of the way, the agent swung a foot onto the edge of the step Opal had vacated and pulled himself up.

All three sat there, catching their breaths. Only the dog seemed unperturbed.

"Thanks," Max said. "You okay?"

Katerina began to nod, then thought better of it. "Just peachy. I have a pounding headache, the whole county thinks I'm a crook, somebody is out to make an even bigger mess of my life than it already is, my ex sent a thug after me and we all could have been killed just now, even poor Opal. Otherwise, I guess I'm fine."

"You *guess*?" His tone was gruff.

"Hey, don't snap at me. I just saved your partner."

"Did you get a look at the guy? Was it the same man as at the hospital? All I saw was a black hoodie and jeans."

"I have no idea," Katerina insisted. "He rushed me so fast I hardly knew what was happening. Where was he hiding?"

"Beats me. Must have been in the kitchen. He wasn't in the living room or bedroom." Standing, he reached for her hand. "Come on. You need to go in and see if anything's missing. Since he was still here, I assume he didn't find whatever he was looking for, but you should take a look."

"I'm not going to like what I see, am I?" she asked warily as he pulled her to her feet.

"No, you're not. Watch your step."

Max kept hold of her hand as he led her back into the apartment. Opal followed, no longer acting concerned or even interested. That was a relief. Katerina was actually feeling pretty good until she saw her bedroom. Or what was left of it.

Max was impressed by this young woman's inner strength. Most would have wept over the mess the thieves had made. Someone had destroyed her thin mattress down to the box springs, then torn the covering off it, too. There was no way she was going to be able to sleep there until replacements were found, and even then it wouldn't be safe with the only easy exit missing part of its railing.

"We should leave the evidence as is until a crime scene team can look it over," he said. "I'm not sure how much of your clothing is usable anyway."

"It better be okay. I can't afford to buy new."

"I'm sure your father—"

"Don't even go there," she snapped. "My dad made it very clear that he wanted nothing more to do with me. I am not asking him for a thing."

"Then how about appealing to your fiancé's friends? I'm sure they have plenty of money." Max hated to keep needling her but necessity and training insisted. All he'd need were a few new names and the investigation could head in a fresh direction. Making a seemingly nice young woman spitting mad was a small price to pay considering what he eventually hoped to get out of her.

During the course of most investigations he had no qualms about stirring up volatile emotions. In Katerina's case, however, he found the method personally objectionable. Necessary, but distasteful.

The fire in her gaze and stubborn set of her jaw told him he might have hit the bull's-eye. Instead of telling him off, however, she merely went to the dresser, stuffed a few things into a pillowcase and walked stiffly past him to the door.

"I've reported this incident," Max said. "You can't leave until the police get here."

Katerina wheeled. One hand was clenched around the opening to the pillowcase and the other was fisted at her side. "I'll be in the car."

"Fine. And while you wait, think. What are they looking for? And who blew up the stable? Nobody becomes the focus of continuing attacks without reason. You must have a good idea who's doing this, and the sooner you tell me, the sooner I'll go away."

Her nostrils flared, her cheeks turned red and she glared at him. "Maybe the same criminals did it all."

"As a profiler, I find that highly unlikely, Ms. Garwood. Whoever set the bomb in the barn couldn't have been looking for something you'd hidden there because they'd have taken a chance of losing it forever in an explosion and fire. This apartment, however, was ransacked but not destroyed. That tells me they didn't find what they were searching for."

"They'll be back?" She chewed her lower lip. "Of course they will." Color drained from her face, leaving her so pale Max worried she might be ready to keel over. There was only one thing to do. He phoned Dylan and briefed him, then asked, "Can you get me another room at that hotel where I'm staying? I need a place to put Ms. Garwood, at least for one night."

Dylan's response wasn't as positive as Max had anticipated but the young woman's wide-eyed astonishment helped him decide on an alternative. "All right. Do what you can. If I have to, I'll give her my room and Opal and I will crash in the car. It won't be the first time."

Meeting Katerina's gaze, he was startled to see unshed tears and even more surprised when she said, "You'd do that for me? When you still blame me for the bombing?"

"Let's just say you're a person of interest. Dylan will wrangle another room. Don't worry. He always comes through for the team."

A tear slipped silently down her cheek. She brushed it away. "You're not nearly as tough and mean as you pretend to be, are you, Special Agent West?"

His "No comment" brought a soft laugh from her that reminded him of joy-filled times he'd thought he'd forgotten, times when life had seemed easy.

A few moments of looking into her eyes was almost more than Max's heart could take. He turned away. If an impartial observer had accused him of emotionally closing down he would not have argued.

Katerina Garwood was as dangerous to his mental and emotional stability as the deadliest of criminals. The only thing that would save him was that he knew it.

FOUR

"I hope you're going to tell me that your agency is picking up the tab for both hotel rooms," Katerina said as Max concluded his business with the police and joined her with Opal. "Because if not, I'm going to be the one sleeping in the car."

"Don't worry about it."

She rolled her eyes. "How can I not worry? I've been living from paycheck to paycheck and hoping for good tips ever since the ranch was raided and Vern was arrested. I'd expected my life to change but not the way it has."

"Can't you get a training job at another ranch?"

"Not around here. Not with my undeserved reputation."

"Maybe your dad will mellow and invite you to come home?"

"Maybe. When it snows in Death Valley," Katerina countered. "I'm not holding my breath."

Max started the SUV. "The police don't think the burglar left any clues. Neither do I, but they collected possible clues anyway. Are you sure the guy in your hospital room mentioned Kowalski's name?"

"Yes. And no." Katerina pulled a face and slowly

shook her head. "At the time it happened I was positive. The more I think about how implausible it sounds, the more I doubt myself. I'm sorry. I know it's hard for you to take anything I say at face value so it must be driving you crazy that I can't tell for sure. Believe me, it isn't easy being me right now."

"*That* I can buy," Max replied, with a twinkle in his eye. "I've made arrangements with a local sheriff's deputy to deliver more of your clothing to the hotel after they finish going over the apartment. It's the best I could do."

"Female deputy, I hope." Katerina felt her cheeks warming. "I guess I shouldn't be picky but I'd feel better if a woman did it."

"She's a she."

Katerina sighed and sagged back against the seat. "Good."

"While you're relaxing," the agent said, "Why not close your eyes and try to picture the hospital room incident. Take it slow and let's talk it through. You were sleeping and something woke you, right?"

"Uh-huh." Her sleep-heavy lids lowered. The motion of the vehicle began to lull her. "I remember thinking how the nurses kept coming in to check on me. I heard that whooshing sound of a door opening and sensed a presence."

"What did you see?"

"Nothing, at first. My eyes were closed. I told the person I was tired and wanted to be left alone." She shivered. "That was when he put a hand over my mouth and pressed so hard he made my lip bleed again."

"Could you have bumped it in your sleep, instead?"

"I had one arm strapped down with an IV and was

lying on my back. It would be difficult to hit myself accidentally."

"Okay. Go on."

"I already told you the rest. The guy said Vern had sent him and wanted to talk to me." Sensing Max's attention, Katerina opened her eyes and looked toward him. He was scowling. "What?"

"That can't be right," Max said. "Kowalski's in jail. There's no way this so-called friend of his could have been taking you to him. Besides, why would he? All he'd have to do was tell you Vern wanted you to visit him."

Puzzled, she mirrored his expression of doubt. "You're right. Not that I want anything more to do with Vern or his buddies."

"Are you sure he mentioned your fiancé's name?"

"*Former* fiancé." She grimaced. "Why would anybody pretend to be associated with a criminal? Do you suppose the man thought I was on the wrong side of the law, too?"

"He could have. That does seem to be the accepted opinion around here."

"Don't remind me. If I had the money I'd pack up and move away. Far away. I'm never going to escape my mistake otherwise."

"And what mistake would that be?"

Max's tone was even but the portent of his question chilled Katerina to the bone. "Falling in love, okay? I'm not talking about anything else and I really wish you and everybody else would quit gawking at me as if I were about to steal the family silver. I thought my dad was the worst offender until I met you, Agent West."

To her chagrin her companion quirked a smile. "Glad to be of service."

* * *

As he drove leisurely toward the historic hotel, Max made little further conversation. He wanted to grill his lovely passenger but decided to bide his time and let her fill the silence as most folks tended to do naturally. A lot of criminals were their own worst enemies in that regard. Either they couldn't help boasting or they got to rambling on about something inconsequential and their subconscious led them to reveal clues before they realized they were doing it.

He chanced a sidelong look at Katerina. Sleep seemed to have overcome her. Her eyes were closed and she appeared totally relaxed. Little wonder. Now that the adrenaline rush from encountering the fleeing prowler had worn off he was weary, too. If there had been a café or gas station along the narrow, winding country road, he would have suggested they stop for coffee.

Katerina stirred. Yawned. Stretched, then winced as her bruised muscles obviously objected. "Where are we?"

"GPS says we're halfway to the hotel. Is there any place along here to grab a decent bite to eat? I think we both need a break."

She studied the bright dash screen and pointed to a section of road. "There's a little hole-in-the-wall place there, in Fish Camp. Hard to know if they'll be open, though. It's more likely on weekends when long lines of tourists drive past on their way to Yosemite."

"I understand it's a pretty park."

"*Pretty?*" Katerina shifted sideways and stared at him. "It's amazing. You've never been there?"

"Nope. It was part of my briefing for this assignment but thankfully I've had no reason to go there on business."

"You never get a vacation?"

"I could if I wanted time off. It's not a top priority." He didn't have to be looking at her to interpret the sound of disgust she made.

"I don't believe it," Katerina huffed. "You face death on a daily basis, yet you don't take the time to smell the roses. What kind of life is that?"

"The kind I prefer," he replied, sobering and clenching the wheel more tightly. There had been a time when he'd had plans to start a family, to behave the way so-called normal people did. That idea had ended abruptly when a traffic accident had claimed his fiancée's life. Max had then thrown himself into his work and found the solace that otherwise escaped him. He saw no reason to rethink a lifestyle that had been working well for the past three years.

"Up there." Katerina distracted him by leaning forward and pointing toward his side of the road. "See the weathered red-and-white building? That's it."

Incredulous, he nevertheless slowed and signaled for a left turn. "It's still in business?"

"Last I heard. I don't get out here much these days. Which reminds me. You never said anything about my pickup. Is it totaled?"

"Probably. The local police had it towed into South Fork to clear the scene. I'll find out for you."

"Thanks. *Again*." She pulled a face. "I'm getting sick of having to thank you for helping me when I know you have ulterior motives. I suppose, when you figure out I really am innocent, you'll hit the road and I'll never see you again."

"That is likely. My headquarters is in Billings, Montana."

"And you were sent clear down here? Weren't there any bomb-sniffing dogs in California?"

"I really can't discuss it."

"Can't, or won't?" she asked.

"Both. Let's just say it's classified and drop it, okay?"

Max was concentrating on his rearview mirror as he made the left turn. To his surprise, a battered old dump truck behind them turned and parked by the weathered building, too.

Katerina pressed him. "Well, what *can* you tell me?"

He chose to refrain from explaining his elite FBI unit but he did shrug and try to divert her attention. "Do you recognize that truck? I think it may be following us."

"What do you mean, following us? When did you notice it? Why didn't you tell me?"

"Don't panic. Most criminals prefer better, faster wheels so I doubt it's a problem." He saw her shade her eyes and squint at the rusty, dented truck. If its engine was as decrepit as the rest of it, they had nothing to worry about.

"I don't..." Katerina began before a sharp inhalation. "Oh, no."

"What? What is it?"

"Shadowed like that, the driver reminds me of the man in the hospital. Doesn't he look like the prowler we chased, too?"

"Maybe. There's one good way to find out. Stay here."

Max undid his seat belt and the safety on his holster with one fluid motion, then opened the door on his side and stepped out. Keeping the SUV between himself and the much larger truck, he pivoted toward it and studied the vehicle silently. If the other driver had ignored him he wouldn't have grown more apprehensive. However, instead of proceeding into the snack shop the way a normal traveler would, the man behind the wheel froze and returned Max's steady stare.

That was not a good sign. He started to circle the front of his own vehicle, intent on confronting the truck driver.

A second man occupied the passenger seat. Max rested his palm on the grip of his sidearm. No one spoke.

The engine of the old truck revved, proving that it was far from ancient. The hair at the nape of Max's neck prickled. Something was very wrong. If both men got out and rushed Katerina, could he protect her? He and Opal probably could, although he was loathe to endanger his K-9 partner unless it was absolutely necessary.

Max raised one hand, palm out and open. "Afternoon. Can I help you fellas?"

Neither man responded. Max reached for his badge. "Federal agent. Please keep your hands where I can see them and get out of the vehicle slowly. One at a time. Driver first."

Instead, the men ducked out of sight. Because the cab of the older truck sat so high off the ground, Max was no longer able to see them from where he stood. He started to draw his gun. The engine roared, drowning out his shouted order to stop. No officer of the law would discharge his weapon under those circumstances and apparently the men in the truck knew it. The driver backed into the road, quickly reversed and ground gears to start forward.

Max ran back to Katerina, slid behind the wheel and grabbed his radio to alert local police, then commanded, "Fasten your seat belt."

"We're not going to chase them, are we? I mean,

how fast can they possibly go in that old truck? It's on its last legs."

"Don't be so sure. It sounds as if they have a new engine under their hood. Until reinforcements catch up to us we're going to keep them in sight. If they really are connected to Kowalski I don't want to lose them."

She braced herself as they took off in a squeal of rubber. "You think they *are*, don't you?"

"What I think is unimportant. It's what we discover after they're pulled over and searched that counts."

"I'd rather walk," Katerina yelled. "Let me out."

He couldn't, of course. If the men knew her by sight he'd be able to tell by observing their initial expressions when confronted. If they were merely unrelated lawbreakers he'd see that, too. Katerina had to be with him when the stop was made. This was too perfect a scenario to waste. Besides, if he let her out, she'd be vulnerable.

"We're staying together," Max yelled back at her. "It's safer."

"Doesn't look like it to me!"

Her blue eyes were wide, one hand fisted on the grip above the passenger door, the other grasping the edge of the seat. Yes, Katerina was fearful, but there was also a sense of wild adventure about her. Under different circumstances he might have guessed she was having the kind of fun a lot of folks experienced on a roller coaster.

Had their current situation not had the potential to turn deadly, Max might have chuckled out loud.

Whipped from side to side on tight, fast corners, Katerina kept her lips pressed together despite the awareness that a good, loud scream would feel wonderful.

Freeing.

Speaking of freedom, Max seemed to be gaining on the old truck. "I think we're catching them."

His "Yeah" didn't sound as upbeat as she'd expected.

"What's the problem? We don't want to lose sight of them, do we?"

"No. But I don't want to corner them all by myself, either. This isn't technically my jurisdiction and if the stop didn't go as planned, a lot of bureaucrats could end up twisting in the wind, me included."

"Is that what *special agent in charge* really means? You pay dearly for bad decisions?"

"In this case it may be. Hang on. They're slowing more."

"What are you going to do?"

"Without armed backup? If it were just me and Opal I'd order them out of their vehicle and hold them at gunpoint."

Katerina arched her eyebrows and made a face. "Hey, it's not my fault I'm still here. I told you to let me out and you refused."

"It was the right decision. It simply complicates things at the moment."

"Ya think?" She knew it was wrong to needle him but he'd been so convinced she was on the wrong side of the law that his current dilemma hit her as ironic. And amusing, provided the men in the big truck stayed away until reinforcements had time to arrive.

"Um, is it just my nerves or is the truck stopping?"

"Stopping. In the middle of the road, no less. The first car that takes that next corner too fast is liable to hit head-on."

She noted the hard set to the agent's jaw, the way his big, strong hands gripped the steering wheel. Clearly, he was having to make some crucial decisions and she hoped one of them included turning around and running for their lives.

Max eased his SUV to the far right of center and set the parking break. "You stay put. Lock yourself in. If anything happens to me, use the radio to call for help." He handed her the mic. "Push this button, talk, then release it so you can hear replies."

"Whoa. Where do you think you're going?"

"To order them out of the traffic lanes before they cause an accident."

"I thought we were waiting for backup."

"You are." Taking the mic momentarily he reported his position and plans to the county dispatcher, then stepped out and slammed the door.

"A fine mess this is," Katerina muttered. An answering whine from the rear of the SUV reminded her that Opal was back there. Releasing her seat belt, Katerina flipped onto her knees and shinnied between the backs of the front seats until she was within reach of the portable kennel box. Opal was not only drooling she was wagging her whole rear end.

"If I let you out will you promise to behave?" she asked the dog. "Your partner might need you and I could sure use the company."

Woof.

"That's what I thought. Okay. Here's your leash." She opened the kennel grate and grabbed the dog's harness. "Hold still, will you?"

The friendly canine's antics were enough to take Katerina's mind off the tenuous situation and bring a smile. "Yeah, Opal, I agree. He's the kind of guy to try riding a wild mustang with no saddle or bridle and then wonder how he ended up in a heap on the ground. I'm glad he's your partner, not mine."

Together, they returned to the front seat. Opal took the passenger's place so Katerina eased behind the wheel. The dash resembled an airplane cockpit with gauges she didn't recognize and equipment that looked like multiple radios, not to mention the computer system she'd seen Max use briefly.

Parked to the right rear of the bigger truck, Katerina could no longer see him. Neither could Opal, which clearly disturbed them both. The dog began pawing at the inside of the door.

"No, Opal. Your boss said for us to stay right here and that's what we're going to do unless…" *Unless I hear shots or something equally as bad*, she thought. Her hands rested naturally on the steering wheel and she sighed. "Why didn't I ask exactly what he meant when he told me to call for more help if he needed it. How am I supposed to know?"

Woof.

"My sentiments exactly." Katerina had always talked to animals and was reassured to have Opal beside her. "You're the one with the fancy training. So, what's the standard protocol for this situation?"

Instead of the silly, drooling look the dog had been exhibiting, she began to focus out the windshield and stare at the large truck. Katerina's focus followed Opal's. It almost looked as if the thing was moving. Backward. Toward them. There was little room to spare to the right before the ground fell away into a steep canyon!

A few native live oaks rose above the edge, their canopies giving the false impression that there was solid earth below. Pines, however, clearly demonstrated that they were rooted far below with only their tops visible.

What was the penalty for driving an FBI vehicle without permission? Katerina wondered. There was no time to ask and even less time left to decide. If they stayed where they were, that lumbering old truck could shove them off the road as if they were a child's toy. Either she took matters into her own hands and saved herself and Opal, or Max would be scraping them up at the bottom of the canyon. Looking at the problem that way made it easy to act.

Katerina dropped the idling SUV into reverse and wheeled it out of imminent danger by cutting the back bumper to her left. She was now back in the traffic lanes and could see oncoming cars slowing long before they got close to her. So far, so good. Now where was Max?

The heavy truck kept backing until one set of dual axels was balanced on the edge of the berm. Then it began to jockey sideways in the roadway, clearly intent on reversing directions despite the cramped space.

Katerina muttered a panicky prayer and gripped the wheel. She'd driven trucks pulling horse trailers and handled big vans at the ranch so she was pretty sure she could drive Max's SUV without wrecking it. Steering it down a winding mountain road backward fast enough to stay ahead of an oncoming truck, however, was another story.

Eyeing their surroundings, she looked for a way to slip past their adversary and escape uphill. It was impossible. The truck would soon be pointed straight at them and she'd have nowhere to go. A wall of rock rose to her left at the edge of the pavement. A dropoff into a steep canyon lay to the right. She had lost her chance to mimic the huge truck and make a successful three-point turn before it took up the center of the road.

There was no room left for evasion. They were trapped.

FIVE

Max jumped back, gun in both hands, feet apart in a shooter's stance. "Stop!"

The dump truck kept inching along.

He raced to Katerina before the other vehicle could complete the last of its tight maneuvers, shoved her aside, slid behind the wheel and tromped on the gas. He was just in time.

With the SUV slewing backward he whipped the wheel hard then slammed on the brakes. They skidded in a circle that left blackened swirls of rubber on the road.

Katerina screamed.

Max straightened their trajectory and sped downhill. Ascending traffic was already backed up for quite a distance. All he could hope for at present was that the thugs in the disguised truck would continue to pursue him and ignore innocent civilians.

"Call this in," he ordered Katerina. "Tell them what's happened and give the dispatcher our updated position."

Although her hand was shaking as she reached for the radio, he could tell she had control of herself. Except for that one piercing scream she was actually responding to the crisis so well he couldn't help but be impressed.

"Can't you go faster?" Katerina asked as soon as she'd finished using the radio.

"Yes, but I don't want to lose him."

"Why not?"

"Because it doesn't matter who is doing the chasing. We still need to know where these guys are and being ahead of them is almost as good as following."

"Says who?" She strained to see past Opal to check their outside mirrors.

"Opal. Backseat. Go. Down," Max ordered. The K-9 obeyed instantly.

Katerina took advantage of the space. "Thanks. I wasn't sure if she'd let me move over."

"You shouldn't have opened her kennel."

"Sorry. I was afraid for Opal. If we'd been pushed off the road she might have been trapped inside the car. I wanted her to have the best chance of survival."

He had to give credit where it was due. "That was quick thinking when you backed up. Otherwise I might have had to shoot the truck driver."

"Would you have?"

"Not if there was any other option," Max said solemnly. "I don't suppose you'd like to tell me who you think is in the truck."

"How should I know?"

"Just asking." He continued to monitor the behemoth behind them and was satisfied it was still on their trail.

Ahead, as the road straightened and the countryside opened into valleys and pasture, cars were lined up behind a farmer's tractor and hay bailer in their lane. Max was not pleased. "Uh-oh." He flipped on his red lights and hit the siren, hoping to clear the way. Most of the passenger cars pulled over but the farmer seemed oblivious.

Max saw Katerina's feet brace against the floorboard. Her hands pushed forward to the edge of the dash. "Look out!"

He did the only thing he could since there was no room to pass; he slowed to a crawl. And braced to be hit from behind. "Hang on."

As far as Katerina was concerned, he couldn't have convinced her to let go if he'd tried. Every muscle in her body was taut, every nerve firing. This was scarier than her toughest dressage competition. At least when she was in the show ring she was in charge. Putting her life in this agent's hands was proving to be a poor decision despite his valiant efforts to protect her. Assuming they lived through the next few minutes she intended to thank him, despite the fact he kept giving the impression he thought this predicament was all her fault.

Then again, Katerina reasoned, her thoughts sizzling as they raced like a wildfire, if Max had believed her from the start, his choices might have been different and neither of them would be sitting here like a lame duck waiting to become roadkill.

Horns behind them started honking. Katerina peered into the side mirror. Her jaw gaped. "Where's the truck?"

Instead of answering, Max grabbed for the mic. "This is FBI Special Agent West again. Be advised, we're now southbound and stuck in traffic. Suspect vehicle has turned off on a farm road near mile marker 92, heading west and kicking up a dust cloud. If you have eyes in the sky you may spot the truck. Otherwise, we've lost him."

The radio crackled. "Copy. Do you still need backup?"

Katerina was astonished to hear him say, "Negative," before signing off.

"What do you mean, 'negative'?" She continued to watch the disappearing dust. "Are you just giving up?"

"We need to choose our battles. If those guys were who and what we thought they were, they'll be back. The secret is to stay alert and be ready for anything."

"Easy for you to say," Katerina grumbled. She plopped back in the seat. "What now?"

"We could make another stop." His gaze was less intimidating this time than she had expected. "Are you up for that visit to the scene of the explosion?"

Her wry sense of humor surfaced and helped her cope. "Garwood Ranch? Sure…why not. I was just almost shoved into oblivion on a winding mountain road. After that, how hard can it be to face my grumpy father?"

"On a scale of one to ten?"

She made a face at him. "Very funny."

"Hey, you started it. Would you rather check out the ranch tomorrow? With all our racing around we're actually not far from our hotel."

"Could we put it off?" She hated to give in to fatigue but the stress of the last couple of days had left her easily exhausted. She stifled a yawn.

"Sure. I have some files to look at and I imagine you and Opal could use a good night's sleep."

"Only if I get my own room," Katerina quipped. "I like your dog but I'm too tired to fight her for the bed the way I had to when we shared the front seat. She takes the space she wants and I get whatever is left over."

"She knows how important she is to me," Max said, smiling.

Katerina knew when she was bested and kept her thoughts to herself. Truth to tell, she would have gladly shared any space she had with Opal. At least the dog didn't make judgments about her character. The thing that made Max's actions so unbelievable was knowing that he still believed she was in league with the men who had influenced Vern, yet was willing to help and protect her. At times like this, Katerina actually wished she did know more about her former fiancé's illicit acts. If she'd paid more attention when they were together she might be able to aid law enforcement and be part of the solution instead of part of the problem.

Sighing, she relaxed against the seat and gazed out the window. Summer sun and California drought had browned most of the grass on the rolling hills. Fire danger was already extremely high, which was why the South Fork Founder's Day parade had been temporarily postponed, much to Mayor Garwood's chagrin. She hoped the predictions of upcoming storms would come to fruition and temper the danger despite the fact that she wouldn't be riding Moonlight in the parade for the first time in years.

Mulling over happier times, she had managed to let go of much of her earlier tension when Max asked, "Did you ever hear Kowalski mention the name Dupree?" which set her back on edge as if she had never calmed down.

"No. I read it in the newspaper but Vern never told me he knew them."

"This is a big state but you live in a small town. Surely you must have realized your boyfriend needed a job. What did you think he did?"

"Sold insurance," Katerina said with a frown. "When I asked why he didn't try to sell some to Dad, he said he never mixed business with pleasure." She made a face. "I should have guessed that his relationship with me was part of his *business*."

"What about his living arrangements? If you were still at home, where was Kowalski?"

"He had an apartment in Oakhurst. I thought he was spending his time at the ranch to be with me, not to use my family's transport vans to disperse drugs." She looked to Max for confirmation. "That's what the paper said he was doing. Is there more you're not telling me?"

"All I can say is that the Dupree organization is widespread and can be deadly. Details are classified." Max paused as if making a decision before continuing. "You probably read that we lost track of a member of our team, Jake Morrow."

"Oh, no." Katerina was truly sorry. "That's terrible. Did you find him?"

"Not yet. But we will."

"No wonder you're so determined."

"It's my job," Max countered. "I always do it to the best of my ability no matter what."

"I know," she said soberly. "I just wish I were able to help."

"Yeah." Max's jaw muscles clenched. "So do I."

The hotel named after Bret Harte was as quaint as any B and B in the gold country. Three stories of restored Victorian splendor were nestled in the shade of live oaks and buffered by steep hills to the west. In the canyon behind, where brush and trees had not masked the long-ago activity, Max could see displaced remnants of rocks and soil from placer mining.

He parked in his assigned spot, then let Opal out on a long lead. "Dog first, then we'll go in," he told Katerina.

She had shifted sideways in the seat and drawn her few belongings into her lap. "No hurry. It's kind of embarrassing to check in using a pillowcase for luggage. I suppose I should be thankful it's not a plastic grocery sack."

"They know you're with me and I'm working here. Nobody will think anything of it." He quirked a smile. "I take it your former lifestyle didn't include a lot of making do with what was at hand."

"Don't hold that against me, okay? I'm learning the hard way."

"I can see that. Too bad you don't have extended family you can call on for help."

She huffed and jumped down. "I don't even have many friends these days. The only ones who still speak to me are the folks from my church, and even they seem a little standoffish. I suppose they're as confused as you are."

"You think I'm confused?" He locked the truck and led the way to the front porch past wild poppies, roses and tufts of gray-leafed lavender.

"I think you're deluded," Katerina replied. "You've been around so many lowlife thugs you don't recognize an honest person when you meet one."

"Meaning you?"

"Yes."

They passed through the door into a foyer. Fans kept the warm, dry air moving and made the ambient temperature tolerable. Max checked the box for his room and found a key for an additional room, as Dylan had promised.

He handed it to Katerina. "Here you go. Opal and I are right next door in room 203 so you'll be perfectly safe." A slight smile lifted one corner of his mouth despite his desire to squelch it. "Want help with your luggage?"

"Very funny." Tossing the sack over her shoulder she added, "I feel like a hobo ready to hop a freight."

"No railroad tracks up here in the hills. Sorry," Max quipped. "I'll see you to your room."

"I can manage."

His smile faded. "I know you can. I just want to be certain you get there. The last time I turned my back on you somebody tried to push you off a cliff."

"Surely there's no danger here."

"Opal and I do a sweep of the whole house twice a day," Max told her. "We'll check your room again now."

"You're scaring me."

"Good. I saw you keep a cool head in an emergency today but that's no reason to become complacent. Even smart, capable people can be fooled."

"*Now* you're getting the right idea about me," Katerina said with a grin. "About time."

Max saw no advantage to telling her he'd been citing failures in his own past rather than referring to hers. The scar on his cheek reminded him every morning when he shaved. That wasn't necessarily a bad thing. It paid to stay alert and doubt everything. Everybody. Too bad that hadn't been enough to keep agent Morrow safe.

Forensics proved Jake had been wounded in the shootout during the raid on the Duprees when Reginald Dupree was captured. Since Reginald's uncle Angus had abducted Jake and escaped the dragnet by helicopter, it was surprising there had been no ransom demands. Of course, Jake was resourceful and may have escaped. Max's worry was that he hadn't returned to headquarters or contacted Quantico because he was hurt or otherwise physically unable.

And then there was Esme Dupree. She'd been in witness protection until she'd panicked and run from her handlers, too. Without her testimony it was possible they'd have trouble getting a murder conviction for her brother, Reginald, although he and his underlings were sure to spend time in prison on drug charges. If Max had thought it would be feasible to sway the second sister, Violetta, he'd have felt a lot more positive about satisfactorily wrapping up the entire case. One phone call to her had proved that she intended to be anything but cooperative. The minute he'd asked her about Esme she'd hung up on him. No doubt she feared her family. Too bad she wasn't as brave as her missing sister.

Which focused his thoughts on the crime family and the random bombings. And therefore on Katerina. She was standing in front of the door to her room, key in hand, waiting for him. She looked…

Max set his jaw. She looked as innocent as a lamb with her big, guileless blue eyes and that wavy golden hair. Part of him wanted to believe her. Another part warned that even lambs could hide the spirit of a ravenous wolf.

The room Katerina had been given was charming. It was dwarfed by her boudoir at the ranch but far surpassed it in lovely decor and a sense of home. Moreover, someone had carefully folded and arranged clean clothes for her atop the antique chest of drawers. That, alone, helped boost her spirits. The view from the lace-curtained window did, too. Raising the sash she was able to look out at rolling hills beyond the massive, gnarled oak that framed the scene. Its shade brought relief from the late afternoon sun while a mild breeze ruffled its leaves and soothed her spirit.

A soft knock at her door was startling. "Who is it?"

"Room service."

The deep male voice sounded terribly familiar. When she opened the door a crack to peek out, her suspicions were confirmed. The very special agent stood in the hallway balancing a tray of food.

"I didn't order anything."

"You need to eat. And rest. Under the circumstances I thought it was sensible for you to dine in your room so you could kick back and unwind."

"And so you could keep an eye on me?" Katerina stepped back, holding the door for him.

"That, too." He placed the tray on a small table by the window. "You have to keep up your strength. I've contacted the diner where you work and explained that you'll need a few days off. First thing tomorrow we'll head out to the ranch, get your stuff and look over the scene. My people didn't turn up anything but you may spot changes because the place is so familiar to you."

"Okay." When he hesitated instead of leaving, she wondered if he'd intended to eat with her. "There's enough for two, if you want to join me," she offered with a sweep of her arm.

"No, no. I won't be staying. Lock your door when I leave and keep it that way unless you notify me." He reached into his pocket and produced a small cell phone. "This is for you. My number is already programmed into it. Don't use it for anything else."

"I had a smartphone in my truck. Was that ruined, too?"

"Yes. According to the evidence techs."

She had other ideas. "You guys kept it to check my activity, didn't you? Well, have at it. I have nothing to hide and the sooner you figure that out, the better."

Max was backing toward the open door. "Good night, then. Eat. Please? I really do want you to stay healthy."

"Because a feeble suspect is harder to explain?" Katerina laughed wryly. "Okay, okay. I'll take good care of myself. You won't have to make excuses for mistreating me." A smile remained as she studied the stalwart agent.

He frowned. "What's so funny?"

"Nothing. I was just realizing that I'm starting to like you. Given my terrible record for choosing friends, particularly of the male persuasion, I figure you're probably planning to arrest me soon and throw me in the slammer with good old Vern."

"The *slammer*?" Max chuckled. "You watch too many B movies."

"Old black-and-white ones are the best," Katerina said. "I love those."

"If you want comedy, maybe. Police work is nothing like that anymore."

"Imagine how it would have been if those characters had had cell phones and modern communications the way we do these days."

Max nodded toward the phone he had just given her. He was no longer smiling. "Keep that with you at all times. Understand?"

"Yes." She made a fist around it. "I don't know how to thank you—for this room and everything."

"You can start by naming your boyfriend's associates," he said flatly.

If Katerina had not been taken aback by the abrupt change in his demeanor she would have slammed the door instead of letting him close it quietly behind him.

She had never met anyone, human or animal, as hardheaded and stubborn as that impossible man. The only plus side she could see was that he was undoubtedly thinking the same kinds of thoughts about her. Well, good. It was about time somebody gave her credit for courage and backbone, even if it happened for the wrong reasons.

Circumstances had forced her into independence and the more she experienced, the better she felt about herself. That, alone, was a prime example of good resulting from disaster, just as the Bible promised. If someone had told her a month ago that she would be homeless, practically destitute and in mortal danger she would have laughed at them.

Now, however, she not only was not amused, she found herself calling upon an inner strength, a latent faith and trust in God, that she hadn't realized lay within.

SIX

Balmy night breezes lifted the lacy curtains over the window in Katerina's room. Because of the hilly terrain, semidarkness had arrived before true sunset. She was more than ready to rest. Matter of fact, she'd started to get really sleepy while eating at the small table in front of the window.

Wrapped in the cocoon of the summer night, she went to the canopied bed, stretched out on the cool sheets and let the humming of cicadas lull her to sleep. As long as the buzzing noise rose and fell in cadence, Katerina was at peace. When it abruptly stopped, however...

Her eyelids fluttered. She stirred, shifted position and stretched. "Umm. Thirsty."

There was half a carafe of iced tea left on the table from her evening meal, wasn't there? She yawned, then sat up and swung her legs over the side of the bed, taking a moment to get her bearings and straighten the T-shirt and shorts she'd chosen in lieu of proper nightclothes.

Quiet was welcome, of course, but something about the total silence bothered her. No insects were buzzing and other than the occasional hoot of an owl, night birds were silent, too.

Katerina paused to listen. To think. The narrow road that wound past the B and B was mostly dark but headlights occasionally shined through her window as cars followed the twisted street.

Fine hairs at the nape of her neck prickled a warning. Logic argued against fear yet instinct insisted she take care despite the fact that her door was locked and an FBI agent was lodged in the room next door.

She could hear herself breathing, feel the thump of her pulse as if that, too, were audible. Maybe it was. Her heart was certainly beating hard and fast enough.

A single, deep bark startled her. She tensed even more. The sound had not come from outside; she'd heard it through the wall from Max's room. Opal? Why would she bark when everything else was so seemingly peaceful?

Slowly, cautiously, Katerina began to reach toward the pillow at the head of her bed. The special cell phone was tucked under it. Whether she used the phone or not, it would be comforting to have it in hand.

The rumble of a motor outside grew closer. Another car was passing. Katerina instinctively glanced in the direction of the open window—and saw a shadow.

It froze for a split second, then began to move, to grow larger. It was inside and coming toward her!

She crab-walked backward across the bed. "No! Get away from me."

"Too bad you woke up. I was just going to leave you a note but since you're awake, we can have a little talk."

"No."

A hand snaked out of the dimness and grabbed her ankle. *Caught!*

Twisting and kicking, she clawed to reach the cell phone. The more she fought, the farther away from it the prowler pulled her.

"Let go of me."

Realizing how inane it was to argue with someone who had invaded her room and was threatening her, she resorted to the kind of ear-piercing, inarticulate scream she'd heard only in scary movies—and from herself during the incident in her hospital room.

It caused her attacker to loosen his hold. She continued to screech until he turned and scrambled for the open window.

Intent on escape herself, Katerina ran for help, twisted the bolt, threw the open the door and crashed into her FBI protector.

Max staggered back, kept his balance and grabbed her. "What happened?"

Katerina merely pointed into her room.

Rushing in with Opal at his side, Max checked the small suite in seconds. When he looked back, Katerina was standing in the doorway with her arms folded, hugging herself. "The window," was all she said.

Max leaned out, satisfied himself that the threat had fled, then returned to her. By that time, several other guests of the establishment as well as the concerned owners had gathered in the hallway.

He shooed them away. "It's all right. Everything is under control. It was just a bad dream."

"Bad dream my eye." Katerina was almost shouting. "There was somebody in my room. I saw him. He threatened me and grabbed me."

Slipping an arm around her shoulders, Max sought to comfort and quiet her. "Take it easy, Ms. Garwood.

Opal and I will look after you." Again, he addressed the small group. "You can all go back to sleep. My apologies for the disturbance."

"Well I'm not going to stay in there," Katerina said in a quavering voice as the others left. "Not when somebody has already found me."

Max turned her to face him and spoke quietly. "I understand. You can take my room and I'll sleep in yours. But right now I need more details. Tell me what you saw."

"There was a shadow. It came at me in the dark." She shivered. "I tried to reach the phone to call for help but he grabbed my ankle and started to pull me off the bed."

"Did he say anything?"

"I don't… Yes! He said he'd been about to leave me a note."

"All right. When I checked your room I was looking for a person, not evidence. Stay where you are while I look again."

"Not on your life. Where you and that dog go, I go. I heard her bark when I was about to be attacked. She must have heard something."

"That was what woke me." Unwilling to argue when he could see Katerina trembling with fear, Max led the way into her room, leaving the door ajar. Supper dishes remained on the table by the window. A carafe of tea had been knocked over and liquid was puddled on the floor. Amid the chaos was a folded piece of white paper.

Max pointed. "Is that yours?"

"No, I…" She started to reach for it. He stayed her hand. "Leave it. There may be fingerprints."

Katerina studied her ankle. "I doubt it. I think I felt gloves, not bare skin."

"Whatever." He lifted the folded paper with two

fingers at a corner and laid it on a bare spot atop the dresser, then used a pencil to carefully unfold it. If it had been the kind of threat an innocent person usually received he might have kept Katerina from reading it. Instead, he stepped back and watched her reactions as she scanned the note.

"Turn over the stash and we'll leave you alone?" she read aloud. "What's that supposed to mean? I don't know anything about any stash. Do they mean drugs?"

"Your guess is better than mine," Max countered evenly. "What do you think?"

She threw up her hands and began to pace. "How should I know? I don't have a clue."

"I wish I could believe you."

"Yeah," Katerina said, scowling at the piece of paper, "I wish you could, too."

Max escorted Katerina back to his room and left her there with Opal. She knew he and the local police would be going over her original room with magnifying glasses, looking for clues, and was relieved to have a refuge away from their investigation.

It was also comforting to have the trained K-9 for company, although at the moment Opal was acting more like a house pet than a police officer. "Must be because you're out of uniform, huh?" Katerina said tenderly. "Your partner did say you were different when you knew you were working."

The boxer's stubby tail wagged, making the rear half of her body move in sync. "Australian shepherds are just like you," she cooed. "When they wag they wag all over. You'd like the dogs at the ranch. They're lots of fun."

Perching on the only chair in the room, Katerina let Opal rest her heavy head on her knee. "You're a sweet girl, aren't you? Yes, you are. Does your partner ever scratch behind your ears like this?" She demonstrated. "Do you like that?"

If the boxer could have replied, Katerina knew she'd have agreed, because the expression of pleasure in her dark brown eyes was evident.

Touching the animal helped calm Katerina, too. Medical science had long claimed that stroking a dog or cat had a beneficial effect on the human body. She believed it.

So did having a pet as a companion. If she hadn't had her horses to train and the ranch dogs underfoot when her mother had passed away, she didn't know how she'd have coped.

Yes, she relied on her faith to carry her through trying times, but as far as Katerina was concerned, God used his earthly creatures to augment His ministrations. And why not? They were a part of His creation, just as she was.

That thought brought her musings back to Special Agent West. He was special, all right. The look on his face when she'd run into the hallway had proved his true concern despite words to the contrary. He might put forth the image of a hard-boiled cop but there was a kind man inside. She knew that without question. The element she doubted was whether she'd ever be able to convince him to let down his guard and see her as she truly was—innocent and worthy of befriending.

Or more? she asked herself, blushing. Yes, Max was older than Vern had been but given her disastrous experiences in regard to that relationship, maturity was certainly a plus. Not to mention how good-looking he was.

Could she get past Max's original attacks on her? Others had said far worse and had hurt her deeply. She might not respect her dad the way she once had, but that didn't mean she'd stopped loving him. The same went for her friends. Anybody could make a mistake. She certainly had. Forgiveness was the key.

Sleep eluded Katerina until almost dawn. She wasn't certain Opal was allowed on the bed but decided to permit the welcome company.

Sighing, she started to smile and made eye contact with the dog as it lay on its back, all four legs in the air. "You snore. Did you know that?" The smile grew as the boxer's tongue fell out of the side of her mouth and she started to pant. "Yes, you do so don't try to deny it."

A light rap on wood brought Opal to instant alertness. Tail end wagging, she leaped down, ran to the door and barked once.

"Come in."

"Why didn't you check to see who it was?" Max demanded. "And why wasn't your door locked like I told you?"

"Good morning to you, too, Special Agent Grumpy. I wanted help to be able to get to me if I was threatened again. And Opal was right here to defend me."

"That's actually sort of logical." He raked his fingers through short, damp hair. "Sorry. Long night."

"Same here," Katerina said. "Your dog snores."

"Like a freight train," he agreed, starting to smile. "You up for breakfast? I can take Opal for her walk while you go back to your room and get dressed."

"Fine." She eyed her current attire. "These aren't pj's but they aren't exactly traveling clothes, either. Are we still going back to the ranch today?"

"That was my plan."

Judging by the way he was loitering she assumed

he had more to say. "What is it? You look like a man with a secret."

"I got a match on the prints we took off that warning note from last night."

"Wonderful! Who was it?"

"Vern Kowalski," Max said flatly.

Gaping at him, Katerina stammered, "H-how is that possible?"

"We're not sure. The only way that can be is if Vern handled the paper sometime before he was arrested and left his prints then."

"So whoever wrote the note has to be someone he knew."

"That's what it looks like."

"Then ask him. Your people need to make him talk." She pressed her lips together and gave Max a frigid look. "Just leave me out of it, okay? I never want to lay eyes on the skunk again—apologies to the real animal."

"Normally, that would be a good idea," Max said quietly.

She noted how seriously he seemed to be studying her as he added, "Unfortunately, we can't. Vern Kowalski was murdered in the exercise yard early this morning. Nobody is going to be getting any more information out of him."

Katerina sank back against the edge of the mattress and grabbed the bedpost for support. "No."

"I'm sorry for your loss," Max said gruffly.

Although she was filled with mixed emotions, one rose to prominence. "I'm sorry for *everybody's* loss," she clarified. "Because now there is no way you can find out what's been going on."

She straightened, pulled herself together and met his gaze boldly even though her heart was pounding.

"Worse, there's no chance I'll be exonerated until you catch all the criminals who are involved." An eyebrow arched as she added, "And one of them is *not* me."

"I'm beginning to believe you," Max replied slowly.

Katerina let herself smile in relief. "Well, it's about time."

SEVEN

Max wasted no time loading Opal into the SUV with Katerina and heading for the Garwood Ranch. Now that Kowalski was out of the picture it was possible that Bertrand Garwood would reconsider his harsh stand. On the other hand, there was an equal chance the man would gloat and make things worse for Katerina. She may have washed her hands of her former fiancé but there had to be some lingering sorrow over his demise. After all, she'd been within days of marrying him. That helped explain her reluctance to accept his position in law enforcement, he supposed. Even a totally innocent person would feel uneasy if they found themselves under the microscope of the US government.

In a way, Katerina's situation reminded him of Dylan's fiancee, Zara Fielding, who had become involved in some kind of mystery while training at Quantico. If an honest person like her could wind up embroiled in trouble without being a participant, so could Katrina.

Clouds kept the sun at bay and temperatures temporarily lower than usual. Rain would be welcome on the tinder-dry grass and brush as long as lightning strikes didn't kindle fires. There was always a chance of that, particularly when thunder and lightning preceded any moisture, according to the fire chief.

"Odd weather, isn't it?" he asked.

"Not good. They postponed our South Fork Founder's Day parade at the end of May because bad storms were forecast. As dry as everything is, the last thing we need is a spark to set it all on fire." Max was surprised to see her smile until she added, "Dad was livid. He was supposed to ride in a convertible as mayor and show how important he is."

"Have they rescheduled? Rain or no rain, it could be dangerous for him to put himself out there like that."

"He wouldn't care. Not when he has a chance to flaunt his political position and wave to all the civilians."

Having met the man, Max understood perfectly. "If we haven't managed to arrest whoever has been harassing you before then, I'll try to talk some sense into him."

"Seriously? You'd do that?"

"Sure. Why not?" He paused to regroup his thoughts. "That is if I'm still in California. Opal is technically a bomb detecting K-9. If the threat disappears from here, I'll either go back to Billings or move on to the next assignment."

Katerina turned to study him. "I'm confused. Are you after a gang of drug dealers or chasing bombings?"

"Well…"

"You may as well level with me, Agent West. The internet is full of speculation and so are local newspapers. Their conclusions point to a connection and blame the Dupree crime family for everything."

"That is highly possible."

"Which is where my former—um, where Vern comes in?"

He glanced her way. "He's one common element. He worked for Dupree."

"And Dad's stable just blew up."

"I already told you, Ms. Garwood, I doubt that anybody who was looking for hidden loot, the way the warning note says, would take the chance of setting a bomb anywhere the drugs might be cached. That would be idiotic."

"Are you giving criminals too much credit for using their brains?"

Max shrugged. "Maybe. It's often easier to track a smart crook who's predictable than to find one who acts on a whim. Take these bombings for instance. If you look at them on a map, patterns show up. People don't mean to reveal their inner thoughts but they do so just the same. It's almost impossible for a rational thinker to act in a totally random manner." He wheeled beneath the fancy iron arch and entered Garwood Ranch. "Here we are."

"Yeah." She breathed a noisy sigh. "Well, let's get this over with. I don't want to stay one second longer than I absolutely have to."

"You can't be afraid of your father, not after the way you've handled yourself since we met. You were amazing on the broken stairs. And last night—you didn't get hysterical or even cry."

"I'm less sad about my dad's choices than I am disappointed," Katerina said softly. "I thought he loved me. I thought Vern did, too. Guess I'm not very perceptive."

"There's nothing wrong with putting your trust in someone," Max murmured as he pulled through the yard and parked next to the remnants of the destroyed stable building. "The secret is in choosing who is deserving and who isn't."

"How do *you* do it?" Katerina glanced at the threatening clouds as she got out and joined him.

Max chuckled and shook his head, "Poorly."

"Why? Because you kept doubting me?"

"Yes, and no." He leashed Opal and put her to work while they made small talk. "I tend to doubt everybody. Everything. It's a valuable trait for my job, but it doesn't make for a lot of friends."

"You're not married, are you?"

"No. Why?" The scowl he sent her way was meant to end their conversation. It seemed to have the opposite effect.

"I'm sorry. It must be lonely, traveling all over the country with nobody waiting for you at home. I never realized how much I relied on friends and family until I had to face the loss of most of them. The loneliness is astounding. I hadn't dreamed it would hurt so much."

"I have my job and Opal. That's enough."

Following the K-9 as she skirted the pile of rubble, nose to the ground, Max was glad he wasn't facing Katerina when she said, "No. It isn't."

Katerina sensed friction in the air between her and Max so she kept her distance. It was none of her business what kind of private life Agent West chose to live, she just hated to see anyone unhappy. Oh, he was capable and intelligent and wonderful hero material, but inside he seemed wanting, as if his heart were silently calling for help. For companionship.

"I am certifiable," she muttered to herself. "Why should I care about a guy who was ready to throw me in jail before he even met me?"

Because you both are lonely and need each other, her subconscious answered. Of course there was no way she and Max could ever become a couple. Innocent or not, her name was stained by her prior associations just as her father had claimed. Still, the ruggedly handsome agent was growing more appealing daily and the possibility of romance kept popping into her head.

Letting her thoughts ramble, she wandered behind the part of the stable building left standing and came to an abrupt halt. Katerina stared. Her heart sank and angry, bitter tears filled her eyes.

Two cardboard boxes sat atop a pile of soot, dirt and barn sweepings and in those boxes was the proof of her entire career as a successful trainer and rider. Her trophies were smashed as if someone had taken a hammer to them. And the ribbons and beautiful rosettes? They were mired in filth. How *dare* he!

Katerina spun on her heel and headed for the house. Outrage fueled her courage and anger drove her forward. Behind her she heard Max calling. She ignored him. Bertrand Garwood was going to answer for his vindictive disregard of her feelings. Today.

Max was startled to see Katerina marching across the open space between the house and stables. Her actions went against everything she had told him. If she wanted to avoid confronting her father she was definitely headed in the wrong direction.

Drawing Opal close to his side Max began to jog. "Katerina! Wait."

She didn't slow her pace. If anything, she sped up. Several ranch hands paused to watch her from a distance but nobody else tried to interfere.

Max broke into a run. "Stop!"

He overtook her just as she reached the elaborate front entrance and raised a fist to bang on the door. Max's firm grip on her wrist stopped her. Fury in her glance made him let go. "Take a breath and tell me what's wrong."

"My—my awards," she stammered, her lower lip quivering. "He trashed them all."

"I don't understand."

"I used to compete and show our horses. I was good. I had the trophies and ribbons to prove it." She raised one arm to point toward the stables. "I'd gathered them all up to take with me when I came for the rest of my things. They're back behind the barns in a pile of..."

He gritted his teeth and eyed the roiling clouds. "Wind's coming up. If we intend to salvage anything before it rains we'd better get a move on."

"It's too late. They're all ruined."

"Maybe we can save something." He had to bite back his fury at anyone would destroy the dreams and accomplishments of another the way Garwood had. "Did you dig through and actually make sure, or are you assuming?"

"I couldn't bring myself to look closely," Katerina admitted. "I suppose there could be a few ribbons I can wash and keep as mementos."

He slipped an arm around her shoulders and urged her to turn with him. "Then let's go. I'll help you sort it all out."

"What about looking for clues to the explosion?"

"I'm done. It didn't take Opal long to tell me the area is clean. Whatever residue there may have been was widely scattered when they put out the fire. She showed mild interest in a couple of stalls but that's all."

"It seems pretty impossible for her to find clues at all, let alone after so many people and animals have tramped through your crime scenes."

Max was glad Katerina was starting to calm down

and think more rationally. "That's where her sense of smell comes in handy. I've seen her locate tiny pieces of detonators, for instance, amid whole piles of refuse. She's really amazing."

Thunder rumbled in the distance. Men who had been working inside metal-fenced outdoor pens began to gather their tools. The air was crackling as dangerous lightning sought a connection to the ground. Formerly curious farm dogs scattered and took cover.

Katerina broke into a trot with Max and Opal at her side and led the way. "Back here."

He kept pace until they reached the box of ruined trophies. Opal stopped him with a pull to the left that nearly jerked him off his feet. She'd found a separate box that neither human had noticed.

"Katerina. Wait. Look," Max called. "What's this?"

"My clothes!" She started to reach for the large cardboard carton.

Max's outstretched arm stopped her. "Hold on. Opal thinks there may be something wrong."

"With my stuff?"

He had to tell her, "Yes."

"Terrific. Now what?"

"You take the ribbons into the barn to keep them out of the rain and sort them while I examine this."

"You're trying to get rid of me, aren't you?" Her pulse quickened. "How risky is it?"

"If I thought Opal had actually identified an explosive device I'd be the first one to call for a bomb squad. Unfortunately, there isn't anything like that in South Fork or even Oakhurst so we'd have a long wait."

Her hand gripped his arm, her nails digging in. "It's better than getting blown up."

Max looked to his K-9 partner. She was curious about

the second carton but not behaving as if she smelled volatile substances.

"Don't worry about me," Max said with a reassuring smile. "Whatever she senses in there isn't going to go boom."

"You know that how?"

"I trust Opal. If she were sitting next to it and looking at me for praise, we'd both make a run for it."

"No offense, but I think I'll take your first suggestion and go to the barn. I'd like to say hello to my favorite horse, anyway."

"Fine with me." He handed her the end of the leash. "Take Opal with you."

"Why? I thought you said it was safe out here."

"From the box, not from the storm," Max explained. "I'll join you two in a few minutes."

"You'd better," Katerina warned, "or I'll call Sheriff Tate."

"Just hold your horses."

"Is that a pun?"

His grin widened. "It wasn't intended to be but if you think it's funny, fine. Now go, before we both get soaked."

"Okay, okay. I'm going."

Drops the size of dimes began to dot the dry ground and the partially folded flaps of the box of clothing. Max grabbed a pitchfork and used its tines to push the top farther open. Katerina was right. All there seemed to be was a jumble of shirts and jeans. A hairbrush and toothbrush lay on top, apparently tossed in last.

He stood back and studied the visible contents. Perhaps Opal had smelled Katerina on the items. Then again, maybe he was missing something. But what?

The answer turned out to be close enough to touch.

Max, however, did not. Using a plastic evidence bag between his fingers and the folded piece of paper that was tucked beneath Katerina's hairbrush, he lifted it out. The lab would tell him for sure if this was a note like the one he'd found in her room at the hotel. The paper looked the same. So did the manner in which it was creased. If he chose to open it he'd be able to guess whether or not the handwriting matched. Proper tests would tell him if the paper was tainted with explosives. Or with drugs. Hefting the box, note and all, he headed for the barn where Katerina and Opal waited.

His first instinct was to keep the news of another note to himself but he quickly changed his mind. Nothing the young woman had done or said since he'd met her had indicated guilt, not even by association. Assuming she truly was in danger she deserved to see what was written. This note had been left for her after all, and she had a right to read it.

And there was another benefit. He was going to be able to judge more about her character as he observed her initial reactions.

Katerina was renewing her friendship with Moonlight when Opal began to wiggle, whine and tug on her leash. Max was back. And he had brought the box of clothing.

"Oh, good. I was afraid you were going to say that was evidence and keep it."

"Some of it, I am," he countered grimly.

"Give me a break. What can my clothes have to do with bombs?"

"I don't know yet." Depositing the carton atop stacked hay bales, he said, "The top shirt and the hairbrushes will stay with me. You can have the stuff underneath, providing there aren't more notes tucked in down there."

Her breath caught. "Notes? You found more notes?"

"One. And it's possible that whoever left it had to move your brushes to put it there, so they'll have to be checked for prints before I can let you have them."

"What does this one say?"

"I don't know yet." He displayed the plastic baggie. "I didn't unfold it."

She lunged. "Well, I will," but he was too quick and held it out of reach.

"I'm going to lay a larger sheet of clean plastic on this hay bale, then open the note with tweezers. Before I do, I'll need your promise to not touch it."

"I promise." What choice did she have? He was the federal agent with all the authority. She was a mere civilian. Besides, she didn't want to contaminate possible evidence. Each opportunity took them one step closer to solving the mystery of her stalker.

"Okay. Shut those sliding doors at the end of the aisle so the wind doesn't blow through. It's getting nasty out there."

"Right." Katerina ran to follow his instructions. He was right about the increasing wind. Rain was now being blown against one end of the long, rectangular building and making a staccato patter.

She returned to him. "We should have parked your SUV inside so we wouldn't get wet."

"It wasn't raining when we got here."

"Are you always so logical?"

"I try to be." Although he was concentrating on unfolding the note, he took time to add, "You should try it sometime. It might simplify your life."

She huffed. "Nothing will ever fix my life. You know

it and I know it. Vern's lies have ruined my past, my present and probably my future, and there's nothing I can do about it."

Expecting him to argue, Katerina was disappointed when he didn't. What he did do was smooth the note with another baggie and hold down the closest corner so they could both see the text.

I want the goods, it said. *Turn them over or you'll end up like your boyfriend.*

Katerina took a backward step. "They must think I hid drugs for Vern."

"I'm going to phone the jail and see if anybody was with Kowalski to hear his last words."

"Besides his killer, you mean? Do you think that's why he was murdered? Could he have been tortured for information?"

"If the Duprees think he was double-crossing them, then yes, it's a possibility. He may have tried to skim or steal and died before he revealed where he'd stashed the loot."

Katerina felt woozy. She leaned against the half door of Moonlight's stall and stroked the horse's velvety nose, drawing comfort from the contact while she mulled over her dilemma.

"This drug cartel thinks I know."

"That's how it looks," he said on a rough exhale. "Are you sure he never said anything about keeping some deep dark secret?"

"Not a peep. No clues, no hints, nothing. I thought he sold insurance, remember?"

This time, when Max nodded and looked steadily at her, Katerina could tell he was on her side. That was huge. She had a true ally. A defender. They might not yet be friends, nor were they romantically involved despite her covert appreciation of Max's many fine attributes. But that didn't matter.

God had answered her fervent prayers. She had been sent a special agent who had finally seen the truth and believed in her innocence. She no longer had to stand alone.

EIGHT

As far as Max was concerned he'd remain in California until all threats to Katerina were neutralized. Higher-ups in the FBI, however, disagreed. He was ordered back to Billings when a credible lead to the whereabouts of Jake Morrow was texted to headquarters.

"Are you sure this isn't another wild-goose chase?" he asked when Dylan O'Leary contacted him. "I want to find Jake as much as the next guy but it's really iffy to leave here now."

"Afraid it's out of your hands, Boss. We've had several reliable sightings of Agent Morrow in the past few days besides the latest tip." The tech guru sounded a lot more somber than usual.

"Okay. I trust your judgment. Tell me again what the message said."

Dylan read it verbatim.

"Daddy's home but not for long. Catch him if you can."

"What makes you think that pertains to Jake?" Max demanded. "It could mean anybody."

"True. But think about it. The only daddy directly

involved in the Dupree case is Jake and he was supposedly spotted by several witnesses. It all fits."

"People claim to have seen him all over the country. Prove to me that text has anything to do with the Duprees and I might take it more seriously. Have you been able to trace the source of the message?"

"Not well. It came from a burner phone but the signal did bounce off a tower near the Dupree estate. They may have a snitch in their midst."

"That would be too good to be true." Max made his decision. "All right. I'll fly back and leave my vehicle here. That way I'll have to come back for it."

"Unless they decide to have it transported. When shall we expect you?"

"Book me a direct flight. My closest airport is probably San Jose."

"Affirmative." O'Leary lowered his voice to a personal level. "Listen, buddy, I understand how you feel about leaving Cali right now. It almost killed me when Zara went off to Quantico. And then when her friend went missing, it was worse."

Max's forehead knit. "I don't know what you mean."

"Sure you do. I've been handling all your special requests, remember?" A chuckle. "You've got a thing for that Garwood woman and you know it."

"Don't be ridiculous."

"Suit yourself. You can deny emotional involvement all you want but I've never known you to hesitate one second to follow orders before. If she's not the reason, what is?"

"Opal is being utilized here almost daily. As long as bombs are being set, this is where she belongs."

"Yeah, well, we haven't been napping, either. Harper has canvassed neighbors in the coverage area of the cell tower and she's come up with a few strong leads. We haven't called for a full-out police action because we don't want to tip anyone off."

"I suppose it's possible that whoever placed the call is near where Jake's being held captive."

"True. Plus, Harper has a name and possible location for Morrow's baby mama. She's requested Opal as backup in case there's a problem."

"Why didn't you say so in the first place?" Max was pacing, throwing clothing into a pile on the bed while Opal watched. "I'll be packed in a few minutes and on my way. Allow me three or four hours to drive to the airport."

"Copy. What're you going to do about the Garwood woman?"

Hesitating, Max looked toward Katerina's room as if he could see through the solid wall. "I'm not sure. She's going to want to go back to work soon so I wouldn't be able to watch her 24/7 anyway. I'll need to arrange transportation for her while I'm gone. Something inconspicuous with a powerful engine. See what you can do, will you?"

Dylan chuckled. "You give me a lot of credit. Anything else? Bodyguards, maybe?"

"No, but that is a good idea. I'll speak to the local sheriff and see if he can spare a unit to escort her to and from work. It's not far."

"You are so transparent," the techie said, laughing more. "How many other crime victims have you decided to protect no matter what? One? Two? None?"

"I would have if I'd thought it was necessary," Max argued. "While I'm in Billings I want you to be tracking down leads to who is responsible for offing Kowalski in jail. Find out if the guy lived long enough to have spoken to anybody and see if you can tie that person to the Duprees."

"You think it was more than random prison violence?"

"Absolutely. I've sent the warning notes Ms. Garwood received to Quantico. Find out what they discovered and be sure the report reaches me. Even if there are no readable fingerprints on the paper there may be trace evidence that will help."

"Okay. I'll get back to you as soon as I book your flight."

"Thanks." Max realized he was concerned beyond normal, yet refused to consider that Dylan might be right about his personal involvement. Katerina was not only from a different world, that of wealth and privilege, she was too young for him. Still, he worried about her despite mental arguments to the contrary. It may be the human thing to do but it certainly was not a professional response. Not only was she on his mind almost constantly, he kept having to squelch the urge to pick up the phone and call her for no reason.

Well, *now* he had one. He pushed the button to speeddial the phone he'd given her and prayed she'd understand why he had to virtually abandon her.

The unfamiliar ring startled Katerina. "Hello?"

"How are you this morning?" Max asked cautiously.

The tone of his voice was off somehow. "I'm okay. What's wrong?"

"Nothing, really. Why?"

"Because you don't sound normal. Have you figured out who is stalking me and what they want?"

"I have our best people working on that," he reassured her.

"Good. I want to go back to living my life. First I have to see if they can fix my truck, then I need to either find a new apartment or ask the landlord to repair the damage to my old one."

"I'd like you to stay where you are for the present. I'm making arrangements for a rental car."

She was both astounded and adamant. "No way. I can't afford it. You know that."

"I know. But I have to fly to Montana for a few days and I'd like to know you're safe, with plenty of people around you."

"You're *leaving*?" Part of her heart felt lodged in her throat while the rest plunged into her stomach and lay there like a boulder.

"Orders," he said flatly.

"I—I thought you were the boss. Special agent in charge and all that."

"There are higher-ups who can override my decisions. You'll be fine while I'm gone. I'll speak to the sheriff and have a deputy escort you to and from work."

What could she say? What could she do? She had no real hold on him other than an intense desire to remain in his company. Of course he had to follow orders. That only made sense. What was far less plausible was the ache developing within her as she contemplated his absence.

Katerina pulled herself together. "Of course. I understand. Do you intend to return to South Fork?"

"Definitely. We have the bombing at the ranch to keep looking at, plus the personal threats you've received. This is one time when your connection to the Dupree cartel is working in your favor."

"I guess I could look at it that way. Might as well have something good come out of my mistakes."

"Everybody makes them," Max told her gently.

Cradling the phone against her cheek she pretended he was speaking directly to her and was standing close, letting her draw on his strength the way she had before.

"Is it all right if I use this phone to call you while you're gone?" Katerina held her breath, hoping he'd say yes.

"Of course. I'll be checking in with you on a regular basis, too…" he cleared his throat "…in case you can remember any names or receive further threats. I doubt you'll be bothered with a visible police presence. When I get back we'll dig deeper into the mystery of where Vern hid whatever the stalkers are after."

"Promise?" It galled Katerina that her voice sounded weak at that moment. She was strong and capable. There was no reason to feel so lost while contemplating Max's absence. Yet she did. It was as if someone had blasted away the foundation of her stability, of her courage, and left her trying to stand on loose sand that kept shifting beneath her.

His "I promise" seemed sincere as well as heartfelt. That helped. So did the idea of going back to work soon. Her current situation required gainful employment and her psyche insisted that she make her own way despite obstacles. That was the mindset that had helped her succeed at training hardheaded horses and it would sustain her now.

"When do you leave?" she asked thickly.

"In a few minutes."

"Meet me in the hall so I can say goodbye to Opal?"

"Sure."

There was not a whisper of doubt in Katerina's mind that she wanted to give her staunch protector a parting hug. Whether she would be able to muster the courage to do so or whether Max would accept the gesture was the real question.

She had often pictured herself close to him the way she had been when he'd helped her leave the hospital. Every second he was near she wanted to lean on his broad shoulder or step into his embrace. The desire was more a matter of needing support than anything else, including romance, she insisted. That would be nice, of course, but at this point she mostly craved something that had been sorely lacking in her recent experiences. True moral support.

She did not intend to wilt like a delicate flower on a hot day and throw herself at him. After all, she was much stronger than that. But she also didn't intend to let him leave without conveying a hint of her growing affection. If she scared him away, so be it. He'd probably leave anyway. Eventually. So what did she have to lose—except her self-respect, and there wasn't a whole lot of that left over after recent events.

Grabbing the door handle she twisted the latch and stepped into the hall.

Max was waiting with Opal by his side. The sight of him was so endearing, so incredibly special, Katerina almost ran to him. Supreme effort slowed her pace. She began to smile.

As if they had both read the same script and were acting their parts, he pivoted to face her and opened his arms slightly.

That was all the invitation Katerina needed. Stepping up, she slid her arms around his waist, laid her head on his shoulder and closed her eyes. Words were unnecessary. Actions said all there was to say.

* * *

The flight to Billings was uneventful. By keeping Opal in uniform Max was able to walk her into the passenger compartment at his side without question. They were about to land when he received word from Dylan that Agent Harper Prentiss had verified the name and current location of Jake Morrow's girlfriend and was waiting for him at the airport.

Since he hadn't checked any luggage he was able to deplane and join her without delay.

They shook hands as their dogs sniffed each other and renewed acquaintance. "I hear you think you know where Jake's family is," Max said.

"Yes. It looks good. I'd just rather have Opal check the premises before Star and I go in, especially since the Dupree family is involved." She passed him a white paper sack. "Here you go. Fresh from Petrov's bakery. I know how meager airplane food can be."

Max pulled out a sticky bun and dug in. "My favorite. Thanks." As soon as he'd swallowed, he asked, "Didn't you date Jake at one time?"

"Not exactly. He and I didn't mesh." She shook her head pensively. "He was persistent there for a while, but there was no way. Not for me."

"Interesting." Max tossed his bag into the back of her SUV and instructed Opal to get in one side as Harper put her German shepherd, Star, in the other. The handlers met in the front seat. "Bring me up to speed," Max said. "What all have you managed to put together?"

"Neighbors near the target house where the woman and toddler live have been shown Jake's photo. Some think they saw him inside. A few insisted his hair was darker. They said the man in question was usually wearing dark glasses, even in the house, so they weren't sure about his eye color."

"What can you tell me about the mother and baby?"

"Her name is Penny Potter. She's a single mother raising a toddler son, Kevin, whose father's name is not listed on the birth certificate. That's why we had so much trouble tracking her down."

Max's jaw clenched. "Assuming you have the right woman. And that she knows something that may help us track down the men who kidnapped Jake. It's iffy that their sightings were accurate."

"I know. But I wanted Opal along to make sure we're not walking into a Dupree trap. Other units are going to stage down the street and stand by until we give the all clear. We'll also have overhead coverage from our chopper. If Jake is in there, like some of the neighbors have said, whoever has been holding him may be present, too. I don't understand why Jake would be with the woman, but we can't ignore possibilities, no matter how far-fetched."

"Fair enough." Max drew his fingers down his cheek. "I left in such a hurry I didn't have time to shave."

"Too busy with Ms. Katerina?"

His head snapped around. "O'Leary has a big mouth and a wild imagination."

Harper was smiling. "Hey, don't knock it. There's nothing wrong with romance, especially at our age. The clock is ticking."

"Not for Katerina. She's a lot younger than I am."

"So?" the female agent retorted. "You can't be after her fortune now that she's been disinherited. If you two hit it off, I say go for it."

"It's not that simple. She was mixed up with the wrong crowd. Even planned to marry one of them."

"One little mistake," Harper said with a wry smile.

Max stayed sober. "Her little mistake was murdered while in police custody where he should have been safe. Apparently, before he was arrested, he stole something the Duprees want back."

"Secret files, maybe? Cooked books?"

"Possibly. I had assumed it was drugs until somebody tossed Katerina's apartment and looked in places far too small to conceal a valuable stash. It could be a flash drive, I suppose. Whatever it is, it's not bulky like the packages of drugs or stacks of money she thinks they're after."

"Interesting. You know, if the father of this baby really is Jake Morrow and we can get Penny Potter to talk, she may be able to shed light on a lot of unknowns in this case."

Nodding, Max said, "Remember, Jake is a victim, too. As for the Potter woman, she may have been fooled and taken advantage of just like Katerina was."

"You really do believe the Garwood woman is innocent, don't you?"

"Yes. Even if I wasn't a trained profiler I'd have come to that conclusion. There is no way anybody is a good enough actor to fool me. Katerina is one of the most honest, unassuming people I've ever met. I can just look into her eyes and tell."

The other agent laughed. "Oh, brother, do you have it bad. I can hardly wait to see a hardheaded guy like you take the fall."

"I'm not falling anywhere," Max argued. "This job is all the fulfillment I need or want. Now, shall we talk about something else?"

"Whatever. I thought sure you'd want to call California and see how things are going there." She glanced knowingly at his cell phone.

"I probably should," Max said, doing his best to ignore his companion when she started to snicker quietly.

Katerina answered on the second ring. "Max?"

"Hey. Just checking on you."

"I'm so glad."

There was a breathless quality to her voice that concerned him. "Are you okay?"

"Fine. I called my boss at the Miner's Grub diner and he said they were shorthanded this afternoon so I volunteered to fill in. And here I am. It's good to be back at work. I hated sitting in my room alone."

"Sorry I couldn't leave Opal to keep you company. We needed her here."

"More bombs?" Fear tinged her previously upbeat tone.

"Just taking proper precautions. Are you doing the same? Did they get you a good car? I know they didn't have much to choose from."

"It's fine," Katerina told him. "Big and ugly and powerful enough to earn me speeding tickets. I love everything about it except the color. It's dill pickle–green."

"Picky, picky, picky," he teased. "No problems? No suspicious people lurking?" *Please, say no.*

"Peaceful and quiet." She paused. "I wish the same for you. I've been praying for you since you left."

He was touched—and a little embarrassed for not relying on a faith he used to trust in every instance until it failed him. Twice. "Thanks. Keep your eyes open and don't hesitate to call 9-1-1 if anything looks out of place or makes you nervous. Okay?"

"Okay. Hear that bell? I have an order up. Can't let it get cold. Maybe we can talk again later?"

"You can count on it," he said softly. "Take care."

The moment he broke the connection Harper giggled. "Want to tell me again that you don't have feelings for that woman. I've known you for years and I have never heard that much tenderness in your voice. Never. You've got it bad, Max. Do yourself a favor and admit it before Katerina gets away from you."

NINE

Katerina had told Max the truth. It did feel good to be back at work where she could stay busy and keep from brooding.

The casual ambience of the tiny diner had surprised her when she'd first entered it in search of a job. The Miner's Grub was the kind of blue-collar joint her dad wouldn't have been caught dead in unless he was hunting for votes, which was one reason she had never discovered it herself.

"I was an awful snob," she murmured, smiling because she could now see her character fault and willingly change. These people were kind and friendly and down-to-earth in ways she had overlooked in the past. Now she saw them for the children of God that they were. All were equal and worthy in His sight.

The owner, manager and cook, Xavier Alvarez, pushed open the kitchen door and stuck his balding head through. "You doin' okay, Señorita Kate?"

"Fine. Thanks for letting me come back." She'd been pouring coffee and the distraction of turning to talk to him caused her to slop some onto the long counter. "Oops. Sorry."

He laughed good-naturedly. "I'd say I missed my

best waitress but I know how you feel about telling the whole truth, so I'll just say we're glad for your help."

"I will be the best someday," Katerina promised. "I learned how to make thousand-pound horses behave when I was just a kid. I'm sure I can master a coffeepot."

"*Muy bien.* Very good. How late can you stay? Doris has been sitting up with sick *niños* for two nights. I'm not sure I can talk her into taking second shift."

"I can handle a double," Katerina assured him, and she meant it. What did not occur to her until she'd spoken was having to drive back to the quaint hotel in the dark. The mere idea that she might have to do it without her planned escort gave her the shivers. Nevertheless, she would do what she had to do in order to keep her job and please her boss. Xavier had hired her when she'd known nothing about serving or prepping food. He'd simply seen someone in need and had provided a way for her to survive while retaining her dignity. She would not let him down.

Busing tables by the windows gave her a chance to keep an eye on the ugly green barge Max had rented for her. It was a typical grandma car. Just sitting behind the wheel made her feel fifty years older!

"Which probably helps disguise me," she told herself. But from whom? There was little doubt at this point that her prior association with Vern was at fault. If he had given her anything to keep for him she would have remembered. There was nothing—except her engagement ring, and it was so infinitesimal it had brought expressions of sympathy from some of her highbrow friends. That was another reason she had never questioned him about money or suspected he was raking it in via drug smuggling. Anybody who was that deep into the culture should have had plenty of spare cash to throw around.

A scruffy-looking, twentysomething customer seated at the counter motioned her over. Smiling, Katerina grabbed a fresh pot of coffee and approached him. "Refill?"

"Sure."

She'd topped off his cup and started to turn away when he stopped her with, "You're Vern's girl, aren't you?"

What was the point of denying it? "I used to be."

"That's what I thought. You don't remember me, do you? We met at a party down by the river last spring."

Vague recollections stirred but nothing definitive came to her. "Maybe."

"I'm Kyle," the wiry man said.

Katerina didn't like the way he was staring at her, but he wasn't the first customer who had gotten out of line since she'd started working at the diner. More experienced waitresses had told her to flirt and joke if she wanted good tips. In the case of this man, however, she saw no benefit, particularly since he'd already admitted to being a friend of Vern's. Any friend of Vern's was no friend of hers.

"How about a nice piece of pie with that coffee?" she asked for diversion. "We have apple, cherry, coconut cream…"

He reached for her.

Katerina avoided him with a step backward.

He crooked an index finger. "C'mere. I won't bite. I just want to give you a message from your boyfriend."

"I told you. I don't have a boyfriend."

"Funny. He thinks you do."

Was she the only one who knew that Vern had been killed? She supposed it was possible, but it seemed to her that his cronies should have gotten the news by now, particularly since criminals were privy to their own insider communications.

"Really?"

"Yeah," Kyle said with a half-smile. "And he wants me to pick up the stuff he hid and turn it into cash for him."

"Oh?" Katerina decided to play along and see how far the man would go. He might even reveal some hint that would help her figure out what it was that she was supposed to know about. "What does that have to do with me?"

"He said he told you where he hid it."

"Somebody already trashed my apartment. Maybe they found what Vern wants."

Kyle's smile widened and he briefly averted his glance. "Uh, nope. That was me. Sorry."

"You're *sorry*?" She couldn't help showing ire. "I had to move because of the mess you made."

"Yeah, but you got better digs out of it. That nice big window gives you a great view, too."

To cover the trembling that had begun when he'd insinuated he was her stalker, she set the coffeepot on the prep counter behind her and folded her arms. "That was *you* in my hotel room, too?"

Kyle spread his hands in a gesture meant to convey innocence. Katerina wasn't buying it. "And you have the gall to come here and face me? You people are unbelievable. Haven't you ever heard of *asking*?"

"Hey, I asked. I left notes."

She'd reached the end of her patience. Placing both palms on the counter between them she leaned forward and spoke boldly, never taking her eyes off his disgustingly smug expression.

"Look, mister, I don't know what you want or where

Vern may have left it, but he sure didn't tell me. If he had, I'd have turned it over to the police already. Got that?" It was clear he didn't believe her. "And you can stop pretending that Vern sent you, okay? You and I both know he's dead."

It did her good to see shock on the man's face. "He's what?"

"Dead. Murdered." Katerina had less trouble expressing herself about it now than she had at first. Acknowledging the loss of her imaginary happy future wasn't nearly as painful as it had been, undoubtedly because she had lost all faith in her fiancé long before his demise.

"When?"

"I heard about it yesterday. I'm surprised you don't already know. If you're tied to the same crime bosses he was, you should."

Kyle slid off the stool and began to back up, hands raised. "Hey, I'm just an innocent bystander trying to do a favor for a friend. If you're as smart as you think you are, you'll tell me where to find those rocks and save yourself a boatload of grief. Whoever arranged to off Vern will be after you, too. And your family."

"Rocks?"

Kyle lowered his voice. "You are either the dumbest woman I've ever met or the best liar. The diamonds. Where did he hide them?"

Diamonds? No wonder her adversaries had been so persistent. Katerina's mind was whirling as the past weeks flashed by in memory. What was it that Max had said? Oh, yes. He'd been talking about the lack of reasoning behind the ranch explosion.

"So, if you wanted these diamonds, why did you blow up the stable at my dad's?" Katerina asked.

"What? Me? I didn't blow up nothin'."

Score another point for Special Agent West. She pressed her advantage. "Well, maybe you should find out who did because there's a fair chance that Vern hid what you're looking for at the ranch. He was out there all the time, visiting me and using my father's horse business as a transport for his drug smuggling. If he was going to hide anything he'd have had easy access."

Kyle was cursing under his breath. She could tell he was extremely nervous because his fists were clenched and he was twitching and shuffling like a racehorse in the starting gate.

When he finally made up his mind what to do and hurried toward the door, Katerina reached for his coffee mug, pinched the rim with two fingers and set it aside instead of placing it in the dirty dish bin to be taken to the kitchen and washed. Max would be so proud of her, she thought, particularly if the stalker's fingerprints were on file. She didn't want to wait but the opportunity to present him with the evidence herself and see his smile was just too good to pass up. Besides, by giving it directly to Max she'd be certain the evidence would be processed quickly.

Scanning the small diner she started to feel a bit less vulnerable. If the man who had just left truly had been the one who'd been dogging her, she could identify him. That was good, and bad. Now that he had revealed himself to her, he had nothing more to lose.

Max and Harper parked half a block from Penny Potter's rented house on the outskirts of Billings and donned black Kevlar vests with FBI printed front and back in big white letters. They had considered approaching the house posing as friendly new neighbors but decided against it. The Potter woman would be more likely to cooperate with easily identifiable agents.

Speaking into the mic clipped to his shoulder, Max gave the standby order. "Harper and I will go in first with the dogs. Everybody hold your positions until I give the order to approach. We don't want to scare a possible victim or give anybody advance warning. Leo, you and Ian cover the rear."

As soon as his teammates had radioed confirmation they were in place, he tightened Opal's leash and started toward the unassuming home. The residential street was normally quiet. With both ends blockaded by Billings police cars it looked totally deserted.

The cell phone in his pocket vibrated. Max ignored it. *Almost there.* "I'll go first so Opal can clear the way, then you follow. Keep your eyes open but no guns. Use Star for apprehension if need be. There's supposed to be a little boy in here."

"Affirmative. We've had surveillance in place for the past twenty-four hours. There's been no sign of the resident. Or of Jake."

"That doesn't mean he's not here." Max raised a fist to knock on the door. "Penny Potter. Open up. FBI."

There was no answer. He announced himself again, then prepared to kick the door in. His hand gripped the knob. It turned.

"Front door is unlocked," Max radioed. "Making entry to check resident welfare. Stand by."

Opal and Max led the way with Agent Prentiss waiting in the doorway. He was always on high alert when his dog was searching for explosives. This time, every nerve in his body was firing. If their intelligence was accurate, this place had ties to Morrow's family and was also within cell tower range of the anonymous tips from someone who might be close to the Duprees. Anything that even hinted of the infamous crime family was bad news, particularly since they had admitted to beginning that series of bombings in retaliation for Reginald's arrest.

Nose to the floor, Opal followed an instinctive pattern, disturbed only when Max told her to recheck certain areas, like closets and the toy chest he found in a tiny room that had obviously housed a child.

Every shadow could hide death, every doorway an armed attacker. Had he not relied on his K-9 partner, his progress would have been considerably slower. And more nerve-wracking. It was bad enough as it was, even though Opal acted as if they were playing a wonderful game of hide-and-seek.

They came to the outdated kitchen. A booster seat was balanced on one of the padded chairs at the worn-out table. The floor was scuffed but nevertheless clean. A few dirty dishes remained in the sink; a used frying pan atop the stove. Max opened the cupboards just to be sure. Opal's response assured him there was no bomb.

"All units, approach with caution. The house is clear. No sign of the mother or child but we haven't checked the backyard or garage yet."

A volley of "Copy" came back to him. Harper was at his side in seconds. "Star isn't alerting to anything in here, either. I think our chickens have flown the coop."

"Apparently. We need to check for signs of the male occupant the neighbors reported."

"Copy," Harper said. She sniffed and furrowed her brow. Her big shepherd was straining at the short lead. "Do you smell that?"

"Smell what?"

"Expensive aftershave. It reminds me of the way Jake

used to smell when he kept leaning over my desk and making passes at me."

Max pointed. "The bathroom is that way. Check it first while I do a sweep of the yard."

He hadn't reached the back porch when he heard Harper shout. "Max! In here."

This time he passed Opal. "What is it?"

"A razor, comb and a bottle of that cologne Jake loved." She pointed to a tiny spot of shaving cream on the sink. "This is still wet!"

Max immediately reached for his radio as he headed for the back door with his dog. "Male occupant may be in the area. Use caution."

Opal's nails clicked on the hard floor as she scrambled to keep pace with her partner. He jerked open the kitchen door and burst out. A high board fence enclosed a small yard. Overgrown bushes filled the corners, some abutting the house. He could see flashing lights of patrol cars in the drive on one side. The other looked open.

"Prentiss, backyard. All other units stand by."

Harper appeared immediately, her German shepherd at her side. Max signaled for her to circle wider into the unencumbered grass while he stayed next to the building. He used Opal to warn them of any booby traps. There was no time for a slower, more meticulous search—not if their quarry was getting away.

One realization bothered Max. A lot. Whoever had been with the Potter woman was acting almost as savvy and capable as a trained agent. Taking him into custody was not going to be easy.

Farther out on the lawn, opposite the corner of the house Max was approaching, Harper held Star on a short lead. Max gave her a hand signal to proceed and they coordinated their movements without speaking.

Opal lunged. Star's deep bark echoed off the house and fence. For a split second Max saw a tall, lanky, dark-haired man slip around a corner and disappear.

Harper shouted, "Is that him?"

Both agents were running at top speed. The dogs would have been faster off leash but they didn't dare release them until they were sure of their target.

Max started to reply, "Looked like him," when his words were drowned out by the rev of a motorcycle engine. Tires squealed. Max rounded the corner just in time to see someone speeding off. When the rider turned to look back he was grinning and wearing the mirrored sunglasses typical of federal agents. If Jake had dyed his dirty-blond hair the resemblance would be uncanny.

"Person of interest fleeing west on a motorbike. Possibly red. No helmet. May be armed and dangerous." Sirens in the distance told him there were cars in pursuit.

He turned back to Agent Prentiss. "Bag those clues in the bathroom while Opal and I check the garage, just to be safe."

"Yes, sir."

The cell phone in Max's pocket buzzed again. This time he answered. "West." The moment the caller spoke his already fast pulse shot off the charts.

Katerina sounded breathless. "I saw him. I mean I met him. He came into the diner—"

"Who did?"

"The guy who's been stalking me. I thought he looked a little familiar when I served him but I wasn't sure until he said something."

"Then you can identify him? What's his name?"

"He said it was Kyle."

"No last name?" Max clenched his teeth. He needed

to be there, to look after Katerina. Identifying her stalker face-to-face put her in far more jeopardy than before.

"He didn't say. But I got you something better. I have his prints on his coffee mug."

"Great! Is he still there?"

"No. He left right after I told him about the explosion at the ranch." Max heard her catch her breath. "Oh, and he told me what he's looking for. You aren't going to believe this. He said Vern hid diamonds!"

"What?"

"You heard me. Diamonds. I have no idea where he got them or why he hid them but that's what Kyle is looking for. He thinks Vern told me where they are."

Pausing, Max considered waiting to ask his next question until they were together again, then changed his mind. "*Did* he tell you?"

"Of course not!" Katerina was practically shouting into the phone.

"I had to ask. I hope you understand. I wouldn't be doing my job if I didn't."

Her "Fine" was crisp and her mood hard to interpret.

"Where are you now?"

"Still at work," she said. "I stepped out into the alley to call you so we wouldn't be overheard."

Max checked the time. "Okay. It's going to take me hours to wrap up here and make it back to you. Promise you'll be careful, Katerina. Stay around people. Don't be caught alone unless you're locked in a room at the hotel."

"What shall I do with the fingerprints?"

"Put the mug into a plastic bag and try to keep it from rubbing on the sides. We may get DNA from where the guy drank, too."

"Okay. I promised my boss that I'd work a double shift. I'll stay here until morning unless you come to get me before that."

"Fine. I'll send someone by to pick up the mug so it doesn't get misplaced. Just hang on to it until then."

"Gotcha. How's your investigation going up there?"

"Don't ask," Max said. "Just take care of yourself."

"I…" Her words were cut off by a vibration and boom that was so loud it hurt his ear.

"*Katerina!* Katerina, answer me. What just happened?"

She didn't have to reply for him to know. There had been another explosion in California.

And this time he wasn't there to pick up the pieces.

Or Katerina Garwood.

TEN

The blast rocked Katerina's world, its flash nearly blinding her despite the bright summer sun that beat down. Instinct caused her to drop the cell phone, duck and cover her head. In the background she began to hear shouting and wailing. Shards of the diner's plate-glass windows lay in the street. Its Miner's Grub sign was hanging by one wire, swinging like a bird's broken wing and looking so pitiful she wanted to cry.

A brief mental check of her own physical condition proved she was uninjured, so she straightened and picked her way back inside. The dining area was in shambles. Broken glass and crockery lay scattered on every flat surface. Exterior windows were missing. Seats from a rear booth were shredded like confetti while the table had been upended and lay in the aisle.

She shouted to her boss. "Xavier, are you okay?"

His "Aye, aye, aye, what happened?" echoed from the kitchen.

"I think it was a bomb," she answered. "Come help me if you can. And call 9-1-1. My phone is broken."

The middle-aged man pushed his way out of the kitchen and surveyed the ruins of his diner. A phone was pressed to one ear and he had tears in his eyes.

"They want to know if anybody is hurt," he relayed to Katerina as she tended to an elderly woman with a napkin pressed to her shoulder.

"We didn't have many customers but some do have cuts from the flying glass. They'd better send ambulances."

Firemen in turnouts were first through the opening where the door used to hang. They triaged victims and organized their treatment while uniformed officers tried to get answers. Katerina recognized Sheriff Tate, who was the first to approach her.

Instead of offering sympathy or asking if she was all right, he gestured to one of the patrolmen. "Arrest this young woman until we get everything sorted out," he said, taking Katerina's arm and pulling her away from the victim she'd been comforting. "She was involved in another bombing a few days ago."

"This is not my fault!" Katerina resisted being manhandled and jerked out of his grasp. "Ask the FBI. They'll tell you I'm innocent."

"I don't see any FBI agents," the sheriff said with a mock grin. Handing her over to the police he backed off and dusted his hands together as if removing dirt. "Far as I'm concerned you can keep that girl locked up till she confesses."

"To what?" Katerina shouted.

"Conspiracy to commit murder. I'm sure we can come up with a few other charges but that one'll hold you for now."

Incredulous, she scanned the crowd looking for anyone who would stand up for her. Most seemed to be in shock, although a few were nodding as if they agreed with her accuser. Even Xavier made no move to interfere in her arrest.

Call Max, her mind screamed. But she couldn't. Not only was the cell phone he'd given her lying in the alley with a cracked screen, she had failed to memorize his private number because there had been no need.

He'll come for me, she told herself over and over. He had to have overheard the blast while they'd been talking and would certainly realize she needed his help. Besides, he was trying to track down associates of the Duprees and one of their trademarks had been bombings. Max would be back.

As she was dragged through what was left of the front door, Katerina remembered the clue she'd preserved. She looked back. Everything had been blown off the prep counter. Including the mug with the evidence. Even if she managed to locate the right one in the rubble there would be no way to prove it was Kyle's and check his prints.

The bad guys had won. Again.

Max arranged for an FBI helicopter to pick him up and fly him to an airport. No commercial flight for him this time. He'd insisted on a government jet and got it. By the time he landed and picked up his SUV, barely three hours had elapsed.

Communications with Dylan O'Leary brought him up to speed on the diner explosion as he drove south. Injuries were, thankfully, minor. Because Katerina had been outside talking to him when the bomb went off, she had escaped completely.

"Except that they arrested her," Dylan added grimly.

"*What?* On what charge?"

"You're gonna get a kick out of this. Attempted murder. My sources tell me she was held because the sheriff insisted. They also tell me that particular lawman is a close friend of her daddy's."

"Bertrand Garwood again," Max gritted out. "I'm beginning to see him as a link rather than Katerina."

Dylan chuckled. "Is that because he's not as pretty as his daughter?"

"Hah. Very funny, although true. Her mother must have been a real stunner because she sure doesn't look like her dad."

"I take it that's a plus," the techie said.

"Oh, yeah." Max kept his eyes on the road while his mind took a detour. Visualizing Katerina being put in handcuffs and hauled off to jail was intolerable. How scared she must be. The mere thought of tears pooling in those beautiful, expressive blue eyes pierced his gut like a lance and made him yearn to take her in his arms and assure her that everything was going to be okay. He'd see to it. Somehow.

"Headquarters to Special Agent West," Dylan quipped. "Did you hear what I said?"

"Yeah, but I didn't like it."

"Well, chill. Your girlfriend is safer locked up in a local jail than she'd be on the street right now."

Max exhaled a long, deep breath. "As much as I hate to admit it, I suppose I agree. Have you run across any new threats?"

"A few. That sheriff owes her plenty considering the way he spoke out and blamed her in front of all those bystanders and first responders. It's going to take a while to convince some folks she had nothing to do with the bombing."

"Do you think someone was trying to get her?"

To Max's relief, Dylan said, "No. If they had been

they wouldn't have waited until she was outside before triggering the device."

"Unless it was random and they weren't watching."

"There is that. How far out are you?"

"An hour, give or take. I'm using my lights but no siren."

"This is an emergency?"

Max snorted before answering, "It is to me."

The Mariposa County Jail wasn't all that bad if Katerina compared it to her former apartment, particularly after Kyle had trashed it. At least there was a cot and a blanket and pillow in her cell.

Waiting for Max would have been intolerable if she had not expended so much nervous energy after the blast. As the jolt of adrenaline began to wear off, her body responded with core-deep weariness.

Although she promised herself she'd stay awake and try to figure out who could have planted the explosive device in poor Señor Alvarez's little diner, her body insisted she must rest. That's why she lay down on the cot. And why she was awakened by Max's voice several hours later.

"Katerina! Are you all right?"

Her lids fluttered open in time to watch him demand that the cell door be unlocked. The sight of him brought instantly renewed hope and strength, both of which were sorely needed.

She swung her legs over the side of the cot and sat up. Words were inadequate to express her feelings at that moment. Max was here. He'd come back. She started to stand, wobbled a tiny bit and felt him lift her into his embrace.

Never had she felt so safe. Her arms slipped around

his waist and she held tight. "Oh, Max, they blew up the diner. It was awful." Katerina felt his warm breath on her hair and wondered if she was imagining the rain of kisses, the press of his lips. Tightening her hold she whispered, "I'm so glad you're here."

She heard a catch in his throat when he asked, "Are you sure you're all right?"

"I am now."

"Reports say nobody was killed or badly injured. Is that what you saw?" His hold on her remained firm.

"Yes." After several long moments she raised her face to gaze at him and was rewarded with the soft brush of his lips on hers.

"I nearly died when I heard that blast and you stopped talking."

"I dropped the phone you gave me. It broke. I didn't have your number written down." She glanced to one side. "Tate thinks I'm some kind of mad bomber."

"So I heard." Max began to smile with tenderness. "He may not realize it but he did us a favor. You were far safer waiting for me in this cell than you would have been going back to your hotel room."

"Can you get me out?"

"Already done," he said huskily. "You're now officially in federal custody. Ready to go?"

Katerina kept one arm around his waist and he encircled her shoulders as they turned and left together. Wondering what she would have done, how she could have coped without Max's help made her tremble. There was no way she could deny how desperately she needed him, nor did she want to. It wasn't weakness to acknowledge a need for moral support, it was a matter of setting aside foolish pride and admitting she wasn't as complete as she had imagined.

Oh, she had her faith and believed Jesus was with her in all things, yet there was also an instinctive desire for an earthly friend who would stand by her. Defend her when she was attacked or falsely accused. Just be there.

That was where Max came in. His presence filled her with a sense of strength and rightness that had been missing for as long as she could remember. As she mulled over recent events she was amazed at how, despite efforts to harm her and those she loved, God had turned evil into good. There were still plenty of serious hurdles to overcome, of course, but Max had returned without her asking. And he had sought her out, made arrangements to help her, stood by her even after admitting he'd had doubts about her innocence.

And now, finally, she could help him with his investigation. The fingerprints on the mug were gone, yes, but her memory remained sharp. She could identify the cohort of her late fiancé and give Max something to work with that might tie to others and snowball into solving the entire case.

Then there were the diamonds, assuming Vern hadn't lied about that, too. It was a possibility. After all, if he was being pressed to deliver drugs or money and didn't have it, he might have invented a story about hiding gemstones just to save his own neck.

Which hadn't worked, she thought, realizing that her initial notion about why he'd died may have been right. If he'd been tortured too much and had kept holding back because he had no choice, he could very easily have driven his tormentors to press him too hard. Dead was dead, of course. It just seemed more logical to assume they had not meant to kill Vern until they'd made him talk.

Once in the street, she paused and looked up at Max.

"What if nobody finds any diamonds? What if they don't even exist?"

"One day at a time, honey," he said gently. "I want to get you back to the hotel where we can talk privately and try to sort out the facts as we know them."

Blinking back tears, Katerina never took her eyes off him when she said, "The only thing I know for sure is that I have never been so happy to see anybody as I am to see you."

"Likewise, Ms. Garwood. When I heard that blast over the phone I couldn't stop thinking…"

"Yeah. Me, too. If I'd been clearing off that table instead of calling you, I might have been blown up."

"Can you describe the last customer who was sitting in the booth at the heart of the damage?"

Slowly, thoughtfully, she shook her head. "It's all a blur. The whole afternoon is. I'm sorry."

"Don't worry about it. I have a few tricks we can try to jog your memory. They sometimes help a lot."

"Sometimes?"

Max nodded. "Yes. If one thing doesn't work we try others. My job isn't pure science the way they depict it on TV. It's more like throwing mud at a wall and hoping some of it will stick. Speaking of mud, did you get your prize ribbons clean?"

"Yes. Thanks for asking. They aren't as pretty as they once were but they'll do as mementos."

"I'm glad," Max said softly.

Katerina knew he meant it from the bottom of his heart. Although they had known each other for a very short time, she was already able to read him like a book. For the most part, anyway. No doubt he was hiding parts of his psyche that he felt were too vulnerable to reveal but she could wait. It was enough to know that he cared, to see the tenderness in his gaze and feel the tingle his deep voice brought on when they were speaking privately. The depth and scope of those feelings were new to her. Overwhelming. What was the most unsettling was an assuredness that Vern had never affected her that way. Not even when he'd proposed. Perhaps that was why she had hesitated before agreeing to marry him.

She let Max help her into the car before she closed her eyes and whispered, "Thank You, God, for interfering before I made the second biggest mistake of my life." And speaking of life… "Thank You for preserving mine and keeping the customers safe."

Katerina's subconscious continued the prayer silently as Max slid behind the wheel. Just looking at him made her so thankful it brought tears to her eyes. She dashed them away so he wouldn't notice.

There was no place she'd rather be than right there. And nobody she'd rather be sitting beside. The threatening world outside the SUV no longer terrified her as long as her handsome special agent was nearby.

"You okay?" Max asked as they drove toward the hotel.

"Fine. More than fine," Katerina said, taking the chance that he shared her feelings. "You're here."

Max had to wait for his heart to slow down before he dared try small talk. He had not intended to make Katerina dependent upon him, it had just happened. In this case it was probably beneficial since he did want her compliance and cooperation. He hoped that she understood he was not actually courting her, he was simply doing his job—at least that was what he kept telling himself when his emotions took over.

He chanced a sidelong glance beneath arched eyebrows. "Thanks. Our FBI motto is Fidelity, Bravery, Integrity."

"Nice. I read it on the seal."

"It's not just a pretty logo. It's how we live our lives, Katerina," Max told her.

"So…" She deftly switched gears. "How did everything turn out with the missing agent you were searching for back in Montana?"

"Not sure. We spotted someone who looked a little like him fleeing the scene, but until we get some DNA results back we're just guessing."

"What happened to that poor woman and her baby?"

He saw no reason to withhold information that was no longer classified since they'd used local Billings police in the raid. "Long gone. She may have fled for any number of reasons."

"What do you think?"

"All I know for sure is that I saw a person of interest ride off on a motorbike and he escaped. The only thing that actually ties him to that particular house is who had been living there."

"Even your specially trained dogs couldn't track him?"

Max frowned. "No. The man apparently had an escape plan. The question is, why was he still there when Penny Potter and the child were gone? It was almost as if he was taunting us."

"Maybe he just came looking for them after they were already on the run and he was trying to figure out where they had gone."

"I suppose that is possible."

Katerina grew thoughtful. "What would be this mystery man's reason for taunting you if he didn't know who you and your team were?"

"Are you suggesting he may have really been Jake?"

"I don't know. I don't know the guy. It was just a theory.

"No way. He would have reported to the FBI as soon as he managed to escape from his kidnappers and have asked fellow agents for assistance."

"Fidelity."

"And integrity," Max added. "Jake Morrow has always been something of a loose cannon but he was— is—an excellent agent. He and his younger half brother, Zeke, weren't raised together but Zeke followed him into the FBI. They're both products of dysfunctional families."

"A person isn't necessarily locked in to a personality flaw forever," Katerina agreed softly. "I have high hopes to escape from the kind of prejudice I listened to most of my life. Now that I recognize it, I should be able to put it behind me."

His lips quirked. "You? Flaws?"

"Don't tease. I mean it. I never knew what a stuck-up snob I was until I got to see the world from the other side."

"So, your enemies did you a favor."

"I guess they did." She began to smile again. "We'll see if it was all worth it after the dust settles."

"I come from a big family," Max said. "We all get along pretty well, considering. I suppose it was hard for you, being an only child, after your mother passed away."

When Katerina looked over at him and he saw the glisten of unshed tears he realized he'd touched a nerve. "It was the worst time of my life. And the best. The loneliness and alienation from my dad pushed me to spend more and more time training horses. If I'd been

happy and fulfilled already I might never have become so proficient."

"Pressure turns coal into diamonds," Max observed. "You don't suppose that was what Kowalski meant when he said he had diamonds, do you?"

"Not for a second. He was a crook. He stole from his bosses and paid the ultimate price. I didn't figure into the equation."

"Then we have some work to do," he said soberly.

"I like the way that sounds. The two of us. Together."

"Absolutely." There was no way he was letting Katerina out of his sight if he could help it. As long as his assignment could be made to justify it, he intended to keep her so close she'd probably get claustrophobia.

"Together." Max grinned. "Just you, me and Opal."

ELEVEN

With a weather forecast of bright, clear skies and no hint of impending storms for a least two weeks, the South Fork Chamber of Commerce decided to announce the rescheduling of its Founder's Day picnic and parade. Considering the crime wave she'd been experiencing, Katerina was more concerned about that kind of activity than she was the weather.

"Are we going to visit the ranch again and look for diamonds?" she asked Max over the breakfast provided by the hotel the following morning.

"Yes, why?"

"Because I'd like you to try to talk some sense into my father."

Max chuckled. "You think that highly of my powers of persuasion? I'm flattered."

"Well, he won't even speak to me. He might listen to a man in authority."

"Do you want me to defend your actions and explain that you didn't have anything to do with the bombs?"

Katerina shook her head. "No. I want you to convince him that it's too dangerous for him to participate in the Founder's Day festivities. Particularly riding in the parade in an open car."

"What makes you think he's in danger?"

"Everything. Look at what's happened so far. His stable was blown up, then my apartment was trashed. The awful bombing at the Miner's Grub should convince him of something."

"Not if he assumes it's all tied to you."

"There's more," Katerina said. "It just came to me. When that guy was threatening me at work he mentioned my family. Dad's all I have left."

"You care about him. I get that." Max sighed. "Okay. I'll give it a try. What do you say we take a ride out that way today?"

"You're free?" The instant those words were out of her mouth she likened them to the humorous reply, *No, but I'm reasonable*, and began to blush.

Max noticed immediately. "What's wrong?"

"Nothing. My mind just works in strange ways."

"I've noticed," he said teasingly. "Sometimes you're so far ahead of me it's scary."

"Really?"

"Really. You aced all your classes in school, didn't you?"

Her cheeks felt even warmer. "Yes. At the time I thought I was chasing 4.0 to impress my father but in retrospect I can see it was a matter of personal pride." She sobered. "I hope that's not a sin."

Max laughed. "You are unbelievable. Think about it this way. If you slacked off and didn't do your best, you'd be wasting God-given talent. Isn't that worse?"

"You're right!"

"Always," he quipped. "Now finish your toast and let's get a move on."

Katerina sipped cooling coffee, then blotted her lips with a napkin. "I'm ready when you are. I just wish there was something I could do for Señor Alvarez. He's lost everything thanks to me."

"Stop blaming yourself. If his insurance comes up short I may be able to get him some help from a victims' reparations fund. I heard that the restaurant kitchen is still intact. If he can rebuild the dining room he should be back in business in no time."

Her hand rested at the base of her throat and she fought tears of relief. "Oh, thank God. Literally."

"You've been praying for your boss, too?"

Releasing a quavering breath, she nodded. "Of course I have. And for all the people who were hurt by the debris. That's the easy part."

"There's a hard part about praying?" Max looked confused.

"Oh, yes," Katerina replied solemnly. "It's much harder to make myself pray for my enemies and others who have hurt my feelings or given up on me."

"You really do that?"

"When I can manage to get myself into the right frame of mind for long enough, I do. It's one thing to know I should forgive and another thing to actually accomplish it."

Max's jaw clenched. "So, you think guys like the Duprees, who have ruined countless lives, should be forgiven? That's crazy."

She was shaking her head. "I don't mean that anybody should be free of the consequences of their actions, good or bad. Lawbreakers have to pay. Vern Kowalski paid the ultimate price for his sins. But if I harbor anger and hate in my heart, the only one who suffers is me. Take my father for instance."

"Because he's so mad at you?" Max was rising. Opal stood leashed and ready at his side.

"No," Katerina said. "I've been giving it a lot of thought and I've come to the conclusion Dad is furious with God for taking my mother from him. I'm just collateral damage."

"Very perceptive. And possibly true. Not that there's much you can do about it."

"I know." She pushed back her chair and joined him. "Which is why I'm so thankful for you. I needed an ally and now I have one."

"You must have some local friends who haven't totally abandoned you."

"A few. The time I spent with Vern alienated a lot of them. Besides, they have families and other worries. The last thing I want to do is expose them to the threats that are piling up around me." She smiled and took his free arm. "You, on the other hand, are armed and dangerous. God knew just what I needed."

Her opinion amused Max at first. He had never been called heaven-sent before. Most of the people he encountered who were not part of his team or in other branches of law enforcement treated him with disdain or distrust or both.

"Thanks, I think," he said gruffly, leading the way outside. "But remember, I'm only here temporarily. I could be recalled at any time."

"I understand."

He didn't think she did. Not in the least. She had identified him as a personal answer to her prayers and was going to be devastated when he left. Which he would definitely do. What did she expect? How could she possibly see a positive outcome when his goal had to be to wrap up his current assignment and go back to Montana?

"I will leave, Katerina. It's inevitable."

"I know."

What could she be thinking? Yes, she was an attractive woman and yes, they had grown closer than he got with most of the civilians he met, but that didn't mean he saw a future for them together. There was only one thing to do. He had to put it into words that would make her understand.

"I have a duty to perform. That's why I'm here. It's my job."

The quizzical look on her face told him she was not yet following his line of reasoning.

"My actions and decisions are based on the case I'm working. In this instance it's about the Dupree crime family and their network of underlings. That's why I came to see you. I needed to delve into your relationship with Kowalski and make sure you weren't working with him."

"Okay. And…?"

It was clearly time to get more specific. "And, my job is very dangerous. I could get shot." He hesitated, then plunged ahead. "Plus, I am way too old for you."

To Max's chagrin Katerina began to laugh. He scowled. "What's so funny?"

"You are," she said between giggles. "I wasn't making a pass at you. I was just stating my faith."

"That's not how it sounded."

When her gaze rose to meet his, Max saw pathos in her expression, something he had not expected.

"Are you a believer?" she asked.

"I used to go to church if that's what you mean."

"Not at all." She was slowly shaking her head. "Was there ever a time when you knew, just knew, that God loved you and Jesus did, too?"

Remaining silent, he refused to answer. His subconscious, however, caused his free hand to rise and trace the scar on his cheek.

"How did you get that?" Katerina asked softly. "Was that when your faith was tested and you let it go?"

"That's no concern of yours."

"Yes, it is," she countered, stepping closer and gently cupping his cheek. The touch was barely there, yet it reached all the way into his heart.

Max stopped her by grabbing her wrist and holding tight. "Don't."

She looked up at him, her eyes glistening. "I'm sorry. For a lot of reasons. I wish there was some way I could prove that God never gives up on a believer. He's still here, still caring for you, whether you know it or not."

"That doesn't matter. What happened, happened. Nobody can change the past."

"No, but you can change the way you view it, your reactions to it." Her gaze never wavered. "Look what simmering anger has done to my father."

"It's not the same thing."

"Isn't it?" Katerina stepped back and Max released her wrist.

"No. It isn't," he said flatly. "I got this scar when I failed to accurately profile a supposedly reformed father. A drug lord assumed that man was a snitch and finished him by blowing up his house. My error cost the lives of everybody in the family, including the little boy I had promised to help."

"Oh, Max. How horrible."

Turning away, he shook off the comment rather than reply. *Horrible* didn't begin to cover the feelings he'd had when he'd come to after the explosion and seen the destruction all around him. The scar on his cheek was nothing compared to the loss of life.

As he escorted Katerina to his SUV and put Opal in first, he bit out, "Where was God *then*?"

"Right beside you," she said with tenderness. "I can't begin to explain why bad things happen, I only know I'd be lost without my faith. That's what faith is, sticking with your belief in spite of not knowing. I don't have to be able to explain things on an earthly plane in order to trust God. It's a personal decision."

She paused while he circled the SUV and slid behind the wheel, then continued, "I also believe that once you have turned to Jesus He won't let you go. Even if you give up on Him, He'll stick with you."

He wished he could agree with her theology. His mind didn't work that way. He needed proof and as far as he was concerned, the untimely death of an innocent little boy was a deal breaker. If God wanted his renewed allegiance, He was going to have to do more than send a starry-eyed young woman to preach to him.

A lot more.

Katerina spent the drive to the Garwood Ranch in silent contemplation and prayer. She was no pastor, no Bible scholar. Explaining her faith was something she'd never been asked to do before and she felt woefully ill equipped. What should she have said? What might she add that would help Max get over his heartache and realize how valuable his skills were?

As he wheeled under the archway she realized she was out of time to speak to him in private. *Father, help me say the right thing, the healing thing. Please? I'm way out of my depth here.*

She took a deep breath and plunged ahead. "You're

being too hard on yourself, Max. When you're doing your best, when you're following your calling, all anybody expects is the best you can do. Nobody's perfect."

"I agree. Lots of people fail. The trouble is, when I made a mistake, people died. A child died."

What else could she say? How could she argue that point? He was right, as far as he'd gone. But there was more to it. There had to be. Life might appear random, yet be following a master plan. If the physical world did not operate systematically it would disintegrate. The same was true of human existence.

She decided to try one more time. "Look, I don't have all the answers any more than you do. Evil exists. The same rules that govern the universe apply down here. Think of cause and effect. Consequences are a given. They may vary but they won't vanish like some kind of celestial magic trick. God doesn't break the rules on a whim. But he did give us the Bible for direction and understanding."

"You understand it all?"

She had to smile. "Oh, no. I barely get the simple concepts. If the Lord had spelled out everything for us it wouldn't have helped, either. Our minds are incapable of rising to that level of comprehension. Again, that's where faith comes in. And free will. You either choose to believe or you reject that teaching."

Max had turned away to concentrate on Opal. When he looked back at Katerina she could tell their conversation about spirituality was over. That was actually a big relief to her.

He motioned. "You coming with me?"

"Do I have to?"

"You do," he said with a wry smile. "If I have to face the mayor of South Fork and warn him to call off his parade, you need to be there to back me up. After all, you've been the victim of two explosions."

"Don't remind me." Although she did keep pace with Opal and her partner, she took care to avoid leading the way. Despite the fact that she was courageous and confident, standing at a door and knowing her father was going to be the one to open it unnerved her. She didn't fear him, per se. She merely disliked conflict—and Bertrand Garwood was conflict personified.

When they were all three on the porch, Max rang the bell. Katerina stood her ground in spite of a growing desire to escape to the solitude and safety of the remaining stables. Nobody answered the door.

"Do you intend to put Opal to work again while we're here?" Katerina asked as they waited.

"Might as well. I figured you and I could inspect the barns together after Opal tells me they're safe. That okay with you?"

"Fine." She didn't realize she was wringing her hands until Max looked pointedly at them.

"You nervous?"

"No more than I would be if I were empty-handed and locked in a stall with a mean wild mustang."

"Want to go to the tack room and get a whip?"

"A quirt. That's the little whip a rider holds. It makes noise when you smack the business end and works more to get a horse's attention than to hurt him."

"I doubt we'll have trouble getting your dad's attention," Max said as he pushed the doorbell again. "The problem may be in getting him to ignore us while we conduct a serious search."

Before Katerina had a chance to answer, the object of her worry jerked open the heavy wooden door and bellowed, "What now?"

"Special Agent West," Max said, offering a handshake rather than flashing his badge. "We met when—"

"I know when we met." Bertrand scowled. "Why are you here?"

"A couple of reasons, Mr. Garwood. I understand you're scheduled to ride in a parade this coming weekend. That may be inadvisable."

"What's it to the FBI?"

"Concern for your safety, sir."

"Bah!" He gestured at Katerina. "She put you up to this, didn't she?"

"No, sir. There was another bomb set off in town. Surely you heard about it."

"I heard," the portly older man said. When he looked at Katerina again his expression was unreadable.

"Then you understand why I'm suggesting you keep a lower profile."

"I have friends in the sheriff's department. They'll take care of me."

"Still, since your daughter has apparently been targeted twice, it would be wise to take precautions."

Katerina could almost hear her father's reply before he said, "That has nothing to do with me. Everybody knows I have no daughter," then slammed the door.

That attitude was no surprise to Katerina. It did, however, send her emotions spinning.

"I'm so sorry," Max said. He slipped an arm around her shoulders and gave her a supportive squeeze. "I'll contact Tate personally and fill him in, just in case your father is lying about having proper protection lined up for the whole day."

"Thanks." She was shaking her head and sighed audibly. "Remember what I said about needing to forgive him? Well, it's getting harder and harder to do."

"Good to know you're human," Max said gently. "Come on. Let's make a sweep of the barns with Opal while you look for good hiding places for those diamonds."

Katerina rolled her eyes. "I don't know where to start. I mean, every bale of hay, every sack of grain, every stall is a possibility."

"Not necessarily."

"What do you mean?" She was having to take two steps for every stride of his to keep up.

"The places you just mentioned all have drawbacks. Hay and grain can be fed. Stalls are raked and cleaned out regularly. They're not secure enough."

"So, it needs to be someplace stationary?"

"That's more likely. Even the trucks and trailers are an iffy choice. Suppose your father sold one or shipped it away with horses in it? Then how would Vern have retrieved his stash?"

She brightened. "You're right! And when we find the diamonds you can announce it and get that terrible stalker off my trail."

"That would be the ideal result," Max said pensively.

Katerina saw doubt in his expression. "You don't think it will help?"

"It's not that. My concern is based on what I know of the Dupree crime family. They don't let traitors like Kowalski get away with stealing from them."

"*They* had him killed? I assumed it was some other prisoner who'd heard about the diamonds and wanted to cut himself in."

"It may have been, if Vern was dumb enough to brag, but I doubt it." Max kept working Opal along the edges of the barns as they talked. "Latest word on the street is that Angus Dupree, the uncle of the kingpin

we arrested, had already offered an enormous reward
to anyone who could get the truth out of your old boyfriend. Once he heard about the gemstones, he was livid.
He'd like the loot found and returned, of course, but he
doesn't care about the monetary value nearly as much
as he does the Dupree reputation."

"But—"

"Let me finish." He paused and faced her. "Pride
governs his actions. Pride and a need for retribution.
He can no longer count on making Kowalski pay for his
crimes against the family. Do you see what I'm saying?"

Nodding, Katerina felt the strength flowing out of
her. Vern was gone. There was only one other connection. One other person who could be punished to bring
him satisfaction.

Her.

TWELVE

Failing to get any leads that day, Max brought in Zeke Morrow and his tracking dog, an Australian shepherd named Cheetah, just in case Vern had wrapped the diamonds in something personal of his before hiding them. They got clothing samples from the jail and picked up a waiting warrant for the ranch.

After a thorough search that included the main house, Zeke reported to Max. "Nothing, Boss. Sorry. Even if he used a sock or T-shirt it's been too long."

"I figured. I just thought you'd be glad for a break from all that hassle about your half brother."

"Thanks. I was hoping you and Harper would come up with something helpful at Penny Potter's when you were in Billings."

Max nodded. "Yeah, so did I. Any word from the stakeout of her place?"

"No. Nothing. She did a better job of vanishing on her own than the US Marshals did hiding Esme Dupree."

"That reminds me," Max said. "What about Esme? Do we have any leads on her whereabouts?"

"Not that I've heard. I've been in the field quite a bit lately."

"I get regular briefings on my computer and smartphone," Max said. "I wondered about rumors."

"It's been quiet. They did tell you about the anonymous text messages, didn't they?"

"Messages? Plural? I know about the one we got right before we raided Penny Potter's."

"There were two more after that. The first said something like, 'Nah, nah, you missed him.' The second was even harder to understand. We finally decided they had to be GPS coordinates but they didn't pan out. Led us to a vacant house."

"All right," Max said. "We'll continue to treat the Potter woman as a blameless victim like Esme until we're sure otherwise."

"She really may be innocently caught up in all this, you know."

"I know. That's why we're giving her the benefit of the doubt."

Zeke's dark eyes narrowed on a slim figure in the distance. "What about the Garwood woman? Are you doing the same for her or are you playing her?"

"She's innocent," Max said firmly. "Dupree bombs have come close to ending her life twice already. There's no way anybody with half a brain would put themselves in dangerous situations like that on purpose."

"If you say so." The other agent arched an eyebrow. "I know how easy it can be for a pretty face to turn an agent."

Ignoring the insinuation, Max asked, "Is that what you think may have happened to your half brother?"

Zeke shrugged. "No, no. But he did seem right on track until he got involved with that Penny woman and fathered her kid." He huffed. "Of course, he and I weren't raised together so it's hard for me to specu-

"His friend, Sheriff Tate, is a lot more sensible than Bertrand Garwood. We worked out a cooperative plan. After the parade, Opal and I will stay on scene at the park and circulate to make our presence known, just in case."

"Do you really think there will be more trouble?" The casual atmosphere of the small town seemed so peaceful it was hard to imagine more mayhem—particularly because if it came, it would be because of her.

"Most of my duties are to keep folks safe, not pick up the pieces after a disaster. We can do that, too, we'd just rather head off problems instead."

Main Street was already filling with spectators. Many had brought their own lawn chairs and were staking claim on the best spectator spots along the curb. Katerina ran interference for Opal as she worked the line because so many excited children wanted to rush up and pet her.

"This dog is doing a job now," she explained. "See her vest? When she takes it off you can pet her. Maybe at the picnic, later."

A sweet, red-haired little girl pointed and lisped, "Ith that her name?"

"No. That says FBI. She's like a police officer."

Katerina kept smiling as she watched Max and Opal work their way farther along the street. The boxer's nose was to the ground until she came to a plastic drum that had been placed at a corner to receive extra trash during the celebration.

Max stopped. Opal circled the blue drum once, then sat next to it and panted up at her handler expectantly.

Katerina's heart skipped a beat. That was the sign. Opal had found explosives! And there had to be a dozen innocent little kids close enough to touch both the barrel and the dog.

She saw Max speaking into his radio. Deputies began to converge. Some stayed with Max while others, arms outstretched, began to shoo the crowd away from the corner. Away from possible harm.

"You, too, ma'am," the nearest deputy said. Katerina remembered going to high school with him, but they never really moved in the same circles. "No. I'm with Special Agent West." She pointed to Max. "I have to stay here."

"Orders are to evacuate for half a block. Move along, please." He lowered his voice and leaned closer. "You don't want to start a panic by refusing, do you, Ms. Katerina?"

"Of course not. I…" She had to back up or be overrun. "All right. I'm not going far."

"Down to the sidewalk in front of the hardware store will be fine," he said pleasantly, as if he had not just warned her of real danger.

From where she and the others stood she watched Max and the sheriff confer. Finally an electric cart built like a small truck was brought in and the blue drum loaded gently into the back.

The driver eased the vehicle forward, inches at a time, while Max led Opal a safe distance away and rewarded her with a favorite chew toy.

Patrol cars, lights flashing, flanked the golf cart as it slowly moved off the parade route. Katerina figured the guy who was driving deserved a medal. She just hoped it didn't end up costing him his life in the process.

Given the choices available in South Fork and the narrow window of opportunity during which the barrel had to have been placed, Max figured it had been delivered with the explosives already inside. That probably meant the device was stable enough to move again rather than wait hours for a bomb squad that might have to travel all the way from San Jose, or farther.

He wasn't thrilled with the sheriff's choice to do so but had to admit it made sense. So did leaving the small cardboard box in the bottom where it lay. Since no other trash had been thrown on top of it since it was left there, he figured that the sooner he checked all the other trash barrels, the better. They weren't the only places he intended to look, of course. The first thing he'd do was make a circuit of all the blue barrels, then retrace his route and look for other suspicious objects. Hopefully, whoever had booby-trapped the trash receptacle lacked imagination and had simply repeated himself if he'd planted more bombs.

Katerina jogged toward him. Max stopped before Opal reached the fifth barrel. "You need to go wait with the sheriff's deputies."

"You found a bomb already?"

"Opal says we did. It's been taken out of town and left in a safe place, under guard, just in case."

"What if she's wrong?"

Max huffed. "Opal is never wrong. And she never lies. That's another reason why a K-9 partner is better than a human one."

"So, why are you still looking?"

"Because nothing says that whoever put the device in one trash barrel stopped there. With all the confusion surrounding the celebration, it's highly likely there will be more than what I've already located." He didn't like frightening her. It was just that she seemed to be taking the whole situation too lightly. Having been born and raised in a small town had left Katerina too gull-ible. Too trusting. That mindset had already led her to become involved with a drug smuggler. There was no telling what else she'd have done if the FBI had not sent him to South Fork.

Max gave her his sternest look. "Listen, Katerina. Don't be naive. This is no game. The earlier bombers may have targeted buildings and not cared about an ac-cidental passerby. But the guys who set these bombs wanted to hurt people for sure."

He was relieved to see her shoulders slump and her head nod. "Okay. I'll back off. Can I stay with you and Opal to watch the parade after you're done working? I know there's no way Dad will ever call it off no matter what you find. Not after all this preparation."

What Max should have done, is tell her there was no time during the day when he'd be off duty. Instead, he gave her permission to rejoin him at Main and Park.

Her joyful "All right!" brought a genuine smile.

Max's countenance mirrored her delight. How could a man not be happy when Katerina was around. She was the kind of woman who always saw the glass half-full, the flowers in full bloom, the sun bright in a summer sky. She had been through plenty that should have de-pressed her, yet she seemed to always bounce back, no matter what life threw at her. Such as her father's rejec-tion. His jaw clenched and anger roiled through him. Garwood had a lot to answer for. He was also a prime target because, no matter how obnoxious he got, he was still related to Katerina.

Max finished checking the last trash barrel and ra-dioed Sheriff Tate with his location. "I've checked and cleared the rest of the route. Did somebody go over the floats and cars?"

"Negative. I've posted a guard but some of them were already parked in the staging area when my man went on duty."

"Copy."

"It's not far from where you are," Tate told Max. "Go past the restrooms and you'll see a bunch of cars and tractors pulling decorated trailers."

"On my way," Max replied. He began to jog, purposely leaving Katerina behind despite minor misgivings. As long as she remained in a crowded area he had already inspected she should be all right. The shops and roads were safe. That left only the rolling stock that could be triggered remotely while passing certain bystanders.

Like Katerina.

Max shivered, picturing the first day he'd seen her a scant few weeks ago. Then, they had not yet formed a bond. Now everything was different. *Very* different if he were to listen to his instincts and put aside arguments against caring for her.

No, that wasn't right, he countered. He might care about her welfare the same way he was concerned for any citizen's well-being. He didn't care *for* her. Because that would mean his feelings were too personal, too special. He didn't want to become romantically involved with any woman, particularly not one who was eleven years younger than he was and tainted by her past.

Max could just hear somebody like Katerina preaching to him about forgiveness and second chances. And she'd be right, up to a point. He had come to believe she was truly innocent. However, that didn't mean his bosses in the FBI would be inclined to trust her, and by association, trust him. Not as totally as they once had, at any rate.

His conscience demanded he take Katerina's side and stand up for her. She was young. That was a given. And she had been terribly spoiled by her father before being ostracized. How awful that must feel. Her whole world had crashed around her, somebody was trying to kill her, the man she had loved had been murdered, and thugs were stalking her for a prize that might never be located.

Pausing, he took a deep breath and visualized Katerina's beautiful eyes and bright smile. Most people would have felt beaten down and have given up, yet she had not. On the contrary, she had bounced back every time, she had opened up to him about her faith. It was solid. Reliable. And by comparison, so was she.

A horn honked. Engines revved. Max saw the procession start to move. Out of time to reach them and inspect each vehicle, he stood aside with Opal and let them slowly pass by. Her stiff posture and intense concentration told him she knew she was still working.

Suddenly she lunged. Barked in spite of her training to remain calm when detecting telltale odors.

Max held up a hand and stepped forward to halt the progress of the antique Packard convertible. Ranch foreman Heath McCabe was driving. Sitting on the rear deck, dressed like a country-western singer, was Bertrand Garwood. He waved Max back. "Out of our way."

"I'm sorry, Mr. Mayor. My dog insists I check your car before you proceed."

"Bah. Ridiculous. Where's my…that young woman who is determined to ruin me?"

"Katerina's not here. And I assure you I am only listening to my detection dog. Now, do you want to let us go over the car the easy way, or do you want to wait for a search warrant and maybe be blown to smithereens in the meantime?"

As Max had figured, the older man spoke to McCabe and had the convertible pulled out of line.

"This won't take long. If you'll both get out, please, I'll let my dog do her job."

Garwood was fuming. "This had better not turn out to be some cooked-up false alarm or I'll have your badge."

If Max had not been so intent on watching Opal he might have laughed. There had been more than one time when he'd have gladly handed over his badge if it had meant he wouldn't have to worry about making another deadly mistake.

"Open the trunk, please."

McCabe took the keys from the ignition and handed them to Max. "Not me, man. I like livin'."

"Are you saying there's an explosive device in the trunk?"

"Nope. But I ain't arguing with your dog, either. If she says it's dangerous, I believe her."

"Actually…" Max led Opal around the idling vehicle one more time. She showed some interest in the trunk but not enough to cause him to call a bomb squad. Using a key he popped the lock and lifted the lid.

"Spare tire, jack, jumper cables…all the usual stuff. Looks like we're okay here."

"What about the undercarriage?" McCabe asked.

"Opal isn't interested in the chassis at all." He started to close the trunk. Opal put her front feet up on the bumper and barked.

Max halted, then picked up the jack handle and used it to gingerly move lightweight items. When he speared a dirty rag and moved it, Opal got very excited.

"This?" he asked, holding it out for her to sniff.

The dog went ballistic.

"This? You want this?" Double-checking, he redirected her attention to the car's trunk. She showed zero interest in it. Fixated on the rag she wiggled at his feet.

"Well, well." Max looked to Bertrand. "Where did you get this car, Mr. Garwood?"

"It belongs to me. I only bring it out of storage for parades and such. Why?"

"Because my dog has picked up the odor of an explosive compound on this dirty rag. There's no bomb in your car but somebody who used this rag came in contact with components."

"Well, she's dead wrong. That's the cloth I used this morning to shine the chrome," Bertrand grumbled. "Now, if you're through harassing me, I need to get moving. I'm the parade grand marshal, you know."

Max stepped aside. "Fine by me. Have a nice day."

As the classic Packard pulled away, Max slid the soiled rag into a plastic evidence bag, sealed it and slipped it back in his pocket. If the lab at Quantico could pick out DNA from more than one donor, Garwood might be off the hook. If not, the man had just foolishly admitted to having touched explosives.

Was he vindictive enough to attack his own daughter? Max wondered. He hated to think that but the evidence spoke for itself. Unless there were traces from others on the rag, they may have found their source for at least some of the bombings.

Which brought him back to square one. Components from all but the ranch bomb matched those from other states besides California. Therefore, it was still quite possible that the Duprees' men had bombed the Miner's Grub diner and had probably left the set in the blue trash barrel.

Had Garwood damaged his own stable? The fact that the horses had all been moved out beforehand made it a distinct possibility. But why? Had he known that Katerina was coming back to get her belongings that day?

Max took a deep breath and praised Opal, then put her to work checking all the other floats and cars while he puzzled over the ranch owner's eagerness to admit using the rag. The man wasn't stupid. Why would he incriminate himself when he could have denied knowledge of anything in the trunk? Did he assume law enforcement wouldn't put two and two together? Or was he so sure of his personal connections to the sheriff that he figured he'd never be charged?

That thought settled in the pit of Max's stomach like a sack of placer mine tailings left over from gold mining with water. If he and his team had to arrest Bertrand Garwood, he figured he could quit worrying about his unacceptable feelings for Katerina. She'd never speak to him again.

THIRTEEN

Reluctant to intrude when her father was talking to Max, Katerina waited until he returned to the picnic area with Opal before she approached. "Did you find something odd in Dad's car? I figured it wasn't dangerous when you let him drive on."

"I'm going to send a polishing cloth to the lab to confirm Opal's opinion of it."

"She makes mistakes? I thought trained K-9 cops were infallible."

"Nothing is one hundred percent. It's possible that a solvent in metal polish smells like something Opal's been trained to key in on. The only thing I am sure of is that the little package we found in the bottom of the trash barrel was a bomb. Whether it was set to go off at a certain time or has an electronic detonator is unknown." He released a breath, then went on. "The sheriff didn't want to hold up the festivities so we decided to send it to the town dump and leave it there, under guard. It should be okay until we can get some experts to dismantle it or set it off."

Katerina kept clasping and unclasping her fingers. "This is unbelievable. I mean, no matter what Vern did or didn't do, there's no reason for some distant crime family to target this little town." Wide blue eyes met Max's. "How long is this going to go on? Will we ever get back to normal again?"

She desperately craved solace. Moral support. The sense that someone was there for her. The night that Kyle had entered her hotel room and she'd been so frightened, Max had been her anchor, her comforter. Right now, right here, she was in dire need of a replay.

It seemed wrong to pray for affection so she merely stood still and waited to see what he'd do. Could he sense her neediness? Did he know how disconnected she felt? He must. Whether he was willing to admit it or not, they had an almost tangible emotional connection.

Max stepped near and laid his hand on her arm. "It'll be all right, Katerina. Maybe not today or tomorrow, but things will get better. Trust me. Every time we have an incident and collect more clues we come that much closer to solving this and ending it."

"Do you? The more I learn, the worse it seems."

He moved from the light touch to encircling her shoulders with his free arm and giving her a quick squeeze. "There are a lot of interconnected crimes and suspects that we have to round up before we'll know enough to totally shut down the Duprees. I imagine you saw on the news that various government agencies formed a task force to break up their organization by arresting the big bosses."

"I remember hearing something like that a few months back. I never dreamed you'd still be chasing them."

"One of the big fish got away. He wasn't first in command but he's bad enough. Angus Dupree is the uncle of Reginald, the head of the organization. Reginald is cooling his heels and awaiting trial along with many of his underlings. We'd love to add his uncle Angus to the docket but he's currently on the run. Unfortunately, so is one of our key witnesses."

"You mean the guy who ran when you were in Billings?

"No, a different one. A woman. The question of who fled from Potter's house should be answered as soon as we get back some results of the DNA samples we gathered from the house.

"What about the mother and baby? Are they all right?"

"We don't know yet. One of my agents, Harper Prentiss, thought she smelled a familiar aftershave in the bathroom at the Potter home but there's nothing positive."

"Oh." Katerina tried to hide her surprise. "Some of your teammates are women?"

"Uh-huh. They make great handlers. A lot of K-9 trainers are female, too."

She knew her cheeks were reddening because they felt awfully warm. "That never crossed my mind."

Leaning closer, Max tilted his head to one side and smiled. "Are you jealous?"

Her "Of course not!" was too quick, too high-pitched to be normal and she could tell from his broadening grin that he knew she was flustered.

"I thought you never lied," Max tsked.

"I don't. I—I…"

He laughed heartily. "I get it. We all tell fibs from time to time to save face or be kind, and don't think anything of it."

"I suppose you're right." Sweeping her hair back from her face with her fingers she tucked it behind her ears. "My, it's hot out today."

"California in the summer. What did you expect?"

Relieved to have been given a plausible reason for her flushed cheeks she agreed. "Right. I hope it's not too hard on Opal. Does she have to wear that vest all day?"

"It's bulletproof," Max explained. "If she did accidentally set off an explosion the Kevlar might not be enough to save her but it's all the protection I can give her, other than staying out of harm's way as much as possible."

"I suppose K-9 officers do get wounded, just like human ones. I'd never thought of that before. It's sad."

"Any loss of life is."

Judging by the way he had stopped smiling and set his jaw, she realized she'd triggered a painful memory. Curiosity made her ask, "Would you like to talk about it?"

"We already did," Max said curtly.

"Ah, the family with the child. I remember." Forgetting her pride she reached out to him, touched his hand. "Things like that stay with us forever. I know that. I just wish I could give you peace about it."

"You can't."

Gently, lovingly, Katerina said, "I know. Only God can." However, Max had to be willing to accept it, she added to herself. Just as she needed to come to terms with the betrayal of those she loved, Max had to forgive himself—and God. Once, he had trusted his heavenly Father with his life, then had begun to question the turn of events and want to place blame. That was as natural as breathing. And holding a grudge was as destructive as holding his breath. Something had to give or it would do permanent damage.

Gazing into the depths of his piercing blue eyes she sensed a strong connection, as if he were reading her thoughts and knew she was seeing his raw pain, was pulling some of it into her own heart and sharing the struggle.

She had no adequate words, no healing platitudes. Katerina merely stepped closer, slipped one arm around his waist and laid her head on his shoulder. Whether Max realized it or not, she was telling him she cared. She understood.

Her heart sped as logic flew out the window and she admitted one more thing. She was also falling in love with him.

Max didn't know how to react to her empathy. He didn't want to hurt Katerina's feelings, but he also couldn't afford to present a weak image. His job had to come first, at least outwardly. But what he really wanted to do was pull her closer and tilt her chin up so he could kiss her.

He would not act on his urge, of course. That would be totally out of character for an FBI agent on duty. Instead, he stepped away. "I thought you wanted to watch the parade."

"Only if that's what you're going to do."

Nodding, Max agreed. "It makes sense. You may spot Kyle in the crowd and can point him out to me."

She shivered. "I hope I don't."

"You should be hoping that you do," Max countered. "Without his fingerprints or DNA it's going to be difficult to locate him."

"I know. I have been watching, but mostly because he sounded so determined when he came to the diner. I trust the Lord. I do. I just figure He gave me a brain to use for something besides a place to hang a hat."

"Well put." Max had to chuckle. "You do have a way with words."

"English was going to be my major in college before I decided to become a horse trainer."

Starting off, he paced himself to match Katerina. "What are your plans now?"

She huffed. "You mean besides staying alive? Beats me. I'd like to go back to working at the ranch. Since that's not going to happen, I guess I'll do whatever I have to, to survive. A girl has to eat."

"Maybe you need a pet. Have you thought about getting a watchdog when you move out of the hotel?"

"Another mouth to feed? Not really, although that isn't a bad idea. Not a pup, though. I wouldn't be able to train it while I'm at work." She began to smile wistfully. "I'd ask to adopt that black lab from the ranch if she hadn't recently had a litter. She's sweet and sensible. And not hyper like your Opal."

"I prefer to call it enthusiasm," Max said with a lopsided smile. "I'd give serious consideration to getting a watchdog if I were you."

"Why do I need a dog when I have *you*?" Her eyes twinkled and made him grin until he recalled the parameters of his mission.

"I won't be here much longer," Max warned roughly. "I've already told you that."

"Yeah, I know. I was just teasing. First I have to find a new apartment or talk my former landlord into fixing up the place that was trashed. I actually haven't wanted to think that far ahead."

"Well, you should."

They had traveled the length of Park Street and were approaching Main again. Crowds thickened. Opal stayed close to her partner's left with Katerina on the right. The first few floats had already passed.

"Here comes Dad."

"I see him. And the deputies the sheriff promised as escorts. Everything looks good."

Although he kept scanning the boisterous crowd he was fully aware of the woman beside him. How could he not be? She was making him crazy. Strong and resilient like a warrior and yet soft and gentle as a kitten, she was so close they were almost touching. And *almost* was not enough for him. Not nearly enough. All he'd have to do was lift his arm and it would be around her waist or her shoulders. Katerina had not objected before. He was sure she wouldn't this time, either.

Just as he started to act on the whim she gasped and pointed. "There! Across the street in front of the florist's. See the scruffy-looking guy with the black T-shirt?"

"The one behind the woman with the stroller?"

"Yes! That's Kyle. I know it is."

Max reached for his radio and called in their position. "I'm going to be in foot pursuit. Send somebody to watch Katerina. She's right across Main from the florist shop." He eyed her. "She's going to wait here."

"I am not."

"Yes, you are. I don't want to have to worry about you while I'm taking a prisoner into custody."

"But…"

He gave her his most severe stare. "Do it."

"Yes, sir."

That was good enough for Max. As soon as he spotted the uniform of a deputy coming their way he shouldered through the line of revelers along the curb and jogged across the street. The high school band was marching by and he zigzagged between trumpeters and drummers.

One quick glance ahead told him that his quarry had noticed him and was on the run. So, it was a positive ID. Perfect. The sooner he captured Katerina's stalker and got him to talk, the sooner they could tie up at least a portion of the case. Kyle was the key. Kyle, and the diamonds the Duprees wanted badly enough to kill for.

Katerina stood on tiptoe to watch Max go. One hand shaded her eyes. If she hadn't wanted so desperately to please him she would have broken her coerced promise and followed, although discretely.

If anyone had asked her which marchers had passed since Max's departure she couldn't have said. All she cared about was keeping him in sight. That soon proved impossible. One foot on the base of a lamppost raised her higher and gave her a last glimpse before he passed out of view.

Sighing and resigned to the wait, she let herself down and leaned against the post. An emptiness she had not felt before was impossible to deny. If the sense of loss was this overwhelming just watching him cross the street, what was it going to be like when she had to bid him a final goodbye?

The thought of never seeing Max again settled in her heart and mind to steal any semblance of hope. Of joy. Pride would not let her throw herself at him, particularly when he kept reminding her his presence here in South Fork was temporary. So unless he expressed affection toward her, she was going to have to stand there and hold back her tears as she watched him leave for good.

Did hugs count? she wondered. Nope. Not the kind they had shared so far. He'd simply been comforting her after a crisis. When she'd tried to hug him at the park he'd acted almost embarrassed and had backed away. That was not a good sign. Not good at all. Now, if he had kissed her...

Imagining his kiss made her tremble, made her stomach flutter like butterflies feasting on the bright yellow wild mustard flowers so prevalent on the rolling hills around South Fork.

Someone touched her arm, snapping her from her reverie. She looked around, expecting to see the deputy who was coming to watch over her. A hard metal object poked her in the ribs at the same instant.

"Don't make a sound," Kyle warned, sneering. "You and I are going for a little walk. If you make a fuss and I start shooting, who knows how many kids might get hurt."

She couldn't move, couldn't take a step, until he gave her arm a jerk. Where was Max? Where was the deputy who was supposed to be there with her?

Katerina found her balance and her voice. "All right. Stay calm. I'll go with you."

"Knew you were a smart girl." He signaled with a toss of his head. "This way."

Eyes wide, she desperately cast around for any kind of help that wouldn't cause her abductor to panic and pull the trigger. There was no one except innocent, clueless civilians, so she didn't dare call out or try to escape his painful grasp.

An incoherent prayer for deliverance formed in her mind. No rescuer appeared. She staggered, tripped, tried to think far enough beyond the moment to know what to do.

One thing was certain.

Survival was totally up to her.

FOURTEEN

Max had rendezvoused with several deputies when they got another call. Earpiece receivers kept him from eavesdropping but the grave looks on their faces told him plenty.

"You're sure?" one of them replied before turning to Max to report, "Reynolds is on scene. There's no sign of the Garwood woman where you said she'd be."

"Tell him to look again. She's wearing a pink shirt."

"Sorry, Agent West."

Every nerve in his body was firing. "All right. You men keep searching for the runner in the black T-shirt. I lost him in that alley over there. I'm going back for Katerina. She can't have strayed far."

Time was his enemy, Max concluded as he wheeled and took off with Opal at his side. Had it been long enough since he'd lost sight of Kyle for the man to have doubled back? He doubted it, but this wasn't his town so maybe there was a shortcut.

"Opal, heel." He shouted over the noise of the celebrants, assuming a runner's pace. If only she were a tracking dog like Harper's German shepherd he'd be able to send her to find Katerina. Some K-9s were cross-trained if they showed aptitude but he hadn't seen the need for adding to his dog's repertoire until now.

The partners crossed Main at the corner by Park. Anxiety had sapped some of the stamina he needed to continue. Max paused in the spot where he'd last seen Katerina and scanned the crowd, looking for the right color hair and her neon pink T-shirt. It was like searching for the proverbial needle in a haystack, only he was looking for one special lady in a sea of moving, shifting bodies, many of whom were tall enough to hide her.

"Katerina!"

He turned the opposite direction, cupped a hand around his mouth and shouted again. "Katerina! Where are you?"

Opal had been straining at her leash since they'd reached the familiar corner. Now, she yipped.

Max checked her body language and started to ignore her until he saw the rapid wag of her tail. Dressed to work, she was not usually that amiable. "Katerina?" he repeated.

The eager dog pulled harder, actually scratching at the pavement with her front paws. He took one last look around, then heeded to his canine partner.

"All right, Opal. That's as good a direction to go as any." He keyed his mic. "This is West. I'm headed south on Park. No sign of the Garwood woman yet but my dog is pulling me this way so I'm going to take a chance."

"Copy," someone radioed back. "We're converging on your location. Deputy Reynolds has already found a couple of folks who think they saw Katerina leaving."

"Was she alone?" Max's throat tightened.

"Nobody was sure. Proceed with caution."

As if they had to tell him! Caution was ingrained in any bomb-detecting specialist. Except that he had already broken protocol by racing around as if he and Opal were two ants crossing hot pavement.

All the time his feet and brain were racing he was searching the distance, praying he'd get a glimpse of Katerina.

Over there? Max's hope jumped, then crashed. It wasn't her. *There?* No. Same color clothing but wrong wearer. He had to force himself to inhale and exhale instead of holding his breath every time he thought he saw her.

Opal's nose was to the ground now. Max knew she'd never had actual practice as a tracking dog but apparently her instinct to find her new friend was strong enough to carry her, at least this far.

Rather than give any commands and possibly confuse the dog, he let her run as fast as she could go with him on the other end of her leash. Clearly, she could have outdistanced him without effort but Max had to hold on or he might lose her, too.

His legs ached and there was a painful stitch in his side. Nevertheless he pressed on. They crossed the main picnic area, then skirted the restrooms. Beyond lay an overflow parking lot where many of the floats and other participants had gathered after the parade.

Opal suddenly pulled to the side, nearly tripping Max. He spun to follow. And saw Bertrand Garwood's classic Packard.

No, no! Not that. Max's heart fell. Opal was headed straight for the same car she'd alerted on before. If she was after that odd odor instead of following Katerina's trail, he'd wasted precious time.

The ranch foreman was no longer behind the wheel but the mayor was once again polishing chrome. "Did you see her?" Max shouted. "Have you seen Katerina?"

Garwood paused and scowled. "No. Why?"

"I think she's been kidnapped."

"Don't be ridiculous. There's no real crime in this town." His wrinkled deepened. "At least there wasn't until her boyfriend showed up."

Max was in no mood to argue. Expecting Opal to stop to sniff the car's trunk, he was astonished to see her put her nose to the ground again and take off.

"Wait a minute," he called to Garwood. "She went past here. Are you sure you didn't see her?"

"I told you I didn't."

"Where's your foreman? McCabe."

"Filling his gut, I imagine. Check the food tables."

Holding a straining Opal in check, Max radioed his position to the deputies and suggested exactly that. If one of them could locate McCabe, he might be able to tell them more.

"I'm going to follow my K-9 until she finds Katerina or loses the trail," Max said, knowing Garwood was eavesdropping and a little surprised at his interest.

The older man stood back, reached into his pocket and fisted a keychain. "You can borrow my car if you promise to take good care of it."

Well, well. "Thanks, but I need to be on the ground with the dog," Max told him. "If you decide to cruise around and look for her, give us plenty of space. I don't want anything to disturb the scent trail."

He didn't glance back to see what Katerina's father was doing after that. All he cared about was giving Opal the best chance to succeed. When all this was over and they were back in Billings, he was going to suggest she be trained in tracking people as well as detecting explosives. That would work as long as he was able to tell her exactly which job he wanted her to do at any given time.

Right now, all he wanted was Katerina. The nagging notion of losing her, for whatever reason, ate at him until his physical pain and fatigue became secondary.

A shuddering breath filled his lungs. This could not be happening. He'd vowed to look after her and had failed. It didn't matter that he'd thought a deputy was taking over for him. He should have waited with her until the other guard arrived.

Opal barked once. Max faltered, tripped and almost fell. With a mighty lunge the dog ripped the end of the long lead from his hand and began to run like a greyhound chasing a rabbit.

"Opal! Stop! Heel!"

Those commands made her seem to go even faster. Max was both livid and distressed. In all the years they had been working partners, Opal had never failed to come when called. Never. If he lost her it would be his fault. Just as it was his fault he'd lost Katerina.

Instead of slowing him down, the weight of his emotional burdens gave Max his second wind. Without a dog to handle he was free to run at his top speed, arms pumping, knees lifting higher as he pounded through the park.

Drying ground and dead grass made it harder to pick out Opal's coat coloring in the distance but her dark vest stood out. So did the bright white FBI printed on the side. Max saw her slow, circle, then take off again. This time she was giving voice like a hunting hound who was about to tree its prey.

Max interpreted the signs and pressed on until he thought his legs would buckle. Adrenaline fueled his mad dash.

Thoughts of Katerina kept him going.

* * *

There was no doubt in Katerina's mind that Kyle would shoot her if she tried to flee. Fear kept her from thinking logically until he had forced her through the park and tried to push her into his waiting car at the far edge of an overflow parking lot. That snapped her out of it enough to try to reason with him.

"Look, don't you suppose that if I knew where Vern had hidden the diamonds I'd have already gotten them?"

"Maybe you did."

She could tell he was confused. Good. Anything that gave her an edge was a plus. "If I had, do you think I'd still be slinging hash at a diner?"

"You might, if you were smart."

"If I was really smart, I'd have figured out that Vern was a crook long before he got me into so much trouble."

"Yeah, well." The wiry man gestured with the pistol. "Get in. We're goin' for a ride and you're gonna show me where those rocks are, or else."

"Are you listening to me?" Anger began to bolster her courage and she raised her voice. "I have nothing left. No home, barely any personal belongings, nothing. I do not know anything about any diamonds and I never did. Vern wouldn't have trusted me with that information because he knew I was too honest. That was why I was such a good cover for him. People trusted me. And with good reason."

"Well, we don't trust you."

Katerina's eyebrows arched. "*We?* Who's we? I thought you were the one who's been stalking me."

"I was. I am." Looking agitated, he raked his fingers through his rumpled, oily hair. "Are you gonna get in this car or do I have to shoot you?"

"You can't be that dumb."

"Hey, show some respect," Kyle snapped.

"Look," she said, speaking slowly and choosing her words with care, "if you shoot me and I *do* happen to know where Vern hid anything, you're up the creek without a paddle. Who else can you ask? Who else was close enough to him to know his secrets?"

"Okay, we'll split it. If you're as broke as you say, you can use some cash."

Katerina sighed. If she agreed to a split to stall for time until someone could rescue her, she'd be digging her own grave because Kyle would then be sure she knew too much. If she refused, he might soon decide she was useless. Either way, she lost.

Father, I could use some help here, she prayed. *I've always tried to do the right thing, to be a good Christian, but I can't see any way out of this.*

One thing was certain. She was not getting into that car. No, sirree.

A blur of color entered the edge of her vision. It was moving so fast it was airborne before she could react. Fortunately, the same was true of her kidnapper.

Opal hit him so hard in the chest he fell backward and thumped his head on the ground. The gun went flying. Stunned, Katerina stood there gaping. The dog was growling and drooling on Kyle's face. His eyeballs looked as though they were about to pop out of their sockets, and he was thrashing and pushing at her to escape.

Katerina frantically looked for Max. He wasn't in sight. Therefore, she had two choices. She could either try to grab the gun, back Opal and hope Max arrived very soon, or she could run away to save herself, hoping the valiant dog would follow. Given her recent belief that her life was about to end abruptly, she opted for flight.

"Opal, come!" she screeched, rounding the parked car and heading into a grove of live oaks for cover. She didn't dare look back.

Her last call was, "Opal-l-l-l!

She heard a single gunshot. Her heart sank. Grasping the broad, rough trunk of one of the ancient trees, she peeked around just in time to see Kyle's car speed off.

"No, no, no. Not Opal." Katerina was bereft.

She slid to the ground beneath the tree and began to weep. In seconds, a warm, rough tongue was drying her cheeks. "Opal! Oh, baby!"

A quick once-over showed no injuries. Katerina's tears turned to those of pure joy. She hugged the brown-and-white K-9 close, buried her face against its shoulder, and began to sob away all the tension and fear. "Thank you, Jesus."

Max saw the whole thing. Opal downed Katerina's kidnapper but the guy was far from out of the fight. The dog held him as best she could without biting the way an apprehension specialist would. Katerina bolted. The perp wiggled loose. Reached his gun. Raised it.

After that, details blurred and overlapped. Opal and Katerina were both running. The man aimed and fired. Katerina ducked behind a tree but whether she was hit or not was unknown. The same went for Opal. She looked as if she'd stumbled or made a dive for cover. Or been shot.

Max drew his own gun on the run. "Federal agent. Drop your weapon."

Instead, the perp burned rubber in his escape.

"Katerina!" It was more of a gasp than a shout and all Max could manage for the moment.

No one answered. His heart was already at the breaking point. He fought to stay on his feet. Imagination was his worst enemy. In his mind he visualized another terrible loss. Another failure. This couldn't have happened, yet it had.

Lungs ready to burst, head pounding, he once again bellowed, "Katerina! Opal!" in a voice that was breaking despite his efforts to sound forceful and in command.

"Max? Over here!"

His head snapped around. He could manage a few more steps even if they used his last shred of strength.

And then he saw her. She was hurrying toward him, apparently unhurt, and Opal was at her side.

Max used every ounce of self-control to try to keep his reactions in check. He failed. In seconds, he had engulfed Katerina in a smothering embrace. His tears dampened her silky hair. The shuddering of her whole body told him that she, too, was weeping.

And so he held her like that, thanking the God he had once turned his back on and feeling so much abject relief he could hardly process the sensations.

There was joy, of course, but so much more. Peace. Assuredness. Rightness. And above all, a sense of loving and being loved that Max had never dreamed could be so strong. So absolute. So perfect.

Even as deputies began to surround them and ask about the gunshot that had brought them running, Max held tightly to Katerina and felt faithful Opal leaning against his legs, acting possessive and sharing the precious moment.

If he'd had his way, he and Katerina would never have parted.

FIFTEEN

Debriefing seemed to take forever. Katerina couldn't help yawning. She and Max were seated side by side on a weathered wooden bench at the edge of the picnic area while the sheriff interrogated her.

"I told you. I don't know who Kyle is other than he used to be a friend of Vern Kowalski's," she said, sighing wearily because she was sick and tired of answering the same questions over and over. "I don't know his last name, where he lives or who he hangs out with. I only met him one time before he came to the diner and threatened me. If he hadn't reminded me who he was then, I wouldn't have remembered him at all."

"I think we're done here," Max stated. "I'm going to take Ms. Garwood back to her hotel. If you have further questions you can phone me and I'll contact her."

Tate scowled. "Just a second here, Agent West, this is my jurisdiction."

Max stood, pulling Katerina up with him as he took her arm. "Agreed. But this witness is mine. I'm putting her into protective custody."

She could tell the deputies were waiting to see which authority would prevail. No doubt it would be her special agent. Truth to tell, she didn't care who won as long as she got to take a shower and change clothes to rid herself of any traces of Kyle's disgusting touch.

The sheriff backed off. "Okay. Take her to the hotel. I've already put out a BOLO for the car you described. If and when we find it I may need you for a positive ID."

"Our pleasure," Max said brusquely.

Katerina leaned his way ever so slightly. *Our*, he had said. *Our pleasure, as in "the two of us."* Her heart warmed and she might have commented if she had not been too bone-weary to think straight.

As Max led her away, he asked, "Are you okay?"

The urge to tease him about such a ridiculous question popped into her head. She squelched it immediately. He wasn't asking only what his words expressed. He was asking much more. How should she answer? How much truth was he ready to hear?

Playing it safe for the present, she merely nodded and murmured, "I'm fine," then counteracted her assurance by stumbling.

Max caught her in his arms, righted her, then took her hand. "When was the last time you ate?"

"Um, breakfast?"

"That's what I thought." He began to steer her toward the tables of food. "You need a hamburger."

"I need a nap."

"First a burger."

Katerina sighed audibly. "I can't believe you're thinking about food at a time like this." When she glanced up at him he had arched one eyebrow.

"A time like what?" Max asked.

"This." Spreading her arms she included the scene before them. "Most of them may be clueless but you know I just got shot at. My stomach is twisted into knots and I'm so exhausted I can hardly keep putting one foot in front of the other. I am *not* hungry."

"You still need to try to eat," he insisted. "The mistake a lot of people make is letting their stress get in the way of common sense. If you allow your body to suffer because your mind is taxed, you're playing right into the hands of your enemies."

Katerina shook her head and met his steady gaze. "I wish you'd quit making such good sense. All I want to do is crawl into a cave somewhere and hibernate like a bear until this is all over."

"Soon." Max was grinning at an elderly gentleman in a Hawaiian print shirt. He was flipping burgers on a grill. Arrayed on a long table beside him was everything to go with the meat. "Is it all right with you if we grab a couple of burgers to go?"

"Fine by me. Better take beans, too, though. My wife made 'em and she's real proud."

Following his line of sight, Katerina saw a familiar woman dishing up baked beans. "Let's just go. I'll eat something later."

"What's the matter?"

"I want to leave, that's all." To her chagrin he was studying her and obviously seeing more truth than she was comfortable with.

Instead of acquiescing, Max grinned widely and handed her a plate, then moved on. What else could Katerina do? She certainly didn't want to attract more attention than she already had. Head down, she used tongs to put a hamburger patty and bun on her paper plate and stayed close to her protector.

The older woman met Max's smile with one of her own, taking in his uniform and Opal's vest. "We're so glad to see the FBI helping out in South Fork," she said. "About time, considering. Beans?"

Katerina looked up. Saw the woman's countenance change, her smile vanish.

"Yes, thanks," Max said, presenting his plate. "And I'm glad to have the help of a trustworthy citizen like Ms. Garwood. She's been a tremendous help to our investigation. I don't know what we'd do without her."

Katerina was not too worn-out to see the humor in the woman's reactions. Her jaw sagged, along with the spoonful of baked beans she'd been about to serve. The only reason it landed on a plate was because Max moved his in time to catch the spill.

"Mercy," the woman said when she finally found her voice, "I had no idea."

Max wasn't done. His admiring gaze rested on Katerina and made her blush more when he said, "Absolutely. As a matter of fact, when all this is over, I plan to recommend her for a citizen's commendation."

"On second thought, I believe I will have some beans," Katerina said with a demure smile. "Thank you."

As they made their way to a nearby table to eat, she couldn't help enjoying the sense of triumph. "How did you know she was one of my worst critics?"

"I'm a profiler, remember?"

Katerina huffed. "You'd hardly need professional training to tell how she felt. Did you see the dirty look she gave me?"

"Yes, and I took advantage of the opportunity to praise you. I hope you don't mind."

"Only if you truly meant those nice things you said. I have been trying to help. There just isn't much I can do and it's terribly frustrating."

"I know. You get high points for trying." He stepped away from the table for a moment to pick up two bottles of water and handed one to her.

"Thanks." As soon as she had slaked her thirst, Katerina took a few bites of her hamburger, then asked, "Is there really a special commendation for helpful citizens?"

When he almost choked on his food she knew the answer. As soon as he stopped coughing, he said, "Not exactly."

Her laugh was easy and joyful. "You are so bad, Special Agent West. Aren't you ashamed of yourself?"

"Not much." Max laid his hand over hers and smiled with evident fondness. "Anything I can do to make your life better after I'm gone is worth it."

The mention of his leaving dampened Katerina's good mood the way a heavy rainstorm would have wiped out the picnic atmosphere. Although she didn't pull her hand away she did tense. He was like a loop of tape, always coming back to the fact he was only a temporary fixture in her life. She knew that. She did. It was painful enough without constant reminders.

And, considering what she had just gone through— and survived—she figured she had nothing to lose if she said, "I wish you didn't have to go. I'm really going to miss… Opal."

At the mention of her name, the panting dog peeked out from her cooler spot under the table. She was drooling.

Max released Katerina's hand and abruptly got to his feet. "You two wait here. I'm going to go see if they have an extra burger or two that I can feed to my partner."

Laying a hand on the boxer's broad, smooth head,

Katerina made a sound of disgust that caught the dog's attention, so she talked directly to her. "Yes, girl, that was a romantic overture I was trying to make. He sure ducked it fast, didn't he?"

The happy dog panted more. "You look like you're smiling. Are you? Have you heard other women throw themselves at your partner? I imagine you have. He's a real hunk, isn't he? Mature and sensible but not stuffy. Don't tell him I said so, but he's just about perfect."

A voice behind her asked, "What's perfect?" Max had returned.

"Your K-9," Katerina said, feeling her cheeks flame.

"Can't argue with that," Max said. He resumed his seat on the bench and was starting to break off pieces of a plain burger patty for Opal when he suddenly stopped moving and canted his head slightly.

Katerina had seen him receive radio messages often enough to know he was listening through the earpiece. Her eyes never left his face until she heard him say, "Copy," and start to get up.

"Bring your plate and let's go," Max said. "I'll feed Opal the rest after we're in the car."

"Why? What happened?" The gravity of his expression gave her the shivers. So did the stiffness of his movements and the way he kept scanning the crowd, not that he had ever stopped. But he had been acting a bit less paranoid for the past half hour or so.

"They think they located the car that tried to take you. We'll swing by their location on our way to the hotel and you can make a positive identification."

"I hope I can," Katerina said. She had to take two steps for every one of his and ended up almost jogging. Max had been right. Eating had helped her recover her stamina.

"Think. Did you touch the vehicle at all? Anywhere? Maybe when he tried to shove you in?"

"I—I might have. It all happened so fast I'm not positive. I do know I resisted."

"That may be enough," Max said. "When we get there we'll see if you left any fingerprints on the side where he stopped with you. After they have the car towed to the police garage they can have techs go over it more thoroughly, but if we can make an ID sooner, all the better."

"What about Kyle? Did they catch him?"

Max was stoic. He was also on full guard. "No. Just the car. And the engine was fairly cool. In this heat it's impossible to tell how long it may have been parked."

"Meaning, he could have doubled back to town again?"

It didn't give her a shred of comfort when Max nodded and said, "That's exactly what the sheriff thinks. They scoured the woods and didn't find any sign of him."

Katerina and Max joined the only deputy left to guard the car. It had been abandoned near the entrance to Yosemite Park. Max had to admit the high country was beautiful. If it had not been hiding a stalker and erstwhile kidnapper, he figured he would have appreciated the gorgeous scenery a lot more.

Beside him in the SUV, Katerina gasped and pointed. "There. That's it."

"Looks right to me. Anything special grab you?"

"Yes. Now that I see it, I remember a half-peeled window decal. It's a picture of Half Dome. I think it was in the corner of the left rear window." She leaned forward to peer through the windshield. "There! See?"

"Yes," Max said. "But we're going to need more proof than that. I imagine those decals are common around here."

"I don't think so. Mostly tourists buy them."

"A good point." He brought his black vehicle to a stop behind the patrol car, got out and introduced himself. "Special Agent Max West," he said, offering his hand and checking out the man's badge and name tag as he approached. "You may be the only local law officer I haven't already met, Deputy Cox."

"I've been working the highways," the deputy said. "Might not have noticed this if the guy had left it inside the park. This time of year is so busy up here it's ridiculous. Come the Fourth of July the traffic will be backed up for miles."

"No sign of the driver?"

"Nope. Just the car."

"Okay," Max said. "Have you checked for prints or trace evidence yet?"

"Sheriff Tate said to wait for you."

Max could tell the young man was probably a rookie. He sure was nervous enough to be. "Okay. No problem. I'll see if I can find a few prints on the outside before you have it towed."

"Yes, sir."

"Keep a sharp eye on my SUV and passenger, will you? I'd hate to lose either."

"You got a police dog in there, too?"

"Yes." Max nodded as he went to work. He'd told Katerina to stay in his car but there was no telling what she might actually do. She was the best and worst kind of woman. She didn't take orders well at all, yet was intelligent and savvy enough to figure things out on her own, so she wasn't as helpless as she looked. Her guileless blue eyes and fair skin beneath a wreath of golden hair gave her an air of innocence that was totally false. Not only was she brave, she was also so smart she sometimes scared him.

And that wasn't the only thing that had him on edge. He scanned the nearby forest, watching for movement. Open, hilly fields colored yellow by dry grass were bad enough. Spotting a predator lurking amid stands of Ponderosa pines and live oaks was next to impossible.

If a perp fired on them they'd never see it coming, Max concluded. The hair at the nape of his neck prickled at the thought. He listened to his gut and tensed, prepared to duck.

The instant he started to turn he heard the crack and whine of a high-caliber rifle cartridge slicing the air.

Max hollered, "Get down!"

His heart nearly pounded out of his chest when Katerina let out an ear-piercing scream.

SIXTEEN

Katerina saw Max fall.

He dropped as though his legs had been knocked out from under him.

Opal set up a terrible racket, her barks and growls echoing inside the closed SUV as she screamed.

Whether it was because of Max's shouted order or by sheer instinct, she flatted herself to the seat as best she could considering all the specialized electronic equipment that was in the way.

Long seconds passed. She could feel her pulse thrumming in her temples, coursing through her veins. Was it over? Was it safe to look, to see if Max was wounded?

She knew better than to show herself too soon. She also knew that the man she loved might be injured. Might need her. At this point she didn't care whether the special agent returned her affection or not. His life might be ebbing away while she lay there, too petrified to act.

That was not going to happen, Katerina vowed. She wasn't foolish enough to simply sit up and present another target, but she could still slip out of the SUV on the opposite side and crawl around it until she got a better look at the scene.

Opal was still carrying on as if they were under attack so she chose to leave the dog behind for its own safety.

The first thing Katerina did was drop to all fours, look beneath the high vehicle and locate Max. He was moving fluidly. And his gun was drawn. He was okay!

"Thank you, God," she whispered, meaning the simple prayer with all her heart.

What about the young deputy? All she could see were his feet and legs sticking out from behind the open door of his car. He was closer than Max so she made a dash for him. And saw that he was gritting his teeth and grasping his bloody arm!

"How can I help you?" Katerina asked, realizing that adrenaline had boosted the strength of her voice as soon as Max shouted back at her.

"Nothing. Stay put," he yelled.

"The deputy's hit!" she answered. "What should I do?"

Max's reply was the human equivalent of Opal's growling. Katerina didn't care. She'd doctored enough animals to know that her first move should be to stop or slow the bleeding with pressure, not a tourniquet. There were no rags handy but she did spot a handful of napkins on the seat, apparently left over from the deputy's lunch. That would be a start.

Stripping off his tie, too, she struggled to get him to listen to her. "Let go and let me pad it," she said. "See? Napkins. We have to stop the bleeding."

Although he nodded and seemed to understand, his hand was clamped so tightly to his injury she couldn't pry it loose. "Let go. Let me help you," she shouted, as if volume might get through his instinct to keep his hand firmly in place.

When a strong arm reached past her and jerked the deputy's hand loose she almost screamed again. Of course it was Max. Who else would have risked his own life to reach the patrol car?

Working together as if trained as a team, Katerina and Max placed the wad of napkins, then wrapped the tie around the man's arm to keep them in place before allowing him to resume his hold.

"I've called for backup and an ambulance," Max told the injured man. "Understand? Help is on the way."

Katerina had expected a little praise, if not another faux award for bravery. Instead, she got Max's most disapproving stare. "What did you think you were doing? Huh? You could have been shot, too."

"But I wasn't."

"Not this time. I'm sure I was the target but considering the shooter's lousy aim he could just as easily have hit you." His scowl was so deep his eyebrows almost met in the middle of his forehead. "Keep your head down. The day isn't over yet."

"Not funny," she countered.

"It wasn't meant to be." Grasping her shoulders he glared so hard she wanted to look away. She couldn't. There was more than one emotion coloring his expression. Anger was obvious, of course, but there was also so much angst it mesmerized her. Not only that, he was right. She had acted rashly. Yes, she'd had good reason to, but that didn't excuse folly.

Meeting his stern gaze, she nodded. "I'm sorry. You're right. I shouldn't have left the car."

"Well, that's *something*. Did you see him go down?"

Katerina felt that the whole, unvarnished truth was the best course so she held nothing back. "No. When I heard the shot it was you I was watching." Unshed tears pooled. "I—I thought you'd been hit and needed help. That's why I got out. But when I saw you moving and you looked okay, I noticed that the deputy wasn't." She sniffled. "I'm not as good a person as you think I am. I only risked my life because of you."

The agent's expression became unreadable. He released her shoulders and sat back on his haunches. His jaw worked. No words came out. Given his earlier chastisement, Katerina was relieved. And penitent.

"I really am sorry. It was just something I had to do. You should understand. After all, that's how you function."

"No," Max said soberly. "I'm certified to do this job. You're a horse trainer, not an FBI agent or a cop. It's high time you got that through your head."

Katerina was more than willing to let him rant if that was what he chose to do. She deserved a good chewing out. And Max's motives were clear. What he said and did was for her benefit, unlike Bertrand, whose main focus was on himself and his so-called reputation.

"I was wrong," Katerina said, trying again to make peace. "Very wrong. I was thinking about my own feelings instead of assessing the danger. It was stupid. I should have stayed put."

"Yes, you should have." He eyed the injured man. "It's beside the point that you may have saved a life by following the urge to check on this officer."

Sirens in the background grew louder. Backup and medical assistance was near.

The relaxing set of Max's jaw and a softening of his glance gave her hope of forgiveness and the approach of paramedics lifted her spirits. That also loosened her tongue enough to ask, "So do I finally qualify for the good citizen's award you mentioned?"

He rolled his eyes and cautiously peered over the side of the patrol car, watching reinforcements arrive. "You qualify for something, all right. I'm just not sure what to call it. Not in polite company."

Before Katerina could come up with a suitable retort he'd gotten to his feet and holstered his sidearm.

"Is it safe?"

"For me, not for you. Stay down until we've made sure the shooter is long gone."

"He probably is, right? I mean, with all the police cars he must have taken off."

"Assumptions like that can get you killed," Max warned. "Just like the idea that if you're on a rescue mission you can't be shot." His icy stare returned. "You can either stay put right there or I'll have the sheriff's men cuff you and throw you in the back of one of their cars."

"You wouldn't dare!"

She knew otherwise when Max gave her a lopsided smile and said, "Try me."

"I wish I had the whole team here with me," Max told Dylan O'Leary when he finally checked in with headquarters again. "Have you had any success tracking down the owner of the prints I took from the car at the park?"

"Yeah. I think so. I'm sending a mug shot to your computer and cell. There was a petty criminal associated with Kowalski years ago. It was a juvenile offense so the records were sealed until I opened them."

"I do not need details you're not supposed to know," Max told him. "Just give me a last name."

"Take your pick. I found three besides Smith and Jones. He went by Kinder, Farth and Wilson."

"Sounds like a law firm."

The tech chuckled. "That was my first thought. Then I got to thinking he may have added another alias since then. I would have."

"Yes, but you have a devious mind," Max joked. "I don't think this guy is too bright."

"Doesn't have to be bright to be lethal."

"No kidding. He shot a deputy yesterday. At least I think it was him. Makes me wonder why the shooter didn't try for me."

"Maybe he did."

"I thought of that. Trajectory of the bullet makes it a remote possibility."

"What about the girl? Katerina Garwood? Have you gotten any more out of her after this last scare?"

Max sobered. "I already told you. She's given us everything she knows. What we can't figure out is where Kowalski stashed those missing diamonds."

"Or where he got the money to buy them in the first place? It's my guess he stole from Dupree and decided it was easier to hide his sudden wealth as little stones than to lug around a suitcase full of cash."

"I agree. What about a getaway plan? Have you turned up any solid leads?"

"No. If Kowalski intended to skip town before he was arrested, he wasn't going to fly. At least not under his own name. There's no record of ticket purchases." Dylan paused. "Not even a single seat."

"To show he was going alone? I get it. I wish you had found some record. It would uphold Katerina's innocence."

"Hey, you trust her."

"I do. Implicitly. But that doesn't mean the rest of the people in her life feel the same. You wouldn't believe her father's rotten attitude."

"Is that your problem, buddy? Are you thinking of stepping in as an older brother?"

"No way! Besides, I do not think of her as a little sister. She's every bit a grown woman. Boy, is she."

"Uh-oh. Here we go again. Another one bites the dust."

"Don't be ridiculous. She lives here and I do not intend to get involved in a long-distance romance."

Dylan laughed into the phone. "Sounds to me like you already are. Talk to you later."

"Yeah. Later."

Picturing Katerina kneeling beside the bleeding deputy and trying to doctor him, Max had a moment when he yearned to take her in his arms again and hold her tight. She was more than pretty. She was extraordinary. And the more he saw of her, the more his admiration blossomed.

That's all it is, Max insisted. Countering that thought made him clench his jaw. He might be able to fool his team and the general population but he wasn't fooling himself. He loved Katerina Garwood even more than he loved his K-9 partner. And that was a lot.

Katerina didn't spot another note shoved under the door of her hotel room until she'd finished dressing the following morning. Recognizing the paper, she immediately phoned Max.

"West."

"A note. Another note." She was nearly hysterical. "You have to come to my room."

"On my way."

She managed to unlock the door in the seconds before he got there and stood back. The instant he threw open the door she raised both hands. "Stop! Don't step on it."

Max skidded to a halt.

"I didn't touch it," she said, trembling. "How did he get this close?" Her eyes darted to the narrow hallway. "He had to be right here!"

"Not if he paid somebody else to deliver it."

"If that's supposed to be comforting, it isn't."

She stepped back, leaving the door open as the agent used a glove to handle the paper. He took it to the dresser to unfold and read.

Katerina peered past his broad shoulder. Her vision began to blur. It was worse than she'd expected. Not only did it threaten her, it clearly promised death to Bertrand Garwood—and her dear horse Moonlight— if she failed to show up at the ranch at an appointed time and disclose information on the location of the diamond stash.

"What—what can I do?" she asked.

Max was already on the phone to the sheriff's office. Judging by his half of the conversation they were formulating a plan.

"That's right," Max said. "Garwood. I need you to get in touch with him and convince him to leave his ranch for the time being. And tell him to put a guard on his property, particularly the horses."

When Katerina saw Max scowl she assumed he was being told that her father had already refused to comply. That figured. If he was anything, he was stubborn. And proud, which was why he had disowned her in the first place.

"All right. We can filter in on foot, a few at a time. I'll meet you in the lobby of my hotel at eleven and we'll go over strategy. Just make sure everybody stays well hidden. This guy has already wounded one deputy and I know he won't hesitate to shoot another."

"No." Katerina grabbed Max's arm, but he ignored her protest. The note had insisted she come alone. If they broke that rule and arrived like a posse, surely her dad and Moonlight would be killed in retaliation.

"Yes," Max said, looking as if he meant his terse comment for her. He bid the sheriff goodbye and turned to give Katerina his full attention.

She raised her hands, palms out. "We can't do it your way. The note said no police." As she realized the full extent of the command her eyes widened. "That means you, too."

"Oh, no. I'm not letting you go anywhere without me so don't even think of trying it. Understand?" He was scowling.

"Yes, but…"

"No buts. I'll let you phone the ranch and try to convince your dad to leave but you are *not* going out there."

"I have to." Panicky, she pointed to the top of the dresser where the threatening note lay. "They still think I know where Vern hid the diamonds. It's them I need to convince, not my father."

Quietly, calmly, Max cupped her shoulders. "Only if we can be absolutely positive he didn't have anything to do with the illegal operations taking place out of his ranch."

Katerina jerked free. "Of course he didn't! Look at how he's been treating me since you raided the place."

"That might be a good way to cover up his guilt."

She whirled. Paced, then turned. "No way. Not him. He may be a pompous…never mind…but he isn't crooked. I'd stake my life on it."

"I believe you, Katerina. Which is why I've decided

you're not going with us when we gather at the ranch again. It's too dangerous. You have nothing to add except to put yourself in unnecessary danger. We'll close in after Kyle gets on scene and grab him. There will be no need for you to leave this room."

Gaping at him, she stared. "You must be joking."

"I have never been more serious."

She fisted her hands on her hips and glared at him. "Give me one good reason why I should take orders from you."

Hesitation on his part took her aback. What did he know about the planned attack that he wasn't revealing? Was it really going to be as dangerous as he'd indicated to the sheriff or was he merely trying to control her? Yes, she loved his powerful persona and forthright way of doing things, but it galled when it was directed at her.

"You can't go. That's all there is to it."

"Not for me, it isn't all. Either you share your reasoning or I'm going, whether you like it or not."

Max came closer. His expression was grim, his gaze steady and uncompromising. When he reached for her again she almost fled. Almost, but not quite.

The touch of his hands on her shoulders was gentle but firm. "It's time for you to put your trust in me the way you want me to trust you."

"I have. I do. I just want…"

In a low, rumbling voice he asked, "What? What do you want, Katerina?"

The intimacy of the moment was so powerful, despite the open door, it wiped her mind of answers the way rain washed summer's dust from the petals of a flower.

Max urged her closer with the slightest pressure.

She slipped her arms around his waist and waited. It

was up to him this time. He'd rejected her in the park and she wasn't going to set herself up for another failure.

He lifted her chin with his forefinger and her heart raced as anticipation flooded through her. His lips brushed hers so gently she wondered if her imagination was playing tricks.

Then he whispered her name with such tenderness she melted into his embrace.

At that moment she would gladly have promised him the moon and then tried to deliver it.

Their kiss deepened. Lingered. Left Max trembling almost as much as Katerina was. The thrill of finally knowing he cared for her was so encompassing she willingly lost herself in it.

Before she could fully regain her senses, Max broke contact, stepped to the door and said, "*That's* why you have to stay here."

Alone, she leaned against the dresser for support. He'd as much as said he loved her. And that kiss... Oh, my. No wonder she had been so unsure about marrying Vern. There was no comparison between the two men. Max was the one. Now all she had to do was... what? Follow his orders?

Breathing deeply and pulling herself together, Katerina realized that letting him walk into danger on her behalf was the *last* thing she'd do. When he had taken her in his arms and kissed her that way he had given her undeniable reasons to stand by his side. Katerina folded her arms and hugged herself, smiling as she recalled every moment of that captivating embrace. Max might be a hotshot government profiler but he didn't have a clue what a woman in love might do. A woman like her.

She glanced at the digital clock on the bedside table. She had hours to come up with her own perfect plan and put it in motion. Or talk herself out of doing something so stupid she'd be forever sorry.

Given her heightened emotions and the way she was unable to force herself to consider staying back while Max risked his life, she figured she was bound to choose with her heart rather than her head. That was okay up to a point. The point where she put herself in real danger.

Ideally, she could reach the ranch early and remove both her mare and her father from the premises before any harm came to them. Or to her.

And then Max would be free to arrest Kyle without incident.

SEVENTEEN

Katerina's mare, Moonlight, was both the easiest potential victim for her to reach and also the most tractable, so she began her rescue efforts there.

Since Kyle expected her to show up to meet him anyway she didn't try to hide the green muscle car the FBI had rented for her. Instead, she parked it in roughly the same place she'd left her ruined truck, one building over. Arriving very early for their appointment did impart a positive feeling but it wasn't nearly as reassuring as being with Max had been.

There were no grooms bustling around, she noticed. That was a little strange but she chalked it up to hot weather and the aftermath of the daylong celebration and parade. Anyone who had partied much at the park or elsewhere was liable to be sleeping it off, and that included the ranch foreman.

Heath McCabe usually managed the Garwood barns pretty well even if he was under the weather. She couldn't remember one instance when he hadn't at least shown up to make sure that the valuable animals were fed and watered adequately no matter what.

Keeping her eye out for Heath so she could warn him to steer clear for a while, just in case, she checked the chart in the tack room listing Moonlight's new stall and headed straight for it. Each step seemed more perilous. This idea had seemed sound back at the hotel. Now, as the minutes ticked by, the doubts started to creep in.

Reaching the stall, Katerina gazed fondly at Moonlight and took several deep, calming breaths. Her beloved, dapple gray mare had darker ears, nose and long black eyelashes, making her even more striking than she would have been in solid gray. Her beautiful coat had always reminded Katerina of moonlight on snow, although there was precious little of that where they lived. The agile mare's Arabian roots showed in her fine bone and facial features, as did the cross with a Standardbred for greater size.

Although Katerina wasn't the only trainer and rider who could handle her she was definitely the person the horse preferred. That affinity came in handy at times like these. Times when she needed to put a halter on the horse in a hurry.

Had she had more advance notice she might have considered camouflaging the mottled gray with hair dye. Sadly, coloring an entire horse was not a job to be done in haste. Besides, if anybody saw her with Moonlight the coat color wouldn't matter as much as the mare's attitude. She dearly loved Katerina. And the feeling was mutual.

She spoke softly, cajoling as she entered the stall and displayed the blue halter. "Here you go, baby. That's a good girl."

Moonlight's upper lip quivered. Her nostrils flared. Then, to Katerina's astonishment, she tossed her head and snorted.

"You are so spoiled," Katerina said, reaching to stroke the silky neck beneath the mane. "Come on. Be a good girl for me. I'm not going to hurt you but I am in a hurry."

That was the problem, she realized with a start. The sensitive animal was picking up on her nervousness and it had caused a negative reaction. She paused and breathed deeply again in another attempt to calm herself, as well as the mare, before trying again.

Although the horse did back up a little more and shuffle her feet in the bedding scattered on the floor, this time she let herself be haltered. Katerina buckled the chin strap and clipped a lead rope to the D ring. All the while she kept up the affectionate banter Moonlight had become accustomed to when they had trained and competed as a team.

Thick, braided rope in hand, she peeked out of the stall to check the aisle. It was empty except for a couple of the ranch dogs who were going about their usual business, napping, scratching or yawning with boredom.

"A little boredom would be nice right now, wouldn't it, girl?"

Moonlight nickered quietly, blowing hard enough to lift her upper lip and make it quiver.

Katerina shushed her with a hand on her velvety nose. "Easy, girl. That's it. Come on. I need to get you out of here so you're safe."

Where she was going to hide a thousand-pound animal was the biggest conundrum. There wasn't time to hook up a trailer and take her away, even if Katerina still had a pickup truck, and she wasn't about to help herself to one of her father's transport vehicles because she had no desire to be arrested for auto theft. A bareback ride might be the best answer once they reached a place where she could stand higher to pull herself onto the horse's back.

An uneven cadence of the hooves hitting the packed dirt got her attention. "Whoa." Katerina stared at all four legs. Hocks and pasterns looked good. Nothing seemed swollen. Still, *something* was wrong.

With her back to Moonlight's head, she bent and tried to lift a foreleg. "Foot." Not only did the mare resist, she tossed her head and began to fight the halter.

Katerina stopped. If Moonlight jerked the rope out of her hand and escaped there would be no way to make sure she was out of harm's way. Her grip tightened. She cast around, knowing what she should do yet reluctant to rethink her escape plans. Time was passing faster than a fractious colt who had thrown his rider.

"Okay, back to your stall so I can use both hands to figure out what's wrong with you," Katerina told the nervous animal. "I don't want to ruin you for life by making you run."

She grabbed a metal hoof pick that hung on a nail, pocketed it and retraced their path. Hands shaking, she checked her cell phone for the time. She could probably count on about an hour before Max and the other lawmen arrived. That would be enough time to figure out what was wrong with her horse. It would have to be.

Katerina's heart went out to the mare. Heath McCabe was supposed to make sure all the horses were groomed regularly, including having their feet cleaned. He'd been taking Moonlight in for a vet check the day the other barn had exploded. How could this problem have shown up so quickly or been missed in the past?

"Well, whatever's ailing you, I'll fix it, baby," she promised Moonlight. Drawing a hand along the horse's side and giving its rump a pat she urged it back into its stall and shut the bottom half of the door so she could work without an assistant. There weren't many show horses Katerina trusted enough to doctor them alone. This one was the exception.

Bending again, she asked Moonlight to raise one foot. The horse shifted her weight. "That's it, girl. That's what I want."

She was reaching for the hoof pick when one of the ranch dogs started barking. The whole pack immediately joined in.

Katerina froze. It was too early for Kyle. Max might be here already but if so, why were the dogs barking when they had gotten to know him? Her heart thudded painfully in her chest.

Without rising, she released her hold on the mare's foreleg and crouched in the stall. The barking was getting worse. Closer. And she was trapped with the very animal she'd come there to rescue.

Max had stationed himself in the hotel lobby to wait for his backup early so he'd be certain Katerina was behaving herself upstairs.

Maybe he shouldn't have kissed her at all, but his raw emotions had finally won that battle. What he was or wasn't going to do about it later was a whole other dilemma. The way he figured, one catastrophe at a time. Maybe, once she felt safe and stopped feeling like a victim, she wouldn't be interested in a romance with him at all.

"Well, that's a depressing thought," he grumbled to himself as several black-and-white patrol cars pulled up in front. Max could see that some hotel guests were uneasy about such a strong police presence so he went to meet the others in the driveway. Opal was by his side.

"My dog's coming in case we need her," Max announced. "May as well be covered."

"Three units of city police went on ahead," the closest deputy informed him. "Our boss went with them to make sure they don't act like old-time cowboys on a Saturday night spree and shoot up the place."

"Sounds good to me." He'd started for his SUV when the deputy leaned out the window of his cruiser and called, "What happened to your pretty sidekick?"

"She's right here," Max said, indicating Opal and pretending he didn't know who the man was asking about.

"Right," someone else drawled. "Personally, I like the ones that look like Ms. Katerina. Thought you did, too."

"I have a job to do. We all do," Max said tersely. "Let's get a move on."

He huffed as he climbed into his SUV. So, his personal feelings were that obvious. Big surprise. It seemed that he and Katerina were the only ones missing the signals. Had she been sending them to him? Undoubtedly. He even recalled rebuffing her at least once when she'd tried to hug him. That kind of casual exchange of affection had begun as no more than the innocent moral support of one human being for another. When had it changed, grown into something so much more? Perhaps the metamorphosis had been so subtle that neither of them had noticed. Or maybe they had both been denying their mutual attraction for different reasons.

Joining the convoy bound for the Garwood ranch, Max had plenty of time to mull over his feelings for Katerina. He had admired her from the moment when she'd tried to ignore her own injuries to go check on the welfare of animals. She'd have done it, too, if he had not forced her to accept medical attention. That kind of self-sacrificing attitude was commendable as long as it didn't get her hurt.

Somehow, after that, he'd started to take a personal interest in her welfare. He hadn't purposely decided to do so, it had simply happened, which was the main reason he'd ordered her to stay in her hotel room. Yes, she was mad at him. And yes, she might hold a grudge. But he'd had to do it. As long as his attention was divided, his success was in jeopardy. More than one agent had ended a promising career that way—and not necessarily by retiring at a ripe old age.

Max instinctively knew he'd be willing to sacrifice himself for Katerina, he just didn't want to. Not if he could look forward to spending the rest of his life with her.

That conclusion hit him hard. There was the key to settling all their manageable conflicts. At least he hoped so. If he confessed his love and she didn't reciprocate, he didn't know how he'd take it. She had to care for him. She had to. And it had to be love, not anything else, such as a desire to escape her critical parent or leave a town that had turned against her.

He began to smile as the convoy neared the Garwood Ranch. After he'd bared his heart he planned to tell her all about his ranch in Montana. She'd love it there. It wasn't a big spread but it was all his, his and his brothers'. There was plenty of room for another house, too, if it came to that.

But for right now… Max slowed and parked out of sight in a grove of trees while the sheriff's men spread out and found their own places to hide.

Since he and Katerina had been seen together so often he hoped the sight of him, if he were spotted, would not put Kyle off and endanger the horses or Garwood. Of all the lawmen present, he was the most easily identifiable, the only one working a dog.

He led the boxer up the driveway, keeping to the edges in case they were being watched. The first long, rectangular block of stalls was occupied by horses, he knew, but Opal's body language did not yet indicate the presence of strangers. Not that he was positive she was reliable in that capacity. All he had to go by was the instinct she'd displayed after the parade.

Max's jaw clenched and a shiver shot up his spine. Of all the actions he'd taken since arriving in South Fork, the smartest had to be his decision to insist that Katerina stay out of this final showdown.

There was a good chance someone would die today.

He didn't want it to be her.

Crouching out of sight and trusting Moonlight to avoid stepping on her, Katerina listened, hoping to pick up clues to who was nearby. The barking of the ranch dogs kept her from hearing clearly but she knew they wouldn't bother raising a fuss over any of the regular employees. Therefore, either the police were already here or Kyle had outsmarted them all.

"Please, Father," she whispered, "make it one of the good guys."

Her arms and legs felt as weak as if she'd just run miles. She was weaponless. Hemmed in. And as useless as a saddle without a horse.

"Lord, I'm sorry," she said, her lips barely moving. Unshed tears blurred her vision as she thought of the man she loved and added, "I'm so sorry, Max."

Moonlight's ears swiveled forward. Her deep brown eyes widened until Katerina could see white rims around the pupils. The horse was getting frightened. And, as a result of animal's signals, so was Katerina.

She duckwalked over to the front wall of the stall and pressed an ear to the wood. Men were talking. If only those dogs would shut up she might be able to figure out who it was and what was being said.

A deep voice shouted. Something metallic crashed against the wall. A bucket had been thrown, probably at the pack of excited dogs, because their barking quieted.

"You stay here and mind the horse while I go take care of Garwood," one of the men said.

Breathless, Katerina heard a muted rebuttal. "What about the other? You know."

"Taken care of. One push of a button."

"I don't like that idea." The voice was gravely, as if the speaker was nursing a sore throat.

"Too bad. I'm the one with the gun so that makes me boss. Now do as you're told or you'll get the first bullet instead of the old man."

Dad! Katerina's emotions churned. She felt ill. *Why didn't I start with the house?* One glance at the horse towering over her and she knew she had chosen wisely. If she had stayed her course, at least one of the threats against those she loved would have been thwarted.

It was suddenly easy to identify with Max and see why he blamed himself for prior mistakes in judgment. She'd had more than one choice this morning and had taken the wrong path. Her motives had been good but her conduct was not nearly as honorable as it should have been. She had let a lie of omission stop her from making wise decisions. False pride had brought her here.

Katerina bit her lip to keep from weeping. She wasn't nearly as clever as she'd thought she was and it was almost time to pay a high price for her inflated opinion of herself.

As she sagged against the front wall of the stall, the exposed end of the metal hoof pick in her back pocket bumped against the wood. A tapping sound that would normally have been almost inaudible seemed to echo like the thrown bucket had.

She held her breath. Froze. Prayed silently that whoever was in the aisle had not noticed. If he came any closer and looked down he might be able to see her despite the barred top half of the wall.

Seconds dragged by. Katerina didn't move. Maybe she was safe. Maybe she'd gotten away with accidentally making the tiny noise.

Then, her dapple gray mare started to move. Careful to avoid stepping on Katerina she ambled to the open half door and put her head through the opening as she always did when greeting friends or begging for treats.

Shadows above told the story. A man was coming closer, reaching out, stroking the horse's forehead and scratching between her ears.

Moonlight knows him! Katerina realized. And suddenly she did, too. The shirtsleeve was familiar. So was the crooning tone he was now using. One of her enemies was Heath McCabe!

As soon as he realized Moonlight should not be wearing a halter, he'd know exactly who had put it on her and would start searching.

The game was over. She'd lost.

EIGHTEEN

Max spotted Kyle in the distance. He was about to follow when Opal began to pull him in a different direction. The radio earpiece kept incoming transmissions muted so he called in his location and reported the situation.

"We have men coming up on the back of the ranch house now. Hold your position," was the reply.

He didn't intend to argue command hierarchy, particularly not when Opal was so intent on leading him to the barns. Whatever the dog wanted at this point was fine with Max. If she happened to turn up another bomb, so be it. If not, he could work his way into position to intercept Kyle if and when he headed back that way.

They rounded the first rectangular barn. Opal began straining at the leash and wagging her stub of a tail along with the rest of her rear half.

For the briefest of moments, Max was so thunderstruck he couldn't make himself believe his eyes. His jaw dropped open. "No. No, no, no."

"You okay, Agent West?" This time it was Sheriff Tate, himself, who was asking.

"No. Have somebody bring my car to me. Park it in plain view."

"Keys?"

Max recited the code for the locked door. "Keys are in the ignition."

"You sure? I thought we'd agreed to do this covertly."

"That was before I saw this." Max snapped a quick photo of Katerina's rented car and sent it to the sheriff.

The older man's reaction was as expected. He cursed. "I thought you were sure that young woman wasn't mixed up in all of this. If she's innocent, why did she come to warn her buddies?"

"They aren't her friends," Max insisted, keeping his voice down and letting Opal approach to sniff the green car. "If anything, Katerina's in deep trouble already. That's why I want my car brought up. We were sneaking around to protect her. Since she's already here I want her to know that I am, too."

"Okay, if you say so. Just remember, this is your party, not mine."

That verbal transfer of authority and therefore blame, struck Max as ironic. Truth to tell, he didn't care who was in charge. All he cared about was finding Katerina and spiriting her out of harm's way. Later, when he had her alone and could express himself without having it broadcast all over the county, he intended to have words with her. And unless he managed to calm down before then, they were probably going to be very harsh words.

Providing she's all right, he added silently. If something happened to steal her from him the way his first fiancée had been taken years before, he didn't know if his heart—or his mind—would survive.

Terror filled Katerina. Moonlight sensed her distress and shied away from the ranch foreman, her ears laid back and her eyes once again wild-looking. That helped expose Katerina's hiding place. There wasn't a thing she could do about it except remain very still, hold her breath and mentally call out to God. It wasn't the way she'd been taught to pray by her late mother but at the moment it was the best she could do. At least she was already on her knees.

The noisy rumble of a diesel engine drifted to her. There were several trucks on the ranch that ran on diesel fuel but that one sounded more powerful. Like Max's SUV!

Confirmation came from McCabe. "Well, well, well. Look who's here. Mr. FBI himself."

To her relief, the foreman stepped away from the stall. She stretched her cramped legs by pulling herself up and peeking through the bars. When Moonlight came up behind her and breathed down her neck she reached around and gave the mare a pat.

There had to be something close by she could use to defend herself until help arrived. But what? The hooked end of the hoof pick in her pocket was blunted to keep from hurting the tender center of a horse's hoof called the frog, so it was useless for self-defense.

A pitchfork might work. If there was one around. Given her father's strict rules about keeping a tidy barn she doubted it.

"Keep going," she whispered, watching McCabe cautiously working his way down the aisle to the far door. If he left the barn she might get a chance to make a run for it. And if she reached her car and made a lot of noise driving away, Heath and the man she assumed was Kyle might give chase.

Someone shouted. Katerina ducked down, holding her shaky breath and clenching her fists. Another man yelled, his words so faint she figured he had to be much farther away.

"Far is good," she muttered. "Just give me a little distance. That's all I ask."

Braced with her hand on the latch to the stall door, she waited and listened. Her fingers tightened. The horse behind her whinnied softly, as if joining in the moment of decision. Almost time. Almost time…

A bang cracked the still air like a hammer breaking a brittle rock.

Katerina fell back, shocked speechless. Horses panicked, kicking at their stalls and calling to each other. That was a gunshot. She knew it was. And since it had rattled every fiber of her being, she knew it had originated in the barn.

Max's name was in her heart and almost on her lips. If they had hurt him she was going to attack them with her bare hands. Pound them with her fists. She was…

Reality overwhelmed her and sapped her strength. She wasn't going to do a thing. She had behaved as if she belonged in a bad movie and had walked into this mess with her eyes open. Now she was going to have to face her fate the same way, like it or not.

Standing tall, she dashed away tears. The air was still, the atmosphere fraught with anxiety. Moonlight was almost as upset as the other horses so she offered comfort, wondering if this was the last time she'd have an opportunity to show love to the magnificent animal.

"Easy, girl. Easy." Katerina began with soft, calming strokes, then laid her cheek against the horse's sleek neck and hugged her, weeping, the way she had so many times in the past. They had shared a lot of good days, a lot of wonderful memories. Her only regret was that those days were probably about to come to an abrupt end.

Thoughts of mounting bareback and charging out of the barn in a daring escape flitted through Katerina's mind. Moonlight might survive that way even if she didn't. Then again, knowing how horses behaved, she knew it wouldn't be long until memories of a cozy stall and plenty of alfalfa hay drew her back home. Then what would become of her with no protector, especially if McCabe chose to take his frustration out on the helpless mare?

As the horse quieted, it became clear that a race to safety was totally out of the question. Shuffling around in fright had noticeably worsened the mare's sore foot. She came to a stop with one foreleg resting on the leading edge of that hoof, as though she were a ballerina on point.

Katerina gave the aisle a quick glance, saw that it was empty and took out the hoof pick. This might be her last chance to minister to her sweet companion and she wasn't going to waste it.

Tears clouded her vision and dripped onto the underside of the hoof as she cleaned it out. There was a big rock wedged between the tender frog and the inside edge of the shoe. No wonder poor Moonlight was limping.

Katerina dashed away her tears, sniffled and persisted. McCabe and his buddy were probably going to shoot her anyway so she was going to give him a piece of her mind. Leaving an obstruction like this was shameful.

Raking at the rock she cleared away everything else that was packed around it. The gray color reminded her of Half Dome in Yosemite Park. The shape, however was odd.

Suddenly it all came to her. Vern had hung around the stables a lot. She'd thought he was there to keep her company but maybe he'd had ulterior motives. If Heath had been telling the truth about taking horses to the vet, this clump of material would have been discovered already. Since it was still here, there was a good chance he'd lied and was merely clearing out the barn before the planned destruction.

Did that mean he hadn't known about the diamonds at that time? It must, because, as Max had speculated, he had blown up a place where they may have been hidden.

So where did Kyle come in? Had he and Vern really been close friends? Or had he been sent by a higher-up to retrieve Vern's stash?

Finally, Katerina got the nose of the pick under an edge of the gray glob and heard it pop loose. The noise startled Moonlight.

Was this what everybody had been looking for? Almost afraid to find out she was wrong, Katerina slowly reached beneath the horse's belly and fisted the object. On the bottom, where it had met the hoof and been protected, she could see sparkling beneath a sheet of clear plastic. This was it! She'd found the hidden treasure!

Before she could straighten she heard a masculine hoot of triumph behind her.

They knew.

Max had heard a shot, seen it shatter the windshield in his SUV and had checked with Sheriff Tate to make sure nobody was injured.

"My deputy bailed out on the passenger side and

made a run for it," was the reply. "He's fine. Sorry about the car."

"It's replaceable. People aren't. Don't worry."

"What now?"

"I'm behind the first barn with Katerina's car. I don't see her yet. Opal and I are going to check the next one. I think that's where the shot came from."

"Affirmative. Be advised. Bertrand Garwood is there, too. One of the guys we're after just brought him out of the house and perp-walked him your direction."

"Copy." Max gritted his teeth. It was becoming more a question of who *wasn't* there than who was. The only thing more ironic would be the addition of drug lord Angus Dupree, missing agent Jake Morrow and maybe runaway witness Esme Dupree. That would make the roster just about complete.

Of course, not being absolutely positive which side Jake was on these days might complicate matters. So did having Katerina's father on scene. Max was pretty sure Garwood was innocent but that didn't guarantee his safety. Nothing could. When Kyle found out that Vern's secret had died with him, bullets were likely to start flying. At this point, Max wasn't sure whether he was angry at Katerina or merely petrified of losing her.

Pulling Opal to heel on a tight leash, he drew his sidearm and began to edge forward.

Someone began to cheer and whoop it up.

Max's gut twisted. He picked up the pace. Reached the rear barn door.

And saw two men slapping each other on the back while Bertrand stood by and stared.

Three accounted for. Why were they so ecstatic? And where was Katerina?

* * *

Standing between the threat and Moonlight, Katerina let Kyle and Heath celebrate all they wanted. She didn't care one whit about hidden diamonds. All she cared about was Max, her beloved horse—and her father.

In that order? she asked herself, answering *yes* with the addition of her heavenly Father as number one. The way she saw the future, her fate could tip either way and the longer her enemies gloated, the better for all concerned.

From her position inside the stall she couldn't see much beyond her father. Hoping for at least a modicum of moral support, she caught Bertrand's attention and tried to smile before mouthing, "I love you."

His response was chilling. "This is all your fault, Katerina. I hope you're happy. Why didn't you put an end to it before it escalated and turn over the diamonds?"

"Because I didn't know where they were."

"Bah. You expect me to believe that?"

She stood tall. "I don't care if you do or not. If any of you do. The only reason I discovered Vern's hiding place is because Moonlight was limping."

Kyle punched Heath in the shoulder. Hard. "Amateurs! I told you it was a mistake to just take those horses for a ride and bring them straight back. You should of had them vet-checked like you said you were going to."

"Yeah, well, if you'd gotten closer to Vern before he was arrested we wouldn't be standin' here at all."

"I wasn't sent here in time." Fists raised, Kyle squared off on Heath. "You brought the feds. You and that dumb idea to teach your boss a lesson by setting off a little explosion. Some little explosion. The whole barn went."

"Only because it caught fire. Besides, you were keeping the diamonds a secret back when I did that. How was I supposed to know it was a stupid idea?"

"If you had a brain under that cowboy hat you'd have figured it out for yourself."

"Fine." Heath backed down and glanced toward the open stall. "What're we gonna do now?"

"Clean up this mess."

"How? We can't just shoot 'em."

"Maybe you can't, but I can."

The ranch manager held up his hands. "Hold on. I didn't sign up for murder. Vern gettin' killed in jail is one thing. This ain't the same. Not a bit."

Katerina saw Kyle's expression harden, his eyes narrowing. "You have no idea who I am, do you?"

When Heath didn't reply Katerina wanted to jump in and ask for her own sake. Kyle had led her to believe they had met months ago. Now she doubted whether or not that was true. He'd spoken and acted like a local good ol' boy before. Now he sounded totally different and far too intelligent. She studied the man, waiting, wondering.

Bertrand Garwood cursed, directing most of his tirade toward Kyle, and Katerina realized immediately that it was a big mistake. She edged backward until her shoulders touched Moonlight's. She and the horse weren't the only ones nervous enough to tremble. Heath was doing a perfect impression of a sapling being buffeted by Santa Ana winds and it served him right. Only her father acted clueless, perhaps because he hadn't realized how deep a pile of manure he was figuratively standing in. "He's saying he's a gangster, Dad. I'd cool it if I were you."

"Don't be ridiculous. This isn't the 1940s or '50s. That era is long gone."

"Correct," Kyle said with a leering smile. "I work for businessmen. That's all they do. Business. We have connections all over the world and once in a while one of our deliveries goes missing. That's where I come in. I see that justice is done." He laughed. "I just do it my way."

"Dupree," Katerina whispered before realizing she'd said it aloud.

Kyle turned on her. "Smart. I knew you were. That's too bad."

She raised her hands, palms forward, to fend him off. "Go. Take the diamonds, all of them. We won't say a word, will we?"

Her eyes pled with the other two men, each in turn. Heath seemed ready to cave but Bertrand was his usual bombastic self. "After all you've done? All you and your kind have cost me? Not on your life."

"How about on *your* life?" Kyle drawled.

The older man blustered. "Do you know who I am? I'm the mayor of South Fork. Sheriff Tate is a personal friend of mine."

"Then you'll have plenty of mourners at your funeral, Mr. Mayor." Waving the pistol, Kyle used it to point at the stall where Katerina and Moonlight stood. "Everybody in. Now. I want to do this right to impress the feds and I haven't got all day."

Nobody moved.

All Katerina could think of was Max, praying he hadn't been shot. When he hadn't returned fire she'd feared the worst, yet held on to the hope that he'd chosen to merely take cover, not suspecting that she or anyone else was in jeopardy.

That had to be it. He could not be gone forever. They had to meet again, if only long enough for her to tell him how much she loved him.

NINETEEN

Max overheard everything. It was all he could do to hold himself back. He'd advised Tate of the situation and was waiting until more officers were in position before giving the order to storm the barn.

His elite team would have had a better chance of success. Trouble was, they weren't there. He was essentially on his own. And he didn't like it. Superheroes were a fantasy. Real men, real agents, used their brains and technology to outwit criminals, they didn't go charging into danger dodging a hail of bullets.

Or running through a minefield, he added. It was time to activate some of their usual precautions. He turned his back on the open door, hunched over his cell phone and called Dylan O'Leary.

"What's up," the tech guru said. "I see it's you but I can hardly hear your voice, Max."

He cupped the small device and tried again. "Can you kill all cell signals from the relay towers around my location?" In the background he could hear computer keys clacking.

"I can, but you'll lose the ability to talk to me."

"We can communicate by police radio, relaying via a landline at their station, if we have to."

"Do we have time to ask for permission?"

"No."

"That's what I figured. Can you at least fill me in so I'm prepared when they threaten to fire me again?"

"A Dupree hitman is holding people at gunpoint and I can't figure out why he hasn't shot them yet. If he's the same one who's been planting bombs around here, he may not need to. The place may already be wired."

"Copy. Works for me. How long do I have?"

"Time is already up," Max said. "Just do your best."

Katerina was out of ideas. Apparently her father was, too. Kyle gave him a hard push and he ended up inside the stall.

"You, too," the Dupree cohort said to Heath.

"Hey, wait a minute, man. You and I are in this to-gether."

"Right. Do you really think I'd join forces with the likes of you? I needed help on the inside, that's all. I don't need you anymore." He motioned with the gun barrel again. "Move it."

If Katerina had not been so disappointed in the fore-man she might have felt sorrier for him. As it was, she could hardly bear to be near him.

"You were like an uncle to me," she rasped. "How *could* you?"

"It was comin' to me. I ain't had a raise in five years. A man's gotta eat."

Bertrand interrupted. "There was nothing coming to you that you deserved."

Shocked, Katerina turned on her father. "This is partly your fault, after all. When are you going to learn to treat everybody fairly?"

The stall door started to swing closed with the gunman on the outside. "Don't hold your breath, lady," he taunted. "There won't be time for any of you to reform."

Pleading and weeping openly, McCabe dropped to his knees in what was left of the opening. That was enough distraction for Katerina to duck, crawl beneath Moonlight's belly and pull out the cell phone Max had given her. The only number entered in it was his so she opted to dial 9-1-1.

What she had not counted on was the loud "Nine-one-one. What is your emergency?" reply.

Kyle shouted obscenities and started shoving the others aside to get to her.

Katerina screamed. Slipped her phone beneath the straw bedding. And heard glass break when Moonlight sidestepped in fright and crushed it.

Bedlam ensued. Katerina rolled aside, hoping to keep from being grabbed or shot. Heath scrambled out the open stall door like the crabs she'd seen crossing hot sand along the Pacific coast, twenty miles due west.

Bertrand Garwood went for the gun and failed. Kyle's punch flattened him.

Breathing hard, the hired thug kept his back to the side wall and the pistol trained on his remaining captives while he pulled out his own cell phone.

"Okay, this is how it's going to be," he said with a sneer before glancing at his revolver. "I like this piece so I was trying to keep from leaving ballistics but sometimes you have to make sacrifices. I can always pick up another one like it on the street."

He cocked the hammer with his thumb. "I'll do the horse first so it doesn't get in my way again."

"No!" Katerina launched herself at him.

Moonlight reared. Her hooves grazed Kyle's arm and deflected the bullet he fired as a reflex.

Katerina shrieked. Was she hit? Was her mare? Was her father?

The pistol barrel came up again, pointed right at Moonlight. Screaming unintelligibly, Katerina lurched toward it.

Instead of firing this time, Kyle used it to bat her away, the blow propelling her across the stall where she slammed into a solid plank wall. Reality dimmed. She began to feel as if she were floating above the conflict, a feather in the wind.

Another shot echoed. Katerina was too groggy to react. Sliding to the straw in a heap she closed her eyes and passed out.

Max was running full out. So was Opal. He'd heard the loud response from the emergency operator and had anticipated a negative result. Boy, had he been right.

Plastering himself against the outer wall of the stall where the battle was taking place, he commanded Opal and the gathering lawmen to wait while he made a silent entry. Sweat dotted his forehead, His hands were slippery. He wiped them dry on his jeans and braced for counterattack, then whipped around the corner and came face-to-face with the armed criminal.

Instead of firing, Max hesitated. This man had admitted working for the Duprees. His insider knowledge might be invaluable—if he could bring him in alive.

"Drop the gun."

"Sure." He tossed it aside.

That didn't fit the profile. What was Max missing? He didn't dare take his focus off Kyle to check the Garwoods. Both were down and out, although neither showed signs of serious injury.

It took Max only a few heartbeats to deduce the prob-

lem. Kyle no longer needed his gun because he had another weapon in hand. His cell phone. He was holding
it in front of him, pointing it like a laser. There was
only one logical conclusion. He was preparing to deto-
nate more bombs. On the ranch. And these weren't like
Heath's meager efforts. These were seriously deadly.

"Don't," Max warned, eyeing the phone.

"Then get out of my way and let me go."

Had Dylan succeeded in cutting off the cell signals?
Katerina had gotten through to 9-1-1 so if he had managed to kill the phones it had happened within the last
couple of minutes. Max couldn't take the chance. He re-
treated in the direction of Katerina's still form, although
he didn't turn his back on the hired killer.

Katerina began to stir. Blinked and looked up at him.
"Max. You're alive."

"Yes." There was nothing more he could do to prevent the planted bombs from exploding. If this was his
final second on earth he was exactly where he needed
to be. With his woman. Best of all, she was smiling up
at him, He knelt to cradle her head and shoulders.

"I need to tell you," she began.

"Hush, honey. Everything's fine. I've got you."

There was no way for him to tell if his back and vest
would shield her enough to keep her alive during an explosion but he intended to try.

She slipped one arm around his neck. "I have to say
it. I love you, Max."

"I love you, too."

Pulling her closer he gave Kyle a sidelong glance and
saw his evil grin as he dramatically pushed one of the
buttons on the phone he held.

Nothing happened!

Max wanted to cheer.

* * *

Katerina was so focused on being back in Max's strong arms she was late noticing how intently he was watching Kyle. When she saw the criminal's sinister expression and the way he was handling his phone, she realized what was going on.

"Freeze," Max shouted. "Hands on your head."

Instead, Kyle threw the phone, pulled a second gun from a holster strapped to his ankle and ran.

"Get him!" Katerina screeched.

"Are you…?"

"Fine. *Stop* him. He works for the Dupree crime family."

"I know. See to your dad."

Katerina had no trouble doing that. Bertrand was very subdued, sitting on the floor and holding his head. "Dad?"

"He shot me!"

"Apparently." She gently pulled his hand away from his forehead. "It's just a scratch. Your hard head must have deflected the bullet."

The confused look he gave her wasn't conciliatory but it wasn't angry, either. Maybe there was hope for them, at least to the point where they stopped being avowed enemies.

"Are you okay?" Bertrand asked hoarsely. "I saw him pitch you across the stall."

"Guess I have a hard head, too," Katerina said. "It runs in the family."

They paused to exchange quizzical looks just as a volley of shots echoed through the barn.

Katerina gasped. "Max."

Bertrand patted her hand. "He'll be okay. Listen. I can hear him yelling orders."

"You're right." Although she managed a smile, there were tears of gratitude to God in her eyes.

"I sure like this one better than Kowalski."

She sniffled and shook her head. "I'm so used to doing the opposite of whatever you want I hardly know what to say."

"Never mind me. When he asks you, say yes."

"What if he doesn't want to get married?"

"Then you convince him." The older man started to chuckle and winced. "Ouch."

"You'll probably have a dandy headache, Dad."

"Not as bad as the headaches you gave me trying to raise you without a mother. I was scared to death of making a mistake. When you said you wanted to marry that oddball, Kowalski, I figured I'd failed big-time."

"*That's* what turned you against me? I thought you were ashamed of me."

"I was. And of myself for not being a better father." He started to frown, then moaned and grabbed his forehead again. "I thought, when I said it was him or me, you'd come to your senses."

"And when I didn't, you stuck to your guns."

"Of course I did. What other choice did I have?"

Katerina had absorbed all the regret she could handle so she grabbed Moonlight's lead rope and led the mare out into the wide aisle at the center of the long rectangular barn. Thankfully, the limp was almost gone.

What had happened to the diamonds? Katerina could not have cared less. Wealth was not the answer to happiness. Oh, it could mask deficiencies for a while but in the end, a person needed much more. Like love and companionship. A mare like Moonlight. And, she thought, glancing at the knot of men gathered at the open barn door and spotting the FBI logo on Max's vest, she needed him.

Just then he turned and saw her. His wide grin spoke volumes as he broke away from the group and started to hurry her way. Moonlight whinnied. Katerina dropped the halter rope and rushed toward Max.

They met, arms open for each other, and held tight.

He stroked her back. "It's over, honey. It's all over. As soon as Opal and I clear out any hidden explosives this threat will end."

She desperately wanted his conclusion to prove true. "How can you be sure?"

"Because I'm going to announce finding the diamonds and explain that they have been turned over to the prosecutor as additional evidence of motive in Reginald Dupree's and Kyle's trials. Even if the US Marshals can't find Esme Dupree so we can put her on the witness stand, we'll have a concrete reason why Kowalski was killed."

"And the drug charges?"

"Yes. Those, too."

"Thank the Lord."

"I have been," Max confessed. "You were right about my needing to come back to my faith. I'm real good at telling everybody else to accept the bad with the good. I just wasn't as good at taking my own advice." His smile softened and he tenderly kissed her.

"Which am I?" Katerina asked, hoping with all her heart for a positive answer.

"Good," Max whispered against her lips. "Very good."

Sighing and enjoying their closeness, Katerina tried to wait for what she thought was coming. Three amazing kisses later Max relaxed his hold and started to say, "Well, I guess Opal and I…"

"Hold it, Special Agent West. You've forgotten something."

"I don't think so."

"Yes, you have. Aren't you going to ask me to marry you and go to Montana?"

A stunned look replaced his smile.

"Uh-oh." Katerina felt like weeping. "I was mistaken?"

After seconds that felt like hours to her, Max recovered and quirked a smile. "That might be the only way I can keep you out of trouble." He eyed the open stall. "That was not the smartest move you've ever made."

"I did it for the right reasons, though."

His smile spread. "That's debatable. So, could you ever bring yourself to leave California?"

That was a very positive sign. "Watch how fast I can pack."

"You haven't asked me anything about my plans for the future or where I live or what my job entails. How do you know you'd be happy?"

"I'll be with you. What else matters?"

Judging by the way his shoulders relaxed and his smile returned, this conversation was going to end well.

Gazing deeply into her eyes, Max said, "I have a ranch in Montana. My brothers and I are co-owners but they pretty much let me do my own thing. There's even room for your horse."

"There is?" Squealing with delight she threw her arms around Max's neck. He swung Katerina in a circle and kissed her again.

"Does that mean your answer is *yes*," he teased.

"Well…" Katerina was so happy she was giddy. Bursting into laughter she managed a quick "Yes!"

It didn't surprise Max to see that most of the remaining law officers were grinning at him and Katerina. If he'd witnessed their interchange he would have been, too. As it was, he had trouble wiping the smile off his face long enough to do a thorough search of the Garwood Ranch.

An encounter with Bertrand as paramedics treated his superficial wound gave him a chance to ask about buying Katerina's horse.

"No need," the older man said. "It's hers. I heard you two talking in the barn. She can take the mare and I'll throw in a new truck and trailer for the trip."

"Really?"

Garwood nodded. "Yes. She earned it with all the work she did around here as a teenager. I paid her entry fees and outfitted her and the horse, but she never got wages the way the other trainers did. It's recently been pointed out to me that I wasn't a fair boss."

"It's true that your foreman set the first bomb here. We found components in his pickup."

"Ah, so that's why his room was so clean. I wondered."

"He'll have to be tried."

"I'll think about getting him a lawyer. We do go way back." He winced. "Ouch."

The paramedic merely smiled as if enjoying doctoring the usually pompous mayor.

"Have you been over the whole ranch yet?"

"Yes," Max said. "Opal and I located three sets. If Kyle had been able to get a cell signal when he tried, there wouldn't be much left of this place but it's safe now." Looking around and taking in the bucolic setting, Max added, "Have you seen Katerina?"

"Yeah. She's in the barn where we had all the fun. I saw her go in there with one of the farm dogs."

"Thanks."

"You treat her good, you hear."

Max saluted casually. "It will be my pleasure." In retrospect he wasn't totally sure how he'd gotten himself engaged so fast but he wasn't going to complain. They didn't have to rush into a wedding although he had no qualms about doing it. Katerina was perfect for him. He'd known that from their first meeting and had not changed his mind since.

He went straight to the barn and began searching stalls. If not for Opal he might have missed spotting her in the shadowy rear corner of one unoccupied by a horse. What it did hold, besides the love of his life, was the black lab she had mentioned before. The dog was happily nursing a squirming litter.

"Pups! How many?"

"Five." Katerina smiled up at him.

Max crouched next to her, blocking Opal so she wouldn't bother the new mother. "What's her name?"

"Dad usually called her something else, but to me she's Baby."

"Since she's a lab, her temperament is probably unsuited for attack or protection, but those pups may have what it takes to be trackers. When we finish an assignment, my team always brings back one or more new prospects for the trainers to test. Would you mind if we adopted a couple of these little guys?"

"I think that would be wonderful. I'd already decided to ask Dad to let me take the mama with me."

Chuckling, Max said, "Well, if you're going to ask him, do it while he's in such a good mood."

"What do you mean?"

"I offered to buy your mare for you and your dad told me he was giving her to you. Her and a rig for hauling her. He called it back wages."

Her eyes widened. "You're serious?"

"Totally. Now all we have to do is plan for you to follow me back to Billings."

He saw her sober as she glanced at the puppies and their mother. Although she didn't say so, he figured she was worried about them if she left too soon.

"Why don't we do this?" Max began. "I'll stay here as long as my assignment can be extended. If no more problems surface now that the Dupree hired gun is in jail, I'll arrange to fly back to visit as often as possible until you and these little guys are ready to travel."

"What excuse can you possibly use?"

"The truth should do it. If not, I'll claim I also need to evaluate these pups before I make a final selection."

"Okay, as long as your choice of a wife doesn't change."

"Honey," Max rasped, afraid his emotions would give away how close he was to weeping with joy. "I have never had a woman propose to me before. I wouldn't dare change my mind. You already have me scared silly."

"You? The self-important, special agent in the protective vest with your calling printed big enough to read from outer space? You? Scared of me?"

Max pulled her gently to her feet and wrapped her in his embrace. "Only of losing you," he whispered against her hair. "I want us to be together for eternity."

"I couldn't agree more," Katerina said softy.

With pups making contented sounds and the two adult dogs panting in the background, Max closed his eyes and kissed the woman who would soon be his bride.

EPILOGUE

Katerina had no doubt Max would keep his word, and he did. They spent many happy hours working with the young lab puppies and he chose two. She adopted the mother dog and couldn't wait to take them all with her to their new home in Montana.

All three canines, plus Opal and several of the other FBI K-9 officers, attended their outdoor nuptials in Yosemite National Park. The weather was perfect and except for a wild whitetail deer who decided to crash the party and nearly created chaos amidst the dogs, the ceremony went off without a hitch.

Afternoon sun reflected off Half Dome. A breeze ruffled Katerina's veil. Wildflowers bloomed in abundance thanks to a few brief showers in weeks prior. And, wonder of wonders, Bertrand Garwood gave the bride away.

Dylan O'Leary was Max's best man. Katerina hardly noticed him as the music began and she started walking toward her destiny. The *best* man in the world was her very own Special Agent Max West.

He beamed the moment he caught sight of her and never took his eyes off her until she stood beside him, holding his hand, and handed her bouquet to maid of honor, Zara Fielding, Dylan's betrothed.

"I can't believe this is happening," Katerina whispered to Max.

"You still want to go through with it so soon?"

"Yes." She smiled behind the thin white veil. "I've dreamed of being married here since I was a little girl. Thank you for agreeing instead of telling me I was being silly the way everybody else did."

Max was grinning. "All right, then. Let's do it."

Max hadn't had to coerce his family members to attend. They were all delighted, not only that he had found someone like Katerina but that they also got to make a vacation out of the trip.

As they posed for professional photos in the shade of a mighty oak, he gave his bride a quick hug. "I told you my family would love you."

"I was less worried about them than I was my own dad. He sounded more mellow right after the barn shooting but I wasn't sure that change would last."

"I know. I had a little talk with him."

Katerina began to giggle.

"What's so funny?"

"I thought the father of the bride was supposed to have that talk with the groom, not the other way around."

Max appreciated her humor. "Ah, but I was already perfect. He was the one who needed an attitude adjustment."

"You're modest, too, I see."

"Absolutely."

Katerina sobered slightly. "I'm sorry your whole unit couldn't be here. Last-minute assignments?"

"Yes. Harper was the most upset to miss seeing us get married. They got another hot tip on Penny Potter and she had to go follow up."

"The brother of the missing agent?"

"Yes. We figured he'd be the most likely to recognize Jake from a distance, in case he's no longer being held captive as some are starting to suggest. Plus, Harper needed the backup."

"Backup? Besides that gorgeous German shepherd I saw in the picture with her? I can't imagine why. He looks ferocious."

Max noticed his bride smiling at the little coal-black pups following their mother and tripping over tufts of soft grass. "Those two sure don't look mean."

"I know," Katerina agreed. "They're adorable. I'll have to really work to keep from spoiling them."

"Our trainers will teach you how."

She sighed and nodded, leaning closer to tuck herself under his arm. "Know what the best part is?"

"No, what?"

"We'll all have homes where we're loved and accepted just as we are." She gazed up at him with love. "Even me."

* * * * *

Lynette Eason is an award-winning author who lives in South Carolina with her husband and two teenage children. She enjoys traveling, spending time with her family and teaching at writing conferences around the country. She is a member of RWA (Romance Writers of America) and ACFW (American Christian Fiction Writers). You can find her at Facebook.com/lynette.eason and on Twitter, @lynetteeason.

Books by Lynette Eason

Love Inspired Suspense

Wrangler's Corner

The Lawman Returns
Rodeo Rescuer
Protecting Her Daughter

Capitol K-9 Unit

Trail of Evidence

Family Reunions

Hide and Seek
Christmas Cover-Up
Her Stolen Past

Rose Mountain Refuge

Agent Undercover
Holiday Hideout
Danger on the Mountain

Visit the Author Profile page
at Harlequin.com for more titles.

BOUNTY HUNTER

Lynette Eason

Do not take revenge, my dear friends,
but leave room for God's wrath, for it is written:
"It is mine to avenge; I will repay," says the Lord.
—*Romans* 12:19

Dedicated to all of the K-9 officers,
two- and four-legged, who put their lives on the line
on a daily basis.

ONE

A simple twitch of his finger and his sister's killer would be gone. His two-month quest to find Van Blackman would be over. Riley Martelli took one more long look at the man in his sights then lowered the weapon.

But he could never kill someone in cold blood. Not even the man who'd murdered his sister and put his six-year-old nephew, Asher, in the hospital with a bullet lodged near his spine.

Being a bounty hunter could be a dangerous line of work. Sometimes more dangerous than his days of being a beat cop.

It definitely had its ups and downs. Bringing in fugitives topped his list of things that made life worth living. But the stakes had never been higher. He just had to figure out how to capture Blackman without getting killed.

In the last year since changing professions, he'd been through some tough times and barely escaped with his life.

And yet none of that had dampened his determination to bring those fleeing the law to justice.

Especially this one. This one was personal.

Which was why he now found himself outside the

small town of Drum Creek, Colorado, just as the sun was getting ready to go down. With little daylight left, Riley needed to quickly figure out how to approach the man and safely bring him in.

Van knelt, but Riley couldn't see what he was doing. Soon, small puffs of smoke drifted from the patch of ground. Was he building a fire? Did that mean he was planning to stay for a while?

Riley settled the gun back on his shoulder and got a better look with the scope. Van crouched over the small flame, pushing the contents as though trying to encourage a larger blaze. Riley lowered the weapon.

Now, in a very secluded area of Colorado's Rocky Mountain National Park, Van moved to stand next to a black SUV just a few yards ahead of him. Grand Lake was calm and serene behind him. A sense of peace and satisfaction flooded Riley even as his adrenaline spiked. It might be July in Colorado, but it was cold at night, dropping into the forties. Van wore a black ski cap pulled low over his ears, but his tall height and broad shoulders were harder to disguise. Riley's heart pounded. Finally, he was going to make his sister's killer pay. He shifted the rifle on his shoulder for one more look through the scope. He scanned his prey's body, watched the way he held his hands. His target kept touching his hip, which meant he probably had a gun there.

The man turned and Riley now had a full-on view of his face—and his heart stuttered.

It wasn't Van Blackman.

Disappointment shot through him. He had the wrong man. Riley lowered the rifle with a frustrated sigh. Then frowned and lifted it to stare through the scope once again. The man's face was familiar. Where had he seen him before? Television? Yeah, that was it. Could it be—? He focused again.

Yep. That was the missing FBI agent that had been all over the news lately. Morrow was his last name. Jack? Jeff? No, Jake. Jake Morrow. And there was a hundred thousand dollars being offered as a reward for his safe return.

It had been reported that he'd been kidnapped by the Dupree crime family and that he might have escaped, but still needed help.

The Dupree family had long been on the FBI's Most Wanted list, and from what Riley had been able to piece together, the feds had almost managed to capture them. Only things had gone wrong in a raid on a warehouse in Los Angeles.

While tracking Reginald Dupree and his uncle Angus Dupree, Morrow had disappeared from the warehouse. From what Riley remembered, a Dupree helicopter was able to get away during the shootout. It was suspected that Morrow was on that chopper, held against his will by Angus. Reginald and two of his associates had subsequently been arrested and were still in custody.

The weird thing was, Jake had been spotted all over the country, but the last report had him near Billings, Montana. So, of all places for him to show up, why here?

Riley lowered the rifle yet again and stood. "Special Agent Jake Morrow?"

The man froze and Riley raised his hands, along with the rifle, over his head and started walking slowly toward him. He stayed on the path that led to the little campsite clearing, bypassing the large rocks and tangled bushes as well as enormous trees. "I'm Riley Martelli. I'm a bounty hunter and I've been tracking a guy. I thought you were him. Imagine my surprise when you turned—"

The man palmed his weapon in a move so fast Riley didn't have time to blink. Morrow aimed the gun at him. Riley's street training didn't allow him to freeze, he just dove behind the nearest tree as the gun cracked.

The bullet pinged off the large trunk, sending debris stinging against his face. "Hey! I'm one of the good guys! What are you doing?" Another bullet zipped past him and he raised his own rifle to his shoulder once again. "Stop shooting! I'm not trying to hurt you!" He peered around the rock, his blood pumping. His eyes met Morrow's and the man glared at him for another few seconds before he raised his weapon once again to aim it at Riley's face.

Riley pulled back just as another pop sounded then he heard the engine of the SUV roar to life.

Riley rose to his feet once again and watched the agent drive away while his heart thundered in his ears. Why had Agent Morrow reacted that way? Had he not heard him calling out to him? Of course he'd heard and *still* opened fire. His aim had been deliberate. Close shots that meant business. If the look in his eyes meant anything, Jake Morrow wasn't lost and he definitely didn't want to be found.

Riley reached for his cell phone, checked that he had a signal, and went to the news website. The number he'd seen on the television last night regarding reporting tips for Jake Morrow sightings was on the home page. He tapped the number and lifted his phone to his ear.

FBI Special Agent Harper Prentiss lowered her feet from her desk and leaned forward, her attention totally focused on what she was hearing. She'd been about to walk out the door to head home for the evening when the call had come through. Could this finally be the tip they were waiting for? "Tell me again. I want to make sure I didn't miss anything." And that his story didn't change.

The man on the other side of the conversation had identified himself as Riley Martelli and said he'd spotted Jake Morrow in Drum Creek, Colorado. Skepticism was her first reaction. They'd had so many bogus tips that her head hadn't stopped spinning with all the information she'd had to sift through. But the more this guy talked, the more she wondered if he'd really seen Jake.

He repeated the story word for word. The details didn't change. Nothing left out, nothing added.

They had to check it out.

"Hold on a second."

"Sure."

She did a quick Google search. It was about a ten-hour drive to Drum Creek. If they left within the hour, they'd have time for a couple of hours of sleep before jumping on the case. She pondered taking the choppers, but they'd need their vehicles for the dogs.

Then again, she wanted to get there before too much time passed and Jake had a chance to move on. Or, there was another option. One that made the most logistical sense. "All right, I'll tell you what. If I take a chopper, I can be there within a couple of hours. The others drive up with the vehicles and meet me there, but at least I can start searching."

"No sense in hurrying," Riley Martelli answered. "You're going to want to start your search where I last saw him, I'm sure. There's no searching in the dark. Not in that area, trust me."

"Give me the location."

"Rocky Mountain National Park. It's about an hour and forty minutes from Denver and about fifteen minutes from Drum Creek. It's got tons of camping areas, lakes and other great hiding places. I repeat, you won't find him in the dark."

Harper bit her lip, her frustration raging. She didn't want to have to wait until morning to start looking for Jake, but apparently she wasn't going to have a choice. They could chopper in lights and other equipment, but that was still risky. They could miss something important on the fringes of the light.

No, they'd have to start the search at dawn. "All right, we can be there first thing in the morning. Can you recommend a place to stay that can accommodate six team members and six dogs?"

"Sure. There's a hotel in downtown Drum Creek. I'm staying there right now. The owner is a friend of mine. What do you need? Six rooms?"

"Yes." Harper worried her bottom lip with her teeth. They had to be careful how they approached this. They still didn't know what they were dealing with. Was Special Agent Morrow an agent in need of help or was he a double agent, actually working for the very mafia kingpin they'd been trying to put away for months now? She just didn't know. But she was going to find out.

"Keep this confidential, will you? We're going to make a big enough splash with our vehicles and the dogs, but if you can help us fly as far under the radar as possible, that would be great."

Keeping the press and the public unaware of their classified missions was the only way to ensure the success of the team. However, with the dogs, the handlers had to be identifiable in certain situations so the FBI provided a variety of uniforms and gear for different occasions. Max West, their team leader, would have to figure out the best option for this situation.

"I'll do my best and I'll reserve the rooms for you," the bounty hunter was saying. "Like I said, the guy who owns the hotel and works the early morning desk is a friend of mine. He can keep his mouth shut—and if you park in the back, your vehicles won't be seen from the main road."

"Perfect."

"I'll meet you in the lobby at 5:30 sharp. Sunrise is around 5:45. If we get out of town and head into the park early, there won't be a lot of traffic or inquiries."

"Good. Our vehicles are black Suburbans. No flashy logos or anything." But the dogs would attract attention. They gathered stares wherever they went. She sighed. Well, they could only do their best.

"Sounds good."

"Thank you, Mr. Martelli."

"Call me Riley."

"All right, Riley, see you in the morning."

She hung up and sent an email to her team. She was a member of the elite FBI Tactical K-9 Unit. While the FBI started its K-9 program many years ago, the Tactical K-9 Unit was started by the agency ten years ago in response to the increased levels of terrorism haunting the country. They ultimately answered to the FBI Director, but her team was special in that they had very little micromanaging from above. They were good at their jobs and the director knew it. He left them alone, only requiring debriefs as necessary from their team leader.

Harper's computer dinged as the responses came in. Good, everyone would be ready to leave by five this afternoon. They'd drive to Colorado, check into the hotel, sleep a couple of hours and be ready to roll by 5:30 a.m. She shut the laptop and placed it in her bag.

They had to find Jake. He'd disappeared in the shoot-out with the Dupree kingpin and his uncle, Angus Dupree, in Los Angeles, California. Jake's Malinois, Buddy, was injured in the shootout and was slowly recovering. Unfortunately, as smart as he was, he couldn't talk and tell them what happened or where his partner went. It was up to Jake's team to find him and bring him home.

Or bring him to justice.

Riley glanced at his watch. 5:28. On any other morning, it would be too early for the motel to have breakfast ready, but he had requested that pastries and juice be available for the team. Since the two of them were friends, the manager had been happy to oblige and had even added scrambled eggs and bacon to the spread. Special agents milled around the buffet, their expressions solemn, determined and ready for anything. Each one had a highly trained, working dog. He didn't see how they would be able to fly under the radar, but working in the early morning hours while most people still slept or late into the evening would help.

His gaze moved back to the woman who had captured his interest the moment she'd entered the breakfast area. She was one of two females in the group and he assumed she was the one he'd spoken to on the phone yesterday.

Harper Prentiss. He liked her name and thought it suited her. She looked to be in her late twenties. Her dark hair was cut short, but in a style that flattered her face. Her blue eyes had locked with his just moments before and he figured she'd be heading his way after she finished her bagel. He swallowed another sip of coffee. He hadn't expected her to be so pretty.

Special Agent Prentiss took her last bite and walked over. Her German shepherd stayed at her heel and sat when Harper stopped in front of him. "Riley Martelli?"

He stood and held out a hand. "Yes, ma'am."

"You're here early."

"I like to be prepared."

A faint smile curved her lips and small creases formed at the corners of her eyes. "Thank you for reserving the rooms. We needed them by the time we got here."

"Hope you got some rest."

"A few hours, but we're used to going without when we have to." She looked around and he noticed the others clearing their trash. Her gaze landed back on his. "We'll be ready to roll in just a few minutes."

"All right. Your vehicles look like they'll hold up to the rugged terrain."

"They will." She paused. "This is an afterthought, but I don't suppose you got a picture of the guy you saw?"

"Nope, but his face has been plastered all over the news and that was the guy."

"And he shot at you," she murmured.

"He did. And kept shooting even after I identified myself with my arms up and my weapon held over my head. Trust me, he wasn't interested in being helped. The bullets he fired weren't warning shots. They were way too close for comfort. If he could have killed me, he would have. He wanted me dead."

She frowned and exchanged a look of concern with the man on her left. He'd been listening to the exchange and now he nodded and stood. "Guys? Let's do a quick introduction and get going. You all about ready?"

A chorus of yeses answered him. One by one, each team member stepped up to introduce himself and his partner. A tall, green-eyed agent with short blond hair held out a hand. "I'm Leo Gallagher." He gestured to the chocolate Lab at his side. "This is True. Nice to meet you."

Riley nodded. Next was the other pretty woman on the team. "Julianne Martinez and Thunder." The foxhound's ears twitched at his name and he looked up at her. She patted his head and they followed Leo out the door.

"Max West." He was the one who'd stood and told them all to head out. Max was tall with short blond hair and blue eyes. He had a wicked-looking scar on his left cheek and Riley couldn't help but wonder what had happened. "This is Opal."

Riley shook his hand.

Harper leaned over as Max headed out the door. "Max is the boss," she whispered. "Everything goes through him."

"Right."

All of the agents were friendly enough, but the walls were there. Riley didn't take it personally. He'd been in law enforcement once upon a time so he got it. They didn't know anything about him. He could be some thrill seeker who got his kicks by calling in false leads and making everyone jump through hoops. He'd have to prove himself, or at least prove he wasn't mistaken—or lying—about spotting Morrow.

Another tall, muscular man stepped up and held out a hand. "Ian Slade." He scratched the ears of the Belgian Malinois at his side. "This is King. Thanks for your help." He moved on toward the door.

"And last, but not least, I'm Zeke Morrow and this guy here is Cheetah." The Australian shepherd was a gorgeous animal. All of the dogs were.

"Morrow?" Riley asked.

"Jake's my brother."

"Okay, then. I hope we find him fast."

"That makes all of us." Zeke's lips flattened and he walked out the door.

Harper sighed and met Riley's gaze. "He's having a hard time."

"I'm sure," Riley murmured.

"Now that you've met the team, we can get going. We're all ready to find Jake and put this case to bed. Why don't you ride with me? Star here has her own area in the vehicle."

He nodded and followed her out the door to climb into the passenger seat. Star slipped into the back and Harper slid into the driver's seat. Leo and True walked over. "Is there room for us? There's no reason to take all the vehicles."

"Of course. There's room for True in there with Star for this ride. It's not that long a trip according to the GPS." They climbed in and True settled into the designated area with Star. The custom-designed vehicle came with a climate-controlled spot where the dogs had been trained to ride.

The other agents and dogs dispersed themselves between two of the other vehicles. Harper cranked the Chevy and pulled out of the hotel parking lot.

For the next twenty minutes, the three of them made small talk and he learned Harper had graduated from high school and then gone straight into the army. "You didn't want to make a career of it?"

"Nope, just wanted my degree in Criminal Justice. As soon as I had that and the loans paid off I got out and applied to the FBI. I had pretty decent grades in high school, but nothing that stood out so the army made sense for me. My dad took off when I was little and my mom found her comfort at the bottom of a bottle and eventually died from alcohol poisoning." She slid a glance at him. "My options were pretty limited. I just knew I didn't want to be like either of my parents."

"You're pretty open about all that."

She shrugged and smiled. "I've come to grips with it. Every once in a while I'll get asked to do a demonstration at a school and instead of just making it all about the dog, I decided that sharing about my past might help someone make better decisions for their future. Kind of a 'you might have it bad right now at home, but that doesn't have to define your future' thing."

Riley found himself fascinated by Harper after that short snippet. Fascinated and wanting to know more about her. Which made him leery. He'd just met her so why did she hold such attraction for him? "Where'd you grow up?" he asked before he could bite his tongue on the question.

"In San Diego."

"Any brothers and sisters?"

"No, I'm an only child." Her lips twisted. "I was kind of sad about it when I was younger, but all things considered, it was better that way." She shot him a glance. "What about you?"

His heart aching, he cleared his throat. "I had a sister. She was killed two months ago by Van Blackman, the guy I'm chasing."

She snapped her head around to look at him then jerked her gaze back to the road. He heard Leo let out a slow breath in the backseat.

"I'm sorry," Harper said softly.

Leo reached forward and patted him on the shoulder. "I am, too."

"Thanks. She's the reason I'm in Drum Creek. I'm originally from Denver, but I got word that my sister's killer was spotted around this vicinity so headed over the night before last. I thought I saw Van coming out of the general store and followed him. Turned out to be your guy. He looks real similar to Jake Morrow—big build, a few inches over six feet, same hair color..." He shrugged. "Dress them in practically identical clothing and they could almost pass for twins."

"You left out some of the story last night."

He shrugged. "The parts I left out weren't important at the time." He pointed. "Turn here."

She did and followed the dirt path around the lake and to a small area where he directed her to park. "This is where I parked the other day or I would have been able to follow him out of the park. I'm familiar with this area so knew he wasn't going far once he got past that boulder up there. Unfortunately, he drove and was able to get away." The trees swayed in the summer breeze and right now, the area looked like something one would see on a postcard. Harper shut off the engine and the others behind her did the same.

Once they were all out of the vehicles, they let the dogs take care of business then Harper pulled a baseball cap from a plastic bag and held it in front of Star's nose. The dog got a good whiff and Harper replaced the hat in the bag then turned to Riley. "I see what you mean about not searching at night. The terrain is rugged. It

would be pitch-black at night. Even with large lights
and other equipment brought in to help with the search,
there'd be no guarantee you wouldn't miss something."

"Exactly."

"All right, lead the way."

Riley made his way down the trail he'd followed
Morrow on yesterday just before lunch. The others fell
into step behind him, fanning out, letting their animals
sniff and search along the way.

Riley finally reached the area where he'd seen Morrow. "Tell the others to stay back. You don't want to
compromise the scene."

She lifted a brow but turned and did as he asked.
The others stopped.

"Sorry," he said. "I guess you know how to work a
scene."

"We do."

She opened the bag and held the hat out to her shepherd again. After she got a whiff, the dog stepped forward, nose to the ground, then in the air. Star went a
little ways then sat and gave a low bark right next to
the remains of the small campfire. She seemed almost
disappointed that it had been so easy and not a chal-
lenge to her superior skills.

Special Agent Harper Prentiss turned those electric
blue eyes on him. "Well, well, what do you know?" She
turned to the others. "He was here."

"Good," Riley said. "Because I really need that reward money."

Harper blinked in surprise, but didn't pursue the matter. "Okay. Well then, I guess we'll have to see that you
get it. Hopefully, between the seven of us, we'll pin-
point Jake's location before nightfall. And you'll get
your reward money."

Riley grimaced. He'd sounded very greedy but he'd have to explain his reasons for his desperation later. He grasped her arm in a gentle grip. "I don't mind staying with you and helping guide you in this area, but you need to know something."

"What?"

"Your danger level is going to skyrocket if you hang around me."

"Because…?"

"Van Blackman's not only my sister's killer, he's vowed to kill me, too."

TWO

Harper's eyes widened. "Why is he gunning for you?"

"Blackman knows I won't rest until he's either in prison or dead. And he knows I'm the one that's most determined to see that one of those two things happen. He's just as insistent that they won't. He sent me a note saying that if I continued to come after him, he'd see me dead, but if I let him go, he'd disappear and I'd never hear from him again."

"I see. And you can't let him go."

"That's not even on the radar. And not just because he killed my sister and shot my nephew, although that's a huge part of it."

"What's the other part?" she asked.

Riley's jaw clenched and his brown eyes flashed. "He'll do it again if he isn't stopped."

"Yeah." She drew in a breath. "All right, thanks for the warning. I'll talk to Max, but I have a feeling he'll say that we'll take our chances. You know this area and we need someone that can help guide us." She paused. "Why is he hanging around here? Why doesn't he just leave?"

Riley shook his head. "Believe me, I've asked myself that same question. He has a vehicle, but I'm not sure how much money he has. The only thing I can figure is that he knows Denver and the park like the back of his hand. He's comfortable here. He also knows that if he leaves, I'll be right behind him. I think he's tired of running and just wants to see me dead so he can get on with his life."

She nodded slowly. "Makes sense."

"Yeah. It actually makes things easier for me, believe it or not." He turned to walk toward Ian and she frowned while she stared at the bounty hunter's broad back. His blunt statement that he needed the reward money bothered her. Sure, a hundred grand was a lot of money, a fortune for some people. But still…

Disappointment streaked through her. She didn't know why she expected Riley to be different. But she did. What was it that made her want to hold him to a higher standard? She shook her head.

Then wariness flowed through her as another thought surfaced. Could this be some sort of a setup? A distraction from what they needed to be focused on? According to Star, Jake had definitely been in the area—and recently. But what if Riley was working with Morrow? Could he be a part of the Dupree crime family himself? She pulled her phone from the clip on her belt and sent a text to Dylan O'Leary: Background on Riley Martelli needed ASAP. Dylan was the unit's technical guru. Based in Billings, Montana, he kept the unit running smoothly. He could do anything with a computer and find just about any information needed.

She discreetly snapped a picture of Riley while he was talking with Ian then sent that to Dylan as well.

On it.

She smiled at his immediate response and knew she'd have everything she needed before too long. She turned her attention back to Riley. He was looking her way and motioned her over.

Harper clipped her phone back to her belt and went to see what they'd found. Star stayed at her side.

"Where are we?"

Ian nodded to a small area on the ground. "Someone built a fire here and Star says it was Jake."

"He was camping out here." It wasn't a question.

"Maybe, but when I followed him to this spot, he didn't have any kind of camping gear set up," Riley replied. "He simply started a fire."

Harper frowned. "But why?"

"Maybe he was bored and passing the time. Who knows?"

Harper squatted next to the doused fire. "Or he was burning something he didn't want anyone else to see." She picked up a small stick and separated the ashes. Bits of white paper were noticeable. "A note?"

"Again…maybe," Riley responded.

"Some of the pieces aren't completely burned and have writing on them." She glanced up at him. "You might have had him running before he could finish the job." Using the stick, she managed to flip one of the larger pieces of paper. "Potter," she said, then gasped. "Hey, this could have something to do with Penny."

"Who's Penny?" Riley asked.

"The mother of Jake Morrow's child."

"Whoa."

"Yeah." Harper sighed and stood. "We've been looking for her and her son, Kevin, because we figure she can lead us to Jake. He was spotted at her home near Billings just a few days ago, but ran when we got there."

"Wait a minute, if he was at her house—and here at the national park—then he's definitely not a captive of the Dupree family. And if he's not a captive and needs help—because he sure didn't want mine yesterday—then what's he doing? Why isn't he reaching out to you?"

"We've pondered all of that, of course, but we just don't know." She had her thoughts, but kept them to herself for now. "He's not a captive," Harper said. "That much we *do* know." The question was, was he a double agent? As much as she didn't want to believe it, she couldn't help but think he might be working for the Duprees. She just couldn't figure out any other reason for Jake to be acting the way he was.

Even if he was worried about Penny and needed to find her, all he had to do was ask and they'd all join in the search for her. As a team. But he was working alone and seemed to want to keep it that way.

"So, like you said, you stay on her trail and let her lead you to Morrow—or in this case, let Morrow come to you if you catch up with Penny first," Riley mused.

"That's the plan."

"All right," Max said. He motioned for the team to gather round. "Let's get this area processed. We'll do it ourselves and make sure it's done right." They retrieved the necessary supplies from the vehicles, moved in and got busy working on it.

Harper's phone buzzed and she pulled it up to look at the screen.

A message from Dylan. Still working on your request, but this anonymous text just came in and wanted to get it to you straightaway. Forwarding it now.

She waited. The team had been receiving anonymous texts leading them to various places around the country. The person sending the texts seemed to want to help find Jake. However, remaining anonymous was obviously more important to the sender. And they were very skilled at making sure they stayed that way. Even Dylan hadn't been able to track the texts.

The buzz came again. Find Morrow's toddler and find Jake. That simple.

She resisted the urge to snort. Right…that simple. If only. Harper pondered the fact that Penny had run when all the trouble with Jake started and they had figured out that the missing agent was most likely looking for her. Only a month ago, they'd gone to Penny's house and had run into Jake doing the same thing. Only he'd bolted when he saw them. Which made no sense to her.

So if Jake was in the park, that was a good indication that Penny and her child were here as well. But where? And why Colorado? She glanced back at the pile of ashes then texted Dylan again. See if Penny has any connections here in Colorado, please. Let me know ASAP.

Sure thing.

Thanks. So how are the wedding plans progressing? Dylan was madly in love with Zara Fielding. Zara was a former team intern who was currently training at Quantico to become an agent. She was also Dylan's fiancée.

Beautifully. Haven't talked to her in a couple of days so I'm going through withdrawal. If you talk to her, tell her to call me.

Will do.

TTYL.

"Hey guys," she called, "we've gotten another anonymous text." The others gathered around her and she shared the message.

"I'd really like to know who's sending these," Ian muttered.

"Dylan will figure it out eventually. Let's finish up here and see what the lab can come up with."

For the next three hours, they worked the scene, but Morrow was obviously long gone and nothing else turned up that she would consider helpful. Finally, Harper sighed and walked over to Max. "I think we're done here, what do you think?"

"I think you're right." He motioned the others over. When everyone was within hearing distance, he asked, "Anyone else hungry? My breakfast wore off long ago."

Chimes of agreement rolled in and Harper looked at Riley. "Any place in town you can recommend?"

"Of course. The motel opens their restaurant for lunch. Then there's the Drum Creek Café that serves burgers, fries, shakes and salads. Or if you want something a bit fancier, there's Twilights right on the edge of town overlooking a small lake." His eyes held hers. "It's a great place for a date."

Ian had a coughing fit. Max snorted. Harper blinked and heat invaded her cheeks. "I don't need fancy since I don't do dates," she said. "The café works for me. What about you guys?"

They swallowed their mirth and nodded. Harper could almost see Ian biting holes in his tongue to keep from commenting. She shot him a warning glare. He grinned then turned to help gather their gear and together they hiked back to the vehicles. Riley walked with Max, the two of them talking. Max would fill her in later if it was something she needed to know.

But what was that comment about a date? Seriously?

Ian stepped over beside her and nudged her with a small grin. "It's a good place for a date," he drawled. "Wonder if he has anyone in mind?"

She slugged him in the arm and he laughed while he jogged ahead. At least he'd waited until he was out of Riley's earshot before he let loose with the teasing.

While she walked, Harper pushed Ian's ribbing aside and pondered her reaction to the good-looking bounty hunter. She admitted her attraction and questioned her sanity at the same time. She had no business letting herself be drawn to this man since she still had questions about his motives and whether or not he could be working with Jake. She didn't really *think* so, but…

Harper gave herself a mental shake and held the door for Star to hop in. She was *not* attracted to him. There.

Riley settled into the passenger seat with Leo and True behind them again. Once Harper was in the driver's seat and headed down the road, she glanced at her handsome passenger. "Are you going to eat with us?"

"No. I have something I need to take care of."

"What's that?"

He shrugged. "Just…something. Personal stuff."

She raised a brow but kept silent. It was none of her business after all. A short time later, she pulled in front of the café and Riley opened his door. He turned back to her. "Let me know if there's anything else I can do to help."

"I will. Thank you for leading us out there today."

"You're welcome." He glanced at his watch. "I've got to get going." He shifted then rubbed a hand over his chin. "Will you let me know if I can collect the reward money?"

Harper frowned. "Sure. If we find Jake here due to your call, we'll get your money to you."

He flushed. "I know I sound money-hungry. It's not that, it's just my—"

"It's really not my business. I'll be in touch."

Riley nodded then exhaled sharply. "Right. Thanks." He climbed out and shut the door. She watched him walk to his car and sighed. Why had she interrupted him?

Because his *great place for a date* comment still rang in her ears. And because she didn't think she'd mind one bit going on a date with him.

Even though she didn't date. And even though she might want to. No, she didn't. Because she was *not* attracted to him, she reminded herself. She had a job to do. Period.

A rap on her window made her jump. When she turned, Max was waiting for her. She lowered the window. "You coming?" he asked.

She turned to see Riley pull away from the parking lot and made up her mind. "I want to check on something first if that's all right."

He frowned. "What?"

"I'm going to follow him. I want to see where he's going. I'm still not a hundred percent convinced he's not somehow working with Jake."

Max gave a slow nod. "Might not be a bad idea. You want some backup?"

"Not yet. I'll call if I need you."

Riley cruised down I-70 toward Denver and thought about the morning. He was hungry but would get something in the hospital cafeteria. His need to see his nephew ate at him. And he needed an update from the doctors.

But he couldn't help the groan that slipped from his throat. "A great place for a date? Really?" His eyes had locked on Harper's and that was what he'd thought. And that was what had come out of his mouth. He shook his head. He wasn't usually so free with his words. But there was just something about her...

He sighed.

He didn't need to focus on that. Instead, he needed to keep his attention on his nephew and helping him heal. A budding attraction for the pretty FBI agent would only distract him and neither he nor his nephew needed that right now. Priorities, he reminded himself. Priorities.

An hour and forty-five minutes later, he arrived in Denver and pulled into the hospital parking lot. He turned the vehicle off and simply sat there a moment. He wanted to pray, to beg God for guidance, money and healing for his nephew, but...

He wanted to believe that God was who He said He was. But so much had happened in the last year that made him question his faith. Made him wonder if he believed in a God who either wasn't all-powerful or just didn't really care about what was going on with him personally. He pushed out of his truck. No time to ponder the heavy stuff. Asher was waiting for him.

Riley walked through the doors of the hospital. He made his way to Asher's floor and headed for the child's room. As he passed the nursing station, the men and women greeted him. "Glad to see you back. Asher's been asking for you. His teacher is here, too."

"Thanks."

He opened the door and found his mother sitting in

the chair she'd occupied since his sister's death and Asher's admittance into the hospital. Her needles clicked softly and a ball of yarn spilled from the bag next to her chair. A dark haired, dark-eyed woman sat on the edge of Asher's bed. The little guy held a card in his hand and others spilled over his lap and the smile on his face was worth more than gold.

"Hi, I didn't realize he had company," Riley said as he leaned over and kissed the top of his mother's head.

"I'm Beth Smith," the woman said. "I was Asher's first grade teacher last year. I heard about what happened and about two weeks ago rounded up his classmates and friends. We had a card-making party for Asher and I was very excited to be able to bring them to him today."

Riley shook her hand. "That's very kind."

"I miss them, Uncle Riley."

He smoothed the child's hair from his forehead. "I know you do, buddy. Maybe some of them can come see you soon since you're feeling better."

"That would be awesome."

Riley smiled at the enthusiasm.

"Can I have a puppy, too?"

"A puppy?"

Asher turned those thick-lashed blue eyes on him. "I really think I need a puppy. It can keep me company and make me feel like laughing again."

Mrs. Smith gasped and Riley saw tears in her eyes before she looked away.

His heart clenched and he found it hard to draw in breath around the grief that filled him. He cleared his throat. "We'll have to see. I'm not making any promises, but we'll talk about it when you get out of the hospital. Deal?"

"Deal."

And Riley was going to do whatever it took to make sure Asher felt like laughing again.

"Hey, you know what?" he said.

"What?"

"I met someone who has a dog. You want me to ask her to bring it up here?"

Asher's eyes widened. "Today?"

"Probably not today, but maybe soon?"

"Yes, please, Uncle Riley. That would be double awesome!"

"Okay, then."

"What kind of dog?" he asked.

"She's a police dog. She helps sniff out the bad guys."

"Wow," Asher breathed.

"A police dog?" Mrs. Smith asked.

Riley nodded. "Yes."

"I have a group of summer campers who are thinking about going into law enforcement. Their favorite topic has been K-9s and their work with the different areas of law enforcement."

"Where are you doing the camp?"

"Out at the national park. We're in the part where they have cabins and decent restroom facilities."

"Roughing it, huh?"

She laughed. "Not too bad."

"I wish I could go to camp," Asher said softly.

Riley squeezed the boy's shoulder. "Let's aim for next summer, okay?"

Asher nodded. "Where I can go and learn about being a police officer so I can catch the bad guys?"

"Sure."

Mrs. Smith kissed Asher's cheek and rose. "Well, I suppose I need to say my goodbyes." She gathered her purse and walked toward the door. "I only managed to slip away from the camp for a short time and need to get back. Asher, I'll check back in on you soon."

Asher waved. "Bye, Mrs. Smith. Thank you for coming to see me."

"You're welcome, sweetheart." She smiled and Asher's lids drooped. The visit had tired him out. Riley said one more goodbye to Mrs. Smith then sat with Asher and held him until he dozed off. It didn't take long. He slid off the bed and turned to his mother who still worked with the needle and yarn. "Another blanket?"

"Yes." She looked up and gave him a weary smile. "It keeps me busy and helps me think. And besides, they're selling pretty well at the little consignment store Sheila runs. She keeps asking for more."

Sheila, his mother's best friend, worked at a consignment store in downtown Denver. She'd encouraged his mother to let her sell some of her items and to everyone's surprise, it had turned into a full-time job keeping up with the demand.

"Now that we're alone, is there any change? Any updates?" His gaze went back to Asher, who was dwarfed by the large bed. The boy appeared to be sleeping comfortably.

His mother laid her knitting aside and rubbed her eyes. "No, son, you know nothing's going to change without the surgery. The doctor said he's strong enough for it now—he's recovered nicely from the bullet in his shoulder and now they just need to get in and get the other one out."

He nodded. Of course he knew that, but each day that went by, he hoped. Hoped his nephew's spine would heal on its own, that he would sit up in the bed, whole and happy again. Riley vaguely wondered how long it took for hope to finally dry up. "I wish Dad was here."

Tears sprang to his mother's eyes and Riley wished he'd kept his mouth shut. His father had passed away two years ago after a short battle with brain cancer.

She swiped a stray tear. "I do, too, son. Are you any closer to catching Van?" she asked.

He rubbed his eyes. "Yes. I think so. I have a good idea where to look for him now." He fell silent for a moment. "That was nice of Mrs. Smith to drop by."

"Very nice. Asher looked forward to it all morning."

Riley reached for her hand and held it, noticing the texture of her still-smooth skin, feeling the warmth of her fingers. A hand that had wiped his tears and cleaned his little boy knees and elbows, had cradled him in her arms when his prom date had stood him up. He was a man who still wanted—if not needed—his mother and her comfort. He wondered if he should be ashamed to admit that. "How are you feeling? Are you taking your medicine?"

"I am." She had a heart condition that required daily medication. One reason she felt she couldn't handle full custody of Asher and why Riley had agreed to be the one to take him should anything happen to his sister. He'd never thought he would be in the position he now found himself. He swallowed and stepped next to the child to run a hand over Asher's sweet face. The boy opened his eyes.

And smiled. "You're still here."

Riley's heart tripped over itself at the love and trust reflected there. He leaned closer and pressed a kiss to Asher's forehead. "Sure I am. How are you doing, Champ?"

"I want to go outside and play."

Riley's throat tightened on the tears that wanted to flow on behalf of the little boy he loved so much. "Soon, Asher. I sure hope you can do that soon."

"Me, too."

"Maybe we can get a wheelchair and roll you outside in a little while."

"Okay." Asher closed his eyes again then opened them when the door opened and the doctor walked in. The boy reached for Riley's hand and held on but there was no fear in his blue eyes. For that Riley was grateful. He'd promised Asher that everyone in the hospital was there to help him walk again and Asher believed him. For now.

The doctor started to speak and Riley fingered one of the tubes running out of the little guy's body. Fresh fury rocked him. He drew in a deep breath. *God, where are You? Where were You? Why didn't You protect them?*

THREE

Harper frowned as she waited on Riley to come back out of the room he'd entered.

They were on the pediatric floor and Harper would admit, once she realized he was heading for the hospital, she'd thought he might be meeting a woman who worked there. A girlfriend nurse or doctor. Then she wondered why that was her first thought. She finally admitted it was because she wanted to know if there was someone special in his life. She grimaced. Why did it matter? It was not like she wanted him to act on his subtle hint about going to the restaurant on a date. Not with her, anyway. Did she?

She did.

And she didn't.

She loved her job and knew she was good at it, but deep down, in a place she would only admit to herself, she wanted more. But she was afraid she just wasn't meant to have a family of her own. And right now wasn't the time to think about it. Conflicted, she pushed the thoughts away and focused on the reason she was there.

Once they'd arrived on the floor, the fact that everyone greeted Riley warmly seemed to support the theory that he was a regular visitor. But he hadn't spoken to any of the women there other than to offer a brief wave and a smile. He'd gone into one of the rooms followed by the doctor shortly thereafter. Her curiosity ramped up into high gear.

But one thing was settled. He definitely wasn't meeting Jake Morrow. So who? The woman who'd walked out wiping tears from her cheeks? She definitely looked like someone who might be Riley's type. Pretty, with a sweet smile she'd shot at the nursing station as she'd passed by.

Harper stayed where she could see the door and waited. Ten minutes later, her patience paid off. The doctor stepped out and she waited for him to walk her way. "Excuse me?"

He stopped. "Yes?" He looked to be in his midforties and was a good-looking guy with kind green eyes.

Harper flashed her badge. "I'm investigating a case. Do you know Riley Martelli?"

"Of course. He's Asher's uncle. A better guy you'll never meet."

The glowing endorsement eased her nerves a bit. "That's good to hear. And your patient is Asher?"

The kind eyes hardened. "Yes."

"Can you tell me what happened to him?"

"No. HIPAA laws and all that." Harper frowned and the doc lifted a brow. "But it was all over the news. You didn't see it?"

"I'm not from around here. Can you fill me in?"

He hesitated and shrugged. "I can tell you what was on the news. Asher caught two bullets when a stalker went after his mother."

Harper gasped. "That's horrible." Even though she'd

seen a lot of awful in her line of work, she would never become numb to murder.

He nodded. "Charlotte, Asher's mother, died almost instantly with a bullet that went through her heart. Asher pulled through. One of the bullets is lodged very near his spine and he needs some pretty tricky surgery to remove it. The one that went through his shoulder did some damage, but nothing major."

"But he'll be all right?"

"He's already pretty well recovered from that one. Until we can get the bullet from his back, though, he won't be able to walk. And yes, all of that was on the news—well, on television in a press conference, I guess you would say. After Charlotte was killed, her mother went on television and told the story. She then begged people to be on the lookout for Van Blackman and to call the police if he was spotted."

"Did it help? Her plea?"

The doctor shrugged. "They got some leads but nothing that panned out." His nostrils flared. "And so he's walking around a free man while that little boy now has no mother and can't get out of that bed." His eyes flashed in fury at the injustice and Harper tried to process the words and push aside her shock.

"When is he supposed to have the surgery?" she asked.

"We've been waiting for him to heal enough to handle it. When he first got here, we didn't think he was going to make it, but he's pulled through like a champ." He smiled proudly. "In fact, that's his new nickname around here. Champ. We're still waiting to see when we can schedule the surgery."

"Doctor? Special Agent Prentiss?"

She froze and grimaced. Busted. She turned to find Riley staring at her. "I told you to call me Harper."

He raised a brow. "Harper. What are you doing here?"

She opened her mouth then shut it. What could she say?

His hands went to his hips and he frowned. "Did you follow me?"

"Yes."

"But…why?"

Harper glanced at the doctor who looked decidedly uncomfortable. She offered him a small smile. "Thank you."

"Sure." He escaped quickly.

Harper looked back at the glowering Riley. "I don't blame you for being mad. I just had to make sure you weren't meeting with Jake Morrow."

"Meeting with Ja—" He ran a hand through his red-dish blond hair. "Why would I be meeting with the man who shot at me?"

He was either truly confused or an Oscar worthy performer. "I don't want to take you away from your nephew, but is there somewhere we can go to talk? When you're finished?" Her phone buzzed but she ignored it for the moment.

He stared at her a moment longer then shrugged. "Let me tell my mother and Asher what I'm doing. We can go down to the cafeteria and get a sandwich. I'm starving."

"Sure."

He started to walk away then turned back. "Hey, do you have Star with you?"

"Yes. She's in the car. Why?" She'd wanted to remain inconspicuous. Walking in with Star would have made her stand out like a sore thumb. The dog was fine in the temperature-controlled area of the vehicle.

"I'll tell you in a minute."

He was gone all of thirty seconds before he returned. "I was going to ask you to bring Star up to see Asher, but he's sleeping deeply. I don't want to disturb him."

"I'm happy to bring Star to see him. Just let me know when." They walked to the elevator. "So the doctor told me a little bit about what happened. He said Asher is your nephew."

"Yes."

"And Van Blackman, the man you mentioned, killed your sister. He shot your nephew, too." The doctor had given her the information, but she wanted to hear it from Riley. Guilt pierced her. She remembered him trying to tell her why he wanted the reward money and she'd cut him off.

"Yes. He stalked her for months before he finally snapped and opened fire on them in the grocery store parking lot. She died and I now have custody of Asher."

"I'm so sorry."

He nodded and a muscle ticked in his jaw. "I am, too."

Harper bit her lip. "Asher's why you need the money, isn't he?"

"Yeah. The medical bills are piling up. The insurance plan my sister had wasn't a very good one and Asher needs surgery. Extensive, expensive surgery. We've had a few people donate to a fund that was set up, but that money's running out and it's getting harder and harder to pay the bills."

Her heart went out to him. How awful.

Harper's phone rang again and this time she pulled it from the clip on her belt. "Excuse me. Why don't you get in line and get your food? Go ahead and eat if I'm not back in time."

"You want anything? You didn't have time to eat if you followed me here."

"Get me whatever you're having. I'm not picky."

"Chicken salad?"

"Sure, and don't wait on me to eat. I never know how long I'll be when I get on the phone with Dylan." She hit the button to answer the phone before it could go to voice mail. "Prentiss here."

"Harper, this is Dylan."

"What do you have?"

"Your guy, Riley Martelli, is clean. I couldn't come up with anything that connected him with Jake Morrow or anyone else that would throw up red flags. He was actually a cop for several years before he became a bounty hunter."

"What? He never mentioned that." She cut her eyes to him as he stood at the counter placing his order. Yeah, she could see him in some form of law enforcement. He had that aura about him.

"Yep. A decorated officer, too."

"Why'd he quit?"

"I don't know. There's nothing in his record to indicate what made him change careers. Whatever the reason, he's still catching the bad guys and putting them away. I did find out that his sister was murdered—"

"I know that part. He told me."

"He told you she had a stalker? And that he has sole custody of his nephew?"

"Yes."

"All right, then. Let's move to Penny."

"What about her?"

"Nothing. Meaning I couldn't find anything that might connect her to Colorado. No relatives, no job, no credit card action."

Harper pressed her thumb to her forehead where the beginning of a headache gathered. "Which might be exactly why she came here. For the very fact there was nothing in her past or present to lead anyone to think she'd run here."

"True. What else do you need?"

"Nothing. I needed what you just gave me." The assurance that Riley was on the up and up being the most important piece of intel. She was rather surprised at the intense relief that flowed through her.

"Great. Then I've got one more thing for you."

"I'm ready."

"I just got off the phone with Max. We've got the evidence in house and will be going through it shortly."

"Keep me updated."

"Of course."

"Thanks, Dylan."

She hung up. The fact that the evidence was already back at headquarters amazed her although it really shouldn't. Their unit's resources by far surpassed anyone else's. By helicopter, the flight time was probably slightly over an hour. Which meant they should have more information about the evidence by dinnertime.

In the meantime, assuming she had Max's okay, she needed to see how Riley felt about striking a deal with the FBI.

FOUR

Riley finished off his sandwich and sweet tea then leaned back to watch Harper get started on hers. She'd settled into her chair and eyed his empty plate. "Guess you were hungry?"

"I know you told me not to wait, but I still feel guilty for finishing before you even sat down. Guess I was starved."

"I'm glad you went ahead and ate."

He munched an apple while he waited for her to eat then say whatever was on her mind. Halfway through her sandwich, she finally looked up. "Sorry, looks like I was hungry, too."

He fell silent, thinking. She got up to refill her drink and when she came back he caught her eye. "Why would you think I was working with Morrow?" he asked.

She sighed. "You were so focused on the money." A shrug. "I don't know. I thought maybe you were helping him somehow."

"What do you think now?"

"I think you need the money for Asher. I'm sorry I was so suspicious and so quick to judge. I guess I so rarely come across someone who isn't willing to do just

about anything for money that I can't recognize someone who doesn't have dollar signs in his eyes."

"The dollar signs are there, just not for personal gain.
Unless seeing my nephew walk again falls into that category." His eyes narrowed on her. "I'm guessing my
background check came back clean?"

She huffed out a low laugh. "Yes, it did. It also revealed something interesting about you."

"That I was a cop?"

"Are you a mind reader, too?"

He shook his head with a small smile. "No, it's just
common sense—and it's not a secret. A simple background check would reveal it."

It was. "So, why the career change?"

He sighed and shrugged. "For several reasons. There
wasn't any dramatic thing that happened. No specific
incident that compelled me to turn in my resignation,
I just…got tired."

"Of?"

"Recycling the criminals."

"Oh."

"I would arrest someone and then see them back on
the street a week later. I was like, what's the point? So
I started thinking about what I could do that would really make a real difference."

"But you *were* making a difference. Just the very na-
ture of your presence, in your uniform, would be a de-
terrent to some people thinking of committing a crime."

He nodded. "I know. I agree. Uniformed officers
are important and I'm not knocking them or what they
do. I'm just saying for me, personally, I wanted to do
something a little different. And being a bounty hunter
seemed to fit the bill."

She took another bite of the sandwich then ate a handful of chips. "Do you miss it?"

"I miss certain aspects of it. You know how it is. When you're a cop, you're a part of a team. A whole culture that you can only be a part of if you're wearing the badge. You know what I mean?"

"Yes, I do," she murmured.

"I miss that connection with the others. Bounty hunting can be a lonely profession."

"You think you'll ever go back?"

Riley paused then nodded. "Maybe. One day." He stood. "But right now I've got to focus on finding my sister's killer. I hope you find Morrow."

She held up a hand. "Wait, don't leave yet. Sit back down, please?"

Curious, he sank back into the chair. "What is it?"

"Do you think we could help each other?"

He lifted a brow. "What do you have in mind?"

"Morrow was last seen by you. No more tips have come in since yours. You know those woods and the mountains out there, don't you?"

He gave a slow nod. "I've been going camping there since I could walk. First with my dad and uncles then with friends. Certain areas of it anyway. Why?"

"I have a feeling Jake's hiding out there."

"Well, I know for a fact Blackman is out here somewhere. I had a tip that he'd been spotted in Drum Creek. I've made a lot of friends in Drum Creek over the years. The owner of the general store, Paul Nelson, and my dad were good friends. Paul called me yesterday and said he'd seen Blackman in the store and he'd bought camping supplies. Said he was going to be hanging around until his business was finished."

"What business?"

"Good question. I haven't really figured that out yet, but…" He shrugged. "Anyway, the national park is the only place around Drum Creek that one would need camping supplies so I'm going to search every last acre if that's what it takes."

Harper frowned. "That could take a long time."

He sighed. "The truth is, there are so many places to hide it would be like looking for a needle in a haystack. Same thing with your guy. It's going to take time."

"I realize that, but we have to do something. Sitting around waiting on leads to come in isn't an option. Not when we know there's a good possibility Jake is hiding nearby." She rubbed her forehead. "My question is why he's sticking around here when he knows he's been spotted. What is his purpose in staying unless he doesn't think he needs to leave? Or doesn't care that he's been seen?"

"He cared enough to shoot at me."

"What if he didn't believe you were who you said you were? What if he thought you were working with the men who kidnapped him?"

"I suppose that's a possibility," he conceded.

"The anonymous person sending the texts seemed to think Jake was looking for Penny."

He quirked a brow. "Is Penny here in Colorado?"

"Not that we know of. What we do know is that Jake's not going to come to us, so we're just going to have to go find him. If you'll help us comb that area and lead us to where he might find a hiding place, I'll do my best to make all of our resources available to you to help find your sister's killer. I'll have to have my boss okay that, of course, but I don't see why he wouldn't."

He studied her then looked away for a brief moment while he considered the idea. *All of her resources at his disposal.* That would be a huge help. He nodded and captured her gaze with his. "All right," he said and held out his hand. "If your boss agrees, I'm willing to go with that."

She shook his hand and the feel of her soft fingers within his grasp made him wonder if his heart would survive the deal.

Riley looked up from Harper's pretty blue eyes. If he stared into them for too long, she muddled his thoughts.

His gaze landed on a figure near the door and he froze for half a second then leaped to his feet.

Harper jerked. "What is it?"

"Van Blackman." He bolted from the table and the man spun on his heels to dart out the door.

He heard Harper give chase as well. "Blackman, stop!"

"Federal agent," Harper called. "Stop now!"

Blackman kept going. Riley pounded after him. What was he doing at the hospital? Had he come to do something to Asher? To finish him off? Fury nearly blinded him and threatened to steal his common sense and self-control. Riley didn't slow, but Blackman was fast. Van pushed past people in the hospital, grabbed one man and shoved him in front of Riley. Riley caught the elderly man on a stumble. "Sorry, sir. Are you all right?"

"I think so."

Riley made sure the gentleman had his balance, losing precious seconds of the chase while Blackman lunged out of the hospital exit.

Harper raced past him. Riley fell in behind her and together they dashed out into the hot Colorado sun and ran down the sidewalk. He rounded the corner just in time to see Van jump into a car and speed off.

"No!" Riley skidded to a stop and tried to see the license plate, but Blackman was already turning the corner. "No," he rasped as he caught his breath.

Harper had run farther than he, only now she was walking back toward him, speaking into her phone. "…green Ford. Four doors, older model. Heading south on Platte Street. Right." She stopped in front of him. "Are you okay?"

"Just mad he got away again. I can't believe he showed up here. He's following me. He's doing his best to push my buttons." He drew in a deep breath. "I refuse to let him do that."

"Good. Let's get Blackman's picture to hospital security and ask them to keep an eye out for him. Especially when you're in the building."

"That's a good idea." Riley clenched his fingers into fists. "He waited until I saw him. Stood there and simply waited for me to look up. He wanted me to know he was there, watching."

"He's definitely taunting you if that's the case."

"It's the case." Riley rubbed a hand over his face and pictured him catching Van and pummeling him into oblivion. No, death would be too easy for the man. He wanted him in prison for the rest of his life where Riley would make sure he constantly reminded the man why he was there. He planned to make prison worse than death for Blackman.

An uncomfortable niggle at his conscience reminded him that it wasn't his place to extract revenge for his sister's murder. It was just his job to bring the man in.

Right. He had a feeling he was going to have to keep telling himself that over and over before he had Blackman in custody.

* * *

Harper sat on the bed in her hotel room back in Drum Creek and opened the laptop she was never without. She'd shed her gear and flexed her shoulders. The vest weighed quite a bit, but she refused to go without it when on duty. And right now, she wondered if she should even take it off at all.

Jake Morrow was an outlier. She had no idea what he might or might not do. If he would shoot at a man who'd clearly identified himself as trying to help him, he might decide he didn't want her—or the team's—help, either.

Her ankle knife and service weapon lay on top of the vest within easy reach should she need them.

Star lounged at the foot of the bed, her head on her paws, eyes following Harper's every move. Harper scratched her faithful partner's ears then logged in to the secure software that she had access to. She pulled up the profile of the man she'd been looking for. His blue eyes stared back at her and she desperately searched her memory for even just one good thing to remember about him. But the mental search turned up nothing. As it did every time.

She sighed and shut the laptop. Her father was gone from her life. He'd chosen to leave when she was four. Not only leave, but he'd apparently never looked back. So why did she care about where he was, what he was doing—and if he had other children? She'd made something of her life without his help and was proud of that fact.

Still, when she was honest with herself, she would admit the rejection hurt. And that made it hard to picture herself married with children. And while she was being honest, she would also admit it was what she wanted. A husband to love and who loved her. A house full of children and a couple of dogs.

She had Star, of course, and loved the animal, but she wanted a puppy, maybe even several puppies. She smiled at the image then frowned. There was no need to go down that emotional road. It was a dream that had very little chance of coming true. After all, where would she find someone who understood her profession? And not only understood it, but would be willing to put up with it?

Riley's face came to the forefront of her mind and she grimaced. She didn't need to think about Riley. Because if she did, she'd have to admit to the attraction she knew was there. Okay, she could admit it.

But the timing was all wrong. Pursuing a romance at this moment was not an option. Her goal, first and foremost, was to find Jake Morrow.

Unfortunately, her mind wanted to investigate the attraction she'd just acknowledged.

Fine. She leaned back and closed her eyes, picturing the bounty hunter with the chocolate-colored eyes that could draw her in and make her want to stay.

Riley Martelli. How would she describe him?

He was a fighter, a survivor. She liked that about him. After all he'd been through with his nephew in the hospital and needing surgery, and his sister killed by a stalker, he pushed through his grief. Or allowed the grief to push *him*?

Maybe.

He was good-looking in a rugged sort of way, intelligent, loyal, compassionate. And loved fiercely and fully. And he'd lost greatly.

Compared to him, she didn't think she'd had it quite so bad. Her father may have left her, but at least he was still alive somewhere. *God, I'm struggling. Struggling with You, and with this case. I need Your help, and I almost don't even want to ask for it because part of me is simply afraid You're not listening.* But she knew better than that. God was there. He was real and He cared about what she was going through. She had to believe that no matter what.

She sighed and let her mind jump to Jake Morrow.

She'd never liked him all that much even though she'd admired his skills as an agent. He'd definitely been one of the best agents she'd worked with. But as a person, a man? Not so much.

One of her earlier encounters popped to the forefront of her mind. He'd pressed her to go out with him and when she'd refused, he'd continued to push until she'd told him in no uncertain terms that she wasn't interested. He'd laughed and backed off, hands held as though she were aiming a weapon at him. "Chill, Harper. Man, you're uptight, aren't you? Loosen up and live a little." His words had been light, but the look in his eye had stayed with her and she'd slept with her gun nearby for several weeks after that incident. But he'd left her alone, seemed to forget all about it, and they'd worked well together in spite of the incident.

She sent a group text to the team. Have any of you guys heard from Zara? I think Dylan's missing her. He said something about going through withdrawals earlier today.

Nope.

Nada.

Negative.

Each response made her frown, but Zara was in training at Quantico. The rigorous schedule didn't leave much room for anything else.

But surely she could send a text to her fiancé.

Harper sent the woman a text of her own. Call Dylan. He misses you.

Her eyes grew heavy and she drifted.

Until she heard something at her door. The knob jiggled. Her adrenaline immediately spiked and she sat up. Star was already on the floor facing the door. She gave a low woof. Harper put a hand on the animal's neck. "Stay," she whispered. Star didn't move. Harper glanced at the bedside clock. She'd been asleep most of the night still dressed in yesterday's clothes. Now it was close to six in the morning.

And someone was lurking outside her door.

She slipped to the window and moved the curtain enough so she could see outside.

Nothing was visible in her line of sight. She wrapped her fingers tighter around the butt of her weapon and stood to the side of the door.

Her phone buzzed on the nightstand and she jerked, her heart pounding in her chest.

Star lunged at the door and barked. Harper spun back to pay attention. Someone was out there. But who? She strode to the end table, grabbed her phone, then sent both Ian and Riley a group text: Someone's at my door. Can you see who it is?

Looking now, came Riley's response.

Don't see anything, Ian's text read. Coming out of my room now.

Got my door open and don't see anything, Riley said.

Harper snapped Star's leash on her collar and,

using the hem of her shirt, slowly opened the door. She pointed to the knob. "Find, girl." The German shepherd sniffed the area Harper indicated then bolted from the room. Harper kept a tight grip on the leash, stepped out and shut the door behind her.

Ian and Riley were already there.

"Nothing here," Ian said. He held the leash to King, the energetic Malinois. The dog was ready to work.

Star pulled at the leash, too. "Star says differently." She and Ian let the dogs have their lead. Harper, with Ian right beside her, followed the animals along the edge of the building, passing room after room. The men trailed behind her and she knew they had her back.

Star came to the end of the building and rounded the corner. Harper went more cautiously, gripping the leash with her left hand and her weapon with her right. She glanced at Ian and he nodded. Star whined and headed for the bushes across the parking lot. King joined her. A man shot out from behind them.

"Federal agent! Stop!"

Ian gave the same command.

The fleeing figure, dressed in jeans and a short-sleeved black shirt, ignored them both and darted toward a dark pickup truck parked at the edge of the hotel asphalt lot. Star and King gave chase, but he threw himself behind the wheel and the engine roared to life.

Riley raced past her and reached for the passenger side door handle. The truck swerved, throwing him sideways. He lost his grip, hit the ground with a grunt and rolled. Ian flew past, chasing the truck.

"Riley!" Harper hurried to him. He drew himself up on all fours and shook his head. "Are you all right?" she gasped.

"Yes. I'm fine." He got to his feet and winced.

"Did you get the plate?" Harper asked.

"I got part of it, but I don't need it."

Ian jogged over to them. "I got it." He pulled his phone from the clip on his belt and tapped a message. "Sent it to Dylan. We'll know something soon enough."

"I know who it is," Riley said. He bolted for his truck. Harper ran after him.

"Who is it?"

"Van Blackman." He yanked open the door and threw himself into the driver's seat.

Harper ran around to the other side and jumped into the passenger seat. Star leaped up and settled herself in the middle as Riley was backing out of the parking spot.

"How do you know it was Blackman?" she asked. "It looked like Jake to me."

"And I'm telling you, they look very similar." He pulled out of the parking lot with a squeal of rubber on asphalt. Harper looked back to see two black SUVs in pursuit as well. Her teammates weren't convinced it wasn't Jake, either.

"Open the glove box and pull out the picture there."

She did. A man and a woman, who had to be his sister, and a young boy about four years old grinned at her.

"See the guy on the left holding Asher?"

"Oh. Yeah. Wow, there really is a resemblance."

"Exactly."

"So how do you know the guy in the truck is Blackman and not Morrow?" she asked.

"I saw his eyes. Their eyes are different colors. Van's are green. The guy I spotted in the park had blue eyes. Very blue eyes."

"That sounds like Jake for sure." She'd been the recipient of his blue-eyed laser stare more than she cared to remember.

He drove with precision, knuckles white on the wheel, eyes scanning.

"Do you see him?" she asked.

"No. I'm just going in the direction he went." Riley slapped the wheel. "I wasn't fast enough."

"Keep driving and looking. We need a chopper," she muttered. "Should have brought one in and held on to it for times like this." She made a mental note to suggest it to Max when they got back.

Riley drove another few miles then sighed. A sound filled with defeat. "I guess he's gone."

"Looks like it. I'm sorry." Her heart broke for him. He was working so hard to find his sister's killer and each time it looked like he might succeed, he got slapped down. He made a three-point turn and headed back to the motel. Harper noted that the others passed them. "They're going to keep searching."

"Good, I hope they find him."

"He'll show up again when he's ready."

He fell silent and Harper let him have the moments with his thoughts. When he pulled back into the parking lot of the motel, they climbed out of his truck and Ian jogged over to them. "Julianne and Zeke are still chasing him. They'll be in touch if they find him."

Harper nodded and Ian looked at Riley. "You're positive that it was Blackman and not Morrow?"

Riley shot him a dark look. "I'm sure. He's following us…me."

"But why would he try to get in my room?" Harper asked.

Ian tucked his weapon away. "Might have just gotten the wrong room. After all, you guys are right next to each other."

"Maybe."

Ian shrugged. "Or he thought you had something that he needed."

"Like what?"

"I don't know but hopefully we'll find out once we catch up with him again," Riley said. His gaze was locked on the direction in which the man had fled. "He's headed toward the park," he murmured.

"Could be," Harper said.

"He's hiding out there."

"Along with Jake Morrow."

Riley nodded. "We'll find them."

She walked back to her room to shut the door and noticed a piece of paper just inside on the floor. A piece of tape held it faceup. She started to pick it up and stopped. She walked over and grabbed a pair of gloves from her bag and slid them on. Then she went back to the piece of paper and lifted it up. *Martelli is a walking dead man. Stay away from him if you don't want to end up like his sister.*

Her heart thudded.

"What is it?" Riley asked from behind her.

She held it up and let him read it. "Looks like you were right," she said. "It was Blackman. It also looks like he doesn't like us hanging out together." She held the letter by the edge. "Threatening a federal agent. Wow, this guy wants his grave dug deeper than six feet, doesn't he?"

Riley's jaw tightened and for a moment she thought she heard his molars grinding. He took a deep breath. "Well, that explains why he was at your door." He gave her a tight smile. "But this is rather encouraging in a weird sort of way."

"What do you mean?"

"He thinks we're after him." She lifted a brow and he

went on. "He doesn't know you're really here because of Jake Morrow," he explained. "Blackman thinks you're here for him." He gave a low laugh. "Oh, this is perfect. He thinks we're working together to catch him—and it worries him. I like that." His smile slipped into a frown as he stared at the note. "I don't like this, though."

She nodded. "Sounds reasonable."

He planted his hands on his hips and shook his head. "This was stupid on his part. Hopefully stupid will eventually trip him up."

"It usually does. We just need to give him a little time to get careless."

"Yes. So what are you going to do with the note?"

"Send it to Dylan." She smiled. "He's one of ours back in Billings and can find out just about anything and everything, but even I don't think he'll get anything off of this. Then again, you never know. There's a piece of tape that was probably supposed to hold it on the door. Maybe there'll be a print on that." She walked into her room while Riley waited in the open door. From her black carry-on, she pulled an evidence bag and slipped the note inside. Once sealed, she placed it on the desk.

Her phone buzzed and she glanced at the screen. "It's Dylan." She lifted the device to her ear. "What are you doing there so late?"

"You know me. I never sleep until my work is done." He kept his voice light, but she heard something beneath. "What do you have for me?"

"I've got something off of those scraps of paper you sent in. Well, the lab got something. I volunteered to call and fill you in."

"Great. What is it?"

"The last name Potter was obvious."

"Right. We're going on the assumption it's Penny."

"Your assumption would be correct. Looks like the rest of it is an address. I ran what I could make out through the system and it came back with several possibilities, but there was one that caught my attention. It's an address that belongs to an old ski chalet that's not too far from Drum Creek."

"Give me the address."

He did and she typed it into her phone. "Thanks, we'll head that way as soon as I round up the team."

"Hope it pans out."

"Me, too."

"I got Ian's license plate number. Should have something on that in the next little while."

"Excellent. Even though we know who was driving, maybe the plate will lead us to him. I'm also sending you a note that I found in my room." She filled him in on their early morning adventure. "See if the lab can pull any prints if you don't mind."

"Of course. I'll be looking for it."

"And I'll be looking forward to hearing from you." She hesitated. "Hey...did Zara contact you?"

"Nope. But I'm sure she's fine. I hope anyway."

There it was again. That odd note in his voice she'd heard when she first answered.

"What does that mean? You hope?"

He sighed. "Just that I still haven't heard from her. I'm getting a little worried."

"Not calling or being in contact doesn't sound like her."

"It's not."

"Let me know if you don't hear something soon and I'll see what I can find out," she said.

"Great. I'll give her a couple of more days. I know things are pretty intense at Quantico right now."

"She'll call or text when she can."

"I know. Thanks, Harper."

"Anytime." She hung up and sent a group text to the others, asking them to gather in the lobby of the hotel in fifteen minutes.

Once they'd assembled, Max gave her a nod and Harper brought everyone up to date on the incident in the parking lot. She also gave them the address Dylan had provided. Max motioned for her to continue taking the lead. "We think Penny Potter could be staying there. If she is, then Jake's probably not far behind. Evidence and that anonymous text lends support to that theory. He could even be with her right now."

Julianne leaned forward. "Come on, Max, tell us what you think about Jake. You really think he'd turn traitor?"

Max rubbed his eyes. "We've talked about this, discussed it until we're blue in the face and I still don't know the answer. I'm in contact on a daily basis with the director and he's as concerned as we are about Jake. Unfortunately, at the present time, we just don't know what's going on with him." He exhaled roughly. "I don't want to believe the worst, but the fact that he shot at Riley who wanted to help him doesn't bode well in his favor."

No, it doesn't, Harper thought.

Their team captain cleared his throat. "Plus, Jake's been seen all over the country so we know he's not in Dupree's clutches, and yet he hasn't reported in to let anyone know he's safe. He also seems to be tracking Penny. I'm going to assume it's because she has his child—which I can understand, but to not call us for help? Something definitely isn't adding up. It goes against everything I want to believe, but it's certainly possible that Jake is a double agent. For now," he said slowly, "I think we need to treat Jake like he's acting— a criminal on the run."

Frowns appeared on the agents' faces and Max held up a hand before the protests could start. "I don't like it, either, but I'm telling you, be careful if he contacts you. Don't trust him. Until he can explain his actions, he's an agent gone bad and wanted by the FBI. But that's classified. The press will keep airing the cover story we've released to them. In the meantime, keep these suspicions under your hat."

Silence fell over the group and Harper's emotions stepped onto the roller coaster. As hard as it was to admit, she'd already come to the conclusion that Jake was a bad agent herself. "We need a chopper out here, Max. That's a lot of territory to cover and I think we need air support that can be at our fingertips in a moment's notice."

He nodded. "I've already thought of that. One is on standby about ten minutes away at an old private airstrip."

"Good. The next thing on our list should be finding Penny—and fast," she said. "For her sake."

The others nodded. She saw Riley rub a hand across his eyes.

Harper drew in a breath and let it out slowly. "Which means our next stop is the address I just gave you. Dylan got the results from the lab and sent me the address from the charred piece of paper. I looked it up on Google Maps—it's an old ski chalet not too far from here. We need to be smart and careful, there's a child involved here. Everyone ready?"

"Ready."

"All in."

"Let's find her."

Harper nodded. "Follow me."

FIVE

Riley waited until the others filed out with their dogs then touched Harper's shoulder to get her attention. Her tension translated itself into the rock-hard muscle beneath his palm. "I'm going, too."

"I'm not so sure that's a good idea."

"I won't get in the way, but I want to be there. Jake's my nephew's ticket to surgery. I know it sounds bloodthirsty and I don't mean it that way, but I just—"

"You're already getting credit for the tip, Riley. Don't worry about it."

"I'm coming."

Harper frowned. They were the last ones left in the lobby. "You're just going to follow me if I say no, aren't you?"

He shrugged.

She sighed. "Fine, but if you get in the way, I'll throw you in jail, understood?"

"Understood."

Harper settled Star into her spot in the vehicle and the dog quivered with the excitement of going to work. Riley could tell the canine was born for this kind of work. Harper climbed into the driver's seat as Riley finished buckling his seat belt.

They pulled out of the parking lot, staying behind one of the other agents. The powerful SUVs didn't have any trouble on the winding mountainous roads that took them back to Rocky Mountain National Park so it didn't take long to reach the ski chalet.

Riley wasn't as familiar with this area as he was with the place where he'd spotted Jake so he took in the surroundings with interest. Harper parked a good distance away, but he could see the house perched on the side of the mountain. It looked like one could simply walk out the back door and ski down the slope. Nice. "No cars out front, but there's a detached garage."

"We'll check it out." She turned to him. "Stay put. Please."

He nodded. "I promise."

Harper studied him for a moment and he wondered what she was thinking. Then she blinked and turned to let Star out. The dog jumped to the ground and sat, her eyes on Harper, tail wagging. "Just a minute, girl. Stay."

Ian and King approached as well as Max and Opal. "We don't need to go in too fast," Max told them. "If Jake's in there with Penny and the child, we need to approach with caution."

"I agree," Harper said. Riley silently added his agreement.

"Harper, you and I and the dogs will take the front. Ian, you and King take the back. Check the garage and let us know what you see. Let the others know we'll signal if we need help and to go ahead and put their earpieces in."

"You got it," Ian said.

Ian and King turned away to go tell the others and Max looked at Harper. "Let's give them a minute to get ready."

Max waited about sixty seconds then asked, "Everybody hear me? You got your earpieces on?"

"Yes, sir."

They listened another second then their boss's lips thinned and he drew in a breath. "That's everyone. Ian, what do you see with the garage?"

"No vehicles in sight. No people, either."

"All right. Are you ready?" he asked Harper.

"More than."

Max nodded and turned to lead the way. Riley settled back into the seat to watch and wait. He itched to be there with them, but it wasn't his place. Not this time. It might kill him, but he'd be patient and let them do their job.

Harper and Max approached the home with weapons ready. The dogs padded alongside them, noses twitching, ears alert to any command that might be uttered. Star alternated sniffing the ground and the air. King did the same. Max stopped at the front porch and Harper followed his lead. "Ian?"

"It's clear back here," he responded, his voice sounding like he was standing right next to her. "And the door is cracked. Looks like someone left in a hurry."

Max reached out a gloved hand and tried the door. "Front door is locked. Harper's coming around to back you up as you enter. I'll stay here in case someone decides to come out this way."

Harper and Star took off to the back of the house. She approached Ian and nodded.

"Entering the premises," he said and used a hand to push the door open slowly. Harper's adrenaline spiked, but she kept control over her breathing even while her pulse pounded. "Star, search."

"Careful." Max's voice came into her ear.

Ian held King back. Star would alert if there was any-one there. Harper looked around the large open living area and found it to be nice and homey. A sofa against the wall. A coffee table and two end tables. Lamps on the end tables in their upright positions. The large area rug was clean and matched the quilted throw someone had thrown into the recliner opposite the fireplace. No sign of a struggle, no sign of anything other than that the occupants weren't there. "Clear in here."

Star headed down the hall, nose in the air, tail wag-ging. She returned a moment later and sat in front of Harper, tongue hanging from the side of her mouth. "Good girl, Star." Harper relaxed her defensive stance. "It's clear. There's no one in here."

Ian lowered his weapon and nodded to the kitchen. "Glasses on the counter."

Harper unlocked the front door and Max and Opal stepped inside. "Sit," Max told the dog. She sat. "Stay."

Harper walked over to look in the refrigerator. She pulled out a pack of ham. "Expires two weeks from now." She uncapped the milk and sniffed. "Still good."

"So someone *has* been living here. I'm going to check the closets."

He disappeared down the hall toward the bedrooms. Max placed his hands on his hips and pursed his lips. "All right, let's search the rest of this place and see what we can find."

Harper pulled the bag from her belt and opened it. Inside was a scarf that they'd taken from Penny's home for the dogs to use for tracking. She took it from the bag and held it out to Star. "Search, Star. Find Penny." Star sniffed the item then went to work once again.

"Search."

Star went straight to the wingback chair next to the fireplace and sat next to it. "She was here," Harper said. She praised the dog and offered her some food. Once Star devoured the treat, Harper encouraged her to search more. The canine covered every inch of the house, noting that Penny had been in each room. She then made her way to the sofa where she stopped and sniffed again. Then moved to the back of the couch and pawed at it. Harper pulled the cushions off.

Nothing.

"Max?"

"Yes?" He stood in the kitchen going through the rest of the items in the refrigerator.

"Help me move the couch, please?"

He headed over and together they moved the sofa away from the wall. Harper spotted what had gotten Star's attention. She picked up the cell phone with her gloved hand. "What do we have here?" She scratched the dog's ears. "Good girl, Star."

Max took the phone from her. "We'll get Dylan to work with this and see if he can trace it back to the owner."

"Could have been there awhile."

"True."

Harper pulled the packet of dog food from her pocket and gave Star some more. The dog ate it and then sat, ready to go to work again whenever Harper was ready.

Max tapped the screen. "Battery is low, but it's not dead. And it's not password-protected." He held it up and shook it slightly. "Between the food in the refrigerator and this, I'd say we missed Penny by a day or so."

"If not hours," Harper said. "We can send the phone off with the note that was left on my motel door earlier."

A knock on the door sounded and Riley poked his head in. "Is it all right if I come in?"

"Thought you promised to wait in the car."

He frowned. "I did, but Julianne said it was all clear and I could approach."

Harper shrugged. "The house is empty but they were here. Penny was anyway. The evidence shows we didn't miss them by much."

Max focused back on the phone. "Last number called was just two hours ago." He looked at Harper. "You nailed that one. We missed her by hours."

He dialed the number and put it on speaker. "Red Robin Inn, would you like to make a reservation?"

"Possibly," Max said. "Could you give me directions on how to find you?"

The man did so. Max thanked him and hung up. He looked at Harper, Ian and Riley. "I don't want to ask him anything about Penny or Jake over the phone, but that must be where she's headed. I don't want any possibility that he could tip them off. It's about thirty minutes from here. Let's get over there and see if she's checked in." He paused. "And don't everyone pull in the parking lot. Stay against the curb in the street. Harper…"

"Yes?"

"You talk to the guy at the front desk. I'll back you up. Ian, you and Julianne take the back of the building in case she somehow gets tipped off that we're coming." He frowned. "I'm tired of being one step behind. Let's go."

The team and their dogs once again piled back into the vehicle and caravanned it out onto the highway that would lead them to the motel. Harper eyed a stone-silent Riley in the passenger seat. "You okay?"

He glanced at her. "Sure. Why?"

"You seem quiet."

"Just thinking, I guess."

"About?"

"About my nephew and all he's been through over the past few months. I'm thinking how innocent people get caught up in things that can quickly spiral out of control through no fault of their own—and thinking that it's really not fair at all and that I hate feeling powerless to do anything about it. I really can't stand injustice."

She nodded. "I know. I see it all the time. Life definitely isn't fair, but we haven't been promised fair, just that we don't have to walk this journey alone."

"You're talking about God, I guess."

"I am."

"I'll admit, I've been pretty mad at Him for letting it all happen," he gritted out.

She shot him a glance then focused back on the road. "That's understandable."

"Maybe. You told me about your past, growing up with a dad who bailed on you and your mom. That had to have been hard."

"I'm sure it was. I don't remember much about it, to be honest. I just remember the fights stopped and that made me glad. It wasn't until I got older that I pieced together the whole story from relatives and my mom's drunken ramblings."

He gave her a contemplative look. "You ever get mad at God about it? Wonder why He didn't do something about it?"

"Sure, I've been there."

"But now?"

She shrugged. "I've made my peace with Him—and my past. In spite of my lousy upbringing, He's proved none of it took Him by surprise and now I can see how He's worked through the bad to bring good."

Riley fell silent again and Harper wished she could read his thoughts. "I don't think any good can come out of my sister's murder."

"I'm sure it looks that way now—and it may always look that way to you—us." She sighed. "I don't pretend to understand the ways or thoughts of God. I just know that *He* is good. He delights in us even in our imperfections and He despises evil." She cleared her throat. "And He's a just God. If I didn't believe that, I wouldn't do what I do. But murder is evil and you may never see any good in your sister's death."

"Seriously, what good could come of it?" he asked harshly.

She hesitated then lifted her shoulder in a slight shrug. "Maybe it's not a matter of looking for the good that can come from it, maybe it's more of just not letting Blackman win."

"And how do I do that?"

"As long as you and those who loved her become better people in spite of the pain that he's caused you by his evil actions, then he doesn't win. As long as you don't allow him to steal your joy and your love of life, then he doesn't win. If you go around hating him and being bitter the rest of your life, then essentially, he manages to kill you along with your sister." She released a breath. "You're not the same person now that you were before she died simply because what happened is a life-altering thing. But that difference doesn't have to define you or your future. You can still have a good life, Riley."

He swallowed hard but nodded for her to go on.

"Remember Charlotte and all she meant to you, teach

Asher about her and keep her memory alive for him because he'll want to know more and more about her the older he gets. Don't let hating Blackman steal those moments that are sure to come."

Silence dropped between them. "I…never thought of it like that," he whispered. "I can't see past her death."

"It's only been a couple of months. It will take time. And when I said that good can actually come from bad," she said softly, "I suppose what I mean, in my case anyway, was that I chose to use that bad to bring good into the lives of others."

"Can you explain that?"

She drew in a deep breath. "I was faced with choices just like anyone else. Certain choices would bring good things. I could help others who were going through what I had already been through. I could give others hope that they could come out of their situation and be able to smile again, to be happy and…free." She sighed. "Or I could choose to go a different route and let anger and bitterness dictate my life. I didn't want to choose that route. But, because of what I've been through, I have a perspective that others don't have and I can help people in the same situations deal with their emotions and feelings in a constructive way."

"You became a better person in spite of your parents."

"Yes. That was a really rambling way of trying to make my point. I hope it made sense."

"It did." He fell silent yet again. Every so often she glanced at him, wondering what he was thinking. Her life hadn't been a bed of roses, for sure, but she was in a good place, proud of what she'd overcome and determined that she'd share her story with anyone she thought it could help.

She felt his gaze on her and glanced at him. "What?"

"You're different."

"What do you mean?"

He shrugged and let out a low laugh. "I'm not sure what I mean, to be honest. I just don't think I've ever met anyone like you."

"So is that a good thing?"

He smiled. "Yeah. It's a good thing."

Harper's insides twisted at his words. Why was he able to do that to her? Why did she have to meet him now when everything was in chaos? He needed to find Van and she needed to find Jake. Romance, attraction, dating…whatever. It was all a bad idea at this point in time and the thought saddened her more than she wanted to admit.

She concentrated on the driving and keeping her mouth shut. The more she opened it and shared with this man, the closer she grew to him. The more she talked, the more she invited him in to know the real her. Which kind of scared her.

Would he run away or stick around if he got to know her on a deeper-than-shallow-friendship level? Did she want to find out?

Yes.

No.

Maybe.

She wasn't going to answer that mental question right now. She was going to focus on her job.

The minutes passed and Harper finally pulled into the parking lot of the Red Robin Inn.

The others followed orders and parked on the street. She climbed from the vehicle and Riley did the same. Together they walked into the lobby of the motel with

Star trotting at her side. "You don't get to go to the room, Riley."

"I know. I'll get back in the car when you tell me to."

Harper nodded and noted the motel smelled of cleaning solution and chlorine. To the right was the entrance to the indoor pool. To the left was the registration desk. A young man in his midtwenties chatted on the phone, his back to them.

Harper approached the desk and waited a moment. Then she slapped the old-fashioned bell sitting on the counter. The clerk jumped and spun. Then flushed. "I gotta go, Jess. Talk to you later." He hung up and cleared his throat. "Ah, sorry about that. What can I do for you?"

He seemed nice enough, just young.

You're not that much older, her inner voice mocked.

In reality, she might not be but a few years older in numbers, but in life experience, chances were she was light-years away from this guy. She flashed her badge, which was overkill since the khaki pants and shirt with the FBI logo emblazoned on it stood out. Star sat at her side and waited for her orders. "I'm looking for a young woman by the name of Penny Potter. She would have been traveling with a little boy. A toddler."

The clerk, Jason, according to his nameplate, swallowed again and his eyes shifted to the door. "Ah, who? Oh, um, yeah, Ms. Potter. Let me check." He clicked a few keys on the computer while his eyes kept going toward the door then down to the phone.

"Something wrong?" Riley asked.

"What? Wrong?" He let out a nervous laugh. "No. Why?"

"Because you're awfully jumpy." Harper frowned. "Is Ms. Potter in your system or not?"

"Um. Yes. Yes, she is. She's right here. Yep. Here she is. She…ah…checked in about two hours ago. With a toddler." Another nerve-grating laugh.

What was wrong with this guy? "Give me her room number and a key, please," Harper said.

He flinched. "A key? And her room number? Why?"

"Because I asked for it. I'm working a case. You want to interfere with it?"

"Um. No. Of course not." With shaky fingers, he pulled a key from the stack and ran it through the machine. "There. 104. Just…um…around the corner."

Harper took the key. "Thanks."

Ian stepped inside. "Max sent me in to see if you needed any help."

Harper nodded at the clerk. "As a matter of fact, I need you to babysit for a few minutes. Make sure our friend here doesn't touch that phone until I give the all-clear, okay?"

"Sure thing." King settled himself beside Ian while Harper and Star readied themselves to head toward the room.

Harper drew in a deep breath. "Finally."

"What?" Riley asked. He walked beside her and stopped at the vehicle where he would wait.

"We're going to get some answers."

SIX

Riley sure hoped so. He was ready for this wild chase to be done with so he could get the money and head back to the hospital to be with Asher.

But until then…

He stayed back as ordered. It made his nerves itch to wait. He wanted to be in on the action, but while he was a former cop while living in Denver, until he earned a badge in this area, he'd have to hang back.

At least he had a good view of the room. He sat in the SUV with Max and Opal with the vehicle's windows down. Leo and True followed close behind Harper and Star. The other team members were poised for action as well, but would keep their distance until needed. Riley understood Max's desire for staunch caution. They didn't want to go bursting into the room without knowing where Penny and Kevin were—and where Jake might be with his gun.

Harper knocked on the door. "Housekeeping!"

No answer.

She tried again.

Again, nothing.

"Penny? You in there?"

She nodded at Leo. He nodded back. Harper swiped the key card and then they were in the room.

Riley realized he was holding his breath and forced himself to draw air into his lungs. For a moment all was quiet. Then Harper appeared in the doorway, her weapon lowered. "All clear," she called.

Max slammed a fist against the dash and Riley jumped then raised a brow. "Tense much?"

The man shot him a wry smile. "A little." Then he was out of the vehicle and joining the others.

Riley followed at a slower pace. Once at the room, he looked inside. Harper held the bag with Penny's scarf in her hand. Star continued to sniff the floor, the perfectly made beds, the chairs, the bathroom. Then she came to her handler and sat in front of her.

Harper let out a sigh. "She was never here." She swept a hand at the room. "I almost don't even need Star to tell me that. Look at this place. It's been cleaned and is ready for the next occupant."

"What?" Riley said. "I thought that guy said she checked in two hours ago."

"Obviously he lied. Or if she checked in, she never came to the room. I'm leaning toward him lying. Let's find out." Her nostrils flared and Riley was surprised he didn't actually see steam escape. She marched out of the room and down the sidewalk to the lobby. Riley stayed right behind her. No way was he missing this.

Harper strode past Ian and planted her hands on the chest-high counter. The young clerk gulped and took a step back. "Um…yes?"

"She was never in that room."

"Well…ah…why do you say that? Of course she was."

"Star says she wasn't. And my dog is never wrong. Which means you're lying and I want to know why."

He opened his mouth and she held up a hand. "Did she pay with credit card or cash?"

The man snapped his lips together.

Harper narrowed her eyes. "And before you answer, let me just help you out here. This is a federal investigation—one that is very important and is costing a lot of money. Now, you just sent us on a wild-goose chase. If you don't want to be arrested for obstructing justice, you'll tell me what you know and you won't leave out a single detail. Including the truth about whether or not Penny Potter and her son checked into that room."

The more she talked, the wider Jason's eyes grew. His Adam's apple bobbed continuously in his skinny throat while he listened to Harper's tirade. Finally, he held up his hands as though to ward her off. "I… I don't want any trouble."

"Good. Talk."

"A…um…a woman called a little while earlier and said if anyone came looking for her and a kid to tell them that she'd checked in. She said if I did, she'd give me a hundred bucks. I said okay. I didn't know it was the cops looking for her. I promise."

"You knew it when I walked in here."

He dropped his eyes to the counter and rubbed his chin. Then he gave a slight nod. "I did. I'm sorry. I wanted to help her—and I'll admit I could use the hundred dollars."

Harper's shoulders relaxed a fraction at his apology. Riley thought the guy certainly seemed sincere. "All right. Thanks for your…belated…help." She paused. "How was she going to get the hundred dollars to you?"

"She said she'd check in with me every once in a while."

"But she didn't give you a number?"

"No."

"And you really think she's going to check in with you so she can bring you a hundred bucks?"

Jason lowered his eyes and gave a small shrug. "It was worth a shot. And she called about thirty minutes before you got here to check."

Harper handed the young man a card. "If she calls again, you arrange to get your money, then you call me, you understand?"

"Um…sure."

"I mean it. I'm not kidding around here."

"No, ma'am. I believe you're not kidding around one bit. I'll call you if she calls me."

"Good. Now, I want the number she called from. Is it in your system?"

"Yes." At this point, he seemed eager to help. Probably wanted to do anything he had to in order to satisfy them and get them out of his hotel.

Harper wrote the number down and texted it to Dylan. She looked at Riley. "It's time to regroup, I would think. Let's check with Max and see where he wants to go from here."

Riley, impressed beyond measure and with a new respect for Harper and her ability to do her job, followed her out to join the rest of the waiting team who'd gathered in the parking lot. Before they reached them, he leaned over to whisper in her ear. "That was incredible."

"What?"

"You. Your interaction with him. That was some of the finest interrogating I've ever seen. And I've seen a lot."

A flush crept up into her cheeks and she gave a low laugh. "It was kind of fun, wasn't it? In the end. Initially, he just made me mad. I can't stand to be lied to. That kid gave off weird vibes from the moment we walked in. He better not try to lie on a regular basis, he's lousy at it."

"Which means he's most likely an honest person. Usually."

"I agree. Which made it a lot easier to get the truth out of him."

"Exactly. You would have made a great lawyer."

"Thank you, I'll pass on that one, though. I like my job." She gave small laugh. "Now let's see what Max has to say."

"Sure."

The team leader stepped forward. "All right everyone, let's head back to the motel. We can eat at the little restaurant there and develop a plan. The first thing we need to do is set up shifts. We can't all keep going twenty-four seven."

Harper's phone buzzed and she glanced at it. "That's Dylan. He traced the number Penny called from and it was a throwaway phone."

"Of course it was," Max said. "She seems to have quite a supply of them, doesn't she?"

Harper nodded. "Let's get that food. I'm starving."

Harper stifled a yawn. She was feeling the effects of little sleep. But she also had adrenaline pumping through her. She settled Star in her spot in the vehicle while Riley took the passenger seat.

The drive back to the hotel passed mostly in silence as Riley kept his attention on the mirrors.

Setting up shifts sounded good to her. She needed

some down time. Time to think and get her emotions under control when it came to Riley. Time to check her laptop to see if there were any updates on her father and time to decide what she really wanted from the future. She slid a glance at Riley and knew he was like the man she might *want* in her future, but was afraid to get too attached to the idea that it could possibly be him since it wasn't likely to pan out anyway. But someone like him…yeah, that wouldn't be so bad.

She couldn't help smiling at the thought of being a lawyer, though. Truthfully, the idea didn't bother her nearly as much as it probably should. As a lawyer, she wouldn't be traveling as much. She could stay home with any future children she and her husband might have.

Harper sucked in a breath and put the brakes on that line of thinking. A husband and children were not in her immediate future.

Her phone buzzed and she pressed the button that would send the call to her Bluetooth. "Harper here."

"It's Dylan again."

"Back so soon? That's got to be good. What's up?"

"I checked out that Van Blackman character. He's definitely not one of the good guys."

"I have no doubt about that. Do you have any way of finding him?"

She felt Riley's gaze on her. "No, he seems to have dropped off the grid. If you have a number for him, I might be able to find something through that."

"Let me ask." She looked at Riley. "Do you have a cell number for Blackman?"

He shook his head. "He's using disposable phones. Whatever number I had for him is no longer in service."

"Did you get that, Dylan?" she asked.

"I got it. He's got a credit card he used a couple of weeks ago. It was a large cash advance from one of the banks in Drum Creek so it's definitely possible he's still in the area. I'll keep a watch on the card and let you know if he uses it again."

"Thanks, Dylan." She pulled into the parking lot of the motel, said goodbye to their tech guy and climbed out of the vehicle with Star at her side.

The team gathered in the dining area once again, drawing the stares of everyone already there. Harper noticed and simply acknowledged them with a nod and a smile. So much for staying under the radar. When all six of them were together, it really wasn't possible to be inconspicuous.

A young boy about the age of seven approached and held out a hand. "Can I pet him?"

She smiled. "Sure. But it's very good that you asked first. And Star is a girl."

He grinned and a deep dimple flashed in one cheek. "She's pretty—and *big*." Star relished the child's sweet touch. Harper found Riley watching the pair, longing and despair mingled in his eyes. She could clearly see that he was thinking of his nephew and her heart hurt for him. When the little boy's mother pulled him away from Star, Harper reached for Riley's hand and squeezed it. He smiled his thanks. A sad smile that disappeared when his jaw tightened with determination.

Max's phone rang and he stepped away to answer while the others discussed the next step in the case. When he returned, he cleared his throat. "Riley, could you excuse us for a moment?"

Riley's gaze shifted back and forth between Max

and Harper then he shrugged and stepped out of hearing distance.

"What is it?" Harper asked.

"That was one of the US marshals we're working with. Thomas Grant. Esme Dupree called him."

Harper scratched Star's ears. "She did?"

"Yeah."

Esme Dupree was their star witness in hiding. She had seen her brother, Reginald Dupree, murder someone he worked with. Reginald knew that she'd seen him and was out to make sure she didn't testify against him. By agreeing to testify, Esme had put herself in grave danger.

"Did she say where she was hiding out?" Harper asked. Esme had been in the Witness Protection Program, but after a close call, had ditched the marshals and struck out on her own.

Max sighed. "No, just that she's alive and still planning to testify at the trial."

"But she still refuses to come in?" Ian prodded.

"Yes." Max rubbed his head then shook it.

"We need her testimony to put him away," Harper said impatiently. "Without her, we have no case."

"Well, I can't say I blame her for being a little wary. Being told you were safe and then getting found and almost killed would make anyone doubt the marshal's abilities."

"Not to mention the fact that two women who resembled her were killed."

"Yeah," Ian grunted. "That would have done it for me, for sure."

Max shook his head. "Thomas tried to convince her to come in, but she says she doesn't trust anyone at this point."

"Anything else?" Ian asked.

"The number she was calling from was traced back to a disposable phone," Max said.

"Esme wouldn't call if she thought they'd be able to find her," Harper reminded them. "She's not stupid."

"Except for running away from the program thinking she can take care of herself better than the US Marshals can," Ian said. "That's stupid in my book."

"I don't know," Harper said. "It might be why she's still alive."

Ian frowned at her. "You think someone on the inside is a mole?"

"I don't know that either, but she was found when she shouldn't have been found. The Marshals have a sterling track record. So it does make one wonder."

Max fell silent. They all did while they contemplated her words.

Harper caught Riley's eye from afar and nodded. He approached them as his phone buzzed. "Sorry," he muttered. He glanced at the screen then answered. "Hey, Champ. How are you doing?" A pause. "Of course you can call me. You can call me anytime."

Harper didn't mean to eavesdrop, but Riley didn't seem to require privacy. "A clown came to visit, huh?… Yeah?… And you thought it was me?" He chuckled even as a flash of pain darkened his eyes. "I'll be by to see you soon, kiddo, I promise."

Asher must have said something else because Riley scowled. "No, I haven't caught him yet, but I'm closing in on him… Yeah?… I wish you could help catch him, too, but you just concentrate on getting better, okay?… Okay, then." Another pause. "Yes, I'm still thinking about the puppy you want… Uh-huh… Okay. Love you, Champ."

He listened a moment longer then hung up, jaw working, eyes glittering with suppressed rage.

The team members had grown quiet, listening to the conversation. Harper caught his arm. "He asked you if you'd caught Blackman, didn't he?"

"Yeah. I didn't realize he knew as much…" He drew in a deep breath. "But yes, he asked and said he wanted to help."

"I gathered that."

Riley's fingers curled into fists. "I have to get him, Harper," he said hoarsely.

"I know. I understand." And she did. She might not understand *exactly* how he felt due to the fact she'd never had a sibling killed by someone who was supposed to love her, but she understood the determination to not let someone get away with doing wrong. Jake Morrow had been a trusted member of the unit, a man they'd treated as one of them, someone she would have trusted with her life and even died for.

Now, he was a wanted man. And Harper desperately wanted to find him so she could demand answers from him. She could see that going over well. Arrogant and cocky, Jake wouldn't respond well to demands. He liked to do the demanding. But he'd been an excellent agent and part of the team and, because of that, he deserved a chance to explain himself.

"Van's taunting me," Riley bit out. "Following me then disappearing as though to say, 'You might get close, but you won't catch me.'"

"He'll mess up sooner or later and when he does, you'll be there to grab him. Or we will."

He gave her a faint smile. "Thanks."

Max rubbed a hand over his head. "All right. To recap. Penny's on the run. It looks like Jake's after her.

We've got law enforcement cooperation and Dylan's keeping tabs on his cell phone."

"Which he's not going to use if he doesn't want to be found," Ian muttered.

"And it's looking more and more like he doesn't want to be," Max agreed. "But I want to know why."

Riley's phone buzzed again. He glanced at the screen and frowned. "Let me take this."

"Of course."

This time he stepped away from the group and pressed the phone to his ear.

"Man, that sounds like some tough stuff he's dealing with," Max said in a quiet voice. "What's wrong with his nephew?"

"He was shot when his mother's boyfriend opened fire on them at a grocery store. He killed the mother, Riley's sister, and paralyzed Asher. The poor kid has a bullet lodged near his spine. That's why Riley's so determined to bring in Jake. He needs the money for Asher's surgery to help him walk again."

Max let out a low whistle.

"What if we could help?" Ian said.

Harper lifted a brow. "Help how?"

Ian shrugged. "Why don't I call Dylan and see what we can come up with?"

"I'm on the way," Riley said as he headed toward the front door.

Harper caught up to him. "Everything okay? Is Asher all right?"

"That wasn't about Asher. That was a friend of mine who works at the grocery store up the street. He said Van Blackman was just in there buying some ibuprofen and cold medicine." He took off and Harper rose to go after him then paused to look over her shoulder. "Max?"

"Go," he said. "Watch his back."

"Thanks. Star, heel." The dog bolted to her side and they hurried after a disappearing Riley. She caught up to him crossing the street. "Riley."

He shot her a tight look then entered the store. An older gentleman approached and pointed out the door. "He just left not five minutes ago."

"Which way did he go?"

"North."

Riley turned to look. "Back toward the park," he murmured. "What's he driving?"

"A green Ford pickup."

"We can take my vehicle if you want," Harper said.

He nodded. "I have to try to find him."

"Let's go. We'll call Max and let him know what's going on."

They rushed back to the hotel parking lot where they climbed into her vehicle. Star hopped into her spot and soon Harper was headed down the road in the direction of the park.

Park made it sound small. Searchable. But as Harper had discovered, it was a vast area of acreage with a multitude of hiding places. However, Riley had done the smart thing and asked people to keep an eye out for the man he was hunting. If Blackman was camping out in the park, then he'd have to come into town for supplies every so often—and to search for Riley, apparently.

Whatever the case, it had paid off. Once again someone had spotted him and called it in.

They just had to catch up to him now.

Riley gripped the door handle as Harper took the next turn. The green truck was just ahead but getting ready to disappear around the next curve. He wanted to tell her to hurry, go faster, but he knew she was doing her best to keep them far enough behind so the man ahead wouldn't know they were on his tail. And besides, she could only go so fast on the winding, two-lane road.

They were climbing now, the road slanting upward, the drop-off to Harper's left growing steeper. "Come on," he whispered.

Harper spared him a glance before turning her attention back to the road. Riley hadn't realized he'd spoken aloud.

The green truck disappeared for another moment. Approximately twenty seconds later, when Harper took the next curve, a flash of green to his right caught his eye. "Watch out!" He realized what was going to happen in the split second before the front of the green truck slammed into the passenger door. He jerked against the seat belt then was tossed back against the window.

Harper cried out. The wheel spun out of her hands and the SUV skidded along the edge of the road. The green pickup came again and this time the nudge was almost gentle in comparison. Through the windshield Riley met Van's wild gaze and his gleeful, crazed expression as the man didn't back away, but continued to accelerate and push the big SUV toward the side of the cliff. "Hang on, Harper, we're going over!"

Harper pressed the gas, and the SUV lunged forward, but it was too late.

The big green pickup's engine gave a mighty roar, another surge forward and the SUV went off the road and over the side of the embankment.

Star barked then yelped when the SUV turned onto its driver's side and bumped down the steep cliff. The seat belt kept Riley in his seat, his right hand gripping the handle while he braced himself for impact. Trees flew past, dirt and rocks pinged off the windows, the world tilted and jounced them and he thought he might be sick.

Then came the bone-jarring halt. The slam jerked him hard enough for him to lose his grip on the door handle. And then all was still. For a moment he didn't move, his breathing—and body—suspended, held physically in place by the seat belt. His heart thundered in his ears.

Finally, he was able to catch his breath. "Harper?" He looked over to find her crammed against the driver's door. Her eyes were open, but glazed. "Harper! You okay?"

She blinked. Then blinked again. "Yes. I think so. You?"

"Yeah. Did you hit your head?"

"No. Surprisingly. And I think my vest protected me from having much of a bruise from my seat belt." She grunted and turned, trying to see behind her. "Star? Star!"

A low woof came from the back and he saw her eyes close in relief for a fraction of a second.

"I'm pretty stuck. Can you get out?" she asked.

"I'm not sure. If I unhook my seat belt, I'm going to fall into you."

Her hand patted her hip. "My phone's gone. Must have popped off." She reached for the dangling mic of the radio while Riley searched for his phone. He heard her calling to her coworkers and getting no response. She let go of the mic in disgust. "It's dead."

His fingers closed over the phone that had wedged between the center console and the seat. "What's the number?"

She gave it to him and Max answered on the first

ring. "Max, this is Riley. We got ambushed and could use a little help."

"What's wrong?" the man barked. "Where are you?"

Riley told him as best he could. "Just follow the road and keep looking down. You'll see us." He looked up through the passenger window. "We didn't fall too far. I can see the edge of the road. Maybe about twenty feet?"

"We're on the way. Stay on the phone, we'll track it and make things a lot easier."

"Of course." He should have just suggested that.

A loud crack reached him and the back windshield shattered. Riley hollered and he heard Harper give a startled cry. "He's shooting at us!"

"What's going on?" Max hollered.

Another bullet rocked the vehicle and Riley dropped the phone. Max would have to figure it out for himself. Riley grabbed for the door handle and unbuckled his seat belt. Gravity pulled him toward her and while he did his best not to land fully on top of her with his entire weight, she still gave a grunt when his elbow dug into her side.

Bracing himself on the back of the seat, he climbed into the back so that he was standing on the shattered rear door window. Star lay above him in her secure area, her paws slipping through the barred door. "Come on, Harper, we're sitting ducks. We've got to get out of here." He reached around to release her belt and found she was already moving. "We'll have to go out the back."

"The back that he's shooting at?"

"Afraid so."

Two more bullets pinged off the undercarriage. She flinched, but lifted her chin. "He's moved. Those bullets came from a different direction."

"Yeah. I've got Star. I don't want her walking and cutting her feet on the glass near here." Riley released Star from her cage and caught her in his arms. She wiggled, but he held her tight.

"Star, stay."

The dog flattened her ears, but immediately went still at Harper's command.

Another bullet, then a rapid succession of them battered the bottom of the SUV.

Harper gripped his bicep. "He's aiming for the gas tank. Go!"

SEVEN

Harper's head beat a harsh rhythm in her skull as Riley awkwardly scrambled over into the back with Star still in his arms. She pressed a hand to her temple. She didn't remember hitting her head in the tumble down the side of the cliff.

She figured it was just the rush of adrenaline, combined with her erratic pulse that caused it to pound like a jackhammer. She drew in several deep breaths while she fought her way to the back of the vehicle. Riley stayed at the very edge of the back. All he had to do was step out. She moved close to him. "Ready?"

"Ready when you are."

Star whined in Riley's arms, but continued to let him hold her as long as she could see Harper.

She drew in a steadying breath then nodded. Riley pushed Star out the back and clambered behind her. He turned and reached for Harper's hand and she grasped his fingers to let him help her out.

Sirens sounded from up above, but Harper's quick rush of relief didn't last long as the crack of more gunshots split the air. Bullets pelted the ground and the SUV and Harper expected to feel the slam of one at any second. Or hear the explosion. "Go!"

Together they raced for the trees. Two more pops sounded and a bullet caught her in the upper back. She cried out and went down.

"Harper!"

Pain streaked through her. She couldn't breathe, couldn't move, couldn't speak. Her hands clawed the ground, her lungs strained for air.

"Harper!" He dropped beside her. Star barked. The sound of the engine roaring away echoed through her head. "Let me see. Don't move."

Not moving was not going to be a problem. Finally, a breath caught and she pulled it in eagerly. Then coughed. The sirens screamed louder. She dragged in another desperate breath and grimaced. "He's getting away," she rasped.

"He's just going to have to this time," Riley said. "He shot you."

Harper drew in another breath. "He shot...my vest. Just...knocked the wind...out of me."

Riley raked a shaky hand through his hair and Star padded over to nudge Harper's cheek. She scratched the animal's ear. "Good girl."

Star sat beside her with a woof. Harper continued to concentrate on breathing through the fire shooting through her, waiting for it to ebb. Riley stayed beside her, watching, his weapon ready. She appreciated his vigilance.

"Harper? Riley?"

Max's anxious shout made Harper grimace. She gripped Riley's hand. "Help me sit up." He hesitated and she sighed. "I'm getting up with or without your help. *With* would simply make it easier." She looked up. "Down here, Max!"

Riley's jaw tightened and he pulled her into a sitting position. Fire blazed through her back and stars danced before her eyes, but she'd heard stories from others who'd been shot and hit in the vest so knew the feeling was normal. She'd be fine. Bruised and sore, but fine. Eventually.

But that was okay. It was better than being dead.

Max's head appeared over the drop-off. "You okay?"

"Yes. Need a BOLO for a green truck." She drew in another breath then gave him the license number. Wow. It hurt to yell, too.

"On it. Can you climb up or do we need to come get you?"

"We can climb, I think." She muttered the last two words under her breath and saw that Riley heard them. He lifted a brow. "Let's go," she said before he could suggest they let someone come get them. "It's not that far."

"I'm not going to talk you out of trying, am I?" Riley asked.

"Probably not. Ask me again in a couple of minutes."

"All right then, I'm game if you are."

Together, with Star at her side, they made their way up the dirt hill. Some places were easier to navigate than others, but the drop-off hadn't been straight down, more like a gentle slope. Which was what had saved their lives.

That and the tree.

She didn't want to think about it. She knew the area had some really steep and deadly inclines, and that if one fell—or was run off the road—it could be fatal. Once back up on the road, Max, Ian and Zeke rushed over. A chopper roared overhead and Harper looked up. "We've got him looking for the truck," Max explained.

"Come on," Riley said, "let's have a look at your

back." Harper let him help her off with the vest. She hissed as she moved her shoulder.

Ian stared at her with concern. "You got hit?"

"Yes. Well, the vest did. I'm okay."

She rotated her shoulder and breathed a sigh of relief that nothing felt broken. It hurt like crazy, and was bruised for sure, but it was nothing that would keep her from working.

Max stopped her. "Let me check it."

"It should be all right in time. It's just a bruise."

"Do you mind if I take a look anyway?"

"Of course not."

Harper waited while Max felt the area and in spite of her gasp and groan, he pronounced her correct in her own assessment. "Wouldn't hurt to have it x-rayed to make sure there isn't something small like a fracture, but I won't force it if you say you're good."

She hesitated. "If it's not better in a couple of days, I'll go in."

"You feel up to working?"

"Yes. I'm up to it."

Max nodded. "Good enough, then."

Star sat by her, panting. "Can one of you give her some water?"

"Sure." Ian jogged to his vehicle and grabbed some from the back, along with a bowl. And two more bottles that he handed to Harper and Riley.

Satisfied that Star was fine, Harper could focus on the incident. She took a long swig from the bottle then recapped it. "That was Blackman in that truck. He's quite determined to kill Riley."

"And you along with him, apparently," Max said darkly.

"No, he's not one to worry overmuch about collateral damage," Riley said.

"Well, killing either of us isn't an option." Harper set her jaw and narrowed her eyes. "We just have one more fugitive to catch in addition to Jake."

Max nodded. "All right. We've got the BOLO out on both of them now. I'm not sure why, but neither one seems to be in a hurry to leave this area."

"Well, we know why Jake is still here. It means he believes Penny is close by."

"And Van knows I'll track him wherever he goes," Riley said. "The thing is he's got a good setup here." He rubbed his head. "He's got everything he needs. Water, food and any number of hiding places. I'm pretty sure that's why he's still here. He grew up in this area and knows it like the back of his hand."

"Where's his family now?" Max asked.

"They live near here in Estes Park."

"Have you talked to them?"

Riley nodded. "The detectives talked to them the day she was shot, of course. Then first thing after Charlotte's funeral, I went by to see them." He exhaled a quick breath. "I believe I told you before that he grew up in foster homes. But his family is located here. A scattering of them anyway. They're still in trouble with the law and don't have much use for law enforcement, but his mother seemed pretty horrified when I told her what had happened and cried the whole time I was there. She claimed she hadn't heard from Van in years."

"And yet he stayed in the area."

He nodded. "I wasn't so sure I bought her story so I had several former cop buddies of mine take turns sitting on his home, but he never showed. Either she really did refuse to have anything to with him or he's just smart and figured there would be someone watching to see if he showed up. In any event, he hasn't gone by there since. At least as far as I know. I check in with his mother pretty regularly and I have some buddies that make their presence visible a few times a week."

"So what would keep him here? Why not run as far and as fast as he could?"

Riley shrugged. "No idea. If it's not his mother, it's very possible there was some connection with his dead wife's family. Van and his wife, Susie, met in foster care. She came from an abusive situation as well. The way he talked, it sounded like their similar backgrounds bonded them. And that's about all he would say about his past." He scrubbed a hand across his jaw. "I talked to his last foster mother just a few weeks ago and she just said he wasn't any trouble even as a teenager, but she still wouldn't trust him as far as she could throw him. Said he was just too quiet and introverted and she never knew what he was thinking."

"What happened to his wife? Did he kill her, too?" Harper asked.

"No. She died in childbirth."

"Oh. That's sad."

"Like I said, he refused to talk much about it. Just that he'd been married once. Charlotte told me a little bit about him and I looked up the rest."

"All right, then." Max nodded. "Let's hope someone spots them and calls it in."

Riley's eyes turned toward the national park. "I think it's time for an all-out search of that area. We'll have to do it mostly on foot, though. There are places vehicles can't go. What do you think?"

Harper looked at Max who shrugged. "It's better than anything else we've got right now."

Riley nodded. "The sun's going to be setting soon. First thing in the morning would be a good time to get started."

"If we don't get any tips or anything else before morning, that'll be the plan."

"Works for me," Ian said.

Zeke blew out a breath. "Yeah. Works for me, too."

"What about the chopper?" Harper asked. "Do we need to bring it in?"

"Might not be a bad idea," Max said. "I'll them know."

Zeke ran a hand through his hair and shook his head.

"We'll find him, Zeke," Harper reassured him.

"I know. The question is, who will we find? Simply a rogue agent who needs some serious redirection or a lousy traitor?"

Either one didn't sound good. And Harper knew which one she was leaning toward.

Traitor.

Even thinking the word made her sick to her stomach. She grimaced and prayed no one else would get hurt before they could find Van and Jake.

Sitting in the back of Ian's SUV with King and Star beside him, Riley had to admit he was worried. Worried about his nephew, worried about putting Harper in the crosshairs of a killer. And worried that if she—or someone else—died at Van's hand, it would be Riley's fault.

On the way back to the motel, he called his mother to check in on her.

"No change," she murmured. "He misses his mama."

Tears cloaked her words and Riley shut his eyes against the surge of hate that wanted to take over. He couldn't let it. It would cloud his thinking, make him careless. For now, he had to bury it. "I know. I miss her, too."

"We all do."

He paused. "What should I do, Mom?" he rasped.

"What do you mean?"

He swallowed hard then forced the words from his throat. "Should I quit chasing Blackman? Should I come back and stay with Asher? What would be the best thing to do? The best thing for Asher?" His heart had never felt so torn. He wanted justice for his sister. He wanted Van Blackman behind bars. Or dead. And yet he didn't want it at the expense of his nephew's mental and emotional well-being. Asher came first.

"Asher will be fine," his mother finally said after a lengthy silence. "He sleeps a lot because of the pain medicine. And while he asks about you every day, I think you need to stay after Van. Catch him and put him away so he can't do this to another family."

Riley's heart squeezed with grief and anger. "Right." It was what he'd hoped she'd say and yet, part of him had wanted her permission to quit so he could be there for Asher.

He drew in a deep breath and pictured his sister's pretty face. Smiling, laughing, spinning in circles with the son she'd adored. His resolve hardened. His mother was right. He couldn't let the man move on to find another woman to kill—another family to devastate. And Riley knew with everything in him that Van would do so the minute he thought he was free to pursue another woman without watching over his shoulder for Riley to show up and take him in. "Okay, Mom, give him a hug for me and tell him I love him."

"You know I will." She paused. "And son, please

be careful. I can't lose you, too. I… I don't think I'd survive it."

His heart hurt at her words. "I'll be careful, Mom."

He hung up and dropped his chin to his chest while his mind raced. Okay, so, in the morning, they'd start hunting again. *God, if You're listening, we could use some divine intervention here. Please?*

A rap on the window snagged his attention. He opened the door to Harper's lovely face and clouded eyes. "Are you all right?" she asked.

"I should be asking you that question. You're the one who got shot."

She offered him a faint smile and some of the clouds receded. "I'm still breathing, so I'm grateful and count that as having a good day."

"I know the feeling. So, what's the plan?"

"They're finishing up here, gathering what evidence they can to ship back to Montana for the lab to go over."

"But this doesn't have anything to do with your case."

She smiled again. "But Max agreed to let you have every resource at your disposal for your help in finding Jake. Our state-of-the-art lab is one of those resources."

He nodded. "I appreciate that. Although, I feel like I've got the better end of the deal. We haven't seen or heard anything more about Morrow."

"That's not your fault. We know he was here. We know Penny was here, could possibly still be here. As long as she stays in the area, Morrow will, too, and we'll find him eventually. So," she said, "it looks like you're going to need an extra set of eyes. Now that we know the lengths Blackman will go to get rid of you, we plan to watch out for you and make sure he doesn't have another chance to get at you."

Riley was grateful for the help. He'd been fighting his own emotions for so long, his search for Van a mostly solitary endeavor, that the thought of having backup was a huge relief. "I don't see how you can prevent it, but I sure won't turn down the offer of the resources—and the extra set of eyes."

"Perfect. I guess we can head back to the motel. The tow truck will be here soon."

"What are you going to do for a vehicle?"

She studied him. "What do you drive again?"

He laughed and shook his head as he realized she'd driven them everywhere they'd gone together. He found he didn't mind that at all. Harper was strong, capable—and extremely attractive. "I have a blue pickup with a king cab."

"That'll work."

Riley watched her walk toward one of the other Suburbans and let out a half chuckle. Then sobered. "Wait a minute," he called. "Are you serious?"

EIGHT

Harper was serious. Until another vehicle could be delivered, they would have to improvise. She looked at Riley and smiled. "I would appreciate it, of course, but you don't have to if you don't want to. I'm not twisting your arm."

"But?"

"But it would help us keep the investigation going at full speed if we don't have to worry about someone being left without a ride for the next day or so. We can always rent what we need, but that means heading to the nearest airport or waiting to have something delivered—and then it won't be equipped with everything we might need for a search out here in the middle of nowhere. If we use your truck, I can just transfer the stuff from mine to yours."

His lip quirked into a half grin. "I get it. You don't have to do any arm-twisting. I'll share."

"Thanks."

Once they were finished with the scene, she, Star and Riley climbed into Max's vehicle.

Since half of the backseat was taken up with Opal's area, Harper directed the canine to the very rear. Harper let Riley have the front passenger seat and she settled in next to Opal. Max cranked the Suburban and they headed out.

"All right, let's talk about Jake for a minute. What are we missing?" Harper asked.

Her boss shook his head. "I'm not sure. I think our best course of action is to stick to the plan. We'll pull in the chopper and do a full-on search of the park area tomorrow like we planned. For now, though, let's get some food."

"You don't think the chopper will be too much of a neon sign, saying, 'Hey, we're here and looking for you'?" Riley asked wryly.

Max shook his head. "They know we're here. Maybe if we keep their attention on the sky, they won't see us coming from the ground."

Riley nodded and shrugged. "Works for me."

"All right. We'll start first thing in the morning."

A quick stop at one of the local fast-food places filled their bellies and a short time later Max pulled into the motel parking lot followed by the other four agents. She appreciated their concern and their willingness to rush to the rescue. She worked with good people.

As far as she knew.

Jake was one she just wasn't sure about.

Harper knew one thing. She was tired. She loved her job, no doubt about it, but it was demanding and high stress and she'd admit she was ready to unwind for a little while. Maybe watch some television with Star curled up at her feet.

And Riley at her side.

She blinked. Now where did *that* come from?

She huffed. She might as well admit it. She found him attractive. There. She said it. Well, thought it anyway. But it didn't matter. There was no way she was getting involved with him.

Then again, why not?

Because he hadn't come out and said he was interested? Okay, there was that, but she had a feeling he was.

Then there was the small fact that he lived ten hours away from her.

She thought about her small one-bedroom condo back in Billings, Montana. White walls, a few pictures of her and the team and Star, of course. But mostly stark and blank, it was simply a place to sleep and shower. Longing crashed in on her, threatening to smother her. She wanted more than that. She wanted a home, a family, a place and person to call her own.

Harper drew in a deep breath and pushed aside the feelings. She had a case to solve. Dreams were nice to have if they were one day attainable. Harper wasn't sure hers were. She wasn't even sure she knew how to have a relationship at this point. Her parents hadn't exactly been domestic role models. Although, at least she knew what she *didn't* want in a marriage.

"Harper?"

She blinked. Riley stood in front of her, Star had joined her at her side. And she didn't even remember climbing from the vehicle. She cleared her throat. "Sorry, I was thinking."

"Deeply. You okay?"

"Sure. I'm fine." She looked behind him to see Max studying her, a frown on his face. "I'll see you guys in the morning."

She headed to her room, her heart in conflict. She could have died tonight. But she'd come close to death several times so what made this time different?

The fact that Riley was with her and he could have died, too?

Maybe.

Inside her room, Star settled herself on the bed and Harper removed her gear. She checked her weapon and made sure the safety was on, then unstrapped the knife at her ankle and set it on the end table along with her phone and little black notepad.

As soon as she flopped onto the bed next to Star, her phone buzzed. She groaned and rolled to snag it.

Riley.

Harper sat up. "Hello?"

"I know you're tired and if you'd rather just sleep, I understand, but you want to get a cup of coffee in the lobby?"

"As long as it's decaf."

"I'm ready when you are."

"Give me five."

Harper hung up and swung her legs over the side of the bed. All of a sudden, she wasn't tired at all. She chuckled to herself. If the thought of spending time with Riley could banish her fatigue after a long, tumultuous day, she needed to take him with her on *all* of her assignments.

She ran her fingers through her hair and noticed it had grown quite a bit. When was the last time she'd taken time to have it cut? Harper wondered if Riley preferred long hair or short.

She huffed at her thoughts. What did it matter? They could be friends, nothing more. She wasn't going to do a long-distance relationship assuming Riley was even interested.

So why was she running gloss over her lips?

Ugh. Harper tossed the tube back into her toiletries bag and zipped it.

She donned a light jacket with a side pocket and slipped her weapon inside then checked outside her room using the window and the peephole. Riley stood to the side waiting on her. Harper opened the door and stepped out. Her heart thudded an extra beat at the sight of him. He'd dressed in sweat pants and a dark blue T-shirt that brought out his tan—and stretched nicely over his shoulder muscles. She cleared her throat and realized she was going to have to come to terms with the fact that she was drawn to this man. And not just because he was good-looking, but because she liked him. A lot.

Riley smiled. "That was fast."

"I've learned how to get ready to walk out the door in under a minute. You shouldn't be waiting out here in the open."

"I was only here a few seconds before you opened the door."

"Doesn't take long to pull the trigger once you're in the sights."

"Noted."

They started walking. He stepped around her and she instantly noticed the protective gesture. Harper cut her eyes to him. "I'm not the one he wants to kill," she said softly.

He shrugged and kept walking. "Maybe not, but he won't mind going through you to get to me. I'm going to do my best to make sure that doesn't happen."

Her own protective instincts surged, but she squelched them. Riley was old-fashioned enough to re-spond to his natural instincts when it came to women and danger. And yet he wasn't offensive about it or thought she couldn't take care of herself, he just wanted to do it.

Frankly, Harper was surprised she'd picked up on that aspect of his personality so quickly. And actually liked it. She was always taking care of other people. It might be nice to be taken care of for once.

He opened the door and held it while she stepped inside the lobby. "The problem is," he said, "I can take all the precautions in the world, but eventually, you and I both know that if Blackman wants me dead, if I don't get him first, he'll get me."

"Let's make sure we get him first, then."

They went to the coffee urns and helped themselves. Harper and Star took a seat in the far corner with Harper placing her back to the wall and her front toward the door. It was a habit she knew she'd probably never break.

Riley maneuvered a chair so he could sit next to her. Apparently it was his habit, too. She took a sip of the hot brew and smiled into the cup before looking up. "How's Asher doing?"

"Hanging in there."

"And your mother?"

"The same." He frowned. "I could hear the fatigue in her voice when I called tonight. She rarely goes home and it's taking a toll on her."

"She won't let anyone else sit with Asher?"

He shrugged. "Every once in a while. The ladies in her Bible study group are wonderful. They offer, but she says it's just easier to stay than to worry from a distance. If I were there, she would go home more, I'm sure."

"You're questioning whether you should continue the search or go to Asher."

He raised a brow. "I am." He shrugged. "In fact, I

discussed that with Mom again tonight. She promised to let me know if it gets to be too much for her, but I doubt she will."

"I'm sorry you're having to go through all of this."

He drew in a deep breath and let it out slowly. "I am, too. But once Van is behind bars and Asher has had his surgery, it'll all be uphill from there." He sipped his coffee and stared at the front door and Harper figured his mind was on his nephew.

He blinked and shook his head.

She covered his hand with hers. When he looked up, she said, "Tell me about your sister. What was she like?"

A glow entered his eyes. "She was an amazing big sister and a natural mother. She was three years older than I and, trust me, she practiced her mothering skills on me when we were younger. She liked black licorice and coke when she watched a movie." He grimaced. "I never could stand that stuff. The licorice, I mean. She had a heart for the less fortunate and often volunteered on holidays to feed the homeless."

"What about Asher's father?"

Riley cleared his throat. "Bryce McDowell. He was a good guy. He and Charlotte were high school sweethearts and got married right after graduation, but couldn't figure out what he wanted to do with his life so he joined the military. He wound up serving in the Middle East. Before he left, she got pregnant with Asher, and then he was killed about two months after he was there."

"Oh, how awful for her."

"Yes. Asher never knew his father. Then when Asher was three, Charlotte met Van Blackman. He wooed her and she thought he was the best thing. We all did. One afternoon, about two years after they were together and talking marriage, I came out of a restaurant and saw him coming out of a hotel across the street at the same time. I started to call out to him when a pretty blonde walked up and kissed him." He glanced at her. "And trust me, it wasn't a sisterly kiss."

She grimaced.

"Anyway, I confronted him and he tried to lie his way out of it. I refused to believe him and he took a swing at me."

"How did that work out for him?"

A grim smile pulled his lips flat. "I ducked. He didn't. I told my sister what I saw and she asked him to explain himself. He admitted the woman was a former girlfriend and had asked him to meet her. He did, but said he immediately regretted it and begged her forgiveness. She told him she wanted some time to think about it."

"And he started stalking her?"

"Yes, but she didn't mention it until it was really too late for me to do anything about it. He killed her the next week after I'd started the process to procure a restraining order." He rubbed his eyes. "Some days I wish I'd never said anything."

"Could you really not have told her?"

He shook his head. "No. I had to tell her, I just wish I'd been more careful, more watchful—more aware. I was a cop and I missed it. Completely. It's hard to forgive myself for that."

"She never told you he was stalking her?"

"No. And I'm not sure it occurred to her to label it stalking. She'd mention seeing him in strange places. He'd show up at her job, at her church, at the same restaurant if she was out with friends, but she never said he was stalking her. In hindsight, that's what it was, of course." He cleared his throat and looked away. She let the silence fill the space between them.

He finally looked back at her. "What about you? You told me about your parents and a little about what your childhood was like. Do you have any other family?"

"I have a few aunts and uncles that I never see. They were around some when I was younger, but not anymore. I suppose that's why I want to have a big family one day."

"How big?"

"I don't know. Several kids, I guess. I want the proverbial white picket fence, too." She laughed then sighed. "Maybe I'm asking for too much. I want a guy who's crazy about me, kids and dogs." She shrugged. "One day."

"So you want to quit the Bureau?"

She frowned and pursed her lips then shook her head. "No, not really. I love what I do. It's been my life for a long time now so I'm not sure I could quit even if I wanted to, but I wouldn't mind the option."

"I see."

Riley stiffened. Her words threw his guard up. What was he doing talking about the future? Or even thinking about it? He had a murderer to catch and a nephew to care for. He didn't have time for romance. No matter that the attraction and temptation to get to know her better was strong.

Why her?

"What is it?" she asked.

"What do you mean?"

"You just got all quiet. What are you thinking?"

"A lot of things. Mostly that I wish I could picture that same scenario as part of my future, but don't think

I can." He sighed. "I was thinking that there might be something between us, something that could develop, but I'm just not sure. I don't think I can be that guy in your scenario."

He looked up and saw her sitting there with her jaw nearly on the floor. She set her cup on the table and stood. "Really? And who asked you to be that guy? We've known each other for a matter of days and while I'll admit I'm attracted to you, I'm certainly not ready to walk down the aisle with you. I was just sharing a dream. Something that I'd like to have in the future with *someone*. I wasn't singling you out. Honestly, Riley, you need to get over yourself. I'll see you in the morning." She strode toward the door with Star at her heels.

The heat started in his chest and rose quickly to cover his neck and cheeks. Well-deserved heat to go along with his complete embarrassment. He groaned and dropped his face into his hands. He was an idiot. Pure and simple.

What was it about this woman that made him trip over his words like did when he was around her? Why did he wind up looking like a fool whenever he opened his mouth about any other topic besides business? He really had to work on that.

His phone buzzed.

His mother's text flashed across the screen. Asher's very agitated. Wants to see you. Can you come in the morning?

Yes. I can come now.

No, in the morning is fine. He just drifted back off to sleep.

Text me if he wakes. I'll come whenever he needs me to.

See you in the morning.

His heart heavy, his mind in turmoil, Riley wanted to hit something. Or go for a very long run.

Harper and the team would have to search in the morning without him. His nephew came first.

But he owed Harper an apology.

And he didn't want her to walk back to her room alone. He jumped up and rushed for the door. And stopped.

She was standing just inside, arms crossed, watching him. He raised his brows and she shrugged. "Someone's trying to kill you."

"And doesn't care if you get in the way."

"So you were rushing to escort me back to my room?"

"Couldn't hurt."

"Right."

Star shifted and he looked down at the shepherd then back up at Harper. *Apologize!*

"I can't be a part of the search in the morning. My mother texted and said Asher needs me."

She frowned. "Is he all right?"

He explained the conversation with his mother.

Harper nodded. "Of course. I'll go with you and the others can start the search. If you give them some direction."

"I can do that, but you don't have to go."

"I think I should. Extra eyes, remember?"

"I remember."

Apologize! He really should, but the ice in her eyes made him wonder if she'd even hear it. Or accept it. Uncertainty made him pause. And then it was too late. She turned on her heel and walked out the door.

Riley sighed and caught up with her again. "Hey, hold on a second, will you?"

She didn't bother to turn. "What?"

"I'm sorry. I'm a jerk. An idiot. A presumptive—"

"I get it. Apology accepted. Now let's get inside somewhere so that no one can take shots at us again."

She swiped the key card and shoved the door open. He followed her inside and shut it behind him. "I shouldn't have assumed—"

"No, you shouldn't have, but it's done, you've apologized, we can move on."

"Can we?" Because now he found himself regretting his words. Not that he was ready to walk down the aisle with her any more than she apparently was with him, but dinner out with her might be nice, along with good conversation, good food… "I spoke without thinking—or perhaps, I was just overthinking. I do like you, Harper, a lot."

She continued to meet his gaze without blinking.

He sighed and raked a hand through his hair. "Can we be friends and not let the attraction that's between us interfere with what we've got to do to catch Jake and Van?"

"What attraction?" she asked, her words frigid.

He simply looked at her and her eyes thawed slightly. "Look, I get it, Riley. You've got a killer to catch and I've got a possible traitor to bring in. You're right. We need to focus on that and not let anything else distract us. Especially not a possible mutual attraction."

"Possible?"

"Possible."

He chuckled softly. "Good. Right. Exactly." He was relieved she felt the same way. Wasn't he?

"So…good night."

He frowned. "But we're still friends. We can still work together, can't we?" He had no idea why he needed her reassurance on that. He did know it wasn't just because she was his "in" to the best FBI resources that could possibly help him find Van. No. It was more than that. Way more.

Now she smiled. "Of course we can. Friends it is."

She held out a hand and he shook it. When she let go, he wanted to grab it back and tell her he didn't mean any of what he'd just said. But he couldn't. He owed it to his sister and Asher—and any other innocent women who might stumble into Van's path—to catch him and put him away. So, he simply inclined his head and walked out the door.

He could feel her behind him, watching. And then he was in his room.

Safe.

And alone.

And not nearly as happy as he thought he'd be. As he *should* be. With one more glance out the window, his gaze probing the shadows beyond the parking lot of the motel, he let out a weary sigh. He didn't have time to be distracted and Harper was one huge distraction. *Focus, Riley, focus.*

Where are you Van?

"I'm going to find him, Charlotte," he murmured to the empty room. "I'm going to find him."

He just prayed he kept his wits about him because if Van found him first, Riley was a dead man.

NINE

Early the next morning, Harper, Star and Riley took off for Denver, while Max and Ian and the others headed for the national park to continue the search. The chopper was already in the air and searching in a grid-like pattern. Max promised to update her hourly.

Harper kept her cool where Riley was concerned. He was right. He had jumped to some huge assumptions. The problem was, he'd hit close to the mark. She *had* pictured him in the role of boyfriend then possible husband so when he'd said that role wasn't for him, she'd been hurt and embarrassed for allowing her thoughts to even go there.

What made her even more unsettled was that she didn't normally do that kind of thing. She didn't put men she met or worked with in that role. She simply… didn't. So to do that with Riley was not only surprising, it made her nervous.

But she'd keep her mouth shut and just pretend last night hadn't happened. Riley seemed willing to follow her lead. The drive to Denver passed quickly with Riley at the wheel and Harper watching for anyone who might decide to follow them and finish what he started the day before. But she didn't spot anyone and she soon found herself following Riley into the hospital.

"Are you all right?" she felt compelled to ask. While he'd said some things that sparked her ire, she still cared about what he was feeling.

He held the door for her. "Why?"

"You're tensed up and your jaw looks like it's been poured in concrete."

He ran a hand over his jaw and sighed. "I'm worried about Asher, my mother. The future."

"I can understand that."

"But I'm trying not to."

"God's got this. Try to trust that He's got a plan in all of this."

His expression softened slightly. "That's what I keep telling myself. It's sure hard to believe it, though."

"Yeah, I know."

They made their way to Asher's room and found the little guy awake and coloring while his grandmother dozed in the chair beside him. Crayons littered the floor around her and Harper wondered if they'd just missed a tantrum.

Riley's mother opened her eyes at their entrance and drew in a deep breath. Relief stamped itself plainly on her face. "Asher, look who's here."

Asher looked up and as soon as he saw his uncle, his frown flipped into a huge grin. "Uncle Riley, you came! Mimi said you were coming, but I didn't believe her."

"Well, if Mimi said it, it has to be true." He bent over and kissed his nephew on his head then rested a hand on his small shoulder.

Asher's gaze landed on Harper. "Who are you?"

Harper stepped forward and smiled warmly. "I'm Harper. I'm a friend of your uncle's."

Riley nodded to the older woman. "This is my mother, Maria Martelli."

"Nice to meet you," Mrs. Martelli said.

"And you." She shook hands with his mother then clicked her fingers and Star settled at her side. "I brought another friend, too."

Asher's eyes rounded and his jaw dropped. "A dog," he breathed.

"This is Star."

"Hi, Star."

Harper pointed. "Go tell Asher hello."

Star walked over to Asher and nudged his hand with her nose.

Asher laughed and scratched the animal's ears.

Riley's eyes caught hers and she thought she saw a sheen of tears there before he looked back at Asher. "What's on the schedule for today?"

"Another X-ray to make sure the bullet hasn't moved," his mother said. "Then we'll take him outside if he feels like it."

"I feel like it."

Riley patted Asher's shoulder. "Great. So, Champ, what happened with all the crayons?"

Asher lowered his eyes. "I threw them."

"Why?"

"'Cuz I was mad."

"Mad because you can't get off this bed?"

Asher shook his head.

"Then what?"

"Mad because my mom went away and Mimi said she wasn't ever coming back. She said she was dead and in heaven with Jesus."

Harper winced and almost felt guilty for witnessing the intimate moment between the grieving family.

Riley swallowed then cleared his throat. "I know. It makes me mad, too, but we're going to get the man who…made her go away."

"And put him in jail?"

"Yes."

"And Star is trying to help," Harper said.

Asher turned his attention to her. "She is?"

"Yes. She's specially trained to track down people like the man who hurt your mom."

"How?"

Harper explained it to him in simple terms and he listened, the rapt expression on his face touching her. "So, hopefully, tomorrow, when we go looking, we'll find him."

Asher nodded. For the next two hours, she and Riley entertained the child while his grandmother took a much-needed break. Asher finally yawned and his eyes grew heavy. "Can Star get up on the bed?"

Riley raised a brow at Harper who shrugged. She patted the foot of the bed and Star hopped up, turned three times then settled her head on her paws. Asher giggled. "There's a dog in my bed, Uncle Riley."

"And she can stay there until you go to sleep."

"'Kay. Thanks." Riley held Asher's hand until the boy went to sleep.

Harper's phone buzzed and she glanced at the screen. "It's Max," she whispered.

"Have they found anything?"

She read the message then said softly, "They found several camping areas that could have been used by Jake or Van, but said nothing concrete. He did find one person who thought she recognized Jake's picture so he feels like he's still in the area."

"Good. What about Van?"

"Nothing so far."

He frowned and nodded. "All right. When my mother gets back, let's grab a bite to eat and get back to it."

"Are you sure you want to go? Asher seems to do much better when you're here."

Conflict raged in his eyes and he sighed. "I need to do this. Asher understands. He's six, but he's smart."

"Catch him, Uncle Riley. I'll be okay."

Harper turned to see Asher's sleepy eyes on them. Riley leaned over the child. "Are you sure, Champ? Because I'll stay if you want me to."

"I want you to stay, but I want the man who killed my mom to be in jail more. I won't throw any more crayons."

Riley kissed Asher's forehead and swallowed hard. "All right, then," he said, his voice hoarse, "I'll get him and get back to you. Deal?"

"Deal."

"And you can throw the crayons if it makes you feel better."

They fist-bumped and Asher's eyes closed again.

Emotions ran across Riley's face and Harper almost thought she might be able to feel sorry for Van Blackman if Riley got his hands on him.

Almost.

The door opened and Riley's mother took her place back in the chair and picked up her knitting project.

Harper's phone buzzed again and Harper couldn't stop the gasp that slipped from her lips when she read the message. Then she smiled.

"What is it?" Riley asked.

"Good news."

"What kind?"

"You'll see. You should know in just a few minutes."

Riley's brows rose. "Now I'm really curious."

But she wouldn't tell him and he finally shot her an amused smile and leaned his head back against the chair. Star shifted onto her side and closed her eyes.

Harper was too excited to even think about dozing and if that doctor didn't get himself in the room in the next few minutes, she thought she might burst.

Just when she was ready to go find him, the door opened and the doctor she'd been thinking about stuck his head in. "Mr. Martelli, do you have a minute?"

Riley exchanged glances with Harper and she shrugged, but that smile on her face didn't fade and the twinkle in her eyes made him wonder what she knew that he didn't.

His mother stood as well. The doctor pulled back into the hall and Riley and his mother followed him. Harper rose, but didn't follow.

"Come on out here," Riley said. "You can hear whatever he has to say so I don't have to repeat it."

Harper gave a slow nod and her heart lurched at the notion that he wanted to keep her in the loop about Asher.

Once she joined them in the hall, the doctor gave them a broad smile. "We're taking Asher to surgery."

Riley gasped. "What?"

His mother gripped his forearm and gave a small cry. "When?"

"You've got ten minutes then we're rolling him down."

Riley looked at Harper. The grin on her face rivaled that of the doctor's. "You knew, didn't you?"

"Yep."

"But…how?"

"Let me make a phone call." She had whoever she was calling on speed dial.

"This is Dylan."

"Hi Dylan, I just wanted to let you know that the doctor just told Riley and his mother that Asher's going to get his surgery today."

"Oh, yeah? Hey, that's great!"

"You want to explain how that came about?" She smiled at Riley.

"Am I on speakerphone?"

"Yes."

He laughed. "The team overheard a conversation Riley had with his nephew and decided to take action to get him up and moving. A couple of days ago, I talked to Mrs. Martelli and asked what it would take to get Asher the surgery." His mother pressed her fingers to her lips and nodded. "She gave me the details and I took it from there. Riley, you've brought us really close to finding Jake Morrow so the powers that be felt you earned the reward money. We Tactical K-9 folks pooled our resources and held a fund-raiser here at headquarters the day before yesterday. A lot of us called in favors and asked for donations. We raised the money in a little less than sixteen hours plus enough for some after-surgery costs like physical therapy."

Riley swiped a hand across his eyes. He didn't even care that tears dripped from his chin as well. "I don't know what to say."

His mother swatted him on the arm. "I think thank-you is a good start."

"Yes, yes, of course. Thank you. I'm just blown away."

"We can do that, too, but only to the bad guys. This

was definitely a team effort to help the good guys, so keep us updated on his progress, will you?"

"Absolutely."

"Thanks, Dylan, talk to you later."

"Bye."

Riley pulled Harper into a hug and held on while he tried to get his emotions under control. The doctor walked off with a new spring in his step and his mother slipped back into Asher's room leaving him alone with Harper in the hallway.

Harper, who was still in his arms.

"Oh, sorry." He stepped back, stunned at the realization he'd reached for her without thinking twice about it.

"Don't be." She studied him, the look on her face unreadable.

He cleared his throat. "I'm going to stay here. It's going to be a long night."

"Of course." She grabbed his hand and squeezed. "I'll check with Max, but I'm sure he'll tell me to stay with you."

The hair on Riley's neck stood on end and he froze. Then looked up to see Van Blackman watching from the end of the hall. The man met his eyes, saluted then disappeared through the door with the exit sign above it.

"Blackman's here." He raced down the hall, passing the startled nurses and hit the stairwell at a run. It vaguely occurred to him he should have checked to make sure Van wasn't standing there simply waiting to shoot him when he came through the door, but at this point, he didn't care. The man had shown up on his nephew's floor.

"Riley!" Harper's shout didn't slow him. He continued down the stairs and out the door at the bottom. He held it open while he scanned the area. The hallway to his right held a patient on a gurney and two medical personnel standing next to him talking. The hallway to his left led to the parking garage.

Harper caught up to him and he headed for the parking garage. Then stopped. "Where'd he go?"

"I don't know," Harper said.

"What if he doubled back?" he gritted.

Riley turned on his heel and sprinted back up the stairs, taking them two at a time. Harper followed him once again, on her radio, and asking for backup.

Once back on Asher's floor, Riley beelined for his nephew's room.

He rushed inside to find it empty. "He's got them."

"No," Harper said, trying to catch her breath. "Don't jump to that conclusion. They were coming to get Asher for his surgery, remember?"

Riley turned on his heel and headed for the nurse's desk. "Lisa. Did they come get him? Asher? From room 312?"

"Hey Riley, what's wrong?"

"I need to know where Asher is. *Now.* Please."

"Sure." She sat in front of the computer and time slowed to a snail's pace while she clicked the keys. Finally, she looked up. "Yep. He's in the surgery prep area."

Riley's knees nearly buckled with relief. "And my mother? She's with him?"

"Um. I would assume so."

"No. I can't assume. I need to know."

She must have sensed his intense distress because without another word, she picked up the phone and dialed an extension. "Hey, is Maria Martelli down there with Asher? Uh-huh. Okay, thanks." She hung up. "She's there."

Riley dropped his head into his hands. They were fine. He wasn't going to lose them to Blackman's evil. "Okay, thank you." *Thank you, God, thank you.*

Officers arrived on the floor and Harper directed them to follow Riley. He led them down to the surgical area and found his mother reading a book to Asher who didn't seem to be paying much attention.

It took a moment to get his heartbeat to slow. In its place, fury churned. He tamped it down and forced himself to think logically, clearly.

What was Van doing here?

"We'll have someone stay on Asher and your mother from here on out."

"Yes. I think that would be a good idea."

And then Asher was being rolled back for surgery and Riley prepared himself to wait while others hunted the man who'd gotten away yet again.

TEN

Harper stood at the door of the waiting room and watched Riley sleep. Or rest. Or pray. Whatever he was doing, he had his eyes closed. His mother sat across from him working feverishly on a blanket. Her needles clicked in a soothing rhythm while the television above her head scrolled the stock market report.

Harper slipped into the chair beside Riley and he turned his head to look at her. "Did they find him?"

"Not yet," she said. "The chopper pilot spotted something and sent them to investigate, but it turned out to be a false alarm."

He sighed. "They won't find him. Not until he's ready to be found." He frowned. "Don't you need to be out there looking for Jake?"

"I updated Max on the situation and the fact that Blackman was seen here at the hospital. He told me to stay and find out what I could."

"And?"

"We've got Blackman on video."

She'd made sure Riley's family was covered and safe then gone to check with hospital security about getting a look at the video footage. It had taken five minutes to bring up the picture of Van standing in the hall next to the stairwell door. They'd tracked him back to a handicapped parking spot where he'd pulled in and placed the tag on his rearview mirror before getting out of the green pickup and walking into the hospital.

"The tag on his vehicle was stolen from a Laundromat this morning. We got him on video there, too."

"Why do you think he was here at the hospital? Looking for me?"

She fell silent then gave a slight shrug. "I have my theories."

"Such as?"

She bit her lip then sat beside him. His mother continued to knit, but Harper figured she wasn't missing a word.

Riley waved a hand giving her permission to speak her mind in front of his mother. Harper lowered her voice anyway. "You said Blackman vowed to kill you."

The needles fell silent.

"Yes."

"Because he knows he'll never be able to stop looking over his shoulder. You've promised to bring him to justice no matter how long it takes."

Riley gave a short nod.

"So, that leads me to believe his only recourse is to kill you."

Another nod from Riley.

Harper bit her lip and shrugged. "I think Van might have been trying to get to Asher or your mother."

"But why?"

"I'm not sure. Again, I have theories, but that's all they are."

"I think he's mocking me."

"Could be that."

"It's why he's stayed around close by. I mean, why

not flee the country? Why stay less than two hours away from where your victim was killed?"

"He wants Asher," his mother said softly.

Riley stilled. "*What? Why* would you say that?"

"He was crazy about that boy, you know that."

"Yes, but—"

"I think Asher's why he had such trouble letting go of Charlotte. He lost his first wife and child and once Charlotte started having second thoughts about him, it sent him into a tailspin. He'd already gotten attached to Asher and if Charlotte left him, it would be like losing his wife and child all over again. He begged, he pleaded, he threatened. And when none of that worked, he lost it and killed her." She paused. "I think he had every intention of taking Asher from her that day and disappearing. Only the fact that he was shot, too, kept him from taking him."

"What makes you say that?"

"Charlotte told me he'd threatened that if she left him, he'd take Asher."

Riley gaped at her. "And you didn't think I needed to know that?"

"Well, since Asher was in the hospital and paralyzed—and Van had disappeared, I didn't think it was that important." She bit her lip. "Now I think it's possible he's just been biding his time."

Riley looked away and rubbed his chin. "Maybe."

"It's a good analysis, Mrs. Martelli," Harper said. "Maybe you should apply to work for the FBI." She kept her tone light in the heavy atmosphere.

The woman gave her a sad smile. "It's just called experience."

"Yeah." Harper sank into the seat next to her and joined them in the wait.

For the next six hours, they alternated pacing, dozing, sipping decaf coffee and waiting for the hourly updates on Asher's progress.

A nurse appeared in the doorway and Riley shot to his feet. She held up a hand. "Asher's doing great. The bullet has been removed and they're patching him up now."

Riley blew out a breath and slumped back down into the chair. "Thanks."

"The doctor will be out shortly to talk with you, but it's looking good for Asher."

Riley swallowed and nodded, not even bothering to try to hide the sheen of tears in his eyes. His mother clasped his hand and Harper placed hers over theirs and squeezed.

Finally, the doctor stepped into the waiting room. He removed his surgical mask and gave them a smile accompanied by two thumbs up. "It went perfect. Asher did amazing. The bullet was right where the X-ray showed. It didn't do any damage to the spine, but the tissue around it was so inflamed, it was what temporarily paralyzed Asher. Now that it's gone, once the inflammation goes down and the incision heals, I think there's real hope he'll be able to walk again soon."

His mother began to cry and Riley wrapped an arm around her shaking shoulders. "God came through," she whispered. "Thank you, Jesus."

Harper's phone rang and she stepped away to answer. "Hello?"

"It's Max. Today was a bust. Mostly. We did find someone who recognized Jake from the park's general store, but couldn't tell us where he was camping or if he was still around."

Harper rubbed a weary hand across her eyes. "When did the person see him?"

"Yesterday morning."

"All right. So, I guess we continue going on the assumption that he's staying put for now."

"Yes, but I'm not sure how long that will last," Max said. "He knows we're here looking for him."

"Is there any indication that Penny has left the area?"

"Nothing. No hits on her passport or credit cards."

"Then Jake's probably not going anywhere, either. We need to keep searching."

"I agree. Can you join in first thing in the morning?"

"I can. Where do you want to meet?"

He told her then said, "I've got a vehicle for you. It's being driven here overnight and you'll have it first thing in the morning."

"Perfect." That would help. As much as she knew Riley didn't mind them using his truck, the official vehicle would make things easier all around.

"Now, how's Asher? The team is begging for an update."

She filled him in.

"Glad to hear the boy's doing well. We'll see you in the morning."

"See you then."

When she returned to the waiting room, Riley was pacing and his mother had resumed her knitting. He enveloped her in a hug as soon as he spotted her. "He's going to walk again."

"That's the prayer." She breathed in his masculine scent and found she didn't want to leave his arms. The thought unsettled her.

But she felt powerless to move away.

He finally let her go and cleared his throat. "I'm glad you're here."

She smiled mistily. "I am, too." She settled into the chair beside him. It was going to be a long night.

Harper and Star arrived in the national park just as the sun rose in a brilliant splash of oranges, reds and yellows. Riley pulled in beside her. He'd insisted on driving his truck just in case he had to leave fast and get back to Denver and Asher.

He climbed out of his truck and into the passenger seat. "I never get tired of watching that."

She agreed. The sight nearly took her breath away and she paused for a brief moment to simply savor it.

"Amazing, isn't it?" Riley asked softly.

She nodded. "Absolutely incredible." She paused. "Are you sure you're okay being here instead of with Asher?"

"I'm sure. The doctor said even though Asher is doing fine, they're keeping him sedated while his back heals a bit. He won't know I'm not there and Mom will call if anything comes up. I've got my truck, I'm good."

"All right, then."

He patted the leather armrest. "Nice wheels."

"Only the best for us," she drawled.

He looked at her. "You're not a typical agent, are you? Or group of agents, I guess I should say."

She blinked. "What do you mean?"

"I mean, you're more subtle. You have amazing resources, Max is the leader of your team and he calls the shots, but…" He shrugged. "I don't know. You just seem different than other agents I've known." He snapped his fingers. "For example, you don't have partners. You all work together as a team."

"Nice observation."

"So, what are you?"

She smiled. "Exactly what you see, Riley, I promise. We are special, yes. We do more classified work, I suppose, than other agents. And we have the incredible resources you mentioned. So, yeah."

Max and Ian pulled in beside them, cutting off the explanation. Max rolled down his window and did the same. "Just got a call," Max said. "Jake's been spotted."

Harper tensed. "Where?"

"Over near a campground where some kids are."

Riley blanched. "I wonder if that's the group Asher's teacher referred to while she was visiting Asher."

"Could be," Harper said.

Max shoved his Suburban in gear. "Let's head that way."

"I'll just ride with you," Riley said.

A short time later, she pulled into the campground and noticed the cabins located to her right situated into a nice circle. A building sat in the middle and she assumed that to be the bathhouse. Various vehicles were scattered about and someone had set up an area with a stage and bleachers.

Max and Ian pulled in beside her. First they'd talk to the leaders of the camp and try to get a good idea where Jake had been spotted. Then the searching would commence once again.

Harper stepped out of the vehicle and let Star out of her area. A bell rang and children began to come from the cabins. Harper judged them to be between eight and twelve years old. A few caught sight of her and pointed.

A young woman dressed in jeans and a pullover hoodie spotted her and smiled. It was the same woman she'd seen walking out of Asher's hospital room the other day. She walked toward Harper. "Hi. I'm Beth Smith."

Harper shook the woman's outstretched hand. "I'm Special Agent Harper Prentiss and this is Star. I think you know Riley."

"Pleasure to meet you." Ms. Smith looked at Riley. "And good to see you again, Riley. How's Asher?"

"Doing well." He gave her the short version of how the surgery came about.

"That's wonderful," she said. "I'm so happy to hear that."

Max and Ian and their dogs finally joined them. After Harper made the introductions, she said, "I hear you spotted a man we're looking for."

Ms. Smith rubbed her hands together and looked around. "Yes. He was down near the river getting some water. One of the children and a chaperone, Gary, spotted him. Gary had been in the general store in Drum Creek and saw the news flash on the television that you were looking for him. He told me and we looked up the number and called it in."

"We appreciate that. Could we speak to the chaperone who saw him? Gary, right?"

"Right. He's in the second cabin on the right just past the bathhouse. He'll be helping some of the younger children get ready for the day. We're doing an early morning swim. The brave ones who want to, anyway. It's too cold for me."

"Thanks again," Max said.

They went to the cabin and knocked on the door. A little boy about nine years old opened it. His eyes widened when he saw them. "Dudes! It's the 5-0! And they've got dogs!"

Within seconds, they were surrounded by ten eager

boys ranging in age from eight to ten. Harper and the others let them pet the animals for a moment before their chaperone moved them back into the cabin then stepped outside. "Sorry about that."

"Not a problem," Harper said, flashing him a warm smile.

"Are you Gary?" Max asked.

"I am. You people are fast."

"We're here with one purpose. To find our agent and bring him home," Max said. "So what can you tell us?"

"He was down by the river. I think he was filling a canteen. When he looked up and saw me, he just nodded and walked away."

"Which way?" Max asked.

"North."

"What was he wearing?"

"A pullover sweatshirt and jeans. And he had a ball cap on."

Harper frowned. "And you recognized him?"

"Well, he took the hat off and dunked his head in the water before he pulled the hat back on. That's when I realized who he was."

Max looked at Harper. "We'll head north. You go south just in case he made a U-turn somewhere. Stop everyone you see and show his picture. We'll do the same. Use the radios to stay in touch."

"Got it."

She and Riley headed back to her vehicle while the children and their leaders made their way to the lake for a chilly morning swim.

"Riley?"

He stopped and Harper saw Ms. Smith motioning him back to her. He shrugged. "I'll meet you at the truck in a minute."

Harper nodded and led Star to the Suburban where she turned on her radio. She fitted the earpiece into her right ear. "You guys there?"

"We're here," came Max's instant response. "Are you headed out?"

"Almost. Riley's talking to one of the chaperones. I'll check in shortly."

"10-4."

She looked back to see Riley and the teacher still deep in conversation about thirty yards away. Probably about Asher. They had their backs to her, Riley's dark head bent over hers. The woman placed a hand on his arm and Harper stiffened. Was that really necessary?

She grimaced. She was *not* jealous. She had no right to feel sharp pangs in her gut at the sight of them together. But come on…would the woman ever stop talking? They weren't in a hurry per se, but Harper was ready to get on with the search. She shot the two one more glance and saw them step into the nearest cabin.

"Great."

Harper turned her attention to Star who seemed restless. She paced to the front of the vehicle then back. "What is it, girl?"

The dog sat at her feet and leaned against her. Harper scratched her ears then opened the door for her to hop in. At first Star didn't seem to want to cooperate, but at Harper's urging, she complied. Harper shut the door and reached for the driver's handle. She'd wait for him in the truck; she liked to do her sulking in private.

A cold blade at the base of her throat froze her. "Jake?" she whispered.

"Actually, no. Try Van."

A chill slithered through her. "What do you want?"

"Where's your boyfriend?"

"Excuse me?"

"Riley!" Van yelled. "Where is he? He's always with you, but you're getting ready to leave and he's nowhere to be seen."

Her gaze flicked to the cabin where Riley was and prayed he stayed put. "He's with some of the other agents. He won't be alone. He'll always have someone on him from now on. You won't be able to get to him so you might as well remove that knife from my throat."

Van cursed. A low, menacing slew of words that expressed his severe displeasure. The hand that held the blade was steady. Decisive. She didn't dare yank away. "Well, then, I guess I get to move on to plan B," he finally said.

"Which is?"

"Your friends get you back when I get Riley."

"You're going to kidnap a federal agent?" She grasped her keys in her right hand and let her thumb rove over the controls of the remote.

"Looks that way, doesn't it? Now move before those kids get back and someone has to get hurt."

He reached around her to open the driver's door and she took a chance. She pressed the button that would release Star. The door swung open on command. The knife slipped, nicking her skin, but she ignored the sharp pain, dropped the keys and grabbed Van's wrist that held the knife against her throat.

"Attack!" She yanked his arm, the knife moved from her throat by a mere inch, and Star dove for his leg.

Van cried out and went down. Harper spun away from him. He swung the knife at Star, but the dog moved at the last minute and by chance, he missed. But Harper could see his intent to stab the animal.

"Star, release. Come now!" And just like in their

training exercises, the dog released her victim and darted to Harper's side.

Harper pulled her weapon, but Van was stumbling away. "Stay put, Van!"

He ignored her and continued his fast limp-jog away from her. She could send Star after him, but he still had the knife in his hand and Harper wouldn't take a chance he'd try to stab Star again.

"Harper? What's going on?"

Riley had come out of the cabin and was running toward her. "Get in the car!" She pressed the button on her radio as she raced after Van, Star at her side. "He's here. Van Blackman showed up and attacked me. I'm fine, but he's getting away."

The roar of an engine caught her attention and she crested the hill to see a green pickup speed away, down the dirt trail, kicking up dust as he went.

"He's heading east. I'm going to try and follow him." It took a few precious seconds to get Star back in the vehicle as well as Riley, but she finally was on the road Van had just taken.

And there was no sign of him.

"What happened?" Riley asked.

"Van showed up and attacked me." She made a sharp right turn to stay on the dirt road.

"He did what?" She heard the venomous tone in Riley's voice.

"He caught me by surprise while you were in the cabin with Ms. Smith. Where is he?" she muttered, seeing nothing to indicate the direction he'd gone. "How does he just disappear like he does?" She slowed, unsure where to go.

"He could have turned off any of the little side roads

along here," Riley said. "There's no way to tell which one he might have chosen."

"Harper?" Max asked, his voice coming over the earpiece.

"He's gone," she told them, seething at once more losing the man. It was now personal for her, too. "We're heading back toward Riley's truck."

"10-4 on that," her boss said. "See you in a few minutes."

Riley's phone rang, and he sighed even as he snagged it. "It's my mom." He pressed the button to connect the call. "Hello?"

Ten minutes later, Harper stood beside the vehicle with her weapon at her side while Riley spoke on the phone with his mother. It didn't appear that anything was wrong, she was just passing on an update.

Max and Ian arrived. Max stepped out of the Suburban and came to her. "Are you all right?"

She waved a hand and holstered her weapon. "I'm fine."

In the side mirror, she examined the nick in the side of her neck. It still seeped blood but wasn't deep enough for stitches.

"What happened?" Max demanded. "You said Blackman attacked you?"

"Yeah. He was there at the cabins. Riley and Ms. Smith were still talking so I went on to the truck. They stepped into one of the cabins and Van came up behind me and held a knife to my throat. He was going to take me as a hostage and trade me for Riley. I decided I didn't like that plan and changed it for him."

She rummaged in the truck and found the first aid kit.

Riley had hung up and was listening to the end of

her explanation. He blanched and punched a fist into his opposite palm. "Unbelievable. The man has no fear that he'll be caught."

He took the antibiotic cream from her and used a gauze pad to clean the area then apply the cream. She winced at the sting but didn't move. He was seething but his touch was gentle. She looked into his eyes and saw the conflict raging inside him.

"We barely touched the surface of our initial search before your call came in," Max said. "We'll head north again and you two stick to the original plan and go south."

Harper nodded. "Got it."

Riley affixed a band aid over the area and closed the kit.

"Then let's find these guys and end this thing," Ian said.

Riley nodded. "I'm all for that."

Harper went ahead and transferred her equipment into the new Suburban.

The dogs sensed they were going back to work and nearly vibrated with excitement.

Max slammed his door and rolled his window down. "Stay in touch with the radios and let us know if you need backup. We'll do the same."

Harper let her eyes focus on the area where they would search. "I had Blackman in the palm of my hand and he slipped away to disappear in this massive area. It's going to be like a needle in a haystack."

Max blew out a breath. "Yes, but it's the only option we've got for now. Jake's out there, too." He paused then shook his head. "It's brilliant, really. Tons of places to hide. Lots of open areas to see if someone's coming.

Yep. If I were wanting to slip off the radar, this is exactly the type of place I'd pick."

"Well, we know Van's around here," Ian said. "Let's see if we can find them both. I'm ready to head home."

Harper held out the bag that had Jake's baseball cap to Star. The dog sniffed it and lifted her nose. She started walking so Harper and Riley fell in behind her. "See you in a while."

She and Riley walked several miles, stopping each time they came across a camper or an RV to question the occupants and to show them Jake's and Van's pictures.

On their way to the next stop, Riley took her hand. She looked up. "What?"

"Are you sure you're okay?"

"Yes, I'm sure." His concern touched her.

"I'm sorry," he murmured.

"Sorry? For?"

"For whatever part I've played in making you one of Van's targets."

Harper stopped walking and turned to face him. "Riley, stop. This is not your fault. None of it. You're tracking a criminal. It's what we do. Sometimes danger is a result. But it's not your fault."

He gave a slow nod, his eyes never leaving hers. Then he sighed. "I know that. Mentally."

"Good. You ready to keep going?"

"Sure."

Finally, after losing count of how many people she'd talked to, Harper showed the pictures to an elderly man who scratched his balding head. "I think I recognize him." He pointed to Jake. "I was coming out of the general store over in Drum Creek and ran across that fellow. He was kind enough to help me change my tire."

"Did he say what his name was?"

"Nope. He seemed to be in a hurry, so I just thanked him. I offered him a twenty and he just shook his head and told me to have a good day."

"But you haven't seen either one of these guys around the park?" Riley asked.

The old man shook his head. "No, not around here." He shrugged. "Doesn't mean they're not out here, though. Lots of places to camp. It would be easy to miss them."

"Of course." Harper put the picture away and rubbed a hand over her eyes. Then smiled. "Thank you for your time."

"I hope you find them."

"Me, too."

The man paused. "Should we be worried? Should we pack up and leave?"

Harper hesitated then shook her head. "I don't think so. They're not attacking random people. They're mostly wanting to just stay hidden and off the radar. But you'll have to make up your mind about whether you feel safe enough to stay."

He shrugged. "I'll think about it."

Harper walked off and Riley and Star followed. She turned and looked around. "You know, we're down here in the valley area where it makes sense to camp what with the fresh water streams and the lake. But what if Jake and Van are hiding out up there?" She pointed to the higher elevation area. Mountainous terrain that wouldn't be easy to navigate, but would definitely be a great hiding place.

Riley planted his hands on his hips. "It would defi-nitely be a better vantage point to watch from and be able to see if someone was coming up—and then take cover and hide to avoid the searching."

"Star isn't signaling that Jake's been anywhere around here. I say it's time to start going up."

Riley opened the map they'd gotten from the visitor's center. "Look here." He pulled a pen from his pocket and started circling. "All of these are campsites on the map. I think we need to be seeking out places that aren't mapped. Places that are flat, close to water, with an easy route out of the park should he have to run."

"Which one? Jake or Van?"

"Both, probably."

She nodded. "All right, let's go." She clicked to Star and the three of them headed toward where they'd parked her truck. Sweat beaded on her forehead and she grabbed the water bottle from the pouch on her belt. "You know, I did my research. There are four hundred and fifteen square miles to this park. That's a lot of ground to cover."

"I know. Not to mention tons of hiking trails, camping areas and so on."

"There's got to be an easier way to do this," she said.

"Choppers would help."

"Yes, they would. But Jake knows our resources. He's not going to camp out where he'd be visible from the air." She paused. "But Blackman might. He might not realize that our resources are now yours and he might not be quite so careful about staying out of aerial sight range." She got on the radio with Max.

"Have you found anything?" he asked her.

"No, but I'd like to bring in a chopper. Could you request one to make a pass over the area?" She gave him the approximate location.

"We've got one at the Denver Airport. I'll get him out here. Give him an hour."

"Thanks, Max. We'll keep looking."

Once they were inside her Suburban, she put it in gear and rolled toward the road that would take them up as Riley had directed. "Are there camping areas up there?" she asked.

"Yes. Some. They're not quite as popular as the ones near the lake, but there are those who brave the roads to get the view."

They continued to climb, looking for anything that would resemble a place someone might decide to set up camp. She watched him from the corner of her eye as she drove. He rode in silence, his jaw tight, eyes narrowed. He radiated determination—and impatience. She understood that. She wanted this to be over with as well—and she didn't have a sick nephew she was desperate to get back to.

Harper pulled into an area designated for pictures. "If I remember correctly, there's a small creek that runs through the trees behind us. It's not exactly off the beaten path, but it's a good place to start."

"Perfect." Harper climbed from the truck and Star hopped down beside her. Harper let Star have another whiff of Jake's hat and the shepherd dropped her nose to the ground.

They walked for several minutes in silence, following Star's lead. The dog searched bushes, trees and rocks to no avail. Harper stopped. "He's not been around here."

"I don't think so, either." Riley looked around. "I know where I am."

"What?"

"I forgot about this place, but my dad used to bring me and my cousins up here. There's a shallow river that runs at the bottom of that drop-off over there." He pointed.

"There's water over there?"

"Yes. If I remember correctly."

She paused as a faint sound reached her ears. "Do you hear that?"

He listened then frowned. "Yes."

She took two steps to the right, stopped then walked to the left. "I think it's coming from that direction." She pointed to the drop-off he'd indicated just moments earlier.

"Let's check it out."

Harper hurried toward the sounds that grew louder as she approached the edge of the cliff. When she stepped to the ledge, she looked down to find it wasn't a drop-off after all. A large stream of water flowed gently at the bottom. "You were right. There's water down here." Movement caught her eyes and she gasped. "Puppies!"

Riley stepped up beside her. "What?"

"Look."

He did and tensed. "There's a bag with a hole in the side. Someone threw them down there."

"And not too long ago. There's still one in the bag." Harper started down the sloping hill and heard Riley follow her. Star beat them to the bottom and began investigating the little pups. They seemed delighted to see her and one began chewing Star's front paw. She nudged it away only to have it come back and start in again.

Star looked at Harper as though to say, "Really?"

Harper scratched the dog's ears. "It's okay, girl, they're just babies. Baby beagles. Probably only a few weeks old at most."

And someone had tried to drown them. Anger at the heartlessness of some people ate at her as she pulled the last squirming pup from the bag. She held it up to her face and it licked her nose. Another gnawed on her bootlace.

Riley snagged the third one before it tumbled into the water. The fourth sat and watched the excitement, his little tongue hanging out of the side of his mouth. "They could have drowned."

"I think that was the idea," Harper muttered.

"I didn't see anyone on the way up here. Did you?"

"No. It took them some time to chew through the bag. Whoever dumped them is long gone. I'm just glad he has lousy aim and missed the water."

"What are we going to do with them?"

"Take them with us for now."

"Take them with us where?"

"We have a K-9 training unit back in Billings. One of the things we try to do is take a puppy back from each assignment to be trained."

"That's a great thing to do."

"And now we have four here." The fourth puppy that had been sitting got up and limped toward Riley. He picked it up. "This little guy is hurt."

"He might have landed the hardest when the bag hit the ground. He might need an X-ray."

"Yeah. Let's find a vet and get him taken care of."

"As for the others, we'll see if there's a place that takes in strays for now. Like a foster home for them. Maybe someone can keep them until it's our assignment is finished. Then we can pick them up and take them back to Billings."

Riley gave a low sigh. "Well, today was a wash."

"Not really. We rescued four little beagle pups who would have died without us. We're heroes."

"Good point." He offered her a smile that resonated within her. He kept his eyes locked on hers. "Harper…"

Her heart thudded but she refused to let him know it. "What?"

"I—"

The poor guy looked terribly uncomfortable. "What is it?"

"Would you—"

"Spit it out, Riley. What are you trying to say?"

"You're not going to make it easy for me, are you?"

"Make what easy?"

He sighed. "Would you have dinner with me?"

Dinner? He wanted to have dinner. After he'd told her that he wasn't interested in being the guy for her? He really had a lot of nerve. "Riley—"

"We can talk about the case and what the next move needs to be to find Van. And Jake."

They needed to have dinner in order to do that? Harper almost said no, then bit her tongue on the words. He might be confusing, but she was being childish. "Sure, I'd love to have dinner with you."

He blinked. "You would?"

"To talk about the case? Of course."

"Oh…right. The case. Of course."

She didn't want to talk about the case. She wanted to talk about him, be with him, soak in his presence and simply enjoy the time with him. However, uncertainty kept her from voicing those thoughts. But the butterflies in her belly had no trouble expressing their excitement about the whole idea.

Together they walked back to the Suburban, carrying the puppies. She got them settled with Star in the back when the crack of a rifle shattered the silence.

Harper dropped low and pulled her weapon. "Riley! Are you all right?"

He scuttled around the front of the truck to join her. "I'm fine."

"You sure?" Another pop sounded and a bullet hit the driver's window. More pops quickly followed and a slew of bullets shattered the inside console. Harper stayed down, but couldn't help the wince. Max was going to flip at the destruction of the brand-new vehicle. But she'd worry about that later. Right now, they just needed to make sure they didn't get hit.

"Yes, I'm fine, but I saw where he is," he answered. "I think it's Van and I'm going after him."

"How? It's wide-open from here to there. He's got a good spot behind trees and will cut you down before you take two steps."

"I know. We'll have to take the truck. Get in and hunker down."

"Riley."

"Please, Harper, help me catch him."

"All right, but we're going to move fast," she cautioned. "He's got a good angle right into the truck. He'll be able to shoot us as soon as we climb in."

ELEVEN

Riley opened the passenger door and, staying low and hopefully out of sight of the shooter, watched as Harper scooted across to the driver's side, pushing the glass off the seat. Keeping her head below the shattered window, she cranked the vehicle while Riley climbed into the passenger side.

She ordered Star to lie down on the seat. Riley knew the puppies were in the enclosed area and would be protected from any flying bullets. All she had to do was move the truck forward and she would throw off the killer's aim that allowed him to plant bullets inside the vehicle.

"Ready?" she asked.

"Yes, go."

Before she lifted her head, she pressed the gas and the vehicle shot forward. More bullets sounded, but this time pinged off the side of the truck.

Harper sat up and gunned the engine once more. Riley leaned out of the window and fired off a few rounds.

The bullets coming their way fell silent.

"There he goes!" A figure darted away. He'd been tucked behind a tree at about the same level as Riley and Harper so Riley didn't think he was above them by much.

The attacker turned and got off another quick shot. The bullet hit the truck and Harper jerked the wheel then swerved back onto the dirt road. She pressed the gas and quickly closed the distance between them and the shooter. Riley pointed. "There he is!"

"He's running now!"

"At least he's not shooting anymore!"

They had to yell over the wind blowing through the broken window.

The puppies yipped from the back and Riley knew they were being tossed around a bit. But she was driving steady now, closing in on the man who'd shot at them. It had to be Van, didn't it? Or was it Jake? The two men looked so much alike, to be truthful, he really wasn't sure who they were chasing.

It didn't really matter. Whoever it was had to be stopped.

When they could go no farther thanks to the trees blocking the way, she braked and jumped out of the vehicle. Riley did the same. A walking trail led into the trees. Several vehicles were parked along a split-rail fence, but there was no one within sight. "I'm going after him," Riley said.

Harper opened the back door and let Star out. "I'm right behind you."

"Be careful, there's a sheer drop-off not too far into those trees."

She shut the door on the barking puppies and Riley heard her bringing up the rear.

He spotted Van just as he disappeared into a copse of trees. Without pausing, he pounded after him, dodging fallen logs and woody debris. "Van! Stop! This is the end of the line!"

And then Riley heard nothing except Harper and Star behind him. She caught up to him, one hand wrapped around Star's leash, the other holding her weapon. "You find him?"

"No. And I don't know which way he went."

"There's really only two choices here," she said. "There's the walking trail that way and then through the woods to my left. Would he go off the trail?"

Riley ran a hand through his hair and felt the sweat drip down the back of his neck. "I don't know. Maybe. All I know is the longer we stand here talking the farther away he's getting."

"All right. I don't have anything that belongs to Van so Star isn't going to be much help tracking him." She glanced at her phone. "There's still no signal. I hate to split up since we won't be able to communicate with one another."

"Let's just go hunting for him. I'll take the walking trail."

She hesitated then nodded. "Fine. But be careful. Meet back here in fifteen minutes, okay?"

Riley heard her and raised a hand to acknowledge he heard her and moved down the trail at a lope. The problem was, he wasn't sure what Van would do. Would he keep running or do something unexpected like stop and hide? Riley slowed his pace, his head swiveling, hand gripping his weapon while his heart thudded in his chest. Where was he?

He'd go off the trail. Riley wasn't sure how he knew it, but it's what he would do. He ignored the *No Trespassing* signs and hopped the fence.

Something slammed into the middle of his back and

he went down to the ground hard. The breath whooshed from his lungs. A booted foot aimed toward his head and Riley threw himself to the left.

And found himself airborne then crashing down against the side of a steep cliff. Pain exploded through him as he bounced and slid. Desperate to stop his downward descent, he threw his arms out, grasping for a hold on any tree or shrub.

He found nothing and knew if he kept going, he'd go right on down to the rocky bottom below.

Star jerked on her leash and turned with a growl.

Harper slowed and spun. "What is it, girl?" The dog lunged back toward the way they'd come. Over the years, Harper had learned Star had reasons for her behavior. "All right, you're the boss, let's go."

Star took off and Harper jogged behind her, keeping her eyes in the trees and the surrounding area. She wasn't exactly being covert and couldn't let Blackman or Morrow catch her off guard.

A harsh shriek reached her ears. "Riley!"

She picked up her pace and bolted back to the place where she'd left him only to find it empty. But Star knew where she was going and pulled Harper toward the fence. She climbed over, dropped the leash, and Star darted through the middle of the wooden fence.

She raced over to the edge of the cliff Riley had warned her about only moments ago and saw a figure dart away. "Stop! Federal agent!"

The man didn't stop and Harper didn't pursue. She raced to the edge where he'd been only moments before and looked over, heart in her throat, expecting the worst. "Riley!"

He was wedged between a bush and the trunk of a

tree. Star growled and Harper whirled to see Van taking aim at her. She threw herself to the side and heard the bullet hit the ground next to her. She rolled to her stomach, raised her weapon and fired back.

Van yelled, turned and ran. Harper had no time to chase him. She had to get to Riley. She could send Star after Van, but it was possible he'd just shoot her. She couldn't take the chance. "Star, down." The animal dropped to the ground.

Still on her belly, Harper army-crawled to the edge and looked down once more. Riley was still there and he hadn't moved. "Riley, can you answer me?"

"Yeah, yeah!"

She wanted to revel in the relief, but there was no time. "Can you move?"

"Not without falling again. I'm stuck." He paused. "Which might be a good thing."

Harper wanted desperately to be able to call for help, but she had to move quickly. She had no doubt Van would be back to finish the job. "I'll be right back. I'm going to get you up."

"What are you going to do?"

"Go get some gear. Um… I'd say stay put, but…"

"You're a funny woman, Harper."

He was joking, so maybe he hadn't hit his head too hard. Harper really didn't want to leave him alone while she ran back to the truck. What if Van decided to come back while Riley was helpless? She paused then called Star over. "Guard. Guard him, girl. Got it? Stay."

The animal woofed and sat. She wouldn't move until Harper returned. But if Van came back, Star would bark and let Harper know. She took off back the way she'd come, running, but being cautious in case Van was lying in wait. Once at the truck, she made sure the puppies were safe in the temperature-controlled area that held them. They were. They'd be fine until she and Riley could get back. *Please let us get back fast and in one piece.*

The prayer whispered through her mind as she unloaded the items she needed from the back. The Suburban came equipped with a first-aid kit, rappelling gear, listening devices, tear gas and other items she would want at her fingertips should she need them.

She grabbed the rappelling gear and the first-aid kit and headed back toward Riley. Again, she carried the gear in one hand, her weapon in the other so she would be able to defend herself if necessary. It seemed to take her forever, but she made it back to the area where she found Star waiting. The dog shifted at her appearance and Harper felt sure that Van hadn't been back this way. "Good girl, Star." She set the rappelling gear and first-aid kit down and looked around for a sturdy tree that would hold her and Riley on the journey back up the side of the cliff.

She dropped to her knees to check on him. "You still there?" He looked to be about fifty feet down. Close enough to talk to, far enough to need help getting back up.

"Unfortunately."

"Anything hurt?"

"Just about everything."

"Any bleeding?"

"A bit."

Harper bit her lip on blasting him with some harsh words. "Riley, I need to know the extent of your injuries. Covering them up or acting like it's no big deal isn't helping."

"You sound like my mother when she's humoring me."

Harper quit talking. She was going to kill him just as soon as he was safe. Then again, his sarcasm and droll responses gave her hope that he was truly as okay as he sounded. As a former cop, he'd deal with this kind of thing the only way he knew how.

Exactly the way he was doing it. Covering up the fear and staying calm.

She glanced at him again. At least he was alive and, as far as she could tell, not seriously hurt. For the moment. The drop below him meant imminent death.

Harper tested several trees before she found one that she knew would hold both of them for the journey back up. She attached the safety and rappel devices then threw the dynamic-style rope over the edge. Quickly, she donned the gear including the helmet and gloves. "All right, girl," she said to Star, "let me know if anyone comes this way, all right?"

Star looked at her, her tongue hanging from the side of her mouth. She'd sound the alarm if Van or anyone else approached. Harper looked at the first-aid kit. Normally, she'd take it down with her, but since Riley indicated no serious injuries, she opted to leave it. She clipped the hook to her harness then attached the spare harness that Riley would use to the rope. "I'm on my way."

"Wait. What? You're coming down?"

"What did you think I was going to do?"

"Get help."

"I *am* help."

He went silent for a moment and she wondered if he was still conscious.

"Harper?" he called.

"Yeah?"

"My hands are cut up pretty bad. I'll need something to help hold on to the rope on the trip up."

"No problem." She'd have to give him her gloves. They were slightly big on her so maybe he could make them work.

The urge to hurry nearly overwhelmed her and she started down. Her wounded shoulder protested, but she ignored it. "Make yourself useful and watch above me to make sure Van doesn't come back and cut the ropes."

Riley flinched at the thought. He missed his weapon. Unfortunately, it had gone over with him and had hit the rocks below. Then again, with the shape his hands were in, he wasn't sure he'd even be able to hold a weapon much less fire it.

Pain permeated every pore of his body. After a quick inventory, he didn't think anything was broken, but he sure was bruised up—and his hands were raw and bleeding. His left leg throbbed with an insistence that he figured would require stitches. Assuming he made it back to the top and to a doctor. Right now he didn't dare move as he could feel the limbs on the tree beneath him bending. He felt like he was right on the lip of the small protrusion and any shifting on his part would unbalance him and send him to his death. *Please, God, don't let me die. I can't leave Asher yet. Or my mother. You know they need me. Get me out of this. I promised Asher I'd be back, that I'd be there for him. I need to keep that promise, God.*

Harper appeared over the edge once again. "Close your eyes. I'm aiming to come down beside you, but I'll probably knock some debris loose."

"Just come on down," he said. "But be careful. Please.

Be careful." He turned his head slightly so he could still see her, but protect his eyes at the same time.

She jumped over the edge and swung back to the cliff, her feet lightly touching before pushing off again. She took her time, being careful, and Riley kept an eye on the ridge above her. If Van came back, all he could do was warn her. She'd have to pull her weapon and shoot him if it came down to it. And all Riley would be able to do was watch.

Pain raced through him. Up his back and into the base of his skull. His leg throbbed in time with his heart. He swallowed and continued to alternate between watching the ridge and watching her.

He couldn't believe she'd come after him. But like he'd told her when he first met her, she was different. Different, as in she pulled his heart like a magnet. If he got out of this alive, he was going to have to rethink some of his priorities.

And then she was beside him. "Hey," she said softly.

"Hey."

She immediately wrapped the rope under his arms and hooked him to her. At least now if he fell, he'd just dangle instead of die.

"We're going to have to work fast," she said. "I need to get you in the harness then we're going up before Van comes back. Can you walk?"

"Can you check my left leg?"

The fact that he'd asked must have surprised her. She raised a brow then worked her way around to his left side where she took a look and sucked in a breath. "Yikes."

"Bad?"

"Definitely not good. Hold tight, I need to get a better look."

She tugged on his pants leg and fire shot through him. "Ah!" The cry escaped him before he could smother it.

"Whoa. Sorry. Your jeans are pretty shredded and you've lost some meat, but I don't see any bones."

"No, it's not broken." He knew what *that* felt like.

"That's gotta hurt, though."

He gave a low grunt. "It hurts." As he'd just proved by being a wimp and letting out that cry.

"All right. Normally, I'd patch you up hanging here, but one: I'm very nervous about being here too long."

"And two?"

"I left the first-aid kit up above because you were only bleeding 'a bit.'"

"Understatement?"

"A *bit*."

"Yeah, sorry. Honestly, I didn't really feel the leg until you were halfway down. It doesn't matter now. Let's get out of here."

Harper unhooked the extra harness and slipped it up his legs—careful to ease it over the wounded left leg— then around his waist. She balanced on the edge of the ledge while she helped him work his way into it. His hands were a real nuisance and hurt. A lot.

But finally, they got it done.

Once he was safely harnessed and hooked to the rope, Riley drew in the first deep breath he'd taken since the fall.

"All right, let's go," he said. She pulled the rope from under his arms and handed him a pair of gloves.

"I thought these might be big enough, but I see they're not. You'll have to be creative."

He didn't bother to try to put them on. Instead he pressed them into his palms to cushion his hold on the line. Hopefully the blood wouldn't cause them to slip. He grasped the rope he was hooked to and looked up. Still no Van, but he had a feeling time was running out.

"Have you ever done this before?" she asked.

"I have to say this is one sport I've not tried, but it can't be that hard, can it?"

She shot him a perturbed look and he grinned. At least he hoped it was a grin. The pain might have turned it into a grimace.

She shook her head. "Stay with me. Slide your hands up the rope and pull yourself. One step at a time. Keep your good foot against the wall of the cliff. Can you put any weight on the injured one?"

He tried it. Again the fire burned up his leg and sent his head spinning, but he could do it. "I'll make it."

Together they made their way up the side of the cliff. One hand over the other. One foot then the next. He looked up to see Star at the edge looking over. She pranced sideways and whined.

"Get back, girl," Harper commanded. "Back."

The dog disappeared. "Guess Van hasn't shown up." Riley grunted at the next step. "Star only seems worried about you being down here."

"That's the good news."

"Is there bad news?" he asked.

"Other than the fact that he's still out there?"

"Right."

She sighed. "No. That's about it."

The world spun and darkness hovered at the fringes of his consciousness. "I hate to ask but can we stop for just a second?"

She paused and he leaned against the side, his eyes turning upward. They only had about ten feet left until they reached the top. He couldn't pass out now. The inky blackness receded slowly. He drew in breaths through his nose and let them out his mouth.

"You all right?"

Her concern touched him. "I'm all right." He drew in a fortifying breath and nodded. "I'm ready."

She didn't offer him more time.

Riley bit his lip and pushed off the cliff wall. This time while the darkness threatened, he was able to push on. It probably only took them about five more minutes to get to the top, but seemed to take forever. He soon found himself lying on the ground, staring at the blue sky and dragging in great gulps of air. His leg pulsed in time with his heartbeat, his hands throbbed and other cuts and bruises would soon make their presence known.

But he was alive. *Thank you, God, that I'm alive. Please keep me that way.*

Harper dropped beside him. She laid her gun next to him. "Just stay still for a minute."

"We need to get out of here."

"I know." She ran her fingers through his hair. "No bumps."

"Amazing enough, I didn't hit my head. Just let me be for a few seconds."

She backed off and he knew he sounded curt. He hadn't meant to.

A wet tongue swiped across his face and he turned his head to see Star watching him. "Thanks, girl." He shifted his gaze to Harper. She'd pulled off her harness and was tucking it away into the bag. "And thank you."

Harper finished zipping her harness into the carrying bag and set it aside. Star showed no sign that anything was amiss around them so Harper felt like she could focus on Riley for the next several moments. If he would let her. Now that he'd had a chance to catch his breath, she pulled out the first-aid kit and moved to kneel beside him. "So are you going to let me take a look at that leg?"

He shifted and sat up.

Then kissed her.

Harper blinked, her mind thrown into sudden turmoil at the feel of his lips on hers. However, it never occurred to her to protest. She'd grown to care for this stubborn bounty hunter and she couldn't deny she wanted to kiss him, too. So she did.

Seconds later—or maybe it was minutes—he pulled back and said, "We need to get out of here."

"Star will let us know if anyone is around."

"If Van's got a rifle and a scope, we'll be dead before Star gets a whiff."

He was right. Her worry for him clouded her thinking. She gave a mental snort. It wasn't worry that had her mind reeling. That kiss...

She cleared her throat. "Can you walk on the leg?"

"I can walk." He rolled to his feet and air hissed from between his teeth. "Won't feel good, but I can walk."

"You need stitches. Let me at least bandage it."

"No time. Van could be anywhere."

Harper tightened her lips at his stubbornness. "So you had time to kiss me, but there's no time for first aid?"

He flashed her a grin that almost hid the pain she knew he was in. "Priorities. And besides, kissing you helped more than any kind of first aid or bandages would. Now, let's go."

Harper backed off because she didn't entirely disagree with him. Not about the kissing part, but about the danger part. Although the kissing part had been really nice.

She huffed and waited for him to step out of the harness.

Then they were ready.

She tapped her hip. "Star, heel."

Star fell into step beside them and they made their way back to the Suburban. Riley moved slowly, but at least he was moving. She wasn't sure what she would have done if she'd have had to carry him.

She noticed his vigilance even as she kept her senses tuned to the area around them. Why hadn't Van returned? He wanted Riley dead and he'd had the perfect opportunity to make sure he accomplished that. The thought spun on an endless loop.

Unless…

"He thinks he killed you," she said.

She opened the passenger door of the truck and Riley fell into the seat with a groan. "What?"

"That's why he didn't come back. He thinks you fell all the way to the bottom."

Riley went silent and she slammed the door. Star followed her around to the driver's side and hopped in. Harper stared at the dog for a moment then shrugged. There was plenty of room in the front for her, but it was a bit out of character. She knew she rode in the back. Harper glanced at the sleeping pups in Star's area and shook her head. "Don't want to be a mama right now, huh?"

Star didn't look at her.

Harper cranked the truck and pulled away from the

lookout area. She planned to head straight for the nearest hospital.

And pray Van didn't come back to find Riley gone and realize he wasn't dead after all.

TWELVE

Riley looked at his leg in disgust. It had been three days since his roll off the cliff. A pearly white bandage now covered twenty stitches.

He'd lost a good bit of blood, but nothing his body wouldn't take care of in time. Drum Creek's hospital wasn't nearly as large or well-equipped as the one in Denver, but it had been able to take care of his injuries just fine and he refused to be transported to the larger hospital. Van was close by and as soon as they let him leave, he'd be on the hunt again.

He sipped orange juice and nibbled on a hamburger someone had rounded up from the small hospital cafeteria in spite of the fact that he wasn't really hungry. But the red meat was good for him and he needed his strength to continue his search.

He leaned his head back against the pillow and closed his eyes. The painkiller they'd given him was making his head swim and he'd already decided there'd be no more of those.

He'd let his mother know of the accident and that he wouldn't be able to be at the hospital for a few days. She'd wanted to drive out to see him and he'd talked her into staying with Asher. She'd finally given in, but he could tell she hadn't liked it. He figured the only thing that had kept her at the hospital was the fact that he texted or called her on a regular basis. Which was fine with him as she kept him updated on Asher. He was so thankful the little guy continued to improve with each passing day. Soon, they'd get him into therapy and up on his feet. Riley couldn't wait.

The knock on the door jerked him out of a light doze. He hadn't realized he'd fallen asleep. "Come in."

The door opened and Harper stepped inside with Star at her side. "You're being sprung."

The sight of her filled him with a quick rush of gladness. "And you're my ride?"

"You think you'll get a better offer?"

He gave a small laugh. "No. You'll do."

"Thanks." She frowned. "So how do you really feel?"

"Better physically. Mad emotionally." She lifted a brow and he shrugged. "He got away again and almost killed me in the process."

"Well. True." She ran a hand through her short hair and leaned against the sink. "Do you feel up to taking a ride or do you want me to take you back to the hotel?"

"A ride where?"

"I did some research while I was waiting to hear how you were doing and found a beagle rescue right here in Drum Creek. The woman who runs it said she'd take them in and keep them for us as long as we needed her to. Two of the puppies are very hyper. I don't think they'd do well in the training program so she's going to find forever homes for those two."

"No kidding. So where are the puppies now?"

"The team has been taking care of them for the last couple of days. I sent one to the training center back in Billings to be raised and trained as a K-9, but I've got the others in Star's area for now. It's temperature-controlled so there's no hurry to get going if you need more time."

"They gave me a painkiller a little while ago, but I think I'm all right to ride out to a beagle rescue."

"I don't mind dropping you at the hotel."

"No, I'll just brood about Van getting away." He scowled.

"All right, if you're sure."

"I'm sure. What about the little guy who was limping? Is he okay?"

"He's fine. He had a dislocated hip, but the vet was able to set it. He also provided some medication to help keep him calm while it heals. He won't work for the training program, either, so we'll just have to find a good home for him."

"Cool. Let's get out of here."

As soon as he was checked out and loaded into the Suburban that she said had been delivered the day after his tangle with the cliff, he held one of the puppies while she drove. Even with a sore hip and on medication, the little guy was full of energy and liked to nibble on his fingers. "They're cute, aren't they?" he said.

She cast a glance his way. "Adorable."

"Asher wants a puppy."

"All little boys want a puppy. Are you thinking about keeping one for him?"

He sighed. "No. Not yet. The timing is wrong." He lifted the pup and let it lick his chin. "Maybe after his surgery."

She smiled, her sympathy clearly written on her pretty face. "I think that sounds like a great plan."

Riley fell silent thinking about his sister, her son and the man who'd radically altered all of their lives.

God, if You're listening, I need Your help to catch this guy. I can't believe You don't want him to pay for what he's done.

"Do you believe God is really just?"

Harper blinked at the question that came at her from nowhere. She shrugged. "Yes. Why?"

"Even after your childhood and everything I know you've seen while working for the Bureau? You can still believe that?"

She fell silent and thought about his questions. Then nodded. "Yes. And sometimes God doesn't have to do a thing to show it to me. I see it everywhere I look."

"What do you mean?"

"Because of the consequences that come with our actions. Sure, it seems like some people never get caught doing the wrong thing. The illegal thing. But even if the drug addict is never arrested for possession, he's still dying because of his choices. Even if the dealer isn't arrested for supplying drugs, he's still living in a world that is uncertain and death stalks him every day."

"What about the abuser that goes unpunished? The murderer that gets away with killing a mother?"

She nodded slowly. "I've thought about that, too. I don't know how—or why—I decided to think about it this way, but I tried to put myself in their mind."

"Scary."

"Sort of. I tried to think—if I made the choice to kill someone in a jealous rage like Van, how would I feel inside? Do you think he's ever known any kind of real peace since that day? He has to live with what he's done on a daily basis, minute by minute, second by second."

"Good, I hope it keeps him from sleeping, from ever

knowing peace," he gritted out. "He doesn't deserve to feel peace."

"I hear you. Don't get me wrong—I believe in justice. I believe if someone commits a crime, he or she should definitely pay for it in the whole 'be-arrested-go-to-prison' kind of justice. If I didn't believe that, I wouldn't have the job I have." She released a breath. "But I'm not talking about the ones who are caught. I'm talking about the ones we don't catch, the ones that appear to have gotten away with their crime. Part of me wonders if they aren't living with a sort of punishment every day, anyway. A self-inflicted one. That living with what they've done and who they've become is retribution in a sense."

Riley didn't speak for a moment. "It's not enough."

"Yeah. I know."

"What if they feel no remorse? What if they don't care?"

"That's a whole different issue. I'm not talking about psychopaths or sociopaths. I'm not talking about people with a mental illness. I'm talking about people who are in their right mind, who do something they know is wrong and that has severe consequences. And then have to live with that the rest of their lives."

"And you think they regret what they do?" he asked.

"Yes, of course. Some, anyway. Not all. But no one starts out life saying 'I want to be a criminal and go to prison.'"

He pinched the bridge of his nose. "I don't think Van falls into that category. I don't think he has any regrets for what he's done. I think my sister served his purpose for the time they were together."

"Which was what?"

Riley sighed. "Van and I had a long conversation

shortly after he and Charlotte started dating. He was an only child growing up in an abusive situation when Child Services stepped in and put him in a foster home. The first of many."

Harper shot him another glance. "You've learned everything there is to know about this man, haven't you?"

"Everything. It pays to know your enemy."

"So when he aged out of the system he went looking for a family," she guessed.

"When he was eighteen, he married a girl that was in the last foster home where he was living before he aged out. She died giving birth to his son three years later."

"Oh, me. So, that's what your mother meant when she was talking about why Van was having such a hard time letting Charlotte and Asher go."

"Yes. And then when he realized she wasn't going to get back together with him, he just…flipped, I guess." His jaw hardened. "Anyway, after his wife and son died, he seemed to jump from relationship to relationship. Two of the women I've talked to said that he was a great guy in the beginning, but soon took over their lives, smothering them, refusing to let them have friends, cutting them off from their families—and threatening to kill them if they left him. They took their chances and left."

"And he never went after them or killed them."

"No, my sister was his first. And if we don't find him, she won't be his last."

Harper digested his words. She'd known criminals like Blackman, of course. Had caught some and put them away. She also knew Riley was right. If Blackman was allowed to elude capture, he'd just disappear long enough for law enforcement to give up looking for him then continue his deadly romances. He definitely had to be stopped.

She pulled into the drive of the beagle rescue and parked in front of the barn as she'd been instructed by the woman who'd given her directions yesterday. Riley held the now-sleeping puppy tucked into the crook of his arm.

A finger stroked the pup's head and Harper thought she saw bit of wistful longing in his eyes. "You sure you want to leave him?"

Riley cleared his throat. "I'm sure." He sighed and stepped out of the vehicle.

Movement from the barn caught Harper's attention. She opened the driver's door and slid out of her seat. Her boots landed on a mixture of grass and red dirt.

A tall, dark-haired, dark-eyed woman in her early sixties approached them, hand outstretched. "Hi, I'm Justine. You two must be Harper and Riley." Harper shook her hand then Riley did the same. "So glad you brought the pups out here. We have plenty of room for them and will find them a good home."

"Not that I believe everything I read on the internet, but you had a lot of great reviews online," Harper said.

Justine laughed. "Well, you can believe those. I didn't have anything to do with them. I just make sure I have happy animals and customers. As long as I do that, the good reviews pour in. Now, let me see the babies."

Harper opened the back door and pulled the other two sleepy pups from Star's area. Star took advantage of the open door to jump to the ground. Harper noticed the shepherd had rather taken to the puppies over the last two days and thought she might miss them when they were gone.

But she'd be fine. She had work to do.

Justine scratched Star's head and the animal closed her eyes in bliss.

"You just made a lifelong friend," Harper told her.

"She's a beautiful dog."

"Thanks. I think so, too. So—" she held the two puppies in a gentle grasp "—where should we put them?"

"Follow me."

Harper and Riley did as requested and walked behind the woman to enter the barn. "There's a play area over there." She pointed to an octagon-shaped baby-gated area. Fresh chips covered the inside and held bowls of water and food.

Harper placed the puppies inside and they immediately attacked the food and water. "Greedy little things, aren't you?" She'd just fed, watered and let them run shortly before heading to the hospital to get Riley.

"Do you have homes for them yet?" Riley asked. He still held the third puppy.

Justine rubbed the little head and the puppy tried to nip her. Riley chucked him under the chin and he turned his attention to Riley's finger. "No, not yet," Justine said, "but it won't take long. We'll get them checked out by a vet, give them their first round of shots, and by the time we're finished with the open house we have every other month, they'll be with some great forever homes."

"Good." Riley cleared his throat and finally placed the playful puppy in the pen. He yawned and padded over to join his brothers in finishing off the food and water. "He had his hip worked on, did Harper tell you?"

"She did. It's not an uncommon thing. I'll take special care of him."

"Thanks."

Harper pulled her keys from her pants pocket. "Well, I can see they're in good hands. Riley, you ready?"

He looked up from the puppy he'd still been watching. "Yeah. Sure."

"Thanks for rescuing them," Justine said. "I don't know why it's easier to throw a sack of puppies in a river than it is to just bring them to someplace like here."

"It's sad," Harper responded. "And I can't dwell on it or I want to go hunt the heartless jerks down and shake some sense into them. Thanks for everything."

"Of course."

Harper walked out and Riley trailed behind her. "You're thinking about that puppy, aren't you?"

"What? No."

"Liar."

He smiled at her gentle rebuke. "It's just the drugs talking. I'll be fine once they're out of my system."

"Right."

The drive back to the motel didn't take long. She let Riley off with instructions to rest. The fact that he didn't argue told her he wasn't feeling quite as well as he projected.

Harper stepped inside her room and sank onto the end of the bed. Star joined her and settled her head between her paws. Harper checked in with Max and learned the others were still working in the national park, looking for more evidence that Jake was still there. She offered to join them.

"Take a break," Max said. "You'll be back on in the morning."

That was fine with her.

Harper pulled her laptop over and opened it. As she had done numerous times before, she typed in her father's name. Grant Prentiss. She knew she should just give up the search for him, but part of her couldn't. She had to know what happened to him.

When she got a notification of a new message she sat up straight.

"What's this?"

Star lifted her head and blinked at Harper.

Harper scratched the dog's ears but focused on the screen. He was wanted on drug trafficking charges.

Sickness pooled in the pit of her belly and she shut the computer. Harper stared at the wall and lost track of time while she thought about the man whose DNA she shared. She remembered yelling, fights, things crashing in the night while she hid under her bed. And then the long silences before it would all start back up again.

And then he was gone shortly before her fifth birthday.

How could she miss someone who'd never wanted her? Someone who'd hardly acknowledged her existence other than to tell her to get lost?

She shook her head and stood.

Her phone buzzed and she swiped it from the clip where it rested against her hip. A text from Riley.

I've thought of another couple of places that would work as possible hiding places in the park. Let's go tomorrow.

That's the plan. Are you going to feel up to it? she texted back.

Doesn't matter.

Of course it does. You had a bad fall. You're fortunate you weren't killed. You need to rest.

I'll rest once Blackman's behind bars. I'm going. Are you going with me?

I'm going. Max has already said we'd be searching out there again tomorrow.

What time?

First light.

See you then.

Harper texted Max to let him know Riley's idea. He responded with a thumbs-up emoji and a promise to be ready to join them.

She set the phone aside and rubbed her eyes. Another early morning. She prayed it was going to be a successful one and no one ended up shot at or dead.

THIRTEEN

Riley wouldn't complain to anyone, but he had to admit the exhaustion, in addition to the pain from the still-healing injuries, was weighing on him. His hands ached, his leg throbbed, but there was no way he was going to miss the search this morning.

He stepped out of his room to find two Suburbans parked out front. Ian and Max were ready with their dogs in the back. Harper sat in the driver's seat waiting on him. Riley opened the door and slid into the passenger seat.

"Good morning," she said.

"Morning."

"A little sore?"

"A bit," he replied.

"Did you get any rest?"

"Nope."

"You refused to take any pain meds, didn't you?"

"Maybe."

"Gotta work on all that early morning chatter, Martelli, it could get annoying."

He slid her a sideways glance. Then smiled. He couldn't help it. As crabby as he felt, he didn't want to be in a bad mood with her. "I'm sore, but I took some ibuprofen so it'll kick in soon." She looked good decked out in her gear. But she looked good no matter what she wore. He'd known a lot of physically beautiful women, but it was rare to find one with a matching beauty on the inside.

His sister had been one of those women. And Harper was one as well. It drew him like a moth to the flame. "Anyone locate my weapon yet?"

"Yes. They found it yesterday. Two park rangers covered the area where they thought it might have landed and found it."

"Is it toast?"

"Pretty much. I brought one you can use for now."

"Thanks."

While she drove, Riley prayed that today would be the day they'd catch Van Blackman. He knew the others were more concerned about Jake Morrow—and Riley knew the man needed to be caught—but Van was his priority.

Soon, Harper pulled through the gates of the park. "Which way?"

"Keep going until you see the curve that goes up. Like the way we went a couple of days ago. Only before you get to the top, there's a turnoff to the left. I'll point it out to you when we get there."

"Keep an eye out."

"Yes, ma'am."

"And wear this." She reached into the backseat and handed him a Kevlar vest. "No sense in taking chances."

He pulled it on, zipping it up and attaching the Velcro straps. "I'm ready when you are."

They stepped out of the vehicle and he had to admit, he felt better with the vest on. Now he could only hope Blackman continued to be a lousy shot. He grabbed his backpack from the floorboard and slung it over his shoulder with a wince. With each passing day, he discovered new aches and pains. And bruises. His legs were the worst. There'd be no shorts for him anytime soon.

Star circled Harper's leg and sat.

"We'll have to hike up the trail," Riley said. "Once at the top, we'll need to split up. There's a pretty deep river that divides the area in two. On either side there are a few more isolated places to set up camp."

Max nodded. "Ian and I can take one side. You and Harper can take the other."

Harper nodded. "Let's get going, then." She started off and Riley fell into step behind her and Star, with Max and Ian bringing up the rear. Riley slung his rifle over his shoulder and winced again when he pulled other muscles that had been strained in his fall. His bandaged hands still hurt, but they wouldn't stop him from doing what needed to be done. His fingers, although cut and bruised as well, were free.

But that was all right. He only needed one to pull the trigger.

Harper noted Riley's quiet determination. He kept to himself, but she didn't have any trouble reading him. If he saw Van Blackman today, it was going to be over. One way or another.

She didn't blame him. It had been a long hard road for him since his sister's death. He needed closure and to be free to be with Asher.

And you?

She immediately quieted that little voice. As much as she might yearn for the right guy to build a life with, she'd made a commitment to her job. And right now that was to find Jake Morrow.

Blackman and Morrow. Both fleeing the law for various reasons. Harper didn't think the two men were hiding out together, but they'd definitely wound up in the same general vicinity. She hoped by the end of the day, she'd have some closure as well.

They hiked up the sloping incline, passing several others enjoying the early morning sunrise. With each person they saw, she pulled out Blackman's and Morrow's pictures and showed them. With each negative response, Harper's hopes that Riley might be onto something started to diminish.

She heard the river before she saw it. When they stepped around the bend, they stopped to consider their options.

Max pointed. "We'll head this way over the bridge. You two take that side. Keep the radios on. There's no phone signal up here."

Harper nodded and clicked Star to heel. She held out the bag with Jake's hat in it to the dog and Star got the scent. Nose to the ground, she trotted along the path. She and Riley followed in silence for several minutes, listening and watching.

Star stopped. She pranced a little, sniffed again then moved toward an open clearing that looked to be a prime camping spot. Surrounded by large stone cliffs, it was tucked back from the river. They approached it with Star eagerly leading the way.

"Has she got something?" Riley asked.

"Possibly."

Riley nodded. "There's a tent and a bicycle. No sign of a vehicle."

"Can you even get one up here?"

"Yes, I've only been up here a handful of times, but there's a road that you can follow around the edge of the mountain that leads up here. But if we drove, we might miss something. Like all of the hiking paths that branch off around here."

They continued to follow Star to the edge of the campsite. Harper held her weapon ready. Then Star skirted the area and started climbing the rocks behind it. It wasn't quite as steep as it had looked from a distance. "Okay, then, if Star can do it, so can I," she muttered. "Up we go."

Harper stayed behind the dog and climbed. Loose debris tumbled behind her. She turned to see Riley working his way up as well. He placed one bandaged hand on a protruding rock and jerked back with a grimace.

"Why don't you see if there's an easier way up here?"

He scowled up at her. "I can make it."

She stopped Star for a moment and the dog waited, panting, tongue lolling over the side of her mouth. "I'm not questioning that. But it might be better if we come at this from two different angles. If he's up there, we can trap him between us."

Riley hesitated, then nodded. "All right."

He made his way back down and disappeared around the edge of the campsite. She told Star to seek and the two of them continued up the sloping cliff. It wasn't a terribly hard climb, but she was in a sweat by the time she got to the top.

She stopped and took in the view. It was gorgeous to her back, but in front of her there was a small expanse of green, then trees clogged the area. Perfect for hiding if someone got too close. She looked around for Riley, but he wasn't in sight yet. It was possible he had to walk a fair distance in order to find another route to the top.

Should she wait on him?

Star tugged on the leash, trying to get into the trees. "Star, hold."

The dog stilled, but her sides quivered with the desire to go. She had Jake's scent and wanted to follow the trail.

Harper gave one last look over her shoulder. Still no Riley. He couldn't be much longer, could he? She hated to keep waiting and give Jake a chance to get farther away. Star pulled again on the leash. "Okay, girl, we're going." She pressed the button on her radio. "Riley, location?"

"Heading your way."

"Star has Jake's scent. I'm going after him."

"Where are you?" Max asked.

She gave him her approximate location.

"Harper, wait for me," Riley said.

"Just a minute more then I'm going after him."

"I don't know how far away I am. I had to walk awhile."

She dropped a glove to the ground then leaned down to position it. "Keep coming until you see the tree line just ahead of where I climbed up. My glove is on the ground. Follow the direction of the index finger. And bring my glove with you, please."

She headed for the trees, her weapon ready. Star bolted ahead of her, straining against the leash. Harper scanned the area, watching, her nerves tense, senses alert. Star really wanted to race into the woods, but Harper didn't want to let her go. If Jake was in there and he didn't want to be found, he'd shoot the dog. And he wouldn't aim for the vest she wore. No, she'd keep Star with her where she had more control.

Star broke the tree line and Harper followed. She

placed a hand in front of Star who immediately quieted. Harper stood still and simply listened. When she heard nothing, she once again gave Star the order to continue. The shepherd turned right and Harper followed.

And came face to face with Jake Morrow, his weapon aimed at her head. "Hello, Harper."

Riley had to make his way up the cliff in a round-about way, but he finally stepped out onto the top and paused to catch his breath. He'd still had to climb, but not as much as Harper.

So, where was she?

He almost called out then figured he'd better keep the noise to a minimal level. No sense in alerting someone to the fact he was there. He held his weapon in his right hand and lifted his radio with his left. "Harper? Where are you?"

Silence.

Riley frowned. "Harper?"

Still she didn't answer. He knew she had on the earpiece that allowed only her to hear him. So why wasn't she answering?

The options weren't good. Alarm slithered through him.

He walked toward the woods and then realized he was quite a distance from where Harper would have come out at the top of the cliff. Could he simply be out of range of her earpiece? Surely, they had better equipment than that. He started the trek that would take him in her direction.

"Harper?"

Still no answer.

"Riley, is something going on?"

Max's voice in his ear. "I'm not sure. Give me a few

minutes and I'll get back to you." He paused. If Max could hear and answer him, why couldn't Riley?

It took him a good five minutes more to arrive to the place where Harper would have crested the hill. But she wasn't there.

He found the glove she'd told him about and leaned over to pick it up and tuck it in his pocket. He knelt and examined the red dirt that covered the ground. A boot track that could be Harper's led toward the trees. Star's prints were also there, just slightly ahead of Harper's. Exactly as she'd told him.

He took off at a jog and was almost to the tree line when he heard the gunshot.

A split second later, fiery pain raced through his side and he stumbled to the ground. Riley lay still as he tried to breathe. But he knew exactly what had happened. Van Blackman had seen him first. Riley pressed a hand against his bleeding hip and rolled into the cover of the woods just as another bullet kicked up the dirt where he'd been lying. He shoved the top edge of his jeans down and glanced at the wound. Just a graze. It was ugly and would leave another scar to add to his growing collection, but as far as Riley could tell it was nothing too serious. Nothing that would keep him from continuing the hunt.

The gunshot echoed around them and Harper flinched. She turned. "Riley!" She started to head back toward the tree line when Jake held up a hand and jerked the weapon at her. "Keep walking." When she'd first run into him, he'd immediately taken her weapon then forced her to walk with the excuse he wanted to talk to her back at his camping site.

She'd agreed simply because she wasn't sure what

he would do if she refused. Only now Riley could be in trouble and need help.

"I'm going to check on my friend."

"And I said don't move, Harper." He inched the gun up so that it pointed to her forehead.

She froze. Star did the same, looking up and waiting for Harper's next command. "What are you doing Jake? Are you going to shoot me?"

"Not unless you give me a reason to."

"Stop this. Put your weapon away and let's talk."

"Not until I'm sure you'll listen to me first."

"I'll listen, but I need to make sure Riley's all right." Riley would know something was up when she didn't answer. But she didn't want him to walk into trouble without some kind of warning.

Her radio was in her pocket. A mere click of a button would bring help. But if she moved her hands, she wasn't completely confident that Jake wouldn't shoot her. And Agent Morrow would know what she was doing. He'd once worn a radio exactly like hers once upon a time. He'd yanked the earpiece out and forced her to remove her vest and leave it, afraid she'd have some sort of tracker on it when he confronted her so if Max or anyone said anything, she wouldn't know. She did notice that he kept the radio.

"I'm not concerned about your friend. Keep going."

"That was two gunshots, Jake. He could be hurt."

"Or he could have been shooting a snake or a wolf or whatever. Walk!"

Harper's pulse continued its frantic pace but she reluctantly continued to head in the direction Jake ordered. She truly wasn't certain that he wouldn't kill her. And she wouldn't be any good to Riley dead.

But she had to try to warn the others. She slid her hand down toward the radio.

Jake jabbed the weapon at the base of her skull. "Don't. Keep your hands where I can see them."

Harper bit her lip. This wasn't the Jake she'd known when they'd worked together. No, she hadn't liked him all that much as a person, but he'd been a top-notch agent and never hesitated to rush in to help someone in need. "What's happened to you?"

"A bad break in life."

"Can't you see that you don't need the weapon? Put it away. We've talked before without you holding a gun on me." Could he really be a double agent? She was sure leaning in that direction. Trusting him was out of the question at this point.

She bit her lip on the words and prayed that Max or one of the others was trying to get ahold of her and would know something was wrong when she didn't answer.

Finally, Jake directed her to a small shelter. An old cabin that had probably been there for decades sat up on a sloping hill that led down to the river. "Nice spot."

"I like it. Nice, quiet and private." He smirked. "And hard to find unless you know where you're going and what you're looking for."

"What are you doing here in Colorado?"

"Looking for someone."

"Penny?"

"Yeah."

He led her inside and she noted the rustic appearance. A dirt floor, the front door that didn't close all the way, open windows that could use some glass panes. A small cot with a sleeping bag lay next to the far wall.

He'd been roughing it.

Jake motioned to a chair at the round four-person table someone had made from an oak tree. "Have a seat and keep your hands where I can see them." She did and he pulled the radio out of her pocket and tossed it onto the counter. "I don't need any more company until I can convince you why I can't come in yet."

Conflict raged inside of her. "What are you saying, Jake? That you have a good reason for this wild-goose chase you're leading us on?"

She sent up a silent prayer for Riley and settled on the edge of the chair, ready to fight back if she had to.

Jake stood at the old-fashioned hand-pumped kitchen sink, his back to it, watching her with hooded eyes. He kept the gun steady on her head. Where the bullet wouldn't be blocked by her vest. "A good enough reason," he said.

"Like what?"

"Like I managed to escape from Angus Dupree after the shootout in the warehouse in Los Angeles. But while he had me captive, Dupree threatened to kill Penny…" He met her gaze. "And my son."

The raw anger there was real. But were the words? If they were, then maybe there was a valid reason for his behavior after all. And yet, Jake had been a good agent for a reason. He was very skilled at playing whatever part he had to. "So you went after them."

"Yes. Then you guys showed up at her house and she ran."

"And so did you."

"I didn't have time to stay and explain my actions. I had to catch up with Penny."

That made sense in a weird sort of way. "And did you?"

"Yes. I told her about Dupree and the threats and

sent her away. I told her I'd catch up to her later. But when I went to meet her as planned, she'd disappeared."

"That doesn't really make sense. Why not go with her?"

"I wanted to circle back and make sure no one was following her. I finally tracked her here, using informants I've made over the years. I don't trust Dupree. I'm sure he's hunting her just as I am and I'm scared to death he's going to catch up to her before I can find her and convince her that I just want to keep her and Kevin safe."

"Why haven't you asked for our help? You're a part of this team. We'd back you in a minute and you know it."

"I know. But I couldn't involve the team. This was personal. You had enough to do trying to track down Dupree and his goons. I couldn't pull your attention from that for something like this. I needed to take care of this by myself."

Now that sounded more like the Jake she knew. Or thought she knew. "I get that Penny's on the run from Dupree, but why run from you? Hide from you? It makes no sense."

He raked a hand through his hair. "She doesn't trust me. I think she's afraid of me."

"Why?"

He shrugged. "Who knows? The stuff on the news, probably. The whole story's not there and I know the director's only releasing what he deems relevant, but Penny knows I'm not with Dupree any longer and she knows I haven't gone in for help. I guess it doesn't look good to her."

"It doesn't look good to anyone." She paused. "The team thinks you're a double agent."

His nostrils flared. "A double agent?" He laughed.

A short sound that held no humor. "No. No way." He waved the weapon. "See? That's why I need this. I didn't want it to get ugly between us with me answering all your questions and you having to apologize. This way, we just cut out the harsh part."

"Then prove yourself."

"What do you mean?"

"Let me cuff you and put you in custody," she proposed. "I'll take you in and we'll get all this sorted out back in Billings."

"Take me in? Seriously?" Star shifted beside Harper and Jake's eyes flicked to the animal then back to Harper. "That's what it's going to take? Harper, come on."

For a moment she wavered. Then stiffened her spine. "Yes, that's what it's going to take."

He sighed and dropped his head for a moment, all the while still holding the gun on her. Different thoughts raced through her mind. Visions of diving across the table and taking him down danced with him surrendering. What would he do?

"All right."

"All right, what?"

"Take me in." He set his weapon on the table and held out his hands. "Cuff me."

She hesitated, watching his eyes. But they were shuttered. Hooded. Everything in her warned her not to trust him. "Move the gun farther away."

He rolled his eyes and shoved it off the table. It hit the floor with a thud. "Satisfied?"

"Somewhat."

He held his hands back out to her.

Lips tight, she stood, pulled the cuffs from the case on her belt, and slid them across the table. "Put them on."

He took them and clicked one around his wrist then fumbled with the other. He tried again and almost got it—until he dropped it. He held his arms back out. "Just get this over with, will you?"

Still she hesitated, searching his face, his body language. Unable to get a clear reading on him, her internal alarms screaming at her, she decided she really had no choice. If he went for the weapon that was now on the floor, she'd have time to stop him. Then again, he could have another on him. "Pull your pants legs up from the ankle."

"You think I have another weapon?"

"Just do it."

With a grunt, he leaned over and did as she asked. He looked clean. When he straightened, he held his hands out yet again, the one cuff dangling from his right hand.

"Not yet. Turn around and let me see your back. Pull your shirt up."

He laughed. "Turn my back on you? Are you kidding? No way. You're cuffing my hands in front of me. Pretty sure I'm not going to be able to reach a weapon at my back."

She stared at him and he sighed. He kept an eye on her over his shoulder, but did as she asked. He lifted the hem of his shirt and clearly had no more weapons on him. He turned full circle and held out his hands.

She stepped forward and reached for the cuff to finish the job.

His arm swung and the cuff caught her in the forehead. Pain shot through her and she cried out, falling to her knees. Her vision went dark for a second.

Jake dove for the gun. Star barked and lunged at Jake. Harper blinked and saw him grab the weapon he'd tossed and turn it on Star. Star latched onto his arm. Jake cried out. "Call her off or I'll shoot her!"

"Star, release!"

Star stopped her attack and released her grip on his arm, but she didn't back away from Jake. She kept herself between him and Harper.

"Sit, Star."

The well-trained animal sat, her gaze bouncing between Harper and Jake.

Jake stumbled away from Star and cursed.

Harper raised a hand to her bleeding forehead. She'd ignored her better judgment and paid for it. "Guess you're not going in peacefully after all, huh? Did that whole story you just spun have any truth at all in it?"

Jake sighed, walked over and grabbed her arm. "Shut up, Harper." Star growled and rose to her feet.

"Star, stay." Harper quickly threw out the command before Jake could turn the gun back on the dog and possibly pull the trigger.

Jake pulled her to her feet then shoved her back into the chair. He reached behind him and grabbed a coil of rope from the counter. "Well, I was going to use this to do a little rappelling, but guess I can use it to keep you out of the way instead. And I've got to get out of here. I'm sure someone's looking for you."

He bound her hands, then bent to tie her feet. She kicked out and caught him in the shoulder. He fell backward with a shouted curse and she lunged from the chair toward the door.

A hard hand wrapped around her left ankle and pulled her back toward the chair. She slid across the floor like a sled on ice. He was big and much stronger than she. "You are one feisty little thing, aren't you?"

He picked her up as though she weighed no more

than a bag of sugar and tossed her back into the chair. This time he turned her sideways and tied her hands to the back of the chair.

"Harper!"

Harper froze at the sound of her name coming from outside the cabin. "Harper! Where are you?"

Riley.

Jake pointed the weapon at her. "Call out and you die. And he'll be next."

She snapped her lips closed and fumed. Jake knelt and finished tying her ankles together. "We're going to find you, you know."

"No, you won't. Which is why there's no point in killing you. I'm just trying to slow you down so I can get a head start and disappear."

Riley called out once more, but this time his voice sounded fainter. He was walking away from her and Jake and the cabin.

Which was good. It might just save his life.

Her head throbbed where the cuffs had cut the skin and warm blood trickled down her cheek. "They'll be here soon, Jake. They're looking for me even now and you know it."

"I know."

"So everything you just told me was a lie."

"Not everything, just most of it." He shrugged. "I was trying to get of here peacefully, but you weren't going to cooperate."

"You're just going to leave me here?"

He leaned in and lifted a finger to stroke her cheek. She bit back the gag reflex and glared at him. "I'm not like the Duprees," he said softly. "I don't just kill to kill."

"You just kill if you think you're going to be caught and brought in."

He narrowed his eyes and Harper wondered if she'd gone too far. Then he shrugged. "But, I *have* been… *corrupted*, I guess you could say. I've had a taste of true power. I've held millions of dollars in my hands." His eyes took on a strange glow that Harper realized was greed. The sight made her want to cringe. But she refused. "Do you know what that feels like?" he asked.

"No."

He smiled and it was almost sad. "No, you wouldn't. Because once you've felt it, there's no going back." His gaze dropped to her lips. "I could kiss you now, you know. I've always wanted to."

Her heart stuttered and she strained away from him. "You could force it, but I don't want it now any more than I wanted it when we worked together."

His nostrils flared then he smiled and started to lower his head. "Let's see if you feel the same way after."

A noise at the door jerked his attention from her and he swung the weapon around. Harper stiffened, her heart racing. Who could it be?

Morrow raced from the shelter.

FOURTEEN

Riley's side hurt. He'd worn the vest but the bullet had found an unprotected area just below it. He was sure that had been on purpose. Maybe Van was a better marksman than he'd given him credit for. He ignored the burn along with all of his other aches and pains.

Because none of that mattered. He had to find Harper. He'd called her name, but gotten no response. Perhaps she was in trouble, either having met up with Morrow or Blackman. Then again, maybe...

Maybe nothing.

She was in trouble. His gut shouted it.

Max and the others were headed in his direction. He hoped. But he wasn't even sure where he was and could only give them directions based on the location of the sun.

He'd managed to follow Harper's and Star's tracks until he got deep into the wooded area. At that point, he lost them. He had some tracking skills, but they weren't good enough to figure out which way she and the dog had gone once they'd veered off the path.

He did think there was a third person with them, which made him leery and alert.

"Harper? Can you hear me?"

"She's still not answering," Max said, stating the obvious. "We need to find her ASAP."

More of the obvious.

Riley sent up prayers for her safety and his own. Returning to Asher was paramount. He couldn't get killed and break his promise to be there for his nephew. "Priorities," he muttered.

"What was that?" Max asked.

"Nothing. Just reminding myself I can't die."

"Right. Remember that."

Riley came to another clearing along the river and noticed the small cabin set back up on a hill. He started toward it, glancing over his shoulder, hating that he was so exposed.

But if there was anyone in that cabin, they might have seen or heard something that could help lead him to Van or Harper. Right now, he preferred Harper. He was almost desperate to know she was safe.

As he approached the cabin, he looked down and thought he saw paw prints. Star?

"Harper? Harper!"

A footstep behind him.

He spun to see Van Blackman taking aim.

Riley dove behind the nearest tree.

Harper's ears tuned in to the sounds around her even while her head throbbed. Had Riley called her name? "Riley?"

She struggled with the ropes and froze when she heard a sound in the door. Had Jake come back?

A shuffling, snuffling sound reached her. "Jake? Riley?"

A shadow fell across the entryway and a furry head rounded the corner.

Harper sucked in a breath at the sight of the wolf. The animal spotted her and bared its teeth while a low growl rumbled in its chest.

Star went into a barking frenzy and lunged. The wolf bolted and Harper's shoulders slumped. Star returned to her side and nudged her. "I know, girl. We've got to get out of here."

She finally managed to get her hands free of the back of the chair. That piece of the rope dropped to the dirt floor. And while her hands were still tied together, at least she could move. She managed to get hold of the earpiece still dangling over her shoulder and slip it into her ear. She could hear the conversation even though she wouldn't be able to call out until she got her radio in hand. Right now, the team was silent.

Where was Riley?

"You see him?"

Max's voice came to her.

"Negative," Ian said.

"Keep looking. He's shot so he might be passed out somewhere."

Who was shot? *Riley?* Had she heard that right?

She tugged her feet up closer and with her bound hands pulled her pants leg up to expose the knife she kept on, strapped to the inside of her right ankle. It was a good thing Jake had grabbed her left one and not the right one or he would have felt it.

She snagged it and worked it under the ropes holding her ankles together. The sharp blade sliced through the fiber.

Now the tricky part.

Harper sat in the chair and pulled her feet up to rest on the seat. She clasped the handle of the knife between her knees and turned the blade outward. She brought her hands up and slid the rope up and down against the razor-sharp edge until her wrists fell free.

She shoved the knife back into the case then stood. Dizziness hit her and she swayed for a moment while she got her balance. Finally, she thought she could move without falling and stumbled to the counter to grab her radio.

"Max. Ian?"

"Harper! Where are you?"

"I'm not exactly sure, but Jake overpowered me and tied me up in a little cabin where he's been staying. It's near the river and that's about all I know. I'm going to retrace my steps. Where's Riley?"

"Haven't heard from him in a while," Max said. "He let us know he'd been shot and then we lost contact with him."

Shot? "How bad?"

"Not bad. Just a graze."

Another wave of dizziness hit her and she shut her eyes while she waited for it to pass. "All right, I'll start looking."

"Are you hurt?"

"Not as bad as I could have been. Jake got me in the head with my cuffs. If you come across him, don't fall for anything he says. He's definitely a double agent."

"10-4 on that."

His disappointment came through loud and clear. Harper rearmed herself with the weapon Jake had tossed onto the counter then called Star to her side and stepped out of the cabin.

"Riley!" She knew he'd called her name. So where was he?

She sprinted around the side of the little house and stopped when she saw Van Blackman aiming a gun at

Riley. She lifted hers. "Federal agent! Put the weapon down, Blackman, or you die."

The man spun and aimed the weapon at her. She started to squeeze the trigger when Riley leaped out from behind the tree and tackled the man.

Riley threw a solid punch and caught Van in the mouth. Van's head snapped back even as the man rolled and snagged his weapon. As Riley went in for another hit, Van brought the weapon up against the side of Riley's head.

From the corner of his eye, Riley saw Harper, her own weapon trained on Van, and knew the only reason she hadn't shot was because she was afraid of hitting him.

And now Van had him hostage, his harsh breaths echoing in his ear while the barrel of the gun dug into his temple.

"You're a hard man to kill, Martelli," Blackman snarled, pulling Riley to his feet while keeping the gun steady.

Riley stood and swayed. He was running out of strength and gritted his teeth to keep his knees locked. "You're a hard man to find, Blackman," he managed to say, his voice sounding a lot more firm than he'd thought it would.

Blackman laughed. "Well, I guess the hunt is over."

"I guess it is." Weakness and nausea swept over Riley and his side flamed with pain from the bullet wound. Truthfully, it was all he could do to remain standing. But falling or passing out weren't options. "Are you going to come peacefully or am I going to have to shoot you? I know which one I'm hoping for."

Van laughed. "I think you're delusional. I'm the one

with the weapon on you. And if your pretty girlfriend doesn't drop hers, you die."

He let his gaze lock on hers. "Don't drop it."

Rage seethed in the look she shot the man behind him. "Van, I can't drop my gun. You're done. You can't win this."

"Of course I can. It's simple. If I'm going to prison, Riley dies. If you let me go, he lives. Are you willing to sacrifice his life for mine?"

"Don't listen to him. He'll just come back and finish the job later," Riley ground out. "If you drop your weapon, he'll simply shoot both of us." The gun pressed tighter against his head and Riley winced. "Here. What about this? I'll go with you. You can drop me off somewhere and it'll all be done. You'll be free and Harper and I'll be alive. She has nothing to do with this, Van. This is between you and me."

"Not anymore. You brought her here. You brought them all here. You and the local police, I can outrun and outsmart." He shook his head. "The FBI is a different story."

Van seemed to be favoring his left arm. "What's wrong with your arm?"

"Nothing's wrong with my arm."

"I shot him, that's what's wrong with it," Harper said. "So you left a note on my door telling me to stay away because you were mad Riley brought in the FBI?" she said as she moved sideways. "Did you really think that was going to work?"

Van laughed and turned with Riley in front of him. "It was worth a shot."

"So what are you going to do?" Harper asked. "If you shoot him, you'll just have the FBI on your tail even harder than we already are."

"I never planned to kill you in the beginning, Riley. What happened to Charlotte was tragic and I deeply regret it. But I'm not going to jail. You're like a dog with a bone. You just don't give up." He paused and a look of regret crossed his face. "I didn't mean to shoot Asher."

Riley's jaw tightened. With effort, he restrained himself from trying to spin out of the man's grasp so he could tear him apart with his bare hands. "But you did."

"Is he okay?"

"That's none of your business."

"Is he going to be ok—" He broke off with a shout and the weapon slipped from Riley's temple.

"Bite!" Harper yelled the command. Riley let his legs give way and slumped to the ground even as he caught a blur of motion from the corner of his eye.

Van let out another harsh scream and fell to the ground, Star's powerful jaws locked around his forearm.

Riley rolled. Pain held him frozen. Blackness swirled and he had a hard time keeping his eyes open. The moment passed and he was finally able to catch his breath and roll to his side, his gun pressing into his hip.

Van lay on his stomach, silent and still. Harper called Star off and the animal backed up, her focus never wavering from the man on the ground. She had her radio button depressed while she kept her weapon on Van.

"Are you okay, Riley?" she asked.

"What's happening? What's going on? Someone report in now!"

Max's voice came through the headset, but Riley couldn't answer.

"Suspect down," Harper stated. "Approaching him."

Riley took another breath and his vision cleared.

Harper stepped up to Van and he lashed out with a foot, knocking her in the knee. Harper went down once again, dropping her gun. She scrambled to get out of his reach, but Van was too quick, landing a punch in her stomach. The air whooshed from her and she bent, now on all fours.

"Harper!"

Move! Riley's brain issued the order, but his body was slow to respond.

Van grabbed the knife from her now-exposed ankle case and raised it over Harper's head. "You should have listened to my warning."

Riley's fingers fumbled for the weapon beneath him, then grasped it.

He raised it and fired. Then fired again.

Van's eyes widened.

The knife slipped from his suddenly slack grip and he fell to the ground with a thud.

Harper let out a gasp and Riley crawled over to her. She gasped again and made a wheezing sound. "Breathe," Riley said softly, "just breathe."

She nodded and took a few more seconds to get her breath. Then she pushed him away and reached out to lay two fingers on Van's neck. Her eyes lifted to his. "He's dead," she whispered then fell back to the ground with a grunt. "I'll get up…in…a minute."

She lay there for a full minute and a half then rolled into a sitting position.

"I should be glad." He looked at the man who'd been in his nightmares for the past two months. The man who'd killed his sister and altered the lives of his family forever.

"You're not?"

He shook his head. "I don't know what I am, to be honest. Except glad it's over." He sighed heavily. "And sad it came to this." He frowned and touched her fore-head gently. "Are you okay? He got you with a hard hit."

"That was from the cuffs earlier. I'm fine."

"Cuffs?"

She wave a hand in dismissal. "You saved my life."

He shrugged. "I figure I owed you."

She smiled and he looked back at Van and shuddered. He hauled himself to his feet and held out a hand to help her up.

Star watched them, her gaze bouncing from one to the other. Then her ears perked and she turned.

Riley saw Max, Ian and the other dogs heading their way. "Well, better late than never, right?"

Harper grimaced. "Right."

Riley stepped back, nursing his wounds, doing his best to ignore the pain pounding through him while he watched the others gather around Harper and demand to know what had happened.

While she explained, he realized he'd fallen in love with her. In spite of his determined efforts to prevent it from happening, his heart had gone and betrayed him. Her strength had impressed him, her beauty ensnared him. Limitless courage, heart rending compassion, a selfless love for those she put first in her life… all of those traits belonged to Harper, and his heart had fallen. Hard. It had let her in in spite of his resistance.

But he couldn't love her. Loving someone else just wasn't going to happen. Because love hurt.

He'd loved his mother and Asher and he'd be there for them, but that was it. Once he'd made the decision, the pain in his heart actually rivaled the one in his side and the rest of his battered body.

And then he had no more time to think. The team

now surrounded him, questioned him and demanded to know that he was all right.

"I'm fine, really."

"Well, you're going to the hospital."

"I don't need a hospital." He touched his side. "It's just a flesh wound."

"You're going. Period," Max said in a stern tone.

Riley sighed. "Fine, but I'm going to the same hospital where my nephew is."

"Deal." Max nodded to Ian. "Let's get some vehicles up here so we can take care of this mess." He looked down at Van. "And a coroner." His eyes took in the cabin. "Is there a blanket in there?"

Harper nodded. "I'll get it."

"You stay put." Max stepped into the cabin. He was gone so long Harper almost went after him. But he finally reappeared carrying the blanket from the cot.

"That's part of a crime scene, you know," Harper said.

"Yeah. That's why I processed that area before I took the blanket."

They fell silent and simply waited. Harper finally heard the sound of engines heading their way. She glanced at Riley and wondered what was going on with him. He was so closed off and shuttered. She slipped over to him. "You okay?"

"Not really."

"What's wrong?" she asked quietly.

He shook his head. "I just need some time to think."

"About?"

"Everything."

"Want to talk about it?"

"No."

She raised a brow. "All right." She wasn't going to

pry it out of him. If he wanted to talk, he knew where to find her.

He raked a bandaged hand through the hair that already stood on end. He opened his mouth to speak then shut it when Leo pulled up.

With an ambulance right behind him.

Leo climbed from the Suburban. "Any sign of Jake?" Harper asked.

"No, afraid not."

She pursed her lips and nodded. Two paramedics approached and she was surprised Riley didn't argue about being checked out.

When they approached her, she sighed and figured she might as well be a good sport as well.

Three hours later, she sat on a gurney in the emergency department, absently checking her email on her phone and waiting to be released. She had the all-clear healthwise, with simple orders to rest and heal. She had no concussion from the hit with the cuffs, just a cut and a bad knot. It would heal.

She sighed and dialed Dylan's number.

"Hello?"

"Dylan, you sound a little tense."

"Oh. It's you."

A laugh slipped from her. "Sorry to disappoint you."

"No, no. It's okay. I'm sorry. What's up?"

"I just called to say thanks for all your hard work on the fund-raiser for Asher. He's doing really well."

"Aw, you're welcome," he replied. "That was a fun project to do. At least I knew it would have a good outcome."

"So what else is going on? What's gotten you so stressed?"

"It's still Zara. I haven't heard from her in almost a

week. I know she's working hard at Quantico with her training and everything, but she's my fiancée. I need to hear from her."

Harper frowned. "That *is* disturbing." It just occurred to her that Zara hadn't answered the text she'd sent her a few days ago.

"Thank you! See? It's driving me *nuts*. I've called and called and gotten nothing. I'm ready to fly out there and start knocking down doors until someone gives me some answers."

"Let me call Quantico and see what I can find out."

He exhaled an audible sigh of relief. "I would be forever grateful."

"All right, give me a little time. I'll be in touch soon."

She hung up and dialed the number that would take her past all the security and right to the person she needed. When the call center picked up, she said, "This is Harper Prentiss. I'd like to talk to Zara Fielding. She hasn't been in touch with her fiancé for the past week and we're all a little concerned."

"All trainees are indisposed at the moment, but more information will be forthcoming."

"*Indisposed?* What does that mean?"

"I'm sorry, I can't offer anything more than that."

"That's a canned response and you know it. What's going on?"

"As I said, more information will be forthcoming."

Harper sighed. She wasn't going to get anything else out of the woman. "All right, thanks."

"Have a nice day."

"Right. You, too." She hung up and frowned. Something was definitely wrong. She called Dylan back and he answered on the first ring.

"What did you find out?"

She told him her conversation with the attendant.

"I don't like it," he said.

"Okay, here's what I think. I think Zara and her team are probably in some type of safe house or something like that. I really don't think you need to worry. Remember, the best of the best is looking out for her and the other trainees."

"Yeah, but sometimes things can go wrong even for the best of the best."

She had to agree. "Hang in there, Dylan. We'll figure it out."

He blew out a breath. "Thanks for trying, Harper."

"Sure thing."

She disconnected just as a knock on her door brought her head up. "Come in."

Riley stepped inside and shut the door behind him. "Hey."

Still a little miffed at his aloof treatment from earlier, Harper debated about answering him then decided not to be childish. "Hey."

He gestured to the chair next to the bed. "You mind?"

"It's all yours."

He seated himself and closed his eyes for a moment. "It's been a long day."

"Yes."

"I just came from Asher's room."

She softened. She simply couldn't stay mad at him. "How's he doing?"

"Great." His throat worked and she wondered what he was trying to say. "He can feel his feet and wiggle his toes."

Tears filled her eyes. She couldn't help it. She'd come to love Asher in a very short period time. "That's wonderful, Riley."

"Yes. It is."

"How is your head? Do you have a concussion?"

"A slight one, but the scans were clear." He touched his side. "The gunshot wound has been cleaned and stitched up and my hands have new bandages."

"Sounds like you're good to go."

"I am." He paused and ran a hand over his chin. "So what now? Morrow's still out there."

"Which means we're still looking for him."

He nodded. "It just hit me while I was watching Asher that you and your team are really good people. The real deal."

She gave a low laugh. "You just now realized that?"

He shook his head. "This isn't coming out right."

"I'm sorry. Go ahead."

"I think after Charlotte died, I lost what little faith I had in humanity. I closed myself off to all but my mother and Asher."

"Understandable," she murmured.

"Maybe. But wrong, too. Asher wouldn't have had that surgery yet without you and your team. I'll never be able to repay you."

"We'd never ask."

He smiled. "I know. You all have restored my faith that not everyone is just looking out for themselves. Some people actually care about others and look out for them, help them. I needed to see that and guess God knew that."

"He does give us what we need when we need it."

"Even when we don't realize we need it sometimes."

She laughed. "Sometimes it works that way, doesn't it?"

"I…"

"What?"

He cleared his throat then said in a low, rough voice, "I don't want this to be the end."

"Of what?"

"Us."

Her heart sped up. "There's an us?"

"I sure hope so." He settled on the edge of her bed and leaned in, his eyes intense.

Harper swallowed and tried to still her suddenly rapid pulse.

"How do you feel about long-distance relationships?" he asked, taking her hands in his.

"I don't know. I've never had one."

"Well, I don't like them."

She blinked. "Oh. Okay."

"When Asher can travel, I want to bring him and Mom out to Billings and see you."

"Really?" she whispered.

"Really. And then we'll have that dinner date we still haven't had."

"I'll be waiting."

He leaned over and kissed her. Time stopped for that brief moment. She kissed him back and realized how very much she wanted it to work between them. When he pulled back, his eyes were warm, glowing almost. She wondered if hers looked the same.

He smiled. "See you soon."

FIFTEEN

Three weeks later
Billings, Montana
K-9 Headquarters

Riley pressed the phone to his ear. He'd made the call to Max after much pacing and soul-searching. Asher watched him from the sofa across the room. "What do you think? Will you help me?"

"I think it's a great idea," Max said.

"So you think she'll go for it?"

"I guess all you can do is give it your best shot, but yes, I think she will. Did she tell you that she found her father?"

"Yes." He paused. "She went to see him at the prison, didn't she?"

Max sighed. "Yeah, and she wouldn't let anyone go with her. She said this was something she had to do on her own."

"That's what she told me." He'd offered to go with her and she'd turned him down flat. He understood. Sort of. But still didn't like it. "All right, keep this all under your hat and I'll see you soon."

Riley hung up with Max and went back to pacing. Asher giggled. "What's so funny, Champ?"

"You."

"What do you mean?" He swiped a hand across his forehead then rubbed it on his jeans.

"Why are you all sweaty?"

Riley paused, wiped his forehead again then shot him a wry smile. "I guess it's called nerves, kid."

Asher blinked at him. "Huh?"

He sighed. "Can you keep a secret?"

His nephew's eyes went wide. "A secret? Like a real live never-ever-tell secret?"

"Well, we're going to tell it eventually, but yeah."

Asher frowned and puckered his lips. After about a six-second delay, he nodded. "I've thought about it. I can keep a secret."

"Great. So here's what we're going to do…"

Harper sat at the conference table wondering why Max had called her in. Then Ian Slade stepped inside and her confusion mounted. "What's this all about? Do you know?"

"Not a clue. I was hoping you knew something."

She shrugged. "Guess we'll find out soon enough. How are you doing?"

He shrugged. "I want Jake Morrow in custody."

"I know."

"How are you feeling?" he asked.

"Like new. All healed up. No more headaches."

"And Riley?"

Just thinking of him brought a smile to her face. "He's perfect."

Ian laughed. "He's a man. Trust me, he's not perfect."

She lightly punched his shoulder. "He's perfect for

me. We've FaceTimed every day since I've been back here. And Asher is making remarkable progress. He's walking on his own and even running a little."

Ian's expression softened. "That's wonderful."

The door opened and Max stepped inside. "Thanks for coming in, guys."

"We had a choice?" Ian smirked.

"You're a funny guy, Ian."

Ian sobered. "Okay, boss, what's this all about?"

Max looked Ian in the eye and Harper frowned. "I know about your connection to the Duprees."

Ian stiffened and his face went blank. "It's not a secret."

"But you've treated it like one."

"What's going on?" Harper asked.

Max continued to hold Ian's gaze. "I haven't told anyone else, but I wanted Harper to be in on this discussion. She needs to know."

"Know what?"

Ian sighed and nodded. "All right." He met Harper's gaze. "The Duprees killed my parents."

Harper gasped. "What?"

"It's a long story, but it happened when I was sixteen years old. I vowed to bring them down one day."

Max turned his attention to her. "I wouldn't have said anything except we're getting close and I want Ian to have backup and eyes on him at all times. If something happens, I don't want the Duprees to be able to claim Ian acted unprofessionally."

"Boss—"

"I don't think you would. I'm saying I want to be able to back up anything that goes down with an eyewitness. You understand? This isn't about revenge. It's about justice."

Ian nodded and stood. "Sometimes the two are one and the same." He walked to the window and stared out.

Max frowned and Harper could tell he was worried about Ian.

"Are we done here?" Ian asked.

"We're done."

Ian left and Max sighed.

Harper crossed her arms and leaned back in her chair. "Ian's one of the best, Max. He'll be all right."

Max nodded. "I know he is. I just pray that his personal vow to bring in Angus Dupree to join his nephew in prison doesn't get Ian—or anyone else—killed."

She nodded. "I'll keep an eye on him." She turned to leave.

"Hold on a second, will you?"

Harper raised a brow. "Is there something else?"

"No. I mean yes."

Harper frowned then gave a little laugh. "Okay. Which one is it?"

A knock on the door interrupted them. Max's immediate relief had her extremely curious. Harper stood to answer the door since it was closer to her side of the table, but Max beat her to it.

"Harper!"

The little voice wrangled a gasp from her. "Asher? Riley? What are you guys doing here?"

The little boy stepped carefully, placing one foot in front of the other to finally reach her. He grinned up at her and she gently swung him up into her arms with an exaggerated grunt. "You've gained weight since I last saw you."

"Uncle Riley's been feeding me steak."

"Good for him."

Riley and Max shook hands. Then Riley hugged her

and planted a quick hello kiss on her lips. She wanted more, but was as aware of their audience as he was.

"I came to take you to lunch," Riley said. "Can you get away?"

Harper looked at Max and he nodded. "Go. Enjoy."

"Thanks, Max."

Asher refused to let go of her hand after she set him on his feet so she held it and Riley took the other one. Asher walked between them with a smile on his face.

Once out of the building and on the sidewalk, Harper leaned over Asher's head and kissed Riley on the cheek. "How'd you get in and upstairs?"

"I have friends in high places now, remember? Like your coworkers?"

She laughed. "I guess so." She pulled Asher to her in a quick hug, careful not to knock him off balance. "I can't believe you guys are here. I've missed you."

"I missed you, too," Asher said. "But I'm hungry. Can we eat?"

Riley laughed. "Of course. And we're almost there."

"Where?"

"Three more steps and turn right."

Asher counted his steps out loud then made a sharp right nearly causing Riley to stumble. He caught the boy and helped him open the door to a small café that was one of Harper's favorites.

Petrov's Bakery. "Oh, yum. We get pastries here for our meetings. I think if they quit supplying them, we'd quit meeting."

Riley waved a hand to the man behind the counter and he nodded with a smile. "I rented out the back room so we could have it to ourselves."

"What? Oh, how fun."

SIXTEEN

Riley led the way to the back. He'd arranged this all with Max and Max had led him to the café. The table had been set for three and he pulled out the chair for her. She settled into it. At one of the other places, a small bell was next to the water glass. Riley smiled. Perfect.

"Wow," Harper said, "thanks, guys. This is so lovely."

Nerves attacked him and he drew in a deep breath. "I'm glad you like it. Asher and I put a lot of thought into it, didn't we?"

"We sure did. Are you going to show her the—"

He clamped a hand over the child's mouth. "Not yet."

Asher's eyes went wide. Then he giggled. "Okay." He looked at Harper. "It's a secret."

"A secret, huh?" She slid a glance at Riley and he put on his most innocent smile.

She narrowed her eyes and he cleared his throat. The waiter arrived and spared him for a moment. After placing their order, he took a sip of his water then set the glass aside. "Any word on Morrow?"

She shook her head. "No. But we're not giving up. We'll find him."

Harper put the napkin in her lap. "Thank you, this is wonderful."

Asher laughed. "You already said that. Well, actually, I guess you said lovely, but it's the same thing, right?"

Harper grinned. "Yes, I suppose so. But it's true."

Riley smiled as well. "How did your visit with your father go today?"

The joy left her face and Riley could have kicked himself for bringing up the subject. He blamed his nerves for doing so.

Harper sighed. "It went well, I think. I was rather surprised at his reception. He said he'd thought of me often and wondered what I ended up like. You should have seen his face when I told him what I did for a living, though. Now that was quite a sight to see."

"And he didn't get up and walk out?"

"No." She gave an odd smile and he thought she looked amused. "He seemed...proud."

"You expected him to have a different reaction."

"Absolutely. He's spent his life hating cops and their authority and then he winds up with a daughter for one. It was sort of funny. In a weird kind of way."

"So, do you think you'll go see him again?"

Harper nodded. "Yes. I'm working on forgiving him. I asked him if he'd be willing to be transferred here to Billings and he said he would. I told him I'd see if I could arrange it." She drew in a breath. "I think the more I see him, the easier that will be. Maybe."

Riley lifted a brow. "You really think you'll forgive him?"

Harper smiled. "I think it will be a daily journey. But I think, with God's help, it's one that I have to take."

Riley reached over and wrapped a hand around her

warm fingers. "I understand," he said. "And it's a journey you don't have to take alone."

Harper blinked back tears. "You can't know how much that means to me."

Riley grinned. "I might have a pretty good idea."

"Uncle Riley, aren't you going to show her—"

Riley clapped his free hand over Asher's mouth again. "Not yet."

Harper giggled. He didn't think he'd ever heard that sound come from her before. "I think you'd better show me whatever it is you haven't shown me yet."

Riley sighed. If he kept dragging it out, Asher was going to spill the beans. "Well, Asher, Mom and I have decided to move to Billings, Montana."

Harper froze and her eyes went wide. "What?"

He shrugged. "We miss you. And my job is portable. So to speak." She still looked stunned and Riley's palms started to sweat. "Um, is that okay?"

A huge smile spread across her face. "It's more than okay. It's wonderful!"

Riley's heart pounded. "Oh good. We were hoping for that reaction."

"Of course. I couldn't be happier."

Tears stood in her eyes, bolstering his courage for the next part of the conversation. "So, Harper…"

She swiped a stray tear. "Yes?"

"I want to be that man."

She blinked. "What?"

"You remember our conversation where you told me to get over myself?"

She flushed. "I remember."

"You were right. And as soon as I said I didn't want to be that man, I regretted the words. I love you, Harper. We've been through a lot and come out on the other side and it took almost losing you to realize I don't want to live life without you." He glanced at Asher. "Make that *we* don't want to live without you. Right, Champ?"

"Uh-huh. That's right."

The stunned look returned. Then she swallowed. "I didn't think I'd hear those words quite this soon."

He frowned. "Too soon?"

"No. Not at all. I've imagined you saying them almost every day and now…you have."

"Yes. I have."

She swallowed. "I love you, too, Riley. I think I realized it when you held that little puppy all the way to the rescue farm."

He went speechless for a moment. "I…wow."

"Is it time yet?" Asher whispered.

Riley laughed and handed the child the bell. "Go for it."

Gleefully, Asher took the bell and skipped to the door.

Harper blinked. She'd forgotten the bell was there. Asher stood at the entrance into the main part of the restaurant and rang the bell three times. Then he ran back to the table and sat, folding his hands in his lap. Harper swung her gaze back to Riley. "What in the world are you two up to?"

"Mr. Petrov is bringing the—"

Riley clapped his hand back over Asher's mouth. The little guy's eyes crinkled at the corners and Harper laughed. Riley had better hurry up with his surprise or Asher was going to let her in on it.

"Are we ready, Mr. Martelli?"

Mr. Petrov walked into the room carrying a bag. That moved?

The robust man handed it to Riley who quickly set it on the floor. "Thank you."

"Yes sir, I have your food for you when you're ready."

"Just a few more minutes."

"Of course. Take as long as you like." He bustled from the room and Harper blinked as a little yap came from under the table.

Amused, she grinned. "Did that bag just bark?"

Riley sighed and rolled his eyes. "Yes, but just hold on a minute."

"But Uncle Riley—"

"Ash—"

But Asher had already clamped his own hand over his own mouth. Harper lost it. She laughed. A deep belly laugh that rolled all the way up and out of her mouth. Tears leaked from her eyes and it was a good minute before she could control her mirth. Riley handed her a napkin and she dabbed at the wetness trying not to completely destroy the little makeup she had on. "Oh, my, Asher. You're just too much."

Riley, too, was laughing and shaking his head. He reached down and she heard the bag rustle. Then a little black and brown head with floppy ears popped up. Harper gasped. "The puppy."

"Yes."

"You went back and got him."

"I did."

"He's grown a bit."

"That's because he eats more than a fifteen-year-old boy does. Here." He handed the squirming pup over to her. She held the puppy under her chin and he nipped it. He sported a red ribbon and smelled like all little puppies smell. Love and innocence and laughter. She scratched a silky ear and laughed again, marveling that her heart could feel so full.

Something hard bounced against her hand and she looked down. Another gasp slipped from her lips. Her insides turned to mush and her muscles went weak. She met Riley's gaze. And read so many emotions there. Emotions she was sure were mirrored in her own eyes. She lifted the ring that he'd tied into the ribbon and stared at the beautiful diamond.

He lifted a brow. "Do you like it?"

"Of course she likes it," Asher blurted. "Who doesn't like puppies?"

Riley stroked his nephew's head fondly, but his eyes never left hers. With shaking fingers, Harper tucked the little body under her arm and released the ribbon around the puppy's neck.

The diamond slid off the end of the cloth and fell into her palm. "It's beautiful."

"Will you marry me?"

"Us," Asher said. "'Cuz I live with Uncle Riley now. Mimi does too."

"Yes," Riley said, "sorry, us. We're a package deal, I'm afraid."

Tears spilled over her dark lashes. She tried to speak, but realized nothing was coming out. She settled for nodding.

"Yay!" Asher jumped up and pumped a fist in the air. "She said yes, Uncle Riley, she said yes!"

Harper gave another watery laugh. Riley stood and walked around the table to take the puppy from her arms. "Here, Champ, hold Rudolph for a minute."

Harper raised a brow. "Rudolph?"

"Don't ask me why. A six-year-old named him."

"Oh, right."

He held his hand out. "Could I hold the ring?"

"Are you going to give it back?"

He chuckled. "Yes."

"Okay, then." She dropped it into his hand. With his other hand, he raised her to her feet then went down on one knee and looked up at her. "Are you sure?"

"More sure than anything in the world."

He slipped the ring on her finger then stood.

"You gotta kiss her now," Asher stage-whispered.

"Thanks, Champ, I guess I do."

He leaned over and placed his warm lips on hers. Harper's knees wanted to melt so she locked her arms around his neck and kissed him right back with all the love and emotion she had in her heart.

"That's good enough," Asher said impatiently. "I'm hungry."

Harper opened her eyes and looked into Riley's. "I love you. Later?"

"Absolutely."

Asher handed the puppy back to Riley, grabbed the bell and ran to the door to ring it again.

Mr. Petrov entered right away followed by two of his workers carrying their food. The restaurant owner took the puppy. "Enjoy this start of a new life, my friends. I pray many blessings over you and your family."

Harper sucked in a breath. Yes. Family. Prayers and blessings.

God was good.

Prayers were answered and dreams came true.

She knew that for a fact and couldn't wait to see what the future held.

She grinned at her guys and sent up a silent prayer of thanks to the One who'd made it all work out.

Riley's hand reached across the table and gripped

hers and she reached for Asher's hand. He took it then gripped his uncle's.

Harper looked at their hands. Gripped tight in a circle.

A never-ending circle of love.

* * * * *

SPECIAL EXCERPT FROM

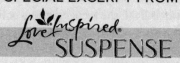

When a guide dog trainer becomes a target
of a dangerous crime ring, a K-9 cop and his loyal
partner will work together to keep her safe.

Read on for a sneak preview of Trail of Danger
by Valerie Hansen, the next exciting installment
to the True Blue K-9 Unit miniseries,
available September 2019 from Love Inspired Suspense.

Abigail Jones stared at the blackening eastern sky and
shivered. She was more afraid of the strangers lingering
in the shadows along the Coney Island boardwalk than
she was of the summer storm brewing over the Atlantic.

Early September humidity made the salty oceanic
atmosphere feel sticky while the wind whipped loose
tendrils of Abigail's long red hair. If sixteen-year-old
Kiera Underhill hadn't insisted where and when their
secret meeting must take place, Abigail would have
stopped to speak with some of the other teens she was
passing. Instead, she made a beeline for the spot where
their favorite little hot dog wagon spent its days.

Besides the groups of partying youth, she skirted
dog walkers, couples strolling hand in hand and an old
woman leaning on a cane. Then there was a tall man and

enormous dog ambling toward her. As they passed beneath an overhead vapor light, she recognized his police uniform and breathed a sigh of relief. Most K-9 patrols in her nearby neighborhood used German shepherds, so seeing the long floppy ears and droopy jowls of a bloodhound brought a smile despite her uneasiness.

Pausing, Abigail rested her back against the fence surrounding a currently closed amusement park, faced into the wind and waited for the K-9 cop to go by. His unexpected presence could be what was delaying Kiera.

"Come on, Kiera. I came alone, just like you wanted," Abigail muttered.

Kiera had sounded panicky when she'd phoned.

"Here. Over here" drifted on the wind. Abigail strained to listen.

The summons seemed to be coming from inside the Luna Park perimeter fence. That was not good since the amusement facility was currently closed. Nevertheless, she cupped her hands around her eyes and peered through the chain-link fence. It was several seconds before she realized the gate was ajar. *Uh-oh. Bad sign.* "Kiera? Is that you?"

A disembodied voice answered faintly. "Help me! Hurry."

Don't miss
Trail of Danger *by Valerie Hansen,*
available September 2019 wherever
Love Inspired® Suspense *books and ebooks are sold.*

www.LoveInspired.com

WE HOPE YOU ENJOYED THIS BOOK!

Love Inspired
SUSPENSE

Uncover the truth in these thrilling
stories of faith in the face of crime
from Love Inspired Suspense.
Discover six new books available
every month, wherever books
are sold!

LISHALO2019